# CREED
## ASHES OF CADIA

WARHAMMER
40,000

# CREED
## ASHES OF CADIA

# JUDE REID

BLACK LIBRARY

## A BLACK LIBRARY PUBLICATION

First published in 2023.
This edition published in Great Britain in 2024 by
Black Library, Games Workshop Ltd., Willow Road,
Nottingham, NG7 2WS, UK.

Represented by: Games Workshop Limited – Irish branch,
Unit 3, Lower Liffey Street, Dublin 1,
D01 K199, Ireland.

10 9 8 7 6 5 4 3 2 1

Produced by Games Workshop in Nottingham.
Cover illustration by Jodie Muir.

A CIP record for this book is available from the British Library.

ISBN 13: 978-1-80407-363-6

See Black Library on the internet at

# blacklibrary.com

Find out more about Games Workshop
and the worlds of Warhammer at

# games-workshop.com

Printed and bound in the UK.

---

*For Rab.*

*'Im Westen nichts Neues.'*

For more than a hundred centuries the Emperor has sat immobile on the Golden Throne of Earth. He is the Master of Mankind. By the might of His inexhaustible armies a million worlds stand against the dark.

Yet, He is a rotting carcass, the Carrion Lord of the Imperium held in life by marvels from the Dark Age of Technology and the thousand souls sacrificed each day so that His may continue to burn.

To be a man in such times is to be one amongst untold billions. It is to live in the cruellest and most bloody regime imaginable. It is to suffer an eternity of carnage and slaughter. It is to have cries of anguish and sorrow drowned by the thirsting laughter of dark gods.

This is a dark and terrible era where you will find little comfort or hope. Forget the power of technology and science. Forget the promise of progress and advancement. Forget any notion of common humanity or compassion.

There is no peace amongst the stars, for in the grim darkness of the far future, there is only war.

# DRAMATIS PERSONAE

## INDOMITUS COMMAND

*Lord Regent Roboute Guilliman*, primarch of the Ultramarines, reborn son of the God-Emperor of Holy Terra

*Lord Admiral Cassandra VanLeskus*, commander of Indomitus Fleet Tertius, the Hero of the Machorta Sound

## THE LORD CASTELLAN AND RETINUE

*Lord Castellan Ursula Creed*, commander-in-chief of the Cadian Armies and lord castellan of the lost fortress world of Cadia

*Lord General Pyoter Valk*, in command of the Cadian Third Armoured Infantry, presently deployed on Tectora Prime

*Major Gideon Argent*, the lord castellan's adjutant

*Enginseer Rho*, assigned to the lord castellan's Capitol Imperialis, the *Wrath of Olympus*

*Lieutenant Wilfret Fletz*, staff officer

## SOLDIERS OF THE EIGHTH REGIMENT

*Colonel Hadrian Aurelius Van Haast*
*Tempestor Valcrev*
*Sergeant Major Domnik Strahl*
*Sergeant Vanatu Harapa*
*Trooper Shael Laskari*
*Trooper Lainn Anka*

## PENAL LEGIONNAIRES

*Mac Ossian,* former regimental chirurgeon, Cadian 477th (disgraced)

*Liga Yager,* former member of the Portside Razerwhips gang.

*Clavie,* an ogryn

## THE 12TH CADIAN SAPPERS, THE 'MOLE RATS'

*Captain Ari Tethys*

*Trooper First Class Zhata Meraq*

*Trooper Amyt Meraq*

## THE ENEMY

*Livor Opilionis,* Death Guard sorcerer, known as *'The Huntsman'*

# PROLOGUE

They say the Emperor's Tarot holds a thousand futures.

Dreams shift and swirl across the little crystal wafers. Images resolve one after another – a hand, a skull, a burning eye – before they are swallowed again into the shimmering mists of time. The diviner has spent a lifetime learning to read the cards, but he knows he sees only the surface. An ocean of mysteries lies beneath, its depths fathomless and terrible.

'Tell me what you see.'

The diviner raises a hand. 'Forgive me. A little longer, if you would.'

The distraction is fleeting, but it takes an effort of will to return his focus to the cards. Already the images are fading, returning to the realms of the merely possible. Readings have been known to fail entirely, and he knows that to lose his grip on the gift now would be a fatal mistake for more reasons than one.

Focus.

He closes his eyes beneath the blindfold and opens his mind

again to possibility. One slow breath, and then another – and there it is, the fulcrum, the hinge, the point on which the future turns.

A sphere of broken rock, its fragments scattering as it spins against a starless void. The diviner's senses flood with borrowed memories of a fallen planet: blood and terror, smoke, the taste of ash.

'The Shattered World.'

His patron gives a snort of impatience. 'Any fool in the Imperium could have told me that.'

'The meaning of the cards is not literal.' Though on this occasion, the diviner thinks, it could hardly be more apt. 'The Shattered World signifies a time of struggle. A great loss. A people divided.'

The cards are turning more clearly now, fate weaving her tapestry as quickly as an auto-loom. A woman in gilded armour. A Valkyrie descending like a falling star. The aimless spinning of a compass needle. Loss. Hunger. Resolve.

'The Pilgrim, reversed. The Fortress of Faith, reversed. An unwelcome journey.'

'And?'

The diviner knows the frustration in his patron's voice, but the Tarot, like the future itself, cannot be hurried.

'The Great Eye above. The Labyrinth beneath.' He shudders. Sweat prickles across his skin, his mouth filling with the taste of decay. 'The Enemy follows close behind.'

Silence. Then: 'Is that all?'

'All that the cards will show me.'

'Then what use are they, or you for that matter?' The anger in his patron's voice is palpable, sharp as the point of a dagger against his ribs. 'Draw another.'

The Tarot resists at first, but the diviner knows better than to argue.

The final card is changing even before it leaves the deck. The diviner's hand hovers over the image as he waits. Is the Tarot simply a looking-glass, he wonders, a mirror that reflects what is to come, or does his art somehow fix the future, turning possibility to certainty in the observer's eye?

The mists part, and the card gives up its secret.

A figure stands on a bloodstained dais, vast, armoured and beautiful, a power maul in its hand, a great scarlet cloak billowing around its shoulders.

'The Warmaster.'

'I trust the meaning is figurative.'

'It means–' The diviner's mouth is bone dry. He swallows, tastes blood. 'Power. Loyalty, gained and lost. Betrayal.' His hands are shaking now, and the ringing in his ears is building to a roar. His patron's hand is heavy on his shoulder, fingertips sharp as teeth where they bite into his flesh. There is only so much longer he can hold the vision – and himself – together. 'Death.'

'But they will succeed? They will find it? He will bring it to me?'

The last vestiges of the vision fade. A bone-deep weariness is settling into every part of the diviner's body.

'What is sought is not all that will be found. More than that I cannot see, or say.'

The diviner removes his blindfold, folds the bloodstains inside and readies himself for whatever form his patron's displeasure will take today.

The cards lie in front of him, blank as vellum, heavy with unwritten deeds.

# ACT ONE

*'I have come to lead you to the other shore;*
*into eternal darkness; into fire and into ice.'*

– Fragment from an ancient text,
kept in the Great Library of Terra

# I

## THE WARLORD

'Lord castellan? They need you.'

The interruption came as she poured the second cup of recaff. The tentative knock at the door was as unwelcome as an ogryn in the mess hall, and as easy to ignore. It was followed by a nervous cough and underscored by the faint scuffling of feet, as if whoever was waiting there had a fair idea of the reception they were about to get.

Ursula Skouros, lord castellan of the lost fortress world of Cadia and commander-in-chief of the Tectora IV campaign, closed her book and took a hasty mouthful of the scalding liquid. The first cup had been purely medicinal, gulped down in a single shot without her noticing the taste, nothing but a jolt of rapid-acting stimulant to take the edge from days of sleep deprivation. Ten minutes of peace to enjoy the second had clearly been too much to ask for.

She sighed. 'Come in, Wilfret.'

The door opened. Lieutenant Wilfret Fletz – nineteen standard

Terran years of age and the newest member of her staff – stood in the open doorway, an apology writ large in every hesitant movement of his spindly frame.

'My apologies, lord castellan.' Fletz looked abashed. 'We have a problem in the strategium.'

'What manner of problem?' Ursula rose to her feet, any lingering fatigue instantly dismissed by a fresh wave of alertness. The assault on the planetary capital was less than two hours away, and her strategy was planned out to the minute. Now was not the time for problems.

'I have no details as yet, lord castellan. Major Argent was quite insistent that it couldn't wait.'

Fletz was already moving through the cramped passageways of the Capitol Imperialis. A faint vibration through the deck plating underfoot was the only sign that the *Wrath of Olympus* was still in motion, rumbling towards the battlefield like the inexorable march of time. Speed wasn't one of its qualities, but the *Wrath*'s portable void shields, adamantine armour plating, Behemoth cannon and array of twin-linked heavy bolters provided adequate compensation, to say nothing of its entourage of Baneblades.

The strategium sat at the very heart of the vehicle, a vast chamber with a high vaulted ceiling lit by an array of sulphur-yellow lumen-globes. One wall was dominated by a huge viewscreen displaying a granular image of the ruined surface of Tectora IV, all detail rendered indistinct by the pre-dawn gloom and the driving rain. Every inch of space was jammed with data-looms, maintenance servitors, the platform's bridge crew and her own staff officers, all of them clustered around the room's focal point: the giant hololithic display of Redemption City projected above the war table in its centre.

'Lord castellan. Forgive the interruption.' Ursula's adjutant snapped a crisp salute.

'Major. Do we have a problem?'

'I fear we do.' Gideon Argent gave a rueful nod.

'Details.'

Argent moved around the flickering blue projection so that his hand hovered over a miniature Imperial tank division on the city's western approach. 'The issue is the Third Armoured infantry under Lord General Valk.'

Pyoter Valk should have been holding position. Instead, his armoured column was trundling forwards with his personal Stormlord in the lead, the battle group following like fawning courtiers in a royal procession.

'I see the general is moving early.' Ursula took a step closer to the table. 'Has he given a reason for that?'

'None. And no answer on the vox.'

Ursula settled back into her command throne and placed her right hand on the sceptre built into its armrest. A needle flicked out like a razor-sharp tongue, aspirated a drop of her blood, then retracted to deliver the sample to its cogitator array. The *Wrath* had a permanent crew of forty-five humans and as many servitors again, but its gene-locked machine-spirit answered to her alone.

She let her eyes rest on the hololithic battlefield. Assuming steady progress over firm ground, Valk's battle group would be in position to assault within half an hour, leaving the rest of the Cadian forces a full ninety minutes behind. Valk wasn't an idiot, which meant either he was moving in response to enemy action – unlikely, but not impossible – or he was enacting a plan of his own that had nothing to do with the overall strategy.

'Time for a word with the lord general,' Ursula said. 'Rho, open a holo-link to *Deus Imperator Vult*. Use my personal channel.'

With a silken rasp of well-oiled metal, the *Wrath*'s enginseer unfurled from between two data-looms and extended a slender mechadendrite towards the hololith.

'Certainly, lord castellan.'

There was a bright binharic chirp, and the hololith went dark, then flickered to life again in a two-dimensional display of the Stormlord's cabin.

*'Lord castellan! What a pleasure to see your face.'* Lord General Pyoter Valk brushed the fall of pale blond hair back from his forehead, all smiles and rakish charm, as if they were face to face at a high-society event and not thirty miles apart on a rain-soaked battlefield. Paired scars traced the high lines of his cheekbones, distinctive despite the poor quality of the projection. *'I trust all is well?'*

'I note you are moving ahead of schedule, general.' Ursula kept her voice flat. 'Is there a reason for that?'

*'Of course, my lord.'* Valk's infuriating smile didn't waver. *'My scouts identified an advantageous position closer to the city walls, a better vantage point to gain intelligence on enemy movements. Under the circumstances, it appears too good an opportunity to miss.'*

Ursula shot a glance at her adjutant. Argent rolled his eyes. His low opinion of the lord general had been an open secret for some time.

'Some effort has been made to acquire adequate intelligence on the enemy already, lord general. Resume your former position. We must hope your enthusiasm has avoided the enemy's notice.'

A burst of static rippled across the projection, and when the image and audio returned Valk was leaning forward in his throne, mid-sentence.

*'...waste of time.'*

'Kindly repeat yourself.'

*'My apologies.'* With the image in monochrome it was impossible to be sure, but she thought Valk's face was flushing red. His tone was urgent. *'Allow me to get into position. This opportunity*

*could bring the battle to a close within hours. I have a hand-picked assault unit ready to follow me through the city's defences to disable its void shields from within. Once that is done, the rest of the division will be in position to force a breach and make its way inside.'*

Ursula allowed a moment of silence to stretch out between them, as if she were actually considering the merits of his plan. 'No, thank you. A valiant offer, but one that will not be necessary on this occasion–'

*'Lord castellan, may I have your permission to speak freely?'*

'By all means.'

Valk was fond of speaking freely, and she was rarely glad to hear what he had to say. A dull sense of weariness crept over her. Right at that moment, she'd have given a month's stipend for a decent cup of recaff.

*'Let me do this, and you can have Redemption City in your hands by noon.'*

The worst thing was that he was probably right. The city would be hers for the taking, albeit with its walls shattered and the streets running with blood.

'Return to your position, lord general. Everything is proceeding according to the established battle plan–'

*'Ah, yes. Your sacred battle plan.'* Valk's thin veneer of charm slipped, exposing the raw contempt beneath. *'With a different strategy we could have conquered this planet in half the time. Instead we're taking it at a crawl and worrying over every shot fired. At this rate it'll be weeks before Redemption falls, when I could be in there right now getting the job done.'*

It was nothing she hadn't heard before. Ursula was perfectly aware that he wasn't the only one of her officers chafing in his harness, but that was a problem that was going to take months to sort, maybe even years.

'Your concerns are noted, general. I'll make time later to

discuss them face to face. *After* we've dealt with the matter at hand.'

'*Your father understood what it meant to be Cadian.*'

The strategium fell still. Cogitators hummed.

'Allow me to remind you that Lord Castellan Creed presided over the greatest defeat in Cadia's history. For myself I prefer victory.' Ursula closed her eyes, counted to three, then opened them again. 'You have your orders. That will be all.'

The enginseer voxed a binharic command. The hololith vanished, and the image of the battlefield returned.

Ursula shot a glare around the bridge. 'Does anyone have anything to add?'

The bridge crew were suddenly fascinated by their data-looms.

Argent shook his head. 'I don't believe so, lord castellan.'

Ursula watched the hololith, waiting for Valk's squad to make their move. For a moment she wondered if he had any intention of obeying her orders, until first the Stormlord then its trailing retinue began the laborious work of retracing their route back into position.

'Excellent.' She settled back into her command throne, and tried to loosen some of the tension from her shoulders. Valk's impromptu plans were becoming all too common an occurrence. This one could hardly have come at a worse time: yet another exhausting battle fought to a stalemate before the first shot against the enemy had even been fired.

Contrary to Pyoter Valk's grim predictions, Redemption City fell just before dusk. The city's void shields had crumpled at the first barrage of artillery, and a hurriedly voxed broadcast of unconditional surrender had followed, accompanied by a white flag wrapped around the key to the city and the former governor's freshly severed head. It had been a textbook conquest from start to finish. Tectora's cities had fallen one after another like an obedient house of cards, setting the planet – and by extension, the sector – on the road of return to full compliance after the isolation of the Long Night.

Ursula looked up again at the statue of the God-Emperor in the *Wrath*'s tiny chapel, and wondered if the uneasy sense of oppression she was feeling was the weight of His disapproval.

'Tell me if this is overstepping the mark,' Gideon Argent said. 'But generally I would expect the successful conqueror of a planet to be wearing a different expression.'

'And what expression am I supposed to be wearing, major?'

'Less disappointed. Less angry.' In public, her adjutant was the soul of deference, but in the privacy of their own company they could speak freely. Any real formality had long since been abraded to nothing by more years of service together than she cared to count.

'Why would I be angry?' Ursula forced a smile onto her face. 'See?'

'You're right. That's worse.'

Argent was right, Ursula thought. She was letting a treacherous sense of anticlimax rob all savour from her victory. Even if the fall of Redemption had been a foregone conclusion, the rebel governor's posturing nothing but a final vainglorious stand long after his people's thirst for war was slaked, that didn't make it any less important. Her plans had come together beautifully in the end, the victory a fitting reward for all her labours.

It still felt hollow.

'Maybe Valk is right,' she said.

Argent snorted. 'If he hears you say that he'll be even more insufferable than he is already.'

'I mean it. Plenty of the old guard are thinking the same. We could have had the conquest over months ago if I was willing

21

to move quicker. Shed more blood. Reduce a few more cities to rubble.'

'Yes, another blasted asteroid is certainly what the Imperium needs. We should reach for the cyclonic warheads every time some idiot provincial governor decides they would be better off not paying their tithe.' Argent withdrew a compact flask from the inside pocket of his tunic and raised it in a toast. 'To your glorious victory. Even if you failed to shed quite enough blood for your generals' tastes.'

'Any fool can turn a planet to ash.' She accepted the offered flask, took a sip of Argent's foul-tasting rotgut and handed it back. 'Having something worthwhile left afterwards is the tricky part.'

The words hung in the air of the chapel like incense. Ursula could guess what her adjutant was thinking. There was only one broken planet that would have brought that solemn, thoughtful expression to his face.

'Between you and me, I suspect Valk has never got over not being there for the Fall.' Argent's voice was bright, but there was something brittle behind the words. Years might have passed, but the wounds left by Cadia's destruction still ran deep. 'To hear him talk, he could have fought the Despoiler and the whole Thirteenth Black Crusade single-handed. We'd all be in Kasr Myrak right now knocking back amasec by the pint. That, and he considers himself the rightful lord castellan of Cadia. If only the High Lords of Terra had seen it that way too.'

'Yes, if you listen to him the whole Guard is a hotbed of nepotism and corruption, and I only have the job because of who my father was.' She rolled her eyes. 'I would be insulted if I thought the man had a single original thought in that golden head of his.'

Decades had passed since the Fall of Cadia and the death

of the former lord castellan. Ursula had been a captain with the 65th Heavy Mechanised Infantry at the time, engaged on Hakeldama against an orkish infestation that for a time had threatened to consume the planet. The first she had heard of Ursarkar Creed's death had been the arrival of a handful of personal effects: a battered cigar case and a signet ring so badly worn that the initials *U.E.C.* were barely legible. They were the relics of a stranger who meant as little to her in death as he had in life, a man who had given her nothing, not even a name.

Worse, he hadn't even had the courtesy of providing a corpse to ease the transition of power to his successor. The last anyone had seen of him was in the thick of the fighting at Kasr Myrak, but no death had been witnessed or corpse recovered. It had taken high command years after his death to agree to reinstate the rank of lord castellan, as if they had been convinced that their old commander might swagger out of Cadia's broken remains at any moment and demand his title back.

In the end, though, the delay had acted in her favour. With years to prepare, by the time the High Lords were ready to appoint another lord castellan, she was prepared to claim the position for her own.

A pool of a hundred suitable senior officers had been reduced to twenty, then ten, then a final three. That was when she had known the battle was won. Ursula Skouros had earned her title with blood, grit and an aptitude for strategy unmatched in the Cadian armies, and she would be damned if she let any one of them – let alone Pyoter bloody Valk – take that achievement from her.

*'My congratulations on another successful conquest, lord castellan,'* Captain Landry Scheer said through Ursula's vox-bead. Scheer's low, pleasant voice was as clear as though they were standing in the chapel and not on the bridge of the troop ship *Undaunted* in orbit five hundred miles overhead.

'Thank you, captain.'

'*I need a moment of your time.*' There was something uncharacteristically hesitant in Scheer's voice. '*We've just been hailed by a vessel midway between the Mandeville point and our present coordinates. The authorisation codes for this vessel carry the highest authority.*'

'To the point, please, captain. Who is it?'

'*The* Omnia Paratus, *under Captain Marcella DeQuervain. A Cobra-class destroyer, most recently assigned to Fleet Primus.*'

Now *that* was interesting. Fleet Primus was the spearpoint of the Indomitus Crusade, a vast armada under the personal command of the reborn primarch Roboute Guilliman, Lord Regent of the Imperium.

'She's a long way from home.'

'*No doubt of that, lord castellan. She's come here with a message. And a request.*'

'What do they want?'

The silence of the vox-channel stretched out into seconds of dead air before the ship's captain spoke.

'*You, lord castellan. They say they're here for you.*'

# II

## THE RAGGED FOOL

It wasn't the worst day of his life, Mac Ossian thought – *that* spot was firmly taken – but it was certainly in the top three. He was one of forty prisoners desperately trying to keep his balance in the back of the freight-truck, packed shoulder to shoulder and struggling to stand upright. The clammy air smelled of cheap disinfectant, vomit and other people's sweat.

The day had started badly, but it had managed to go down-hill from there. It had been his fourth day in the penitentium's oubliette, the hours stretching out so long, empty and dark that he had started to wonder if he had been forgotten entirely, but apparently the Emperor's plans – and those of the Astra Militarum – went beyond leaving him in a hole to rot. Any flicker of hope he had felt when the cell door swung open had been quickly extinguished when a pair of military provosts had jammed the barrel of a lasgun into his ribs and dragged him, filthy, naked and blinking into the light.

'Try something,' the provost had said. 'Go on. See what happens.'

He had frozen on command, waiting while a chirurgeon he didn't recognise slid the gleaming tip of a hypodermic into the median cubital vein of his left arm, and the next half-hour had passed in a state of helpless paralysis. The medicae had taken their time over the examination, scrutinising every inch of his anatomy to satisfy themselves that he was fit for his intended purpose. The inspection ended with a series of painful intra-muscular injections, the juddering of a tattoo needle across his forehead, and a resonant click as a heavy collar snapped shut around his neck.

You could say what you liked about the Astra Militarum Chirurgical Corps, but when it came to processing penal legion-naires they were quick, clinical and startlingly efficient – but then, they'd had a lot of practice.

'What you in for?'

The voice came from the penal trooper to his left, a whipcord-thin woman in a flimsy synthweave jumpsuit that matched his own. The truck lurched, and he almost fell, grating his knuckles painfully against the metal wall as he shoved himself upright again.

'Does it matter?' Ossian shrugged, rattling the chains that bound his wrists and ankles together. A separate chain ran through his cuffs, linking him to the woman on his left and a scrawny kid who looked barely out of his teens on the right. It looked like the kid was the source of the smell of vomit, judg-ing by the nauseous expression on his face and the dark stains down the front of his jumpsuit.

'Just making conversation,' the woman said. The diode on her collar flickered red, and in its half-light he caught a glimpse of her grinning face, her teeth stained yellow from a heavy cotin habit, her left eye red and swollen. 'Bet you're innocent, right? Same as the rest of us.'

Something heavy slammed into the corrugated partition between the driver's compartment and the back of the truck, the sound of the impact reverberating through the enclosed space.

'No talking back there,' a man's voice rasped.

Silence fell. Ossian sat down against the wall, feeling the vibration of the truck's tyres through the metal at his back. The vomiting boy on his right had closed his eyes, his bony chest rising and falling in quick, shallow gasps, his face ghastly pale. Maybe the medicae hadn't been that competent after all.

Ossian stared at the roof and tried to think about nothing at all, but his mind was a storm of swirling thoughts and images. Maybe he should kick up a fuss so that the provosts had to come back here and make good on their promise. At least then he could stop worrying about where they were going. The truck was stiflingly hot after the bone-gnawing cold of the cells, the rocking of the truck over uneven ground almost comforting. If he tried, perhaps the God-Emperor would grant him the gift of sleep...

The truck swerved, jostling his head painfully off the metal behind him. He looked up, startled, as one of the other prisoners stumbled and fell into his lap. He shoved the prisoner away, sending him sprawling across the wiry woman's lap in a confused tangle of limbs.

'Idiot,' he snapped, regretting the sharpness of the words as soon as they were out of his mouth. Losing his temper had got him into this situation, and it was hardly going to improve matters now if he lost it again. He unclenched his fists, took a slow breath and let it out again.

Keep your mouth shut, that was the one rule from life in the Guard that still applied to his new life. Speaking up never failed to get you into trouble. He had learned that lesson the hard way.

The truck braked sharply. Someone else fell, dragging more prisoners down with them. Ossian drew himself upright and pressed his back against the wall. A fight in here would spread like burning promethium. Staying on the ground would get him crushed.

He looped one arm under the scrawny boy's shoulders and dragged him to his feet. The boy wasn't doing much to support himself, but given that he couldn't have weighed more than eight stone soaking wet it didn't take much effort to keep him upright.

'Are you injured?' Ossian asked him.

The boy's eyes opened. His lips parted, but instead of words a fresh trickle of vomit made its way down his chin. The boy's skin was so hot Ossian could feel it through the flimsy synthweave jumpsuits. That wasn't good. If whatever the boy had was contagious, every one of them had already been exposed, the highest dose reserved for those closest by.

Just his luck yet again.

The truck's back door opened and the darkened compartment flooded with light. Ossian closed his eyes a fraction too late, and a dazzling blue after-image danced wildly in his vision.

'Get out, the lot of you.' It was the same voice as before, the one that had shouted for silence in the back of the van. The connecting chain gave a sharp jerk, and Ossian almost fell.

'Can you walk?' he asked, and nudged the boy in the small of the back. The kid didn't speak, but he took a shuffling step forward, then another. It wasn't much, but it was going to have to do.

By some miracle the guards managed to keep the prisoners on their feet, wrangling them out of the truck into a huge open space that Ossian thought at first might be a warehouse of some kind, before he recognised the symbol of the eagle-in-flight stencilled on every wall. They were standing in the cargo compartment of a heavy mass-transit conveyer, while a convoy of trucks lumbered up the ramp to disgorge their cargos and dead-eyed servitors stacked pallets and containers by the walls.

By the time the hold doors slammed shut there were over five hundred convicts lined up in rank and file. Most of them were like the woman chained on his left, the sort of toughs and gangers you'd find on any trip groundside for rest and relaxation, but a handful looked like they'd been soldiers some time in their fairly recent past. There was at least one ogryn, separated from the others at the rear of the compartment and accorded the privilege of one-to-one attention from a provost of her own.

The provost who had shouted before, a balding, heavyset man in his mid-forties, with a sergeant's stripes on his shoulder and the beginnings of a gut, stepped forward and unfastened a shock baton from the loop on his belt. Behind him, a tall woman in a calf-length black coat regarded them from under a peaked cap, one gloved hand resting on her holstered bolt pistol.

Commissars. You could spot them a mile off.

'Listen up.' The provost's voice was jarringly loud, echoes reverberating off the vaulted ceiling of the cargo hold. 'Let me break some bad news to you. As far as the Imperium is concerned, you are all the walking dead. The cowards who lacked the good sense to take a clean death when you were offered it. From now on, you exist for one purpose – to take the weapons you are given and discharge them at the enemy until they die, or you do.'

Ossian glanced at the boy standing next to him. He looked barely conscious, swaying back and forward as if he might topple over at any moment. His skin was flushed and glistening with sweat, and occasionally he let out a weak, hacking cough. The provost and the commissar didn't seem to have noticed, or if they had, neither thought it was worth paying attention to.

'Your old lives are over,' the provost sergeant continued. 'You can put any thoughts of earning your freedom back in the ground where they belong. From now on you eat on command, you shit on command, you think of nothing but your duty, and if you are extremely fortunate the God-Emperor might give you the blessing of a clean death on the battlefield.'

He smiled, light glinting off a gilded tooth. He held up his wrist to display a chrono-sized brass device covered in miniature dials and levers.

'This control module can trigger both of the two mechanisms in those fine necklaces at your throats. This one' – his finger hovered over one switch – 'will deliver a carefully measured dose of frenzon into your jugular vein, sufficient to overcome any cowardly inhibitions you might have when faced with glorious battle. I think you all know what the other switch does. Any questions?'

The boy gave another pathetic cough. Ossian raised his hand.

'Someone has something to say.' Mock-courtesy dripped from the provost sergeant's words. 'What is it, legionnaire? A question to ask? Wisdom to share?'

Ossian kept his eyes fixed directly ahead. Keep calm. The bastard's voice was grating his nerves raw.

'The trooper to my right is sick. He may well be contagious. Untreated, he poses a risk to everyone in this vessel.'

The provost sergeant's footsteps echoed as he walked down the row of prisoners and put his face nose to nose with Ossian's.

'Contagious, is he? Are you an expert on contagious diseases, legionnaire?'

'I have some experience, yes.'

'And how do you come by that?'

Ossian made a quick mental calculation. How much of the truth was he going to tell? He settled for just enough to make a convincing answer. The rest was none of anyone's business.

'I was a field-medicae with the Cadian Four-Seventy-Seventh.'

'Oh, a *Cadian*,' the provost said, lacing the word with contempt. He turned away, playing to the crowd with a gold-toothed grin and a broad sweep of his baton. 'We should have known from the eyes. How honoured I am to be in the presence of a soldier of Cadia. My commiserations on the loss of your planet.'

A sycophantic titter ran through the rows of legionnaires. The provost puffed out his chest.

'Tell me, Cadian, how does that failure feel?'

Ossian kept his mouth shut. He had been stupid to speak up, stupid to get himself noticed. It was always a mistake.

'No answer for that? Let's try an easier question. What's your name, Cadian?'

He straightened his back, standing as close to attention as the chains would allow. If he was going to take flak for being a Cadian, he was damn well going to act like one.

'Oss–'

The baton caught him in the jaw, the impact followed a split second later by a dull electrical impact that shuddered through his brain, short-circuiting speech, balance and hearing in a single flash of light. His ears rang. Lightning bolts shot across his vision. He hadn't felt himself hit the floor, but he was sprawled at the provost's feet, his muscles twitching helplessly as he tried to stand.

'That,' the provost said, sending a fine spray of spit into Ossian's face, 'is the wrong answer. You have no name, no rank, no place of birth. So far as the Guard is concerned, you might as well have been shat out of the warp this morning like the turd you are, do you understand me?'

He tapped the baton to Ossian's forehead. Ossian braced himself for another nerve-shattering shock, but there was only the uncomfortable press of plasteel against the freshly tattooed and tender flesh.

'These three numbers here. These are your name, rank and serial number, unit, regiment and family home.' The provost sergeant punctuated each noun with a rap of the baton on Ossian's aching skull. 'From now until the end of your short, miserable life.'

A hand locked around the collar of Ossian's jumpsuit and pulled him upright. He swayed unsteadily on the spot, ears still ringing, his lips fat and numb. The provost sheathed his baton, and twisted a brazen dial on the control unit on his wrist.

'And just so none of you forget the *other* thing your collars do.'

His finger touched the brass button. Ossian closed his eyes, braced for the explosion that would take his head from his shoulders.

There was a dull thud in his right ear, more like an imploding lumen-bulb than the detonation of an explosive charge. Something warm and wet spattered the side of his face. It was blood, but not his own.

When Ossian opened his eyes, the boy was on the ground, his scrawny torso ending abruptly at the neck. Where the head should have been there was only a wet grey-pink smear on the decking. His left hand was lying palm up, the fingers curled in on themselves like the legs of a dead insect, the thumb still twitching.

'Allow me to be the bearer of glad tidings,' the provost said. 'There is no need to worry about contagion in the penal legions. There are only two ways your new career ends. You die for the Imperium doing your Throne-given duty.' He tapped a finger to the little control unit on his wrist. 'Or you die when I do mine.'

# III

## THE GREAT EYE

On a borrowed desk in borrowed quarters, the parchment scroll lay coiled tightly around its secrets. In the week that the *Omnia Paratus* had been in the warp Ursula had rolled and unrolled it a hundred times, still not quite able to believe its contents no matter how often she inspected them. She had known the document was important from the moment she had set foot on the destroyer and found its captain waiting to hand over the scroll in person, but it was the seal that was the truly extraordinary part: a circle of royal blue wax the size of her palm, embossed with a silver-white inverted omega.

The symbol of the Ultramarines.

She unrolled the scroll again and traced her fingers over the ornate Gothic script. The jagged letters and sweeping quill strokes of the calligrapher's script would have been better suited to a High Gothic litany than the terse series of instructions it contained. A faint scent of incense rose into the air from the disturbed parchment, a breath of sandalwood and attar of roses.

*To the Lord Castellan of Cadia,* the missive began. The letters were illuminated with scrolls and skulls, the two capital 'C's each incorporating a stylised Cadian gate. *You are hereby instructed to take immediate warp passage on His Imperial Majesty's voidship the* Omnia Paratus, *destination classified. Further orders will follow on your arrival.*

There was no date. The scroll might have been prepared a week ago or have spent ten thousand years in a stasis chamber, but the signature, a large, sweeping 'R' at the bottom of the page left no doubt as to the identity of its sender: the lord regent himself, the reborn primarch of the Ultramarines, Roboute Guilliman.

Ursula was no stranger to the battle-brothers of the Adeptus Astartes. In a military career that had taken her to four subsectors through twelve protracted campaigns, the sense of awe she felt in their presence – a wonder that touched the perimeter of fear – had never faded, as intense as the first time she had seen them stride from the fog of war like giants from a fable. They were the Emperor's right hand, avenging angels, come to deal death with a blazing sword, heedless of the lowly mortals locked in combat around them. The thought of the eldest and greatest of them with a quill in his hand to sign her orders in person was an incongruous and unsettling thought, as if she had received orders signed by the God-Emperor Himself.

The smell of incense in the room was cloyingly sweet, but it still wasn't enough to mask the faint scent of burning. Her eye drawn back to the scroll, she watched in disbelief as the letter 'R' blackened and widened, the parchment charring in an expanding ring of green-tinged flames. She reached for something to extinguish the fire – her jacket, her bedroll, anything – but the scroll was already fully ablaze, tiny fragments of charred grey paper drifting upwards in the thick grey smoke. A gust of scalding air caught her full in the face, and as she watched, the flames seemed to light not just the scroll but also everything behind it, burning through reality as if it were nothing more than a painting on a wall. There should have been deck plating, the supports of the table, her own carefully stowed backpack – but instead the hole opened directly into the void, a thousand glittering stars scattered across a vast violet nebula.

Ursula knew that sky. She had been born beneath it, slept beneath it each night for the first twenty years of her life, knew the constellations – the Sword, the Chariot, the Seven Spears – as old friends. She tried to turn away, but her feet were frozen to the floor, her eyes fixed on the hole in reality that was now wide enough to step through. The flames were consuming the room from its deck to its overhead, reality melting away to nothing like a candle tossed into a fire.

The nebula was dazzlingly bright, its unnatural purple-green aura rippling out in great questing strands that spun and coalesced like vast probing tentacles. Something tore in the fabric of space, and a thousand eyes opened in the space beyond the void. The Great Eye. Its gaze pressed against her soul, probing for any cracks through which it might enter and rot her away from the inside.

'No–' she managed. Her lips were numb. Her skin was erupting in blisters, her vision blurring as her eyes ran with tears of blood and pus.

The something behind the eyes laughed, the sound of mockery bypassing her ears, arriving fully formed in her skull.

It spoke only one word.

*'CREED.'*

Ursula sat upright in her bunk, her right hand closing around the sidearm on her nightstand before her eyes had fully opened. A klaxon was blaring, its harsh whoop loud enough that she could hear it despite the thundering of blood in her ears. The scroll was lying intact on her desk, the room empty, the ship's recycled air cold against her skin.

She had been dreaming. She was on board the *Omnia Paratus*, following the lord regent's orders. There had been no fire, no tear in reality, no great eye watching her from the abyss. The thought of it was still enough to send a shudder down her spine.

The klaxons fell silent. The ship's vox-system crackled, and a tinny voice spoke.

*'God-Emperor, save us from the mouth of the wolf.'*

Ursula knew the prayer: one of the litanies for safe warp translation. The dream lingered, clinging to her consciousness the way her sweat-soaked underwear clung to her skin. Her muscles aching as if she'd just finished a close-quarters assault, she slipped a robe around her shoulders and perched on the edge of her bunk. The chem-showers could wait. They were hardly an ideal place to be if the warp translation went less than smoothly.

*'Silence those who would harm us, and call us forth with the blessed.'*

The ship was still, as if even the vessel's mighty machine-spirit had turned its gaze inward in prayer. Leaving the warp intact was a fate to be desperately desired, but as Ursula understood it the points of translation were amongst the most dangerous of the voyage, the times at which a ship might lose its course, or attract unwelcome attention and be lost entirely.

*'Crew and passengers of the* Omnia Paratus, *prepare for warp translation.'* This time it was the captain who spoke, her voice crisp and confident. *'We are in His hands, and there is nothing to fear.'* A pause. *'Navigator, bring us home.'*

The lumens flared red, flickered once, and went dark. The ship lurched sideways in a shift that had nothing to do with physical movement. The eye from her dream flashed into her vision, fear clawing at her guts as the great blazing lids slowly opened...

And then it was over. The lumens resumed their steady glow, and the faint sparkle at the edge of her vision that always accompanied a trip through the empyrean faded to nothing.

*'Praise be to the God-Emperor for His deliverance.'* The tension was gone from the captain's voice. The deck plating resumed its faint vibration as the ship's plasma drives returned to life. *'Heading towards our rendezvous point now. At full burn we should reach our destination in less than two hours, Emperor willing. Crew, to your stations.'*

Two hours.

Time for food, a chem-shower, and then, perhaps, some answers.

# IV

## THE PILGRIM

Cadet Shael Laskari opened her eyes.

The target sat in the centre of her scope as if it had been painted there. She focused on the three concentric rings printed on the parchment, ignoring the scorch marks left by her two previous shots – one off-centre to the left, the other top right. She had one shot left to take, and all the time in the world to take it. She moved her index finger from the trigger-guard and brought it into position. Breathe in. Breathe out. And–

'Take your shot, ratling.'

The target danced wildly in her sights. Laskari lowered her long-las, and shot a glare at the cadet to her right. Lainn Anka was grinning back at her over his own rifle, which glinted in the harsh midday sun.

'I'm not a ratling.'

'Really? That's news to me.' Anka looked her up and down. 'You're short like a ratling, you're scrawny like a ratling, but then I suppose you don't shoot nearly as well as a ratling.'

'I thought you had your own shot to take, Anka?'

'I think you'll find that's Cadet Sergeant Anka to you. Besides, I already have done.' He gestured with the barrel of the long-las down the shooting range. Laskari lifted her scope and focused in on Anka's target. Three shots. Close grouping. No bullseye, but still a decent performance. She'd need to hit her target dead-centre if she wanted to beat his score. Given what was at stake, she'd never wanted anything more in her life.

'I'm telling you, you're going to miss.'

'Why?' Laskari kept her voice light. She already knew the answer. Getting this far in the marksmanship trials had already earned her a black eye and a warning to withdraw her name from the competition lists, but she hadn't backed down then and she wasn't going to start now.

'Just a piece of friendly advice.' Anka's grin widened. 'One you'd do well to follow.' He turned his attention back to his own target half a second before the drill abbot raised a hand for silence.

'Stop wasting time, Laskari,' Drill Abbot Pollek barked. 'Take your shot.'

Laskari turned her attention inwards, focusing on her breathing, trusting her hands to steady on their own. Her target came back into focus. Another breath, in and out, all of the world reduced to three concentric rings on a sheet of vellum. The long-las was an extension of her own hand, the shot already made in her mind's eye.

She squeezed the trigger. A bolt of green energy seared down the shooting range, leaving the sharp scent of ozone in its wake, and a charred brown circle in the very centre of the target.

*Bullseye.*

She held the target in her sights for another second, hardly able to believe the shot she had made. There would be a price to pay in blood and suffering – there always was – but she had won. Anka had lost, and that made up for a hundred insults, a thousand beatings.

Because her victory came with an even sweeter prize, promised by the major to the best shot of the Whiteshields. Promotion to the rank of trooper. Colours and a badge, permission to scrub the white stripe from her helmet, and best of all, transfer off-world. She didn't know where she'd be going, but it had to be better than the endless deserts of Shukret-Dhruv.

The drill abbot called the ceasefire. Laskari lifted her head from her sight and placed the long-las down on the sand at her feet. Anka had done the same, his eyes fixed on the drill abbot as he walked down the shooting range to retrieve the targets. Abbot Pollek unpinned first Anka's then her own, held them up to the light, then rolled both together into a single cylinder. Laskari's nerves were singing, any composure vanished the moment her final shot hit the mark.

'Well shot, both of you.' The drill abbot didn't smile, but then he never did. 'Cadet Sergeant Anka, report to me at eighteen hundred hours for your new assignment. Cadet Laskari, as you were.'

It took a moment for the drill abbot's words to sink in. That wasn't right. The winning score had been hers, not Anka's. The drill abbot had made a terrible mistake.

'Abbot Pollek... please.' The abbot was at the barrack-hall door by the time she caught him, her feet kicking up plumes of sand from the training field. 'I think there must have been an error. I hit the bullseye with my third shot.' She motioned to the vellum targets, rolled up under the drill abbot's arm. 'Check them again, sir. Please.'

The drill abbot unrolled the scrolls and separated the two sheets, holding first one to the light and then the other. The hot yellow sun blazed through her bullseye to cast a vivid circle on the dusty ground.

'There it is, sir. My shot. That one there.'

'Anka shot the bullseye.' Abbot Pollek's voice was flat. 'This target is yours.'

'No, sir. Like I said, there must have been a mistake...'

She stopped. It wasn't a mistake. The drill abbot knew fine well whose target was whose.

'You shot well, Laskari.' He spoke firmly, without a trace of sympathy. 'But Cadet Sergeant Anka shot better.'

'Yes, sir.' A lump of frustration rose in Laskari's throat. She swallowed it down, her eyes dust dry. Just another day. Another disappointment.

She should have known to expect it by now.

The period between noon and three was officially designated for maintenance of equipment, self-edification and, if the necessary permission was obtained, mortification of the flesh by any officially sanctioned technique, but in practice the midday heat made anything but rest impossible. Most of the cadets spent the hours flat on their bunks under a copy of the Imperial Infantryman's Primer, ready to lift it into a reading position if the barrack door should swing unexpectedly open.

Laskari didn't hurry back to barracks. After her conversation with the drill abbot she returned the long-las to the armoury and stripped it down, reciting the litany of cleansing as she worked sacred machine oil into its moving parts. The barrel was cool now, the spirit inside lying sullen and dormant. She didn't blame it. They had both been cheated of their victory today. When she had finished, she took Anka's long-las from where he had tossed it into the weapons locker and cleaned that, too, stopping only when both weapons were gleaming inside and out.

Even in the shade the heat was merciless. She took herself back to the barracks and lay on her mattress, staring at the springs of the bunk above. With a bit of luck Anka would be too busy preparing for his departure off-world to make good on his promise to make her regret her actions, but there would be no shortage of willing volunteers ready to step into the power vacuum his departure would leave behind.

The door opened, and thousands of tiny motes of dust danced in the sunlight. Laskari closed her eyes. Someone nearer to the door groaned and rolled over, then something soft and heavy thumped into her midriff.

'Laskari, the major wants to see you. In her office, right away.'

She sat up and shoved the thrown head-roll onto the ground, her face burning. A soft, mocking 'oo' rose from the other White-shields. It was the traditional response when any of them were summoned to the base commander's office, an invitation usually followed by a dressing down at best, and a flogging at worst. Obviously, a report of her insubordination had reached the major's ears, and the decision had been taken not to let such a thing go unpunished.

Laskari got to her feet and straightened her uniform. In her experience, pain and humiliation were both best dealt with by gritting your teeth and getting it over with.

The major's door was open. Two of the windows were open as well, and a faint breeze was wafting through the building, blowing fine golden dust inside. Keeping the building free of sand was a losing battle, but the movement of the air was refreshing, a partial antidote to the scorching heat of the day.

Laskari struggled to remember the last time she had been inside the major's office – a bare, spartan space, the only signs of individuality a few grainy old picts in ornate metal frames. One showed a much younger major standing in front of a Leman

Russ, while the other was a portrait of an unsmiling child who might have been six or seven Terran years old. Neither pict looked like it had been taken during the last two decades.

'Sit down, cadet.'

The major poured two beakers of water from the metal jug on the desk. Her ocular augmetic telescoped outward with a soft whine, and a muscle twitched in her scarred cheek. The rumour in the base was that the major's battlefield career had ended with the shot that had taken her eye and paralysed half of her face, leaving her with the choice of retirement or over-seeing the training of raw recruits. Now she spent most of her days behind closed doors and left the day-to-day training of the cadets to the drill abbots.

'I heard you shot well today.' The major's voice was hoarse, dust dry, with a metallic twang from her augmetic larynx. Her face twitched again. Laskari kept her gaze on the major's good eye.

'Thank you, sir.'

'I understand you have some concerns about the drill abbot's judgement in the final round.'

'No, major.' Laskari took the offered beaker of water and sipped it, swilling the warm liquid around the inside of her mouth before swallowing it down along with her pride. 'I forgot myself. I misspoke.'

'Did you.' The major's remaining eye narrowed. Laskari thought the iris must have been violet once, but the years and the plan-et's relentless sunlight had faded it to the same dull grey as her hair. How long had the major been stuck here, on a planet where only the poles were habitable and the rest of the world was a sea of molten glass?

'Tell me, cadet.' The major coughed, and took a sip of her own water. A trickle escaped from the scarred side of her mouth. 'What do you understand about the task for which Cadet Sergeant Anka has been selected?'

Laskari racked her brains. There had been so much rumour and gossip that it was difficult to remember any of the facts at all. 'It's a mission off-world, sir. Destination and purpose classified.'

'And you're keen to go? Despite not knowing the slightest detail of what might be required of you?'

'I'm ready to serve, major.' There was no going back now. 'I know they're looking for a good shot, and I'm the best in the company.'

The major's mouth twitched. 'Are you, now?' She took another sip from her goblet, and placed it down between her hands. 'It may surprise you to hear that I know very little more than you do. I have received a request from high command to recommend a cadet for a classified mission into enemy territory. Competence, diligence and obedience are all desirable qualities, along with aptitude for the long-las, but there is one further attribute, considered non-negotiable. The selected trooper must be of Cadian blood.'

Laskari felt her face flush scarlet. 'My grandmother fought with Colour Sergeant Kell on Cadia, major. Both of my parents were born under the Eye of Terror.'

'But you yourself were not.'

'No, major.'

'You have a younger sister, I believe?'

'Yes, major. Drina. She's at the schola. She'll be ready to take up arms in a year.'

The major nodded thoughtfully. 'Cadet Sergeant Anka was born within the wider Cadian System. His family is what is generally referred to as old blood, and I have been informed that his relations would be outraged should a cadet of such' – she gave a short, dry cough – 'obvious potential be overlooked. As regards his lineage, he is the ideal candidate for selection.'

*And what about every other regard?* Laskari thought.

'I take it you have a different opinion of him?'

Laskari paused. 'I don't think my opinion is relevant, sir.'

'Very diplomatic.' The major reached behind her, and pulled a scroll from the columbarium on the wall. 'Anka has been selected for this mission, and will be leaving Shukret-Dhruv tomorrow according to schedule. That much will not change.' She passed over the scroll, sealed with a red wax disc embossed with an image of the Cadian Gate. 'However. Nowhere does it state that I am forbidden to send a second candidate, should I believe they are suited to the task.'

Laskari extended her hand, and let her fingertips rest on the smooth, cool parchment of the scroll.

'Here are your orders, trooper. Go and scrub the stripe off your helmet. You ship out tomorrow.'

# V

## THE FORTRESS OF FAITH

The sheer size of Naval voidships was something Ursula found impossible to comprehend. A mile on the ground was a known quantity, something that could be covered in a fixed unit of time, but once she tried to apply the distance to a structure floating in the endless expanse of space, her brain slid sideways from the concept and failed to make any sense of it at all. No matter how many times she made the journey through voidspace from one warzone to another, she had never adjusted to its scale.

Her first sight of the *Chamberlain Tarasha* had been from the bridge of the *Omnia Paratus*, as the Adeptus Astartes vessel waited for them near the Mandeville point. Its engines had been banked down, and the lights along its jagged flanks were a subdued amber glow.

It was not, by Imperial standards, an enormous ship. At a little over a mile in length, it was less than half the size of her usual troop carrier, but while the *Undaunted* was a beast of burden, the Astartes vessel was a predator, long, sleek and ready to spring. Now, as the gun-cutter ferrying Ursula drew closer on its final approach, its lights picked out the vast gilded aquila on the *Chamberlain*'s flank, the hooded gun-ports of its broadside cannon battery, the glowing aperture of the aft hangar bay.

'Bringing us in now, lord castellan,' the pilot said.

A pair of silver mechadendrites extended from beneath Enginseer Rho's scarlet robe to lift the tech-priest to a standing position. 'This journey would have been twenty-five per cent more efficient had anyone thought to equip the pilot with a mind impulse unit.'

On the other side of the passenger compartment, Argent laughed. 'What's your hurry, Rho?'

A rapid series of binharic chirps sounded from beneath the red-and-white hood. '*You* may not be looking forward to seeing the interior of an Adeptus Astartes vessel, Major Argent, but I most certainly am.'

For a moment, they were weightless. Golden light filled the gun-cutter like a benediction, then a soft thud reverberated through the hull, and gravity reasserted itself.

'Mag-locks engaged. Down-powering engines. Praise the God-Emperor for another safe voyage.'

Ursula got to her feet. 'I'm very glad you're looking forward to it, Rho, but try not to touch anything. Under the circumstances I would prefer not to offend our hosts.'

Rho traced an elegant spiral in the air with one of their articulated steel tentacles. 'I will of course try my best, lord castellan.' They gave a theatrical sigh, the sound tinny and metallic through their vox-speakers. 'But you have to understand that it will take considerable willpower to resist such a unique and tempting opportunity.'

Rho kept an extensive databank of recorded sounds as replacement for the ones their augmetic larynx could no longer make.

Ursula wondered if that particular world-weary sigh had been one of her own. It sounded like it might have been.

'You usually tell me temptation is a sin of the flesh.'

'I admit only to the purest of intellectual curiosity.'

'Compartment repressurised, lord castellan.' The pilot had turned in his chair to face the passenger compartment. 'Shall I open the hatch?'

'Do it.'

Ursula rose to her feet. Argent took up his usual position at her right hand, the tech-priest and Lieutenant Fletz directly behind them. Given the numbers needed to oversee Tectora's return to compliance she had barely been able to spare a handful of troops to act as her personal retinue – which, given Captain DeQuervain's refusal to carry anyone other than the bare minimum, was probably just as well. A squad of armsmen had been assigned as her security detail for the duration of the voyage, but she would have felt considerably more comfortable with a fire-team of Tempestus Scions at her back.

The hatch swung upward. The air in the hangar bay smelled of the same incense as the scroll: sandalwood, Marwaldian pepper and rose attar. Two cowled human figures stood waiting at the bottom of the gun-cutter's down ramp, a man and a woman, dressed in long royal-blue tunics with the symbol of the Ultramarines emblazoned across their chests.

The man pushed back his cowl and stepped forward. 'Welcome aboard, lord castellan. Please come this way. The lord regent is waiting.'

His voice was calm, his Low Gothic precise, accentless and perfectly inflected. Behind him, his companion kept her head bowed, her features obscured by the soft drape of her hood. Chapter-serfs, born and raised to serve the battle-brothers in all things, as their parents had before them and their children would after they were gone. A life of obedience, without independence or self-determination. Her skin crawled at the thought.

'My thanks.'

She stepped out of the gun-cutter and the enormous scale of the vessel struck her again. The *Chamberlain Tarasha*'s hangar bay was the size of a cathedral, Thunderhawk gunships in rows to either side, her borrowed gun-cutter a child's toy by comparison.

Argent gave a low whistle. 'Big, isn't it?'

They passed through a towering doorway into a passageway with walls of unpolished adamantine, which absorbed more than reflected the flickering torchlight. A sharp left turn took them onto a gantry overlooking the belly of the ship below, where blue-robed serfs moved vast macrocannon shells between the *Chamberlain*'s magazine and its battery, a pointed reminder that the Adeptus Astartes were never truly at peace.

'Would you like a moment before we proceed, lord castellan?' the serf asked.

They had reached a simple door at the end of a wood-panelled passageway by the time he spoke, its simplicity almost shocking after the baroque splendour of the rest of the ship.

'No need. I'm ready.'

But ready for what?

If the lord regent intended to strip her of her commission, that could have been done on Tectora, but instead he had seen fit to drag her through the warp to an unspecified location. Logically, the thought should have given her comfort, but the adrenaline flooding her system made her think otherwise. An unpleasant suspicion occurred to her. What if Guilliman had decided to withdraw the Cadian armies from their current objectives, break up the regiments and use them to bolster the forces committed to his great crusade? Her father's lord castellanship had ended with the loss of their home world; was hers to end with the dissolution of their entire culture?

'My lords.' The serf opened the door and bowed. 'I present to you the lord castellan of Cadia.'

Ursula took a step inside. The chamber was dark, with a huge table in the centre, lit by a scattering of free-standing braziers that cast as much shadow as they did light.

A towering figure in blue-and-gold power armour sat at the head of the table. Firelight glinted on the laurel crown around his forehead, highlighting his aquiline profile and deep-set blue eyes. She had never seen him in the flesh before, but there was no doubt in her mind that she was in the presence of the Lord Regent Roboute Guilliman himself.

'Lord castellan, be welcome.'

Ursula had expected his words to come as a deafening thunder, but when the sound arrived it was different – a soft, deep rumble that she felt in her chest as much as heard with her ears. She knew his face from a thousand devotional picts, but no portrait could do the man justice. There was something about the ancient warrior that transcended mere humanity; he was full of a terrible beauty that promised inspiration and devastation in equal measure.

With an effort of will, she turned her attention to the other people in the room. There were four at the table, all of them unaugmented humans, while a pair of fully armoured Ultramarines stood vigil behind their lord's throne.

'Please, enter,' the lord regent said.

Ursula stepped forward, suddenly aware that she had been gawping senselessly on the threshold. One of the seated figures raised a checking hand – a middle-aged man wearing an elaborate black-and-gold frock coat, his long dark hair upswept in an elaborate chignon and topped with a miniature voidship.

'We don't need the retinue, I don't think.' The man's voice was languid. 'The serfs can attend to their needs elsewhere.'

'I was under the impression that my staff were also welcome.' She didn't recognise the man, but from his manner and fashion sense he had to be one of the rogue traders who had committed their fleets to the regent's great crusade.

Lord Guilliman inclined his head. 'I leave that decision in your hands, lord castellan.'

The rogue trader visibly bristled. 'As you command, lord regent. But I would urge the lord castellan to consider that the matters which she has been called here to discuss are of the gravest importance. To set foot upon this vessel is to invite the attention of our enemies. And we have enemies within and without, you may have no doubt of that.'

The image of the burning eye from her warp-dream flooded Ursula's mind. 'If any of my retinue have concerns regarding their personal safety, they are at liberty to leave.'

No one moved, not even Fletz.

'Excellent. My lord regent, I am at your disposal.'

The primarch rose to his feet. Seated he had been tall, but on his feet the size of him defied logic. He might look human, but she was acutely aware that he and his brethren were nothing of the kind. She had seen the Astartes fight often enough to know how that veneer of humanity slipped away when confronted with the enemy, leaving only the devastating weapon the God-Emperor had created them to be. A shiver passed across her skin at the thought of how Guilliman would look in anger. She doubted there were many who had seen that sight and lived.

'I trust you will forgive the necessary secrecy with which this meeting has been arranged. I will not make formal introductions, but each of us in this chamber represents the interests of the Imperium, specifically the Indomitus Crusade.'

The rogue trader raised his glass in a mocking salute. To his left sat a young woman with pale skin and a close-cropped helmet of dust-and-ashes hair, a string of heavy adamantine beads on the table in front of her. To Guilliman's right was another man, wearing Astra Militarum dress uniform, a brigadier from one of the regiments with an over-developed taste for gold braid. He didn't look like someone who'd seen active service for a few decades, but that didn't mean he wasn't dangerous. She searched her memory for a name to fit his description, and came up blank. The Guard was full of old soldiers in fancy uniforms.

The last was a woman in Naval uniform, with a steely expression and an augmetic eye. Ursula knew her from reputation alone: the indomitable Admiral VanLeskus. If the other people at the table were the equivalent of VanLeskus in rank and power, a melta bomb on the table would obliterate the head of Indomitus Command in a single messy blast.

'Cassandra VanLeskus,' the woman said. 'An honour to meet you, lord castellan. I've followed your career with interest over the years.'

'As I have yours, fleetmaster.' Ursula felt her muscles fractionally relax. The Naval commander's straightforward introduction was uncommonly welcome. 'I understand your victory at the Machorta Sound is being extensively studied in the Academies as a flawless example of Naval strategy in action.'

A faint green glow kindled in a darkened recess of the chamber, illuminating a hunched figure in the scarlet robes of the Mechanicus. This tech-priest was huge, so large that she had the feeling that if it stood upright it would have towered over everyone in the room except the primarch.

'I beseech you, Lord Guilliman, we must make haste.' Its voice buzzing like a hive of insects, it raised a skeletal hand into the air.

The room flooded with light. Three servo-skulls shot upwards and beamed a star map onto the vaulted ceiling, the image sharp and clear as if they were outside beneath a night sky. Slowly at first, then with increasing speed, as though seen from a point atop a moving voidship, the image zoomed in on a tangled galaxy, a star system, and finally on a single planet whose continents she knew as well as her own features.

A planet that no longer existed.

'Cadia.' She felt the rumble of Guilliman's voice through the deck plating. 'The greatest of the fortress worlds. For centuries, its people kept the Cadian Gate, the most strategically important navigable route to and from the Eye of Terror. The home world of the finest human soldiers in the Imperium, who were its last line of defence against the abominations that poured from the warp rift.'

The older man in Militarum uniform straightened in his chair, and Ursula felt a brief flicker of pride and satisfaction at the offended look that passed across his face, before returning her attention to the projection. Clouds were rolling across Cadia's surface now, flickering with vivid green lightning.

'Your father was the greatest tactician the Astra Militarum has known since Solar Macharius. Despite all of his efforts, the planet fell to Abaddon the Despoiler.' The primarch's lip curled, as if the name tasted sour, and as if in answer, a vast shadow passed in front of the world. The Blackstone Fortress, an ancient voidship of unknown origin, large enough that its impact had obliterated a planet.

Ursula shifted her restless limbs. The feeling was absurd, but some deep-rooted emotion made her want to turn away from what was about to happen. Countless times she had imagined standing on Cadia's surface as the fortress filled the sky, as it had blotted out the sun, as the planet's inevitable destruction had drawn closer. How had it felt to live through those moments, knowing that all was lost? Not for the first time, she was grateful that tidings of Cadia's destruction had only reached her long after it was over.

'My lord regent, I am sure you have not brought me here merely to revisit my father's final defeat.' She swallowed, her mouth suddenly dry, and the planet exploded, sending pieces spinning out into space like shattered glass. 'His war was fought and lost decades ago.'

'Indeed.' The great leonine head nodded. 'Much was taken that day. Much, but not all.'

A fragment of the planet hung in the empty air, ragged at its edges, magma trailing from the shattered edge where its core had once been. Behind it, in the illusory sky, the Great Rift split the heavens, casting the remains of the Cadian System in an unearthly crimson glow.

'One sizeable part of Cadia Prime remains.'

Ursula drew a sharp, involuntary breath. What the lord regent was saying wasn't possible. Cadia was gone, obliterated, shattered to dust and debris. The last vox-broadcasts from Cadia had told the terrible truth, that the planet was physically breaking apart beneath their feet, torn to shreds by the Despoiler's wrath. That some part of it had endured was unthinkable, impossible, yet here was the truth on the lips of the Emperor's chosen son.

Gideon shifted beside her, and she touched a warning hand to his wrist to forestall whatever he was about to say. 'You must understand, lord regent, this comes as something of a shock,' she said. 'May I ask what is known of those remains?'

Guilliman inclined his head towards the rogue trader in the elaborate headgear. 'The lord captain's vessels have been of tremendous use in scanning what remains of the planetary surface. Lord captain, if you would?'

The rogue trader rose to his full height. Surmounted by the huge headdress he might have been an imposing sight, under other circumstances, but next to the primarch the attempt fell flat.

'It would be my honour, lord regent. My enginseers have cross-referenced the auspex images received to pre-war maps of Cadia. The remnant is composed of approximately one-twentieth of the planet's former mass, the surface covering an area including the Rossvar Mountains, the surrounding land mass and the remains of several fortress cities.'

'And is there any evidence of life on the planet's surface?' Ursula asked.

The rogue trader's face twisted into an unpleasant smile. 'There is certainly abundant activity on the surface. Whether that can be said to be life in any true sense of the word remains to be seen.'

Ursula's temper flared. Why did this overdressed fool have to be so obtuse? She clenched her hands into fists, counted to three and consciously relaxed them. 'Allow me to be more exact, lord captain. I am enquiring as to the presence of human life signs. Specifically, Cadians.'

He shrugged the question casually aside. 'After all this time? I hardly think *that* likely.'

VanLeskus sat forward in her chair. 'To the best of my understanding, what is left of the planet's surface has been utterly overrun by the forces of the Archenemy. The Despoiler may have turned his eye to Holy Terra, but there are many lesser beings of his kind who continue to squabble over Cadia's remains.'

A bitter taste rose into Ursula's mouth, a heady mixture of disgust and anger building in her chest, as though she had been unexpectedly confronted by the rotting corpse of a long-dead relative.

VanLeskus went on. 'Lord Castellan Creed travelled widely across Cadia as part of his final preparations for its defence. He spent time in the vicinity of the Rossvar Mountains not long before the invasion proper began. We believe he was overseeing the creation of a vault, somewhere to leave his final plan for Cadia, to be enacted in the event that his forces were overrun.'

That certainly matched what Ursula knew of her father: always with another plan up his sleeve, never defeated, only moving on to the next great plan that would save the day. Except in the end all of his plans had come to nothing, and Cadia had paid the price.

'What manner of plan, admiral?'

'No one is certain. There were rumours, of course, talk of a weapon powerful enough to strike one decisive blow at the enemy. Something that might, perhaps, have ensured his people's future, but that he never had a chance to deploy.' VanLeskus shrugged. 'I should add that this is for the most part specula-tion. The atmospheric storms make it impossible for the lord captain's auspexes to study much below the surface.'

'Over this last decade, the Indomitus Crusade has been the spearpoint of the Imperium's retaliation against the Great Enemy,' the primarch said. 'Yet those enemies grow stronger and bolder, their territories expand. Their corruption spreads. A weapon of mass destruction of the sort that your father believed could protect Cadia from the Despoiler would be a priceless asset for our cause.'

Ursula blinked. 'Forgive me, my lord, but am I to understand you propose a return to this... this daemon-haunted fragment of Cadia?'

'You understand correctly.'

'My lord.' Ursula ran her tongue over dry lips, choosing her words with care. 'I must urge caution in such an endeavour. An attempt to conquer what remains of a world overrun by the forces of Chaos could all too easily waste thousands of lives in pursuit of a highly uncertain reward, lives that the Imperium cannot easily spare.'

The rogue trader snorted. 'It seems I was right, lord regent. Not exactly her father's daughter, is she?'

Blood rushed to her face. She clasped her hands carefully behind her back, so that she wouldn't be tempted to put them round the popinjay's neck and squeeze the life out of him. She focused her attention on Guilliman instead, who, to her surprise, carried on as though the rogue trader had not spoken.

'In that regard we are in agreement, lord castellan,' Guilliman said. 'I do not propose an invasion. I invite you to consider instead, that with the correct support, a small unit of Cadian soldiers might succeed in their objective where an army would fail.'

That prospect was enough to catch her interest and hold it. 'An interesting challenge, my lord. If you wish me to formulate a strategy, I would require access to the lord captain's auspex data, specifically information on atmosphere and plate tectonics, maps of the relevant fortress cities and the surrounding terrain. I have several experienced officers with the skills for this sort of mission' – her heart sank as she realised exactly how suited to the task Pyoter Valk would be, and how delighted he would be to be asked – 'and following a period of consideration I would be honoured to present you with my recommendations.'

The huge tech-priest made a rhythmic wheezing hum. The fleetmaster leaned forward.

'I think you misunderstand, lord castellan. The recovery of Ursarkar E. Creed's lost weapon would bring us a powerful military asset, and act as a potent symbol of the indomitable Cadian spirit. But for Creed's daughter – for Lord Castellan Ursula *Creed* – to fight her way through the ruins of Cadia, to don her father's mantle, to reclaim his legacy, to continue his great work as leader of his people...'

For the first time during their brief meeting, VanLeskus smiled.

'Think of how potent a symbol *that* would be.'

# VI

### THE GOLDEN GATE, REVERSED

Ossian had given up keeping track of the days. At first, he had used hunger, thirst and fatigue to mark the passage of time, but his physiology had become unreliable. Now he was always hungry, thirsty and weary no matter what he did, restless and bored with no end to the long darkness in sight.

The ogryn had the right of it, he thought. The big abhuman spent her time in meditative silence, rousing only when the cage door opened for delivery of their daily ration of corpse-starch. The provosts made no effort to ensure equitable distribution, and those prisoners too slow or too weak to take and hold what they needed were left without. Ossian followed the ogryn's example: wait patiently close to the cage door for the rations to be thrown in, take his share then retreat to a darkened corner like an animal at bay, glaring with all the ferocity he could muster at anyone who came too close. As long as there were softer targets, he could choke down his unappetising meal in peace.

He broke a piece off the starch-bar, placed it in his mouth and chewed it thoughtfully. It was bland and dry, parchment flavour with a hint of bone-glue and an aftertaste that reminded him of the smell of cauterised skin. It was remarkable how the Imperium produced a consistent product no matter where you went in the galaxy. No matter what luckless bastard had been rendered down for nutrients, they always tasted the same. At least in the Guard you got a packet of Seasoning No. 5 to go with it, its tongue-burning heat a tolerable substitute for actual flavour.

'You going to finish that?'

The voice in his ear came as a surprise. He had started to think of his fellow convicts as a gestalt – a sullen, many-headed beast with an orange synthweave hide, lumbering helpless and resentful towards slaughter – and to hear one of them speak independently was almost a surprise.

The speaker was the same woman who he had been chained to in the truck. Her shaven scalp was dotted with a faint blonde stubble where her hair was starting to grow back. His own scalp itched.

Ossian looked at the unappetising ration bar in his hands. It didn't look like much worth fighting for. 'No. Do you want it?'

'Thanks.' She took it, swallowed down half without bothering to chew and tucked the rest inside the cuff of her jumpsuit before offering him her hand to shake. 'Name's Liga Yager. You're the Cadian, right?'

Ossian sighed. With nothing else to entertain the convicts, the story of his beating in the hangar bay had spread like Catachan razorweed, consuming any unfortunate truths caught in its path.

'Mac Ossian,' he said, and felt a tiny moment of defiant satisfaction. They could take his rank from him, but his name was still his no matter what the provosts said.

'I can call you Mac, right?' She didn't wait for an answer. 'Heard you saying you were a medicae back in the day. That's got to be useful where we're going, right?'

'I doubt it. No one seems to be handing out medkits. I imagine they're working on the principle that legionnaires are cheaper to replace than repair.'

He had hoped his ration would buy him a few minutes of peace, but the woman showed no sign of leaving. She smiled like they were old friends, though she looked young enough to be his daughter. His granddaughter, even.

'Is this purely a social visit, or was there something more than rations that you wanted?'

She laughed. 'Straight to the point, doc. I like it. I'm not after anything, only a medicae's a useful man to know.' Her accent was harsh and nasal, and a gang name – *Portside Razerwhips* – was tattooed along her right forearm. She turned her hand over to reveal an expensive skinplant nestled beneath the skin of her right palm. 'Thief's light. Nice, yeah?'

It was the sort of technology that would have cost a couple of months' stipend for anyone with an honest job.

'If you want my advice, I suggest you keep that covered unless you want to lose the hand.'

Liga shrugged. 'Don't reckon they care much. Long as we don't cause a fuss I reckon we're sitting pretty till we hit dirtside.'

'This?' He couldn't quite stifle a laugh. 'This is what you would call sitting pretty?'

'What's not to like? Warm and dry, food once a day, anyone gives you shit and the provosts come in and blow their head off. Better than back home.'

'You are aware why we're here, yes?'

'Worry about that tomorrow.' Liga leaned forward conspiratorially. 'Listen. I hear they've got something big planned for us. Dropping us into a warzone, fighting heretics, something like that, yeah?'

'A reasonable supposition.'

'Anyway. The guards talk all the time. When they're unloading the chow, checking the collars, all of them talking like we don't even exist. Most of this lot' – with one sweeping gesture she took in the assembled mass of human misery, spraying crumbs of corpse-starch in a fine arc through the air – 'they're going to drop them right in the middle of trouble. But some of us they're going to send down separately. A small squad, one Valkyrie. Fewer legionnaires means fewer provosts, right? Which means we've got a chance to get away.'

As plans went it wasn't the worst one Ossian had ever heard, but it was a close-run thing.

'You understand we are unlikely to be deployed on an Imperial world, don't you? The penal legions are reserved for the worst warzones in the Imperium. The ones where the butcher's bill comes in too steep for even high command to want to pay in regular Guard.'

'Sure.' Liga waved his objection away. 'But the way I see it, right, either we do as we're told like good little troopers and die fighting for His Holiness over there' – Ossian was fairly sure she was referring to the provost sergeant rather than the God-Emperor Himself – 'or we get down there, see what we can sort out and make a run for it. Maybe we die, maybe we don't. I'll take those odds over certain death any day.'

'Which would all be fine, except for our new neckwear.' Ossian tapped a finger to the collar around his neck. 'These are fitted with a proximity trigger. Run too far from whoever's got the control unit and…' He held his hands up to his face and mimed an explosion. 'I've seen them in action. You can take reassurance from the fact that you'll be dead before you have a chance to realise what's happened.'

'Yeah, but they'll have to disable it somehow. That or send an officer down with us dirtside, and somehow I don't think they'll be so keen to die with a bunch of convict scum, do you?'

Maybe she was right. It sounded convincing, but then, he doubted a dockside ganger would be much of an expert on the penal practices of the Astra Militarum.

'Fine. Let's say I believe you. Why are you so keen to have me involved?'

'Like I said. We could use a medicae.' She gave him a yellow-toothed grin. 'That kid back in the loading bay, the one who got his head vaped, he was one of my lot. You tried to do him a solid. I figure you're the right sort to have at my back in a tight spot.'

The blast doors opened. Ossian had known it was coming from the moment the engine note changed from a steady thrum to shorter, lighter bursts. He had been on enough troop ships to know that sound. It meant they were adjusting their course in small, careful increments. The ship was getting ready to establish itself in orbit. They were about to arrive.

'Hands on your head!' Provosts moved into the hold, taking up firing positions between the cages. Liga nudged Ossian forward so that they were standing at the bars, a better place to get noticed, she had said. A better place to volunteer.

Liga's offer had been preying on his mind since she had first made it. He was under no illusions about his chance of surviving regardless of what form his deployment to the planet took, and the more he thought about it the harder it was to find merit in either course of action. Was Liga right? Did they have a better chance of survival in a small group, or was this all a futile attempt to regain some semblance of control over her destiny? Death was certain in either case. Did it matter exactly what form it took?

'Good news, legionnaires,' the provost sergeant said. 'I'm look-ing for a dozen brave souls for a special mission.' He ran the tip of his shock baton along the bars, stopping just at the locked gate. 'Hot rations and a chem-shower for any volunteers, how's that for an offer?'

Liga nudged him again. He shook his head. *Too risky.*

'Here.' The ogryn lumbered forward, one big hand outstretched towards the bars. 'Hot ration? Clavie volunteer for that.'

'There you go.' The loathsome smile was back on the provost sergeant's face. 'That's your ogryn putting you to shame right there.'

'What you want me do?'

'Do exactly as you're told, legionnaire, and you'll be fed and cleaned up quick smart. Anyone else?'

Liga raised her hand. 'I volunteer.'

Scattered hands rose. A provost holding a bunch of auto-keys unlocked the cage further down, releasing a steady trickle of volunteers. Ossian caught a glimpse of a bulky pair of men, shaven-headed and identical, a slight, indistinct figure that was either a ratling or a child, and another ogryn, this one appar-ently male.

'My friend volunteers too, sir,' Liga said.

Ossian tried to back away, but the ogryn was behind him, waiting patiently for the cage door to open. *Shit.* He shook his head again, but Liga ignored him, waving with one hand and pointing at him with the other.

'He's a medicae, sir. Used to be in the Guard, sir.'

'Oh, the Cadian again.' The provost sergeant sounded pleased. 'Volunteering to die for the Emperor like a good little soldier. Looking for a second chance, are we?'

'My thanks, but no–'

'Out you come.' Keys jangled, and the door swung open. Two

provosts stepped in to hold the others back. Liga darted past them through the open door and the ogryn lumbered after. 'No need to be shy, Cadian. We've got a treat for you coming up.'

'See? All going according to plan,' Liga whispered.

Ossian didn't agree.

'Emperor protect,' he muttered.

'Not worry, little man.' The ogryn put her hand on his shoulder and gave him what she probably thought was a gentle pat. Any gentler and she'd have driven him feet first into the deck plating. 'Clavie look after you.'

# VII

### THE STAR

'This is outrageous.' Argent's mouth was close to Ursula's ear, his voice a tight, controlled whisper. 'A potent symbol is right. A symbol of the Imperium throwing Cadians to the wolves yet again.'

'Gideon, this is not the time–'

'This is a suicide mission they're talking about, Ursula, do you understand that?' Her adjutant's voice was shaking, a vein bulging on his forehead. He might think he was keeping his voice down, but the lord regent's posthuman hearing would be attuned to every word. The primarch was yet to react, but that could only be a matter of time. She'd seen Astartes kill for lesser degrees of disrespect.

'That will be all, thank you, major,' she snapped.

Argent's mouth shut.

'Allow me to provide some reassurance. This is not a suicide mission.'

VanLeskus was leaning forward across the table, her hands

clasped in front of her. Clearly there was nothing wrong with her hearing either. Neither she nor Guilliman seemed remotely perturbed by Argent's outburst, though the rogue trader had puffed himself up like an offended blowfish.

'Full support will be provided, both in the form of boots on the ground and aerial surveillance, with a plan in place for early extraction should the need arise. In addition' – VanLeskus' gaze dropped briefly to her hands, and she hesitated for half a breath before continuing – 'the Morale Departmentum is keen to obtain pict-footage of your triumphant return to Cadian soil.'

'Admiral, am I to take it that this is a *propaganda* exercise?' The faint sense of nausea Ursula had felt at the sight of the devastated planet returned. Maybe Gideon was right after all.

'As a secondary objective only.'

Ursula almost laughed. 'And when it goes horribly wrong? Do you really expect watching me getting torn to shreds by a Neverborn – or whatever other abominations are down there – will rally the troops?'

VanLeskus shook her head. 'As I said, risk should be minimal. In addition to what I've already mentioned, we have a distraction planned to draw away any local enemy forces to cover your approach, with a second decoy squad sent into your deployment zone ahead of you to gain intelligence on any hostiles in the area. As for the soldiers under your immediate command, a list of suitable personnel has already been prepared.'

Ursula blinked. 'My apologies, Admiral VanLeskus. I must have misheard you. I could have sworn you said you had already chosen my squad.'

'Not me personally, no.' VanLeskus had the good grace to look slightly abashed. 'It has been deemed necessary that a range of Cadians are represented on the mission. Some born on-world, off-worlders of Cadian heritage, transplants from other regiments. There's a longlist from which you can make your final selection.'

'I see.' Ursula's thoughts were a tangled mess. 'My lord regent, might I have a moment to consider?'

A ripple of surprise ran through the humans in the room. Clearly the notion that she would do anything other than immediately assent to the primarch's plan hadn't occurred to them.

'Certainly, lord castellan.' Guilliman's composure didn't waver. If anything, he seemed pleased by her request. He turned to the Space Marine on his left. 'Brother-Captain Ajax, kindly escort the lord castellan and her retinue to the observatorium. I have often found the serenity of its surroundings conducive to clarity of thought.'

'Thank you, lord regent.' Despite the vaulted ceiling, the air in the room was suddenly close. 'But perhaps you would be kind enough to allow my staff to wait elsewhere.' She glanced at Argent. He was still red in the face, his lips squeezed tightly shut as if holding back a tide of words. 'For the moment, I would prefer to gather my thoughts alone.'

The observatorium was a circular room beneath a transparent armaglass dome, star charts arrayed in columbaria around the walls and a throne in its centre, everything built on a scale large enough to accommodate the primarch. She decided not to sit. If this was where Guilliman came to meditate then casually assuming his chair would be uncomfortably close to blasphemy – and besides, the sheer size of it would have made her feel even more of a child than she already did. Instead she stood beside it and turned her gaze to the stars overhead, aware of the watchful gaze of Captain Ajax as he stood sentinel in the doorway.

This was it. All the decades she had spent squirming out from under her father's legacy, building her own career, her own reputation, her own formidable list of victories, had come to this. Her achievements were of no importance to Lord Guilliman, VanLeskus or any of the others. She thought of the rogue trader's mocking sneer, and her gut clenched tight with anger.

Not exactly her father's daughter, he had said.

That was fine. She had never wanted to be.

The stars overhead were glittering specks of diamond on a velvet cloth. Was Cadia visible from here, a fragment of a dead world orbiting its dying star? She let her eyes unfocus, losing herself in the shifting nebulae, fathomless as her own swirling thoughts.

Argent was right to be angry, but losing his temper in the primarch's presence had been unforgivable. To show disrespect like that to any Space Marine would have been perilous, but the lord regent was the son of the God-Emperor Himself, reborn after the opening of the Great Rift to light the way with his father's fiery blade. But more than that, Guilliman had brought her here for a reason. To hear the plan, certainly, maybe even to meet and get the measure of her, but that hadn't been all. The greatest surprise of all was not that she was to return to Cadia, but that he was giving her a choice in the matter.

That made it a hundred times more difficult.

On the face of it, the decision was easy. All she had to do was decline with the greatest of respect, and she could be on her way back to the Tectora System within hours, putting the finishing touches on a highly efficient campaign. After that, she had a list of systems in need of conquest that would keep her busy for a decade or more, returning the lost to the Emperor's holy light using the skills she had spent a lifetime developing.

Or she could throw it all away: her career, her name, a lifetime of careful planning. The name was the worst part. Becoming 'Ursula Creed' again would be agreeing to live her life in a costume, a mummer in a cheap mystery play: an acknowledge-ment that every achievement of her life was worth less than a dead man's legend. That was a lie she wasn't willing to live, no matter who was asking.

She cleared her throat. 'Captain, I have reached my decision.'

Ajax inclined his vast helmet towards her. 'Very well, lord castellan.'

Ursula stepped forward to follow him from the room, but he lifted a massive gauntleted hand to stop her.

'Wait here. I will inform the lord regent of what you have told me.'

He closed the door with an air of finality. Ursula felt a pang of guilt at the prospect of the look of disappointment that would no doubt appear on the fleetmaster's face. She had *liked* VanLeskus. The rogue trader could take himself and his ludi-crous headwear off to the warp for all she cared.

She waited. Seconds stretched into minutes. A comet streaked across the sky, passing from one side of the armaglass dome to the other and on into darkness. An omen, the preachers would have called it, but then that was their business – finding mean-ing in signs and portents. Making war on a grand scale was hers, and she saw no reason to stay away from it any longer than she already had.

Heavy footsteps echoed down the corridor, then the door opened again. She straightened her tunic, ready to follow the battle-brother from the room, then stopped as she realised who was standing there.

'Lord castellan,' Guilliman said.

'My lord regent.'

The primarch's vast, broad-shouldered frame filled the door-way, and she had to strain her neck to look up at his face. This close, he towered over her, a giant of a man built on a scale as hard to comprehend as that of the voidship on which they stood. Ursula caught her breath, and forced herself to stand her ground. Rationally, she knew she had nothing to fear from him – not here, not today – but there was something about his presence that brought a cold sweat out on her skin, something deep-seated and atavistic, a fear dredged up from ancestral memory like a warning scrawled on a star chart.

*Here be monsters.*

'Captain Ajax tells me you have reached a decision.'

'Lord regent, I am honoured beyond measure by your offer–'

'A moment, please, before you continue.' Guilliman walked past her to the centre of the room and stood beneath the dome. 'You are aware of the name of this vessel?'

Ursula blinked. 'The *Chamberlain Tarasha*, my lord.'

'Indeed.' His bright blue eyes turned to the stars overhead. 'Tarasha Eutan was seneschal to the consul of Macragge some ten thousand years ago. Her name is written in countless histories. But of those who knew her in person, only I remain.'

*Ten thousand years.* An unimaginable span of time, but he spoke of it as easily as if it were days or weeks. What would it be like to remember these distant times with such clarity? To have outlived family, lovers, friends – all lost in ten millennia of stolen years.

'It was under her tutelage that I grew to adulthood. She and my foster-father taught me that which was required of a noble of Macragge. Diplomacy. Leadership. The arts of war. I was an adept pupil.' There was no boastfulness in his words, merely the serene declaration of an unassailable truth. 'I was a grown man by the time my father came to claim me. It would be a lie to say I did not entertain some doubts as to my suitability for the role ordained for me.'

Guilliman's eyes were still fixed on the stars. Ursula studied the planes of his face, features of such classical perfection that they might have been wrought in marble. It was strange to think that he had ever known a moment's doubt. He turned and met her gaze, and it took all her considerable willpower not to look away.

'I tell you this not to counsel you to any course of action. I tell you this because I understand what it is to feel the burden of a father's legacy. It is not always easy to be what the Imperium requires of us.' A frown flickered across his face. 'All the more so in these difficult times.'

He extended his gauntlet, and she took it hand-to-wrist in a warrior's handshake. Fingers that could have crushed her skull like a spent shell-casing closed around her forearm, his hand so large that the ceramite-clad fingertips brushed against her elbow-joint.

'Regardless of your decision, lord castellan, I am glad to have had this chance to meet with you.'

Another shooting star passed across the dome of the observatorium, a cold streak of blue-white fire.

'The council will be waiting,' Guilliman said. 'Are you ready to return and give them your answer?'

'I am, my lord.' The decision that had been so difficult to take mere minutes before was suddenly effortless. 'I will lead the return to Cadia. Under my father's name, if that is what must be done.'

'Then allow me to be the first to thank you by name.' The faintest of smiles crossed the ancient warrior's face. 'Lord Castellan Creed.'

*Ursula Creed.*

Everything about the name felt wrong, like badly fitting armour. Like a dead man's coat pinned around her shoulders.

# VIII

## THE SLAUGHTERED GROX

Four sharpened iron stakes were all it had taken to secure the poxwalker to the ground: one through each wrist and one between the paired bones of each ankle. It lay spreadeagled on the ground, the head and the rotting limbs stretched out like the points of a star. Cords of muscle stood out on its neck as it strained to lift its head from the ground, teeth gnashing furiously in the attempt to break free. The effort was futile. It had been nailed to Cadian ground, and there it would remain.

Livor Opilionis, disciple of Grandfather Nurgle and one-time sworn brother of the Death Guard, raised a final spike in his armoured right hand and leaned down to steady the thrashing head with his left. He waited until the rotting jaws gaped widest, then drove the spike down between the broken yellow teeth, pinning the head to the ground through the back of its skull.

Opilionis turned his gaze to the sky above his head, and the sky glared back. Here, at the highest point of the ruined fortress city, the Eye of Terror, that malign tear in the substance of reality that had burned above the fortress world of Cadia since time immemorial, flared so brightly it seemed only yards out of reach. Beside it, the great glowing wound of the Cicatrix Maledictum tore the void in half, staining the granite towers and spires of the ruined city a deep, unwholesome crimson.

He drew the rusty combat knife from beneath his robes, knelt by the struggling poxwalker, and slit its rotting skin from throat to pelvis in one smooth movement. Bloated entrails burst from the ruptured abdomen in a cloud of noxious gas, tumbling over each other in a grotesque simulacrum of life. The poxwalker continued its useless struggle against its restraints, its glowing red eyes filled with hate and hunger. Opilionis reached inside the abdomen and pulled out a fistful of liver, the necrotic organ disintegrating into mottled red-and-black pulp at the touch of his gauntlet. The gall bladder burst, sending a fountain of pus across the gaping wound. He inspected each in turn, laying out an intricate mosaic of kidneys, intestines, spleen and pancreas on the shattered ground.

The auguries were clear.

Opilionis rose and regarded the pathetic specimen hollowed out before him. The poxwalker had served its turn, and its relentless moaning had become an irritation. He raised one armoured foot and brought it down on its chest, crushing the already liquescent lungs and desiccated muscle of the heart to pulp. The poxwalker still twitched against its restraints, but its groaning ceased.

A huge power scythe lay on the ground at his feet. He stooped, lifted it with reverent hands, and attuned his senses to call upon the warp. Storm clouds raced across the sky towards him, crackling with malign energies, blotting out the stars. Even the light of the Eye grew dim, its baleful gaze obscured to a dull red glow. Wind gusted suddenly, whistling between ruined buildings, carrying a heavy crimson rain as it went.

The storm was only the first step.

Soon the power he had dreamed of would be his, and all those who had scorned him would pay.

# IX

## THE KNIGHT OF DISCORDIA

The cargo bay of the *Oriflamme* was alive with activity, crew in ornate black-and-gold uniforms directing the flow of goods and supplies, shifting crates marked *Munitorum Supplies* and *Caution: Explosive* out of cargo shuttles and onto humming suspensor platforms. Something hit Laskari's backpack and she stumbled forward, almost falling before she managed to right herself by grabbing Anka's arm.

'Watch your step, you clumsy oaf!' he hissed.

'Sorry. Something bumped me.'

Laskari turned, and found herself looking into the dead eyes of a loading servitor. Its arms had been replaced with two lifting claws, the bare flesh a livid, painful-looking purple where skin met metal. It smelled overwhelmingly of bleach, sacred incense and decay.

'Have you never seen a servitor before?' Anka asked.

'Never up this close.' She manoeuvred her backpack so that it was sitting squarely on her shoulders again, then tightened the chest strap.

'What an education this must be for you.' Anka's lip curled. 'Where are we to report?'

Laskari rolled her eyes. 'I'm not your adjutant.'

She had been sick of Anka before they started their warp journey, and nothing had improved by the end. He had spent the time alternately boasting about his own remarkable abilities, denigrating hers and speculating about their mission. After the first day she had made it her business to avoid him, spending hours walking the gantries and passageways of the refinery ship on which they had taken passage.

The servitor continued its uncomplaining progress across the cargo bay. Laskari reached into her pocket and brought out a folded sheet of parchment covered in her own careful handwriting.

'Like I said before. We're to report to a Captain Mariet Thysia on arrival.'

'And does it say where we do that?'

'It says she's part of the Departmento Munitorum.' Laskari scanned the room. 'There's no sign of an officer here. An infantry officer, I mean.'

It was Anka's turn to roll his eyes. 'I hardly think they'll be coming to fetch us in person.'

'I suppose we could ask–'

'In a place this size? We might as well try to find a skull in an ossuary.'

Anka was aggravating, but he was also right. The loading bay was bigger than the entire training camp on Shukret-Dhruv, and the brief glimpse she had seen of the *Oriflamme* through the refinery ship's grubby porthole had left her overwhelmed by its size. She didn't think it was a military vessel; in her limited experience, the Astra Militarum didn't cover every surface with quite so much gold-and-black filigree.

'We can't wait here.' Laskari waved a hand around the cargo bay, noticing a fast-moving Naval rating just in time to avoid smacking him in the face. 'We're getting in the way. If we just get out of the loading bay perhaps we can find someone and ask directions.'

'I'd wager a week's rations we're back here in less than an hour no further forward.'

'I'm not interested in your rations.' Laskari moved in the direction of the doorway on the far side of the cargo bay.

A Naval officer in black and gold stopped them, his lasgun held at ease across his chest. Laskari's own long-las was strapped to her pack, unloaded and carefully padded inside its drab brown carry case.

'You two. What's your authorisation?'

'Trooper Shael Laskari, sir.' She snapped a quick salute.

The armsman gave her a calculating look. 'Cadians, are you? What's your regiment?'

'We don't have one yet, sir. We have orders to report to Captain Thysia on arrival.'

'Don't know them.' He had a curious accent, clipped and sharp, each brief sentence rattled out like a volley of bullets. 'Need to see your orders.'

Laskari unclipped the chest strap of her rucksack and propped the bag on the ground at her feet. The scroll-case containing her orders was packed in tight beside a spare set of fatigues, a bedroll, the remains of a week's rations and the few picts of her family she stored flat inside the pages of her Primer. They were the sum total of her worldly possessions, and they barely filled half a twenty-gallon kitbag.

She pulled out the case, broke the seal and handed the document over for inspection.

'Yours too,' the armsman said to Anka. He scanned both

papers, rolled them up again and handed them back. 'Munitorum delegation's in the aft compartment, deck six. Two flights up, head out into the main deck and turn left. Can't miss it.'

'Aft?' Laskari looked to the armsman for clarification, but his attention was already elsewhere. She shrugged, opened the bulkhead door and stepped into a narrow stairwell, the stairs beyond so steep that they would have been better described as a ladder. Two flights up, the armsman had said.

She hitched the rucksack up on her shoulders, and began to climb.

The provosts made good on their promise of food and chemshowers. Now that the penal legion was safely on board the *Oriflamme*, Ossian got the impression that the provosts had relaxed. That wasn't much of a surprise. They were another step closer to handing over the tiresome responsibility of keeping a few hundred convicts alive until they were ready to be slaughtered for the God-Emperor's glory. Ossian had overheard snippets of conversation about the return voyage, about the provosts' plans for home, the joy-toys they'd visit, the places they'd drink in on their shore leave. He – and every last sweating soul in the hold – would be dead by the time the first glass was poured.

That said, at least the convicts would go to their graves well fed and clean. The showers had been basic: an array of high-powered chem-sprays in the below-deck washroom that left any skin they touched red and gleaming, followed by a burst of depilatory foam to melt away any regrown hair. After that the promised double ration had come in the form of a bowl of grey slop, hot, filling and unlimited in quantity. There had even been flavour packets – a hearty meal for a condemned man.

'Reckon all this is a goodbye present,' Liga said, once they were dried, dressed and back in chains. The female ogryn was at the front, shuffling her way towards a mag-lift with the others in her wake like a reluctant parade, looking like she could win a tug of war against all the rest without breaking a sweat.

'You lot keep it down back there.' A provost Ossian didn't recognise gave the chains a tug. 'There's no need to talk where you're going, understand?'

They shuffled into the elevator. There were four provosts in the detail, standing one to each corner with their backs pressed against the wall. Ossian could feel the tension in the room rising. If the prisoners kicked off a fight in this confined space, and especially if the ogryn got involved, it was anyone's guess how many of the guards would be left when the doors opened again. Of course, the rest of them would be dead too, but maybe a few hours of life was a fair trade for the chance to go down swinging.

Liga leaned in close, her voice so soft he could barely make out the words. She smelled of chemical showers and hot rations. 'Nothing's going to happen till we're off the ship. But the moment we touch ground, that's when we do it, all right? Take out the guards and run.'

'What about the collars?'

'Deal with that later.' She grinned. 'One step at a time, doc.'

The elevator doors opened onto a mezzanine overlooking what had to be the main central deck of the ship. It was more the size of a cathedral than a voidship. A tank regiment could have carried out a full set of manoeuvres without touching the wall, if they didn't mind crushing the hundreds of crew swarming below. On the ceiling, a painted mural depicted warring angels armed with fiery weapons, locked in eternal combat as cherubs and servo-skulls fluttered and buzzed beneath them. Stained armaglass windows reached from floor to sky, constellations shifting slowly as the vessel turned in its orbit.

'Don't get too used to the view,' the provost sergeant said. It was Ossian's old friend again, the one with the gold tooth. 'You're just here for the Munitorum to check you out, make sure you meet their specifications. Special treatment, just like I promised. Then back down into the hole you go to wait for the drop.'

A lieutenant in crumpled service dress stepped forward, his gaze flicking between the prisoners and the data-slate he carried. 'The penal detachment, I take it?' Without waiting for a reply, he looked over his shoulder to address a small blonde woman in an immaculate Munitorum uniform, the golden buttons on her high-collared tunic freshly polished and gleaming. 'Captain Thysia, the penal sub-detachment for Operation Kasarn is here. Did you want to review them in person?'

The captain looked up from her own data-slate, her eyes wide and her finely plucked eyebrows raised. 'Whatever would have made you think that?'

For one wild moment Ossian considered throwing himself on the captain's mercy, then instantly dismissed the thought. What was he expecting? For a mid-ranking Munitorum officer to overturn the verdict of a military tribunal, undo the shackles and return him to normal service? That was as likely as the God-Emperor Himself descending from the Golden Throne with a personally signed pardon.

'Very good, captain,' the lieutenant said, and made a mark on his data-slate.

Two troopers who looked barely old enough to be out of basic training sidled up to the captain. From their uniforms they were Cadian, though their lack of violet eyes told Thysia they were not born on-world. One was a white-skinned boy, burly and tall, the other a slight young woman with a freckled fawn-brown complexion and a head of tight black curls.

'Captain, may I–' the boy began, and the lieutenant cut him off with a wave of his data-slate.

'Wait your turn.'

'Throne-and-damnation.' The immaculate captain snatched the data-slate from her subordinate. 'Provost sergeant, get those legionnaires out of my sight. And you two – stand over there and wait.'

There was a sudden hubbub from below. Ossian looked over the rail to see the crowd parting around a group of Militarum officers, moving in a swirling mass where each individual seemed desperate to push themselves inwards towards the eye of the storm.

'Brilliant. And now *this*,' the captain said. 'Impeccable timing. I *told* them we needed more time to get everything arranged…'

'What're they talking about?' Liga asked.

Ossian leaned forward as much as his chains would allow. For a brief moment the throng parted enough for him to glimpse the figure at its centre: a tall, broad-shouldered woman of about his own age dressed in well-worn Cadian drab. Long ash-brown hair was snagged in a bun at the nape of her neck, the silver strands at her temples glinting as she bent her head over an offered data-slate. The conversation was impossible to hear, but from the sour expression on the woman's face she wasn't best pleased.

'Someone important?' Liga asked.

The lord castellan of Cadia was notorious for avoiding picts, but the resemblance to her legendary father was unmistakable. Both had the same lowered brows, the same pugnacious jut of the jaw, the same glowering deep-set eyes. Give the woman a cigar and a buzz cut and she could have stepped out of a thirty-year-old propaganda poster.

'She's the Cadian commander-in-chief,' Ossian said.

Liga snorted with laughter. 'Didn't know there were enough of you left to be worth commanding.'

The ship continued its steady rotation. Through the windows a planet swung into view – no, not a planet, a storm-wracked remnant of a world, clouds roiling across its surface, simmering with lightning.

The pieces of the puzzle fell into place one after the other. The secrecy, the presence of the lord castellan, the shattered planet below.

The battered rock beneath them was the broken remains of Cadia.

They were sending him home to die.

# X

## THE LORD OF SWORDS

'I feel like a Leman Russ,' Ursula said, as Enginseer Rho fine-tuned the fit of the magnificent silver-and-red suit of power armour for what felt like the thousandth time. The harness was a perfect example of form over function. It was the sort worn by rich aristocrats and planetary governors when they wanted to look good for the crowds, rather than anything designed for war. Guilliman's armour had moved like an extension of his own body, but this felt heavy, clumsy, an impediment instead of an asset. It was undeniably beautiful – if your tastes ran to filigree and gemstones – but she would have traded it for a decent suit of carapace armour in a heartbeat. Apparently playing the hero was only part of it. You had to look like one for the pict-casts as well.

'Kindly repeat yourself for the benefit of my ageing cogitators, lord castellan.'

'Standing here. Being cleaned, polished and readied for battle with no say in any part of the proceedings.'

'I can assure you, lord castellan, you are not a Leman Russ.'

Ursula rolled her eyes. 'No, more's the pity. A tank, for example, is not required to make polite conversation while its plating is being fitted.'

Or to give its nominal agreement to a plan which had clearly been in preparation for months before its arrival, she thought, but left unsaid.

Argent was standing in silence, his back pressed to the armoury wall. He had been uncharacteristically quiet since they had left the *Chamberlain Tarasha*, spending the short, blessedly uneventful warp jump alone in his quarters when his presence wasn't directly requested. She wouldn't have called what he was doing sulking – at least not to his face.

'Magnificent,' Captain Thysia said. She raised a hand and her waiting servo-skull buzzed forward, hovering in front of Ursula's face and snapping off a series of picts. 'A smile, lord castellan?'

Ursula bared her teeth. She was starting to develop a real dislike for the effervescent propagandist.

'Or perhaps not.' Thysia gave a nervous smile of her own. 'Better to stick with stoic and determined.'

*Frustrated and restless, more like.*

Rho played one of their vast collection of sighs. 'Kindly refrain from fidgeting, lord castellan. I have not yet completed the litanies of preparation.'

'How long until we drop?' The lens of the servo-skull made another clattering burst of sound. 'And major, I am not accustomed to repeating myself. Remove that pict-scanner from my vicinity, or I will remove it myself.'

'My apologies, lord castellan.' The propagandist waved the skull away. It took up a position in the far corner of the room with what Ursula imagined was a resentful air. She was fairly sure it was still recording. 'Your descent is scheduled for eighteen hundred hours ship time.'

*Six hours.* It wasn't enough. Under normal circumstances, Ursula would have had everything prepared to the last detail by now, her plans checked, revised, analysed and rediscussed, but this time everything was different. There were only so many times she could review personnel files and second-guess her selections, only so many times she could study planetary scans and ensure they were committed to memory. Thysia had every minute between now and then accounted for, filled with pict-opportunities with the lord captain and inspiring speeches to be given to the troops, with no margin left for error.

Rho gave a disdainful binharic chirp. 'I have done all that I can. The armour is optimised to your biological parameters, lord castellan. I maintain it would have been significantly easier to adjust your organic components to suit the armour.'

'I prefer my organic components as they are, as well you know.' Ursula flexed each armoured joint in turn. The suit weighed several hundred pounds, but the powerful servo-motors built into its joints detected and amplified her movements at the first twitch of muscle. Each movement was accompanied by a gentle whine, soft enough to pass without notice on the battlefield, but just loud enough to grate her nerves raw with every move she made. 'What about my weapons?'

'All anointed and appeased with the appropriate litanies.' Rho waved a mechadendrite, and a servitor lumbered forward, holding a tray laden with weapons. Her power sword was there, a well-balanced sabre with a swept hilt to protect her knuckles, along with her usual hotshot laspistols and a freshly issued bolt pistol, which had been the price she demanded in exchange for agreeing to wear the ridiculous armour. Next to the laspistols it looked comically oversized, but its explosive shells would be a welcome addition to her arsenal.

'Very good, lord castellan.' Thysia reached out a hand towards

Ursula's face as if to smooth back a flyaway strand of hair, then clearly thought better of it. 'All is proceeding according to schedule. Now, if you would be so kind as to follow me, I'll introduce you to the rest of the Eighth.'

'The what?'

'The Eighth Regiment, lord castellan.'

'What are they doing here?' There had been no mention of any of the scattered survivors of the Eighth Regiment in any of the briefing material she had been given.

'Once again, my apologies.' Thysia's feet made quick tapping footsteps on the deck plating as she headed from the armoury. 'The Eighth Regiment, Second Founding, I should have said. Indomitus Command gave their personal authorisation for the regiment to be reinforced to its original strength, and for its colours to be returned to active service.'

Ursula gritted her teeth. 'Generally, a decision of that nature would be in the hands of the lord castellan.' The re-forming of the Eighth was yet another indignity piled on top of the rest, another frustrating addition to the growing sense that she was merely a bystander in someone else's great plan.

'Under normal circumstances the decision would of course have been yours, my lord.' Thysia held the door open and waited for Ursula to follow. 'Time has been so regrettably short on this occasion that we had no choice but to obtain authorisation from a higher authority. I can make the documentation available if you–'

'No, there's no need.' Ursula shook her head. She had never served with the Eighth, and had never wanted to. The regiment's unofficial sobriquets had been enough to put her off: *Creed's Legacy. The Lord Castellan's Own. Ursarkar's Dogs.* No doubt Thysia and the rest of the Logos Historica Verita thought a second founding of the famous regiment would play well to the crowd, and they were probably right. 'And how many of the Eighth do I presently have under my direct command?'

'Ten, my lord. The ones you have personally selected. And yourself, naturally.'

'Naturally. What did you do with the rest, the ones I didn't pick?'

'I really couldn't tell you exactly, lord castellan,' Thysia said smoothly. 'As I understand it, they were redeployed elsewhere.'

Shael Laskari cast a sidelong look around the briefing chamber, trying to see if any of the other members of the squad looked as nervous as she was. In keeping with the decor of the rest of the *Oriflamme*, the walls were painted a deep and glossy black, intricate bas-relief vines and leaves picked out in sheets of gold leaf. A chalice-shaped brazier burned in the centre of the room, secured to the wall by a gilded bracket in the form of a human hand. She was fairly sure that the braziers alone cost more than she would make in her entire career.

There were ten of them in total: Laskari and Anka; a colonel of Hussars in an exquisitely tailored dress uniform of Volpone blue that flattered his dark brown complexion to perfection; a burly tan-skinned soldier whose arms and neck were covered in intricate geometric tattoos; a pale, faded-looking sergeant major in field dress; and a five-strong unit of Tempestus Scions. Seven of them had the telltale Cadian eyes, the exceptions being Laskari herself, Anka and the man with the tattoos.

The burly soldier leaned back, clasped his hands in front of him and stretched them above his head, his mouth opening in a wide yawn. 'Does anyone have the time?' he asked. She didn't recognise his accent, but it wasn't Cadian.

The sergeant major pushed back the left sleeve of his jacket and turned the inside of his wrist upward. Glowing blue digits appeared on his skin. She'd never seen an electoo like that, and instantly wanted one. 'Five minutes overdue.'

The Hussar colonel sniffed. 'More hurry-up-and-wait, I see.'

'If that's the worst thing that happens today I'll take it.' The big man was leaning back, eyes closed, face turned up to the ceiling.

'I will take it, *sir*,' the older man corrected him.

The big man glanced over at Laskari and rolled his eyes. 'Right, sergeant major, sorry. I'll take it, *sir*.'

Laskari hid her smile.

The colonel gave another disdainful sniff. 'I can say with every confidence that will not be the worst thing that happens to any of us today.'

The briefing room door opened. Laskari shot to attention as if she'd been electrocuted, Anka lumbering to his feet beside her a moment later. Her pulse thudded in her throat. This was it. The moment she would meet her commanding officer and undertake her first mission.

Finally she'd be a true Cadian.

Ursula took up a standing position at the end of the table, studied the faces of her new squad, and began her briefing with a lie.

'Allow me to introduce myself. My name is Lord Castellan Ursula Creed.'

Ten pairs of eyes stared back at her.

'I'm delighted to hear you've finally decided to embrace your father's legacy, lord castellan.' She recognised the speaker from his file: Colonel Hadrian Aurelius Van Haast, forty-nine Terran years old, Cadian-born and already the most decorated officer of his former regiment. 'Rather a *volte-face*, no? I thought you had cut yourself off from the old man out of spite.'

'No spite involved.' She had spent much of the warp jump towards Cadia trying in vain to decide on an explanation for her seemingly inexplicable name-change. She settled on a half-truth, and tried to make it sound like she believed it. 'It was suggested to me that the name might be a source of inspiration to those who remembered the former Lord Castellan Creed. A reminder that what went before is not forgotten.'

Van Haast raised an eyebrow. 'I would have thought that the Fall of Cadia was still fresh in the memory of those who lived through it. Though as I recall you were elsewhere at the time, so perhaps your recollections are not so sharp. Certainly my memories of our last retreat remain' – his lip curled – 'vivid.'

She waited until the colonel had finished, then let the silence stretch out a fraction longer than necessary. 'The ten of you have been hand-selected from the Cadian regiments for a mission of the utmost importance. The soul of Cadia is its soldiers – whether born and raised under the Eye of Terror, the children of Cadian parents off-world or transplanted into our regiments from other Imperial forces. Some of you remember Cadia as it was. Others have never set foot on Cadian soil. Today that changes.' She drew a deep breath and squared her shoulders. 'Today, we return to Cadia.'

No one moved.

'I understand this will come as a surprise to you all–'

'A surprise?' Van Haast gave a sharp bark of laughter. 'How exactly do you propose we return to a planet that no longer exists?'

'Cadia was not entirely obliterated by Abaddon's Blackstone Fortress. Intelligence reached me a short time ago that a size-able fragment of the planet remains.'

'How disappointing for you, lord castellan.' The man was visibly pulling himself back together, the momentary loss of composure disappearing behind a veneer of supercilious civility. 'To have been kept in the same state of ignorance as the rest of us for so long.'

She ignored the jibe. Physically Van Haast looked nothing like Pyoter Valk – he was dark where the general was pale, tall and lean where Valk was muscular – but he had the same infuriating arrogance that only came with years of what he no doubt would have referred to as good breeding. She suspected it had more to do with everyone telling you from birth how Throne-damned special you were.

'The remnant of Cadia of which I speak is a wedge incorporating the borderlands between Cadia Primus and Secundus, Kasrs Gallan and Arroch, and the Rossvar range between them.' In her mind's eye, Ursula saw the hololith of the planetary fragment, spinning in an illusory void, its atmosphere and molten core trailing into nothingness like the tail of a comet. 'The impact of the Blackstone Fortress caused considerable distortion of Cadia's crust and mantle, and with that in mind, the *Oriflamme*'s explorators have prepared us a best-guess schematic, superimposing pre-Fall data onto novel topography. Major Argent, if you would.'

Argent stepped smartly to the table and unrolled the map, seared on vellum in the spidery hand of the *Oriflamme*'s explorator.

'Our mission is simple. We are to be deployed by Valkyrie to the planetoid's surface, in order to breach a vault beneath Kasr Gallan and extract its contents. Intelligence suggests that it contains weapons that formed part of Ursarkar Creed's final strategy for the salvation of Cadia, had there been time to deploy them.'

Van Haast waved a languid hand. 'The cities to which you refer were part of my family's holdings. There are at least half a dozen vaults like that in the general vicinity of Kasr Gallan. Add in Kasr Arroch and you can double that number. What makes this particular one more likely than the rest?'

Ursula dropped her right hand to the pommel of her power sword, focusing her attention on the cold metal against her palm. Thysia had been insistent that there was at least one representative of old Cadian blood in the squad, but if Van Haast kept up this behaviour that blood was going to end up spattered on the walls of the *Oriflamme*.

'For the simple reason that the enemy wants it. The *Oriflamme*'s auspex array has detected a heavy concentration of enemy activity around the vault. Evidently we are not the only ones who want what is inside. Add to that, it lies close to Ursarkar Creed's childhood home. Using that location as the base for his final stratagem would seem like exactly the sort of sentimentality the man was famous for.'

Ursula took a step back from the table and folded her arms. What she was going to say next would be as hard to hear as it was to articulate, but giving incomplete information now would be a recipe for failure.

'Since the Fall, Cadia has become a battleground for the Neverborn. The scant images we have of its surface show Cadia to be changed beyond recognition. When the Great Rift opened, Cadia was dragged into hell, and there it has remained in the years since. We will face daemons, Heretic Astartes, horrors the like of which most of you will never have faced. But Cadia is our birthright, and we will take from its ruins that which is ours.'

'Do we know what manner of weapons the vault contains, my lord?' the youngest trooper said. Her file had given her name as Shael Laskari, sixteen Terran years of age, newly graduated from the Whiteshields.

Ursula shook her head. 'Not at present, trooper. But I look forward to finding out.'

The room fell silent again. The Catachan raised his hand.

'Go ahead, Sergeant Harapa.'

'I like a death world just as much as the next soldier, chief,' he said. The man's accent sounded like he was chewing the words up and spitting them out wet. 'No disrespect, but this sort of strike-and-extract sounds like a job for Space Marines, not Astra Militarum.'

Ursula sighed. Vanatu Harapa was, on paper at least, every bit as Cadian as the rest of them, which didn't mean much. He was Catachan born, bred and raised, one of the recent reinforcements from other armies brought into the devastated Cadian regiments. That particular plan had been fraught with problems from the start. The attitude of the aristocracy to the newcomers had led to a failure of integration, resentment among the ranks and poor unit cohesion that had almost brought the attempt to a close – but there was simply no alternative. Without new blood, no matter how much the old guard resented it, there could be no future.

The longlist of transplants from other regiments had contained the big death worlder, the former champion ice-climber of the Valhallan 28th, and a recently promoted Tsegohan tank commander from the 49th Armoured. Given that there hadn't seemed much need for ice-climbing and the Tsegohan was making a fair success of things where she was, the Catachan had been the only reasonable choice – an exemplary soldier, but one who had yet to learn what being Cadian really meant.

'This is not a task for the Adeptus Astartes, no matter how well suited they would be,' she said flatly. 'This is work for Cadians. Our people fought and died for that planet. The very soil is drenched in our blood. If there is a weapon there capable of striking a blow against the enemy then it is our sacred duty to recover it and to use it for what it was intended. We cannot save our home world, but we may yet avenge it.'

'With the greatest of respect, lord castellan, why don't we stop this bombastic nonsense and speak plainly,' Colonel Van Haast said.

Behind her, Argent cleared his throat. 'It would behove you, colonel, to remember in whose company you sit.'

'That's quite all right, major.' Ursula raised a placatory hand, watching the other faces around the table for their reactions. The non-commissioned officer – Sergeant Major Domnik Strahl, formerly of the old Eighth Regiment – was scowling furiously, while Laskari looked as if she were trying to slide unobtrusively under the table. 'Speak your mind, colonel, I'm not afraid to hear it.'

'This is Munitorum nonsense. This isn't a triumphant return to Cadia. No one cares what Ursarkar Creed stashed in that bunker, or even if it's still there.' He tapped one elegant forefinger on the table for emphasis. 'This is to consolidate your position as lord castellan, and personally, I'm insulted you haven't mentioned that key fact already.'

Ursula kept her face blank. She couldn't blame him for his doubts, but she would damn well blame him for articulating them in front of the rest of the squad. She'd learned from years of sparring with Pyoter Valk and his ilk that the only way to deal with aristocrats was to meet them head-on, no matter how exhausting that became. She raised one armoured hand, extended her index finger, and pointed it at the door to her right.

Van Haast frowned. 'I don't take your meaning, lord castellan.'

'The door, colonel. In case you were having difficulty with the navigation. The same goes for the rest of you.' She fixed them with her most pleasant smile, the one that Argent claimed was more terrifying than reassuring. 'Anyone with any reservations about this mission is at liberty to leave. I don't want anyone on this team less than fully committed to the task at hand.'

No one moved. She hadn't really expected any of them to. Van Haast would be a millstone around her neck, but he was only part of the problem.

'I think I speak for us all, lord castellan, when I say how honoured we are to have been chosen for this mission. For myself, I relish the opportunity to return home, no matter how changed we find it.' Sergeant Major Strahl was all stiff grey pomposity, like a drill abbot on inspection day. It was the sort of unctuous servility that made her flesh creep. According to his service record he had known her father personally. No doubt he'd been the same sort of snivelling yes-man back then as well.

'Thank you, sergeant major. Now. If we can return to the task at hand. Kasr Gallan is located here.' She indicated its position on the map. 'Our Valkyrie will bring us down in a patch of clear ground thirty miles south of the city. Three other Valkyries will drop a unit of Scions each in a loose wedge formation – we'll make contact once we're planetside and converge on our destination. Assuming things continue according to plan...'

She glanced up. The Catachan, Harapa, hadn't quite managed to hide his grin quickly enough. Clearly he knew as well as she did that no plan ever survived contact with the enemy.

'*Assuming* things go to plan, we should at no time engage any hostile force in or around Kasr Gallan. If this is unavoidable, our orders are to disengage at the earliest safe opportunity and withdraw. Mobility and silence will be our best defence. Tempestor Valcrev, I understand your vox-operator has already been issued with a long-range beacon.'

The Tempestor gave a crisp nod. 'Yes, lord castellan.'

'Care to give us the information on it?'

The Scion to the Tempestor's right snapped a sharp salute and got to his feet. 'Sir. The beacon can be triggered independently of the standard long-range vox signal. On activation it sends a signal on a narrowband frequency to a continually monitored channel. Estimated response time from beacon activation to arrival of support between ten and fifteen standard minutes.'

The vox-op dropped back into his seat. There was something eerie, almost artificial about the way the Scions moved and spoke, like they had been stamped out on the same production line.

'We've also been issued with a laser targeter, compatible with the Aeronautica's auspex system. If we run into something large, it opens up possibilities for targeting air-to-ground missiles.'

'Thank you,' Ursula said. 'To summarise. We avoid hostile contact, and if it occurs the *Oriflamme* can have us out in a mean time of twelve-and-a-half minutes. Our primary objective is to reach Cadia and add whatever information we can regarding the location and access routes to the bunker, and to return with that information. Anything else is a bonus.'

'An admirable sentiment, lord castellan.' Van Haast again, back to needle at her like a tick in a bedroll. 'And how are we to avoid the attention of multiple hostile forces long enough to carry out our mission, let alone last these twelve minutes should we find ourselves under sustained assault?'

Ursula met his stare. 'That,' she said, 'is where the penal legionnaires come in.'

# XI

## THE LIGHTNING TOWER

'Is it meant to be this loud?'

Even with her mouth at Ossian's ear, Liga was barely audible over the roar of the engines and the relentless buffeting of the wind. The only noise cutting through it was the two-stroke chainsword roar of Clavie the ogryn's snores, and even that was hard to hear. Two of the twelve-strong squad of penal troopers had already puked their guts all over the compartment, and the viscid grey stew looked considerably less appetising on the way up than it had on the way down.

Ossian nodded and focused on holding his own rations down. The drop was louder than any he remembered, but that could have been due to the atmospheric conditions or the dubious condition of the drop-ship, most likely both. That was the sort of combination that brought anyone out in a cold sweat.

'Surprised you're not all deaf in the Guard!'

'Wait until you hear your first bolter.'

'What?'

He shook his head. There was no point in repeating himself. Liga shrugged, tapping a finger to the side of her head.

'Remember the plan,' she mouthed.

It wasn't like it was something he could forget.

Liga's strategy was simple. As soon as they hit the ground, their first task was to work out if the collars were on a distance control. They'd know they were working within a perimeter if a provost got off the drop-ship with them; if not, they'd have at least the distance of low orbit to work with, assuming the officers' plan was for them to survive long enough to be of any use at all. The orders they had been given were simple: spread out, survey the ground, and ensure that all hostiles and environmental features were captured on their gun-picters. According to the provost sergeant they had the honour of being the advance guard, though their briefing had been conspicuously short on detail on how they were to be extracted once their objectives were achieved.

Another day in the Guard. As always, it was an honour to serve.

The male ogryn made a disconsolate braying noise, loud enough to cut through the roar of the falling ship. Ossian's head was splitting. Why did they all have to be so Throne-damned loud?

'Can the lot of you just shut the frekk up for five minutes?'

The drop-ship gave a sudden downward lurch, slamming Ossian's head into the wall then bouncing him forward into his restraints hard enough that they cut into the soft flesh under his arms.

'What the hells was that?' Liga shouted over the drop-ship's roar. Its engine had taken on a new note, a high panicky whine that sent a stream of ice water running down Ossian's back. The craft was canting to the left, spinning in big lazy circles that worsened the tilt at every sweep. The abhuman was braying out big frantic lungfuls of sound that filled the compartment like an air-raid siren. Even Clavie had woken up, staring around herself in dull surprise.

Ossian unfastened his restraints and staggered to the door that separated the rear compartment from the flight deck.

'Hey!' He hammered on the door with both fists. 'If we're going down, you need to tell us where the chutes are!'

Another lurch. The drop-ship filled instantly with the sharp smell of promethium, mixed with a familiar scent so out of place that he didn't recognise it at first.

'We crashin'?' Clavie said. She still looked drowsy, but a hint of fear was creeping across her face.

'Not quite yet, Clavie.' Ossian tried to smile. The last thing they needed was a terrified ogryn blundering about in a confined space.

'That good.'

There was no answer from the flight deck. Ossian knocked again until his hands ached, but the door stayed resolutely shut. How close were they to the ground now? There was another sharp crack, followed seconds later by a deafening thunderclap that he felt as well as heard.

They were going down, and they were going down fast.

*How do you survive a drop-ship crash?* Ossian searched his memory, and came up with a scattering of useless fragments. Imminent death was supposed to focus the mind, but tumbling towards ground at near terminal velocity was making it hard to think. He should be in his restraints for starters, but how that was going to help when they made impact was anyone's guess.

'What do we do?' It was the ratling, his eyes wide and his delicate hands clumsy with panic as he fumbled at the buckle holding the straps across his chest.

'Brace yourself.' Ossian stumbled back towards his seat, the world juddering and rattling around him. 'Stay in your restraints. Get your head forward, grab the bottom of your seat and–'

The drop-ship lurched again, sending him flying backwards. His shoulder hit the wall, and he bounced back, winded, into Clavie's lap. Then, unexpectedly, the drop-ship's dreadful shuddering eased and it levelled out.

'We've stabilised.' Ossian took a deep breath. 'Throne-be-praised, we've stabilised.'

Liga grinned, her expression tight. 'That's good, right?'

'It certainly beats the alternative.'

Now that their flight had resumed its steady downward course, his former panic seemed ludicrous, the sort of idiocy you'd expect from a raw recruit like the rest of them, not a seasoned veteran. A cool breeze blew across his face, soft and soothing on the cold sweat of a moment before, but still carrying with it that strange incongruous blend of promethium and… and what? Something sweet, rank, appallingly familiar. Something that had no place in the rear compartment of a drop-ship.

*Decay.*

The smell was the suppurating sweetness of an infected wound.

The realisation came just as a gap appeared in the rear ramp, a sudden window to the outside that had no business being there. At first there was only darkness, then another burst of lightning illuminated the compartment with a sickly purple glow. Rust was spreading out from the gap in the metal, tarnish and corrosion blossoming into tiny flakes, tugged away like petals by the building maelstrom. First the hole was big enough to admit a finger, then a hand, then wide enough that the ground appeared below them as a distant charcoal blur.

Another flash. A fresh wave of corrosion spread across the fuselage, this one starting from a point directly overhead. The drop-ship was disintegrating around them, the metal struts that gave it integrity exposed like bones, the ground approaching at terrifying speed.

The lumens went out. The abhuman shrieked, a panicky, inhuman sound that drew an answering scream from someone else in the darkness. The pilot's voice came through the cabin vox, her tone calm and unhurried.

*'Brace for emergency landing.'*

Ossian cast a desperate glance through the drop-ship's dissolving floor. Spurs of metal reached up from ferrocrete ruins like grasping fingers, as they hurtled down towards the ruined buildings below. The pilot was coming in shallow, he realised, planning on skimming the terrain with their undercarriage in a last-ditch attempt to decrease the force of the landing.

Ossian looped one arm through his restraints and closed his eyes. Thought was impossible, banished by the screaming around him, the overwhelming smell of decay, the wind like an artillery barrage in his face.

A snare-drum rattled as the drop-ship's undercarriage met the ruined roofs, then came a shriek as the metal plating of the undercarriage tore free.

The howl of an emergency klaxon. Red light on terrified faces. Then impact.

# XII

## THE SHATTERED WORLD

'There are twelve seats on a Valkyrie,' Argent said.

'What did you say?'

Ursula was in the process of rolling up the map when he caught her arm, the rest of the squad already leaving to make their final preparations for the drop.

'I said there are twelve seats.'

'Sorry, Gideon, I don't follow. Why are we discussing flyer schematics?'

'One for each of us. Those ten, you and me, which makes twelve.'

'You're not seriously proposing coming with us, are you?'

'Why not?'

Ursula shook her head. 'Because you're needed here. Someone has to stop Thysia from sending us to our deaths in search of the perfect propaganda shot. Besides, you don't have the skills I need for this mission.'

'Half of the team doesn't have the skills you need for this

mission. Two Whiteshields, an old man and an aristocrat who'll fall to pieces the moment the polish comes off his boots. If it wasn't for the Scions you might as well be going down there on your own.'

'Don't forget the Catachan.'

'Ah, yes, a man from a jungle death world. Just what you need in the ruins of Cadia.' Argent gave her a pleading look. 'Let me come with you. We've fought together for years, Ursula. You know I can do this.'

The silver armour was suddenly heavy on her shoulders. 'We've *worked* together, which isn't the same thing. How long is it since you fought on the front lines? I don't need yet another idiot to babysit along with all the rest.'

Argent flinched as if she had slapped him, and she felt instantly guilty. It was commonly believed – and not wholly without substance – that Argent owed his entire career to her patronage. His failings as a soldier had become apparent during their first days as Whiteshields, but the years had bound his fading star to her rising one with chains of friendship and obligation. In return, she received the reward of his company, his wry sense of humour and his loyal – if admittedly uninspired – service. But just because his reputation was true didn't mean she should rub his nose in it.

'My apologies, Gideon. That was uncalled for on my part.'

He shook his head. 'No apology needed. But surely with such an untried team, you need someone with you who you can trust to watch your back.'

Argent made a valid point. In an ideal world she would have had a team of trusted officers beside her, soldiers who she'd served with for years, people she'd die for and who she'd trust to do the same for her. But then, who would she even have chosen? The comrades from her days in the ranks were scattered, half of them dead, half of them sent to command far-off regiments. Argent was the only one left. That wasn't a good enough reason to take him.

'And what will I say to your wife if you end up dead? Or Dathien?'

Gideon smiled ruefully. 'I doubt Irissa will care much at all. We're not exactly close any longer. And at least Dath would get to know his father died a hero, not sitting behind a desk.'

'The Imperium has no shortage of heroes. What it *needs* is competent professionals.' She shook her head. 'Frankly, this isn't the time for your mid-life crisis.'

Argent pulled himself to stand at attention. 'Lord castellan, I would take it as a personal favour if you would allow me to accompany you on this mission to Cadia.' Then the ridiculous over-formality was gone. 'Please, Ursula. Unless you don't trust me, that is.'

A long, weary sigh escaped her mouth. 'I trust you. Of course, I do. But it is far too late to change things now. The mission parameters are set, our equipment has already been assigned. Adding an extra member to the team at this stage would disrupt everything.'

'It's all taken care of.' He held up his data-slate with a triumphant air. 'You signed it all off yesterday.'

Ursula took the data-slate, the servo-motors of her gauntlet whining as they adjusted the pressure of her fingers against the fragile piece of tech. 'I can assure you I did nothing of the...'

She stopped. There was the file detailing her final selections for the squad with her personal authorisation code below. Eleven names, plus her own. Not the ten she had been expecting.

'You used my holo-seal.'

Argent shrugged, with what he no doubt thought was a winning smile. 'Desperate times call for desperate measures.'

'You should have asked me.' A tight ball of anger was coalescing in the pit of her stomach. She did her best to swallow it down before it could rise into her throat and come out in words she might later regret.

'You were busy.'

'This behaviour is unacceptable.'

'Then please accept my apologies. You've given me your seal in the past when it's been needed. I didn't see the harm on this occasion.'

Ursula shoved the data-slate back at him. 'I'm going to find Thysia and get this fixed. You are not coming and that's–'

'Excuse me.' The voice from the doorway was tentative, accompanied by a knock so soft it was barely audible. Laskari took a hesitant step forward. 'Lord castellan, major – I think I dropped something.' Laskari's eyes were fixed on the floor. 'If I could just–'

'Go ahead, trooper.'

Ursula watched the younger woman searching under her chair on hands and knees, eventually resurfacing with a brass compass. Laskari had been trained on some backwater planet barely worth the effort of holding on to, and according to the recommendation that had accompanied her, she was the second-best shot in her cohort. As if a silver medal were something to be proud of.

Argent was right. They were a total liability, the lot of them.

'Thank you, my lord.' Laskari scurried around the far side of the table, folded in on herself as if she were trying to disappear entirely.

'Carry on, trooper.'

Ursula waited until Laskari had gone before she looked back at her adjutant. He didn't speak, but his expression said it all.

*I told you so.*

She'd have given her right hand to be back on Tectora, caught between a mug of recaff and Pyoter Valk's insubordination instead of this devil's choice: take an ageing staff officer to a death world out of some misplaced sense of debt, or the same journey with an untested rabble of strangers.

'Fine. Consider me convinced.'

'Thank you.' Argent took her hand and shook it vigorously. He looked relieved more than pleased. 'I give you my word, you will not regret this.'

Except she already did.

Consciousness returned, slowly and painfully.

Ossian's face was pressed against something sharp that jabbed into his cheek when he tried to move his head. The left side of his body throbbed like one large bruise, pain skewering between his ribs with every breath. His skin felt sticky, his lips and eyelids glued shut, his mouth full of the taste of copper. You didn't need to be a medicae to know what that meant.

'Mac! Wake up!'

Someone was shouting his name, the words indistinct, like they were drifting through water. Who was it? And for that matter, where was he?

*The drop-ship.* Images came back one after another, flashing through his mind at dizzying speed. He'd been standing, watching in horror as the ground rushed up to meet them and the others screamed in their harnesses. The others. Liga, Clavie and the others...

He prised open his eyelids. Liga was leaning over him, her face filthy, her right eye swollen shut.

'You're not dead. Good. Get up, we haven't got much time.'

Ossian blinked, shook his head and tried to stand. Everything was red, as if he were seeing the world through a flickering curtain of blood. The emergency lights.

'I need a moment.'

He closed his eyes, opened them again and got unsteadily to his feet. The drop-ship had landed at an angle, and the tilted horizon was messing with his balance. Everything was wrong. He looked up and saw his restraints hanging empty above him. He hadn't been in them when they'd crashed. The impact should have killed him, unless something had broken his fall.

'You haven't got a moment.' Liga's voice was urgent. 'We need to get moving. Find weapons. Get away from here.'

'What…?' His head felt thick and stupid. He looked down and saw the body of one of the other troopers beneath him. It was one of the twins who had volunteered back in the cargo hold. The dead man's face had been completely caved in, the flesh reduced to a bloody pulp, the bones shattered like the shell of a dropped egg. Ossian put a hand to his own head, and pulled out something sharp that had lodged in his scalp.

It was a shard of bone.

Dully, Ossian realised what had happened. His gut gave a sudden lurch, and his mouth flooded with bile. The impact of the crash had thrown him into the other trooper, cushioning his fall at the cost of the other man's life.

'Hurry up!' Liga called back. 'You can spew your ring later. There's something outside. I think…' Liga's voice dropped. 'I think they must have heard us come down.'

'What sort of something?'

'I don't know.' She grabbed his arm and pulled. 'I don't want to find out.'

Sometime during the impact the drop-ship had broken in half, half of the walls and most of the deck plating rotted away to nothing. There had been a dozen of them at the start of the drop, but there were only a handful of corpses still inside the ruined craft: the ratling, dangling forward in his harness like a grotesque Candlemas decoration, the second of the twins impaled on a penetrating metal strut that had pierced the drop-ship's chassis.

'Anyone else survive?'

'Clavie. She's beat up, but she's walking. When I woke up she was thrashing about trying to get out of her restraints, so I figured I should get her outside before she did herself any more damage. Thought the drop-ship was going to explode from the smell of it.' She kept her fingers locked around his arm, dragging him towards the hole in the drop-ship's plating. 'But turns out there's nothing left to blow.'

'Any idea where we are?'

She gave a helpless shrug. 'No idea. Nowhere near the landing zone. And everything for about a hundred miles just heard us come down.'

He stepped outside, and a blast of scorching air hit him squarely in the face. He gasped on reflex, and his lungs filled with a pungent blend of sulphur and rot, strong enough to set his eyes watering, his mouth and throat suddenly bone-dry. Green afterimages from the Valkyrie's emergency lighting danced in front of his eyes, and he blinked them away, trying to make sense of the hellscape around him.

The Valkyrie had come down in the midst of what had once been a complex of buildings, tearing apart the perimeter wall and coming to rest in a heap of rubble. The forward section had detached completely and come to a stop nose first in the ground, though it seemed to have kept its integrity more than the passenger compartment. The sky overhead was a swirling mass of blood-coloured cloud so heavy and low that it looked barely out of arm's reach. Somewhere in the distance, an inhuman throat gave a shrill, metallic screech, unpleasantly reminiscent of the sound of nails down slate.

The ogryn was sitting on a twisted fragment of metal that

looked like it had torn free of the Valkyrie's wing. She was staring blankly into the darkness, blood running from a laceration on her shaven scalp down the back of her neck in a dark line like a mercenary's scalp-lock. Her massive shoulders were shuddering, heaving up and down with every breath.

'Clavie? Are you still with us?'

She didn't look up. This close he could see that the scalp wound was going to need attention: nothing complex, just a few stitches. He reached out to touch it, but she jerked her head away like a skittish grox, her face contorting with panic.

'No!'

'All right, big girl, all right.' Liga stroked the ogryn's shoulder reassuringly. 'No one's going to touch you without your say-so.'

'That wound needs to be cleansed and sutured,' Ossian said.

'She's spooked, Mac. You can try once we've got somewhere safe.'

'And where do you have in mind?'

The thing shrieked again. This time it sounded closer, and an answering screech came from the opposite side of the crash site. Clavie flinched, her big head snapping round to stare into the darkness.

'What is it, Clavie?'

The ogryn shook her head. 'Thing behind that wall. Watchin' us.'

'Nothing's watching–'

'There, stupid!' Inhumanly quick and strong she grabbed his head between her hands and turned it sharply to the left.

'Clavie! Let go! Throne…' Ossian fumbled at her fingers in a futile attempt to break her grip before his skull imploded. 'I'm looking!' he managed, and the bone-crushing pressure eased. 'Throne, Clavie, be gentle. I'm on your side, remember.'

Her hands dropped back into her lap, her eyes focused into the dark again. A sudden gust of scorching wind buffeted Ossian's face, and as he turned his face away, a glint of light reflected off what for a moment he thought was a pair of gleaming, over-sized eyes. He drew a sharp breath, and then the eyes were gone.

'Did you see–' Ossian began, but he was interrupted by a blast of sound: the note of a hunting horn, the sort he had heard years ago, when the local aristocrats went out hunting quarry-beasts in the forests. This one had a deeper tone, a raw, resonant rasp to it that made his flesh creep.

The ogryn lumbered to her feet. 'Liga. Time we go. Now. Right?'

'In a minute, big girl.' Liga was scrambling up the Valkyrie's broken nose cone to the flight deck's open entrance hatch. 'Ossian, come up here. We need weapons. They've got to be in here, right? No one was expecting convicts to go out unarmed.'

'Lascarbines, probably.' He scrambled up after her, torn between the urge to run from whatever was making that noise, and the need to feel the weight of a weapon in his hands. 'They won't be fancy.'

'I don't need fancy.' Liga poked her head out of the hatch. 'You keep watch out here, big girl. Anything comes close, you shout and we'll come running with the guns, okay?'

'Anythin' come close, I crump it.'

'That's my girl.'

Ossian swung himself up with his good arm, trying to ignore the pain in his ribs as he squeezed himself inside. Stepping back into the drop-ship, he was struck by how comparatively normal the Valkyrie's interior looked, and how much had changed in the last hour. Setting foot on the planet's surface had been like stepping into a nightmare, a place where the normal rules of reality seemed more tenuous with every moment that passed. This might be all that was left of Cadia, but it wasn't home. Not any more.

'Arms lockers, right?' Liga was already rifling the compartment, undeterred by the tilted horizon. 'I'll go back, you go forward. Pilots should be carrying sidearms.'

Ossian lurched forward towards the cockpit, and stopped as he heard the harsh rasp of laboured breathing. When he leaned around her chair, he saw the pilot slumped back against her headrest, her mind impulse unit disconnected, her face corpse-grey. Blood had soaked through her fatigues from where her legs had been crushed beneath the crumpled instrument panel. Ossian didn't bother to check her co-pilot. The same metal strut that had shattered the drop-ship's canopy had impaled him through the centre of his chest.

'You're all right,' Ossian said, except nothing was, and from the look on the pilot's face she knew that too. Her right hand jerked convulsively towards the sidearm on her hip. Ossian caught her wrist and guided it back to her lap. He took the laspistol as an afterthought, and tucked it into his belt. 'I'm here to help you.'

The pilot nodded, her eyes flicking to the sidearm then back to his face.

'My name's Ossian. I'm a medicae. I'm going to get you out of here. But I need your help if I'm going to do that.'

'Found them!' Liga's voice drifted forward from the rear of the compartment, bright with triumph and relief.

The pilot's eyes narrowed. Ossian wondered what he looked like: blood-soaked and battered, a shaven-headed monster in tattered penal fatigues and a flashing bomb collar. Just the man you want at your side in a tight spot.

'Are there medicae supplies in here?'

The pilot nodded. 'Under the seat.'

He ran a hand under her chair and found a smooth metal case, marked with the staff-and-serpent of the Militarum Chirurgical Corps. A quick inspection showed it was intact and fully stocked. He lifted an autoinjector of morpholox and held it up so she could see it, hating himself already for what he was about to do.

'Painkillers are on their way. Answer my questions, and you can have them. The collar round my neck. How do I get it off?'

'You can't.'

Ossian closed his eyes. 'I can only help you if my head stays where the God-Emperor put it.'

The pilot's gaze moved from his face to the mess of twisted metal and gore below her waist. 'Convict scum.' She took a deep, painful-sounding breath. 'Go fu–'

A lasweapon fired behind him, deafening in the confined space. Superheated grey-pink liquid sprayed from the pilot's forehead, spattering the remains of the canopy and the ruined instrument panel. She slumped to the side, smoke rising from the burned-out sockets of her eyes.

He looked up. Liga was standing behind the pilot's chair, lowering her lascarbine.

'You were right,' she said. 'Nothing fancy, but there's one for each of us.'

'You shot her!' Ossian sprang to his feet and backed up against the remains of the instrument panel. 'Frekk's sake, Liga, you didn't need to–'

'She was going for the detonator.' Liga pointed with the muzzle of the carbine towards the pilot's wrist. The dead woman was wearing an exact copy of the device the provost sergeant had been wearing before. It might even have been the same one. If she'd touched it, he'd be dead.

The air stank of burned flesh. Ossian drew a deep breath, trying to settle his lurching guts. 'What if there had been a dead man's switch on it? You could have killed us all.' His hands were shaking as he unbuckled the control unit from the pilot's arm.

'Calculated risk. If she'd hit that button we were all dead anyway. Can you see the deactivator?' Liga held out a hand for the detonator-unit.

Ossian turned it over. 'I don't think it has one.'

'Better take it then. Like you said, maybe it's rigged to activate at a certain distance. I don't know about you, but I don't much fancy surviving all this only for my head to blow off two miles from the crash site.'

He buckled the strap around his wrist, the metal still warm against his skin.

'First chance we get, we disable the damn thing, okay?' Liga continued. 'We just need time and the right tools. There're kitbags and carbines back there. Half of them got trashed in the landing, but there's more than enough for the three of us. Rations, too.'

The hunting horn sounded again, and as if in answer something banged a heavy fist on the outside of the cockpit's metal plating.

'Liga!' Clavie's deep voice was tight with panic. 'Doc!'

'What is it, big girl? What do you see?'

'Not see. Hear. Lots of them. Getting closer.'

'We're coming!' Liga slung her lascarbine over her shoulder. She leaned across and helped herself to the dead co-pilot's laspistol, checked it, then tucked it into the belt-webbing of her jumpsuit beside a new and vicious-looking combat knife. 'Come on, doc. Time to move.'

# ACT TWO

'*All hope abandon, ye who enter here.*'

– Fragment from an ancient text,
kept in the Great Library of Terra

# XIII

## THE GATHERING STORM

Laskari checked her kitbag for the fiftieth time, confirmed that her compass, spare ammunition and the laser targeting device were indeed still where she had packed them, then stowed it under her seat. The memory of her unscheduled return to the briefing room brought a flush of shame to her cheeks whenever she thought of it. She had been so desperate to make a good impression, but the look of weary frustration on the lord castellan's face had stripped those illusions away. She wasn't here because she was a good soldier or a good shot. She was here because the Munitorum had demanded a Cadian young enough to have been born after the Fall, purely to look fresh-faced on the pict-casts.

'Did you ever see picts?' Anka had finished stowing his own kitbag, and was strapping himself into his restraints.

'Of what?'

'Of Cadia. The way it used to be.' He waved a hand. 'My family held land in Secundus. My grandmother used to show me old picts of their compound.'

'Only the ones in the entertainment 'casts.'

The thought of the broadcasts brought back good memories, evenings spent clustered round the tiny pict-caster in her family's quarters watching whatever was on offer that night: *Heroes of Cadia. Death on the Elysian Fields. Creed's Last Stand.* Full of square-jawed heroes, inspiring speeches and last desperate rolls of the dice.

'Obviously they don't count.'

Laskari had been first on board, but the Valkyrie's compartment was filling up fast. The Scions were checking and stowing each other's gear with well-practised precision and ignoring everyone else. Colonel Van Haast spared them a disdainful look as he took up his seat, as far away from the rest as possible.

'What do you think it'll be like?' Anka dropped his voice to a whisper.

'Honestly? I don't know.' The lord castellan's briefing had been comprehensive on objectives, mission protocol and extraction plans, but light on the details of what Cadia would actually be like. 'I don't suppose anyone knows. Not exactly.'

'We're going to be the first. The first Cadians back home since the Fall. No one even knew it was there any more, and here we are, the first to return.' Anka's broad freckled face lit up. 'I should volunteer to be first out of the Valkyrie. "Lainn Anka, first Cadian to set foot on native soil in a generation." That sort of thing could earn a man a place in the scrolls.'

'You're in the wrong seat for that.' The Catachan sergeant turned from securing his kit in the overhead compartment. In his freshly issued body armour, Harapa looked even bigger than before, though the Cadian drab sat oddly on him. He looked like he'd have been more at home fighting bare-chested with a combat knife held sideways in his teeth. 'I'd leave that to the chief. She's wearing the bullet-catcher.'

Laskari watched as the lord castellan took up her place near the Valkyrie's rear hatch, her helmet and its majestic crimson plume mag-locked to the belt of her gleaming power armour.

'–contact with the penal drop-ship assigned to Operation Kasarn,' Thysia was saying, waving her data-slate. 'The pilot reported a freak energy discharge during the descent, and we lost contact shortly after.'

'Unfortunate.'

'But we're still seeing clear skies over your deployment zone, lord castellan. Clear enough. The main body of legionnaires is safely on the ground on the far side of Kasr Gallan. They're drawing plenty of attention from the Archenemy, exactly as we hoped. The loss of two pilots and a few penitents shouldn't change anything at this stage.'

'Other than the fact we were relying on their intelligence regarding what we are likely to face,' the lord castellan snapped. 'Going in blind is less than ideal.'

'I appreciate that, my lord.' Thysia was speaking quickly, a note in her voice that stopped just a fraction short of desperation. 'I must, however, remind you that the window for this mission is closing. The other Valkyries are already in the air. To abort now...' She paused, gathered herself, and continued. 'The penal legionnaires don't matter in and of themselves, but the effect they have in attracting the attention of the local hostiles will be time-limited. If we withdraw now, all we have done is let the enemy know we're planning something. We have no guarantee that they will take the bait again.'

A scowl passed over the lord castellan's face. Laskari held her breath. If the lord castellan called off their mission now, what would happen? Would they be kept on the *Oriflamme* to try again in days or weeks? Or would she be sent back to Shukret-Dhruv, to be replaced by someone more experienced, and – time to face the truth – actually competent?

'This is the wrong time for this discussion,' the lord castellan said flatly. 'An hour ago we would have had options.'

'And had the information been available then, lord castellan, I can assure you that I would have conveyed it immediately. We can only deal with matters as and when they arise. My advice to you–'

'I did not ask for advice.'

The air temperature in the Valkyrie dropped by a couple of degrees, and Thysia took a step back. Laskari saw Harapa subtly adjust his position, then everything went very still until the lord castellan returned her attention to the data-slate.

'We proceed as planned,' she said. 'Once we are on the surface, you get your picts and whatever soundbites you need to keep the Logos Historica Verita happy. As soon as we move I expect any information you receive to be relayed directly to my personal vox. At the first sign of contact I want the extraction team on standby. In the event of sustained contact we withdraw, whether that means a wasted penal legion or not. Is that clear?'

'Certainly, lord castellan. Is there anything else I can help with before you go?'

'You've done enough.'

'*Take your seats, please.*' The pilot's voice came through the Valkyrie's vox-system, calm and laconic. '*Taking you out in T-minus two minutes. God-Emperor willing, we have clear skies and plain sailing all the way down.*'

Laskari checked her harness again.

'You all right there, trooper?' Harapa said.

She nodded. 'Right as rain, sarge.'

'Good kid.'

Laskari closed her eyes and waited. A soft thrum ran through the Valkyrie's bodywork, its machine-spirit purring with an eagerness to see action that matched her own, like it was Candlemas Eve and she was waiting to open her gift.

*'Arm doors and cross check complete,'* the pilot said. The Valkyrie's docking clamps disengaged with a thud. *'Soldiers of Cadia. It is my honour to escort you home.'*

Ossian picked his way across the broken ground, trying to keep his eyes off the sky. There was no doubt in his mind now that they were being followed, though the regular boom of the hunting horn had been replaced by a wild moaning and whooping that echoed eerily off the tightly clustered ferrocrete walls. It was impossible to be sure, but from the layout and the broken aerials jutting from the earth like shattered ribs, he thought they might be in what remained of a vox-relay station. Now it was a twisting ferrocrete maze of blind turns and dead ends.

'Gettin' closer,' Clavie said. The ogryn had reached a T-junction, her piggy eyes darting from side to side with obvious fear. Liga had insisted she take a lascarbine, but instead of hanging it over her shoulder the big abhuman was holding it like a club. 'Liga, which way we go?'

'Doesn't matter.' Liga was a little distance behind, scanning the darkness for any sign of their pursuers. There was something about the way she moved, how she handled her lascarbine that made Ossian question what she'd said about her past as a ganger. He was fairly sure she wasn't a soldier – not a *Cadian* soldier, anyway – but someone, sometime had taught her how to act like one. 'Try left,' she said. 'Keep moving.'

The space between the walls was narrow enough now that Clavie was blocking it completely. Any narrower and her shoulders would be scraping along the ferrocrete. Ossian risked a glance up, and saw another twisted aerial to his right, twenty feet tall and silhouetted against the heavy crimson sky. Eight human corpses hung from it like grisly trophies, the rusted metal pierced through ragged cloth and the bones beneath.

The skeleton at the top caught his eye, skewered from pelvis to the tip of the skull like a roast on a spit. A few wisps of hair still clung to the skull, stirring with the movement of the air, and for a moment he thought the skull turned its empty sockets towards him. He tore his gaze away, and when he looked back the skull was still. A trick of the light, nothing more. It hadn't moved. It couldn't have.

The hunting horn boomed again, echoing off the broken walls. It sounded closer. Much closer. This time when the skeleton turned its head the movement was undeniable. All eight moved in eerie synchrony, fleshless jaws unhinging to let out a polyphonic shriek that pierced his skull like a white-hot needle.

'Throne–'

'Shut up!' Clavie slammed her hands over her ears and bellowed in pain. 'Shut up!'

'Clavie!' Liga was tugging on the ogryn's arm, her voice a soothing murmur. 'It's just noise. It can't hurt you.'

'Tell her we have to keep moving.' Ossian's ears were still ringing. 'We can't stop–'

'No!' Clavie bellowed, rounding on him with terrifying speed. She slammed one fist into the wall, sending a shower of dust and debris into the air. 'Another–' A second crash, fist against ferrocrete. 'Dead–' The huge knuckles were running with blood, but she hadn't noticed, punching the wall over and over again until a spider web of cracks spread out across its surface. 'End!'

'I hear you, Clavie, I hear you!' Liga shoved past Ossian, inside the range of Clavie's massive haymakers. 'We can get out of here, but you've got to work with me!'

Clavie's massive head looked down at the other woman. Her face was scarlet, her nostrils flaring like those of an angry bull-grox.

'Can you do that for me, big girl?'

126

Clavie's piggy eyes refocused. Her fists unclenched, and her lower lip started to tremble. 'Don't like it here.'

'I don't like it much either.' Liga reached out and took Clavie's hand, turning it to wipe at the blood running from the broken knuckles with her sleeve. The ogryn flinched, but she didn't pull her hand away. 'But don't go hurting yourself. We need each other, right?'

The ogryn's massive head nodded. 'Need each other.'

'That's right.' Liga nodded. 'This way's a dead end, but all we have to do is retrace our steps–'

A lightning bolt seared across the sky. For a split second the thin veil that separated reality from the immaterium was stripped away, revealing a hellscape of writhing daemons, all the horrors of the warp staring back as if through an invisible barrier. Then Ossian's vision cleared, his mouth flooding with the bitterness of rot and ozone. This place was cursed, somewhere the normal rules of reality no longer applied. He blinked his eyes, trying to focus beyond the afterimage bisecting his vision, making out a snarl of twisted metal and razor wire – and beyond it the suggestion of open ground.

'There's our way out!'

Liga whooped with delight. 'There you go, big girl!'

Ossian turned to retrace his steps. Lightning flared again, and the fleeting vision of the warp was followed by the sight of a massive silhouette haloed against the sky. In the moment before the darkness returned Ossian could see that it was human shaped, but colossal, bigger even than Clavie, holding a long hook-topped weapon.

'There's something down there,' he hissed. They were rapidly running out of options, caught between a dead end and an unseen menace approaching with slow footsteps that shook the ground. 'Following us. Through the maze.'

'Back to that T-junction, then,' Liga said. 'If we're quick–'

He strained his eyes into the gloom, but the serrated after-image made it impossible to divide the darkness into substance and shadow. There had been something there, and he could no more have run blindly towards it than taken flight out of their prison. A heavy footstep shook the ground. It was getting closer.

'Too risky,' Ossian said, trying to sound calmer than he felt. 'Clavie, I need you to keep doing what you were doing just there. Break down that wall for me. I know you're strong enough.'

Clavie looked doubtfully at her cracked and bleeding knuckles. 'Liga?'

The ganger shot a look over her shoulder, then lifted up a fist-sized piece of rubble and slammed it against the crack in the wall. 'Use a rock, big girl. You can do it.'

Clavie nodded. She bent over and lifted a piece of astrogranite the size of an ammunition case, twisted her shoulders back then uncoiled herself forward to slam it into the wall. Dust plumed into the air as she drew back and delivered a second thunderous blow, obliterating a segment of wall large enough for them to scramble through.

'You did it!' Liga shouted. 'Clavie, you're amazing!'

Ossian scrambled through the hole in the wall, reaching back in case the ogryn needed coaxing to follow, but she was building up momentum and broke into a lumbering run as soon as she had two massive feet on solid ground. Liga was running too, and he fell into step beside them. The buildings had been more widely spaced here, or perhaps simply more had been destroyed, but there was what looked like clear ground ahead. The urge to turn to look over his shoulder tugged at him like a chain tied to his collar, but he resisted, focusing on the feel of the cracked astrogranite beneath his feet, the acrid rasp of the air across his throat.

The horn sounded again, its bellow muffled by the ruins. They were gaining ground. He thought back to the narrow maze of walls, to the huge silhouette, stark against the blazing sky. Had it all been a trick of the light, conjured up by the gloom and his well-shaken brain?

Clavie skidded to a halt so suddenly that Ossian almost ran into her back. She was staring at the sky, an expression of wonder on her face.

'Look. Shooting star.'

'We're not here for stargazing, big girl. Too cloudy.' Liga's mouth snapped shut. 'Throne. She's right, Mac, look. It's not a star. That's another drop-ship.'

He looked up, trying to plot the trajectory of the falling light. 'Where is it coming down?'

'There must be a landing zone. If we can get there, maybe they can deal with what's following us.'

Ossian tried not to think about the morpholox in his pack. There had been enough in there to draw this nightmare to a close right now for all three of them. Liga's relentless survival instinct was admirable in its way, but surely even she had realised that their chances of getting out of here were narrowing by the minute.

'We find the landing site. We introduce ourselves, and ask politely for extraction. What then?'

'Maybe they give us a ride home. Maybe they shoot us in the head. We'll cross that bridge when we come to it.'

'I wish I had your optimism.' He started moving again. 'For the record, I still think they're going to shoot us the moment they see us.'

'Who shoot us?' A trail of blood oozed from Clavie's scalp, black in the dull red light.

'No one's going to shoot us, big girl,' Liga said.

'Bad place,' Clavie said quietly. 'Scared.'

'You, scared?' Liga shook her head. 'Whoever's out there, they should be scared of *you*.'

# XIV

## THE CITADEL, REVERSED

'*One minute.*'

The pilot's voice cut across the roar of the Valkyrie's engines. Ursula took up her position at the rear ramp, the ever-present servo-skull, doing duty as the propagandist's eyes and ears, hovering at her shoulder.

One minute, she thought. I'm not ready. But then, I'm never going to be ready for this.

Ursula ran her eyes over the rest of the squad. The Scion fire-team were already loaded and standing, and the two green-horns were practically vibrating with anticipation, jostling at each other in their eagerness to get into position. Van Haast was still in his restraints, staring at the door without blinking.

Argent got to his feet. She gave him a nod, and he smiled weakly in return, the expression stopping short of his eyes. He pulled his goggles down, fixed his respirator over his nose and mouth, and flashed a thumbs up.

'*Ready, lord castellan?*' Thysia's voice came through the servo-skull's tinny vox-caster. It bobbed in front of her, its shutter clattering open and closed across its ocular lens.

She reached out a gauntleted hand and shoved it away. 'Keep that thing out of my sight-line.'

The skull spun wildly, narrowly missing Sergeant Harapa's head, then righted itself at a safer distance. *'Of course, lord castellan.'*

Ursula unfastened the helmet from her belt and placed it on her head. The magnificent scarlet plume was so tall it brushed against the Valkyrie's overhead.

'Ready.'

*'Excellent.'* The skull's eyes flared in time with Thysia's words. *'If you'd be good enough to pause just as you leave the Valkyrie so we can capture some more picts–'*

'Fire-team One, on me.' She had to have the damn skull along, but that didn't mean she had to listen to it. 'As soon as we touch the ground I want the landing site cleared and an assessment of our situation. Tempestor Valcrev, your fire-team will secure our perimeter.' She rolled her eyes. 'And try not to get killed in the first minute for the sake of a few propaganda posters.'

The Valkyrie's turbojets changed note, and the horizon tilted. The ramp opened and began its descent, revealing nothing but darkness beyond. Ursula adjusted her helmet's visor to low-light, but the image was barely any clearer, nothing but an indistinct landscape in green and black.

*'Dropping the ramp for you now,'* the pilot said. *'May the Emperor protect you all.'*

The Valkyrie was still a few feet in the air when she jumped, the engines deafening, despite the muffling effects of her helmet. Her armour's servo-motors absorbed the impact with a whirr, and she moved forward as the squad dropped down behind her, the Scions fanning out into the darkness like a single five-limbed creature. One of the Valkyrie's aircrew ran a lumen-stick across its interior and signalled the all-clear, and then the drop-ship was rising again, its ramp still open, the air stirred to a whirlwind by the downdraught of its turbojets.

'Perimeter's secure, lord castellan,' Valcrev voxed. 'By all metrics we've come down perfectly on target.'

'Good work, Tempestor.' Ursula activated her helmet's heads-up display, and took a moment to orientate herself. 'Hold for now. Let's get a feel for this place.'

Runes flashed across her vision, analysing the composition of the air and the ground beneath her feet in detail that would have delighted her enginseer.

'The atmosphere is breathable, my lord,' the Scions' medicae said.

'Excellent news.' Argent unfastened his respirator and let it drop to around his neck. Already the rubber seal had left a red mark around his nose and mouth, giving him the look of some strange muzzled animal. 'I loathe the feel of those things on my face.'

Ursula broke the neck-seal on her helmet and lifted it free. After the helmet's stifling confines she had expected cool air against her skin, but the atmosphere was so arid the sweat on her skin dried instantly to a crust of salt. They were standing in a dried-up riverbed, the remains of ancient engines of war jutting like the wrecks of sunken ships from the hard-packed red earth. The banks had eroded away to shallow slopes, while beyond them a crumbled martyr's wall marked the boundary of what had once been Kasr Gallan. By the looks of it some of its hab-bunkers and fortified towers were still standing, but the longer she looked at it, the more unsettled she became. Something had changed the city, twisted it into a grotesque parody of its former self, but close enough that you might never know the full extent of the deception until its jaws locked around you.

She took her compass from her pouch and flipped its polished brass case open. The needle was swinging aimlessly in a lazy circle. Of course there were no magnetic poles – there were no poles at all, torn away and scattered into the void – and that realisation brought both disorientation and an unexpected pang of sorrow. It was one thing to know that your home world was gone forever, another to learn of its ongoing existence in a blasphemous half-life, but confronting that reality under a blistered scarlet sky was something else entirely.

'Any words to mark this momentous occasion?' Colonel Van Haast shook her from her reverie with venom in his voice.

'Were you expecting a speech?' she snapped back. In fact, the Logos Historica Verita had supplied one, but she'd told them in no uncertain terms exactly what she'd thought of that idea. Now that the Valkyrie was gone, the landing zone was eerily quiet, but that didn't mean she was going to start orating for the viewers at home. 'I hardly think this is the time.'

She gave the sky a last look, slammed the helmet back on her head and sealed it with a hiss. Somewhere beyond the thick pall of cloud was the Eye of Terror, blinded by the storm. She had spent the first decade of her life under its baleful gaze, and she found its absence even more unsettling than its presence. It was like any enemy: the less you saw of them, the more dangerous they were.

A grid of green lines spun and twisted across her heads-up display, resolving into a topographic map of the area. Kasr Gallan was there, a mausoleum of broken towers and overgrown barracks, while behind her the Rossvars rose out of the foothills like a row of jagged teeth. The image flared white as a burst of lightning lit the sky over the kasr. Each energy discharge from the clouds seemed to rip the hole in reality a little wider, each vision of the warp more vivid and intense than the last.

She closed her eyes until it passed. A few seconds later, it was followed by a distant rumble – not thunder, but the sound of an artillery barrage.

'The penal legion must be making contact,' Argent said. 'They won't last long under an assault like that.'

'Spare your pity for someone who deserves it.' The lasrifle resting lazily in Van Haast's hands was an antique hunting piece, the barrel inset with adamantine scroll-work, a gilded aquila on one side of the stock and an aurox rampant on the other. 'Murderers and traitors, every last one of them.'

'I'm not worried about them,' Ursula said. 'But we should make use of the distraction.' She raised her gauntlet and pointed towards the kasr. 'That watchtower there is our first landmark. Valcrev, you're on point.' The two green troopers were still struggling into their backpacks, apparently oblivious to their surroundings or anything she had just said. 'Harapa, you take Anka and Laskari and cover the rear. Rest of you, we're moving in wedge formation, eyes out. Clear?'

'Lord castellan.' Sergeant Major Strahl was at her elbow, standing stiffly to attention. 'Might I have a word?'

'Is now the time?'

A smile flickered across the old man's face. 'It is, my lord.'

'Quickly then.' A moment or two for the team to acclimate to their surroundings was no bad thing, but she could do without hearing more of the old fool's sycophantic drivel. He withdrew a carefully wrapped object the size and shape of a charge-pack from a belt pouch, and held it out to her with an incongruously ceremonial air.

'What is it?'

'I was ordered to give this to you as soon as we arrived.'

She repeated herself through gritted teeth. 'And *what is it*?'

'A journal, sir. Your father's.'

'Thysia, turn that damned pict-caster off.' White-hot anger flared through her. 'What exactly are you thinking?'

'*I assure you, lord castellan, that has nothing to do with me.*' Through the vox, Thysia's tinny voice was all wounded dignity.

'I don't care what you have planned, you turn the damn thing off.' Inside her helmet, her face was burning. 'A little convenient, isn't it, for the long-lost journal of Lord Castellan Creed to come to light at this specific moment?'

'My apologies, sir.' Strahl bowed his head deferentially. 'But my orders were very clear. The parcel was to be returned to you when first you set foot on Cadia, neither sooner nor later.'

'Your orders.' The gift was still in his hands, offered out towards her. 'And from whom did these orders come?'

'Colonel Hellsker.'

She blinked. That wasn't the answer she'd been expecting. The servo-skull flitted back in her peripheral vision, and she slapped it aside with the back of her gauntlet without looking. 'Marda Hellsker? The hero of the Delvian Cleave? *That* Colonel Hellsker?'

'Yes, my lord. Colonel Hellsker said she was given it by your father the last time they spoke on Cadia.'

'But that was *years* ago.' She took the little parcel and turned it over in her hands. It was wrapped in dark brown suedecloth, the edges scuffed bald. 'How could she possibly have known that I would come back here?'

'I regret I do not know, my lord.'

This didn't make sense. Strahl expected her to believe that her long-dead father had anticipated her return to Cadia and arranged for his journal to be delivered – and for what? It was poor compensation for decades of missed name-days, and for all Strahl's denials, this had the fingerprints of the Logos Historica Verita all over it.

She shoved it back at him.

'Keep it.'

'Lord castellan, please–'

'You've kept the damn thing for decades. A few more won't hurt. And if Colonel Hellsker has a problem with that, she can take it up with me herself.'

A brief, troubled frown crossed the sergeant major's face, but he nodded and tucked the journal back into his belt-pouch. 'As you command, my lord.'

'It's not what I was expecting,' Anka said.

They had climbed out of the riverbed and were crossing open ground towards the broken remains of the martyr's wall, picking their way across cracked astrogranite scattered with tufts of unnatural-looking crimson foliage. The toe of Laskari's boot contacted something hard and resonant that rolled away at the touch, and she looked down to see that what she had kicked was the dome of a human skull. A drop of warm liquid trickled down between her shoulder blades, followed by another.

It was starting to rain.

'What *were* you expecting?' Laskari kept her voice low.

'I don't know.' Anka shook his head. He sounded uncertain. 'I thought coming home would feel different. I knew it would be difficult, but to have the chance to see the land our ancestors fought for... I thought it would be special. This feels... wrong.'

Laskari looked at her boots. More raindrops were falling, raising craters in the red earth like the impact-marks of tiny bullets. A metallic smell rose from the dampened earth, intense and sharp like the taste of blood from a split lip.

'It takes time to acclimatise to a new world.' Laskari gestured with her long-las towards the lord castellan, her silver armour reflecting crimson in the half-light. 'That's why we follow protocol.

137

Orientation and preliminary survey, to be carried out at all times, except in case of immediate hostile contact.'

'That's not what I meant.' Anka rubbed a hand across his forehead, then froze.

Laskari flinched. 'What is it?'

'The rain.' Anka held his hand up in front of her eyes. There was a dark smear across the fingertips, and a matching streak above his brow-ridge. 'Look at it.'

She looked up at the sky, at the tiny drops hurtling towards her like shooting stars. The air smelled strange: sharply metallic, with an undercurrent that put her in mind of the dead bird she had found in her bedroll the night she had outshot Anka for the first time. The little corpse had been ripe with decay, the flesh parting like spoiled fruit beneath her fingers, spilling fat white maggots from beneath its carapace of feathers. It had taken days to scrub the smell from her fingers, weeks for her bedroll.

She licked a raindrop from her upper lip, and tasted copper.

'Blood,' she said softly. 'It's raining blood.'

Where could it be coming from? She had learned in the schola where rain came from – how water evaporated from planetary surfaces, cooled into clouds of water vapour only to fall again as rain. How could the same be happening with blood? She held up her hand to inspect the slippery scarlet drops, the copper taste turning sour in her mouth. The last survivors to leave Cadia before the Fall had spoken of seeing the ground soaked in the blood of the dead and dying. Had the sheer volume of blood spilt – the lifeblood of a martyred people – been enough to change the laws of nature in this infernal place?

'You two all right back there?' Harapa said, and Laskari jumped. She turned to see him standing in what, up until a moment before, had been her blind spot. For such a big man, he moved with remarkable stealth. 'Scions are looking twitchy,' he said. 'That's never a good sign.'

'What are they looking at?' Anka asked. In front of them, the wedge had come to a halt. The Scions fanned out, their goggles glowing green, hand signals flashing between the Tempestor and her fire-team at dizzying speed.

'Don't know yet. But I don't reckon we'll have long to wait.'

Valcrev's voice rasped through the vox. 'Lord castellan, we have multiple hostiles approaching on the far side of the martyr's wall.'

'Ready yourselves,' the lord castellan said, and drew her sword.

They had been running through the ruins of the kasr for ten minutes, and Ossian had already fallen twice. The first time he had checked himself by scraping his palms red-raw on a ferro-crete wall, but on the second fall he had caught his ankle in a tangle of rusted razor wire, tearing a chunk of skin out of his right shin and sending him skidding over the blood-slick ground. The raw flesh hurt with every step, but they couldn't slow down. Not now.

He cast another desperate glance over his shoulder – something he tried to do as little as possible – and this time he saw them clearly. Pale shapes moving between the ruined buildings, capering in and out of the swirling scarlet rain, shrieking hunters driven forward by the sonorous note of the hunting horn.

'Can't... run... any... more,' Clavie gasped.

'Did you hear that?' Liga didn't stop running. 'Voices.'

'Imperial?'

'Don't know. Shut up and let me listen.'

Out of the rain ahead came the distinctive crackle of vox-static, followed by a few words too quiet for Ossian to understand.

'Gothic. They're speaking Gothic.' Liga's face lit up, her teeth bright against the blood covering her face. 'We found them. We made it.' She grabbed Clavie's hand, and dragged her on towards the broken perimeter wall in front of them. 'Come on, big girl! Last big sprint and we're safe!'

# XV

## THE MARTYRS

'I have multiple movement signals. Incoming at speed.' Tempestor Valcrev's voice was matter-of-fact. A shiver went down Laskari's spine in spite of the heat.

'What else can you tell me?' The lord castellan sounded every bit as calm as the Tempestor. Laskari wondered how many years it would take to feel half as relaxed under pressure, and if she'd survive long enough to find out.

'Sixty, maybe sixty-five, fairly strung out. Most of them are human-sized, a mixture of warm and cold. At least one larger target.'

'Abhuman?'

'Possibly. One with a power signal, presumably armour and weapons.' The Tempestor shook her helmeted head. 'Something is disturbing the auspex.'

'Large in power armour counts as Heretic Astartes until proven otherwise,' the lord castellan said.

A blurt of laughter forced itself from Laskari's throat. Fallen angels were things of nightmare, legends to scare unruly children who wouldn't go to bed. The Adeptus Astartes were incorruptible, perfect warriors made by the God-Emperor Himself. It wasn't possible that they could fall to Chaos. They couldn't be real. Not even on Cadia.

'That can't be right,' she whispered.

Anka shrugged helplessly. 'You hear rumours.'

'But it's not true. It can't be.'

She shot a look of appeal at Sergeant Harapa, and his grim expression told her all that she needed to know.

'Get ready,' he said.

A hunting horn boomed from the other side of the martyr's wall. She could hear the oncoming horde now, moaning and shrieking in a way that sounded neither human nor sane.

The lord castellan's sword flared into brilliant blue-white light. The Scions moved ahead of her to take up firing positions, while the rest spread out to cover their flanks. Laskari took aim at the darkness beyond the martyr's wall, trying to stop her hands from shaking.

*Don't worry about what's coming. It's just like the shooting range. All you have to do is find your mark, and–*

Something colossal burst through the gap in the wall, its monstrous face streaming with blood, a weapon raised in a colossal fist. Her finger found the trigger, and squeezed, sending a beam of vivid green light spearing from her lasgun. It struck the monster in the right eye, and for one terrible moment Laskari thought it was going to keep running. Its momentum carried it forward, the huge legs still moving long after the brain had been pierced, then it tumbled forward to the bloody ground with an earth-shuddering crash.

It was dead.

She had killed it.

Slowly, the wider world returned. Someone was shouting over the ringing in her ear, a stream of syllables that didn't make sense at all.

'–your fire, Throne-damn-it! I said hold your fire!'

A hand grabbed her arm. Laskari lowered her long-las and refocused her eyes. The giant she had shot was lying face down, two filthy human-sized figures skidding to a halt on either side. One of the humans – a woman, Laskari thought – dropped to the ground beside the dead monster, cradling the ruined head in her outstretched hands. The other one had already dropped his weapon at his feet, and was walking forward, his hands outstretched above his head.

'Hold your fire!' the man shouted. 'We're from the penal legions – we're not the enemy!'

A pair of Scions darted forward, one grabbing the man roughly by the collar of his jumpsuit and dragging him forward, while the other approached the huge figure on the floor and its human companion.

'It's an ogryn,' the Scion said, his voice tinny through his helmet. 'Penal troopers. He's telling the truth.'

Laskari's stomach dropped. She had a profound wish to have the last ten seconds of her life back, anything to undo her stupid, lethal mistake. 'I thought–'

'I know what you *thought*.' The lord castellan's voice was a sharp-edged growl. She pointed the tip of her sword towards the man. 'You. Come forward.'

'We're being followed,' he said. There was a collar around his neck, and a tattered orange jumpsuit was plastered to his body with mud. 'Close. Multiple targets–'

'Shut your mouth, scum.' The nearest Scion smacked him in the mouth with the back of one gauntleted hand. The legionnaire staggered, but he didn't fall.

'That's enough.' The lord castellan raised her hand. 'Both of you, drop those carbines and get behind the firing line. We can sort this mess out once we've dealt with whatever is–'

'Contact is imminent, my lord,' Valcrev said. 'Ten seconds…'

'Make ready.' Lightning crackled down the lord castellan's powerblade, electric blue against the gloom.

The kneeling legionnaire looked up at the martyr's wall, then back at the dead ogryn. Then she got to her feet, cast her carbine to one side and sprinted past the Scions to her surviving companion. Laskari watched her move, and the woman fixed her with an angry glare, her eyes red-rimmed and narrowed with hatred.

'Contact in five…'

'Hold.'

'Four…'

'Take aim.'

'Three…'

The martyr's wall erupted with ragged figures, shambling towards them with arms outstretched. Some of them looked almost human, eyes sunken back into gaunt faces, strings of intestines spilling from gas-ruptured abdomens, while others bore grotesque mutations, weeping sores and horns protruding from grey-green flesh, rusting weapons clutched in taloned hands. All were grinning, lips drawn back in a gleeful rictus that had no place on a human face. The smell of decay spread through the air, mixing with the skinned-meat smell of the bloody rain. Laskari shouldered her long-las and brought her finger up to the trigger-guard, the metal unsettlingly warm and slick to the touch.

The horn blew again, and a monstrous figure moved into sight behind the ranks of the damned.

It was half as tall again as she was, wearing a suit of grey-green power armour, so thick with corrosion that only sorcery could be holding it together. Blood trickled in rivulets over its pockmarked surface, and a wide pair of bone antlers protruded from either side of its visored helmet. In one hand, it held a wickedly curved scythe. As it approached, the rotting-meat smell in the air intensified, so thick that Laskari could taste it in the back of her throat.

'Choose your targets. Make your shots count.' There was no trace of fear in the lord castellan's voice.

The rotting horde stumbled forward. The closest opened its jaw impossibly wide, revealing broken yellow teeth and a bloated black tongue, and let out a low, hungry-sounding moan.

'Two...' Valcrev voxed.

'Give fire.'

The world blazed green. The first rank of shambling horrors fell, but their places were instantly filled. The Scions were moving together, their hotshot weapons laying down a broad arc of fire. Laskari shot the open-mouthed horror, then aimed at the next, fired and aimed again, not stopping to check if any of her shots had hit the mark. There were so many of them, advancing in a rotting, shambling tide.

'I wanted to say I'm sorry,' Anka said.

She killed another leering poxwalker with a shot through the eye.

'What?'

'I'm sorry.' He was at her shoulder, eyes on target, shot after shot finding its mark in rotting flesh. 'For how I treated you.'

'What brought this on?' She had been on the receiving end of Anka's fists often enough that she had learned not to trust a word that came from his mouth.

'This. I thought I knew what being Cadian was. How to behave. How it would feel to come home.' He lowered his long-las and slapped a fresh charge-pack into the magazine well. 'I was wrong about that. And I was wrong to treat you the way I did.'

'They're not stopping, chief!' Sergeant Harapa voxed. 'How many more are we expecting?'

You made my life a living hell for years, Laskari wanted to say. Instead she took a shot that scored a deep furrow through a poxwalker's cranium, stripping away a wide trench of bone and revealing the rotting brains beneath.

'We can talk about this later.'

'Auspex is struggling.' Tempestor Valcrev spat the words like bullets. 'The whole area is coming alive.'

'They're trying to flank us,' Van Haast said. He was walking slowly backwards, choosing his shots with care, each bolt from the exquisitely decorated lasrifle sending another abomination crumpling to the dirt. 'I rather fear they're succeeding.'

'Ursula – lord castellan – we need to fall back.' The note of panic in Argent's voice came as a relief. If the usually confident major was frightened too, maybe the clawing panic in Laskari's own stomach was less of a cause for shame after all.

'Still clear behind us.' Valcrev sent another stream of las-bolts into the horde. 'If we go now–'

The ground under Valcrev's feet erupted around her, and she vanished in a fountain of red earth that showered blood and pus-yellow liquid in all directions. Valcrev's second was caught in the spray and recoiled, the faceplate of his armour sizzling and corroding at terrifying speed. He screamed, clawing at his helmet, but as soon as the liquid touched his gauntlets they began to dissolve, eating away at metal and flesh until his fingers were nothing but stumps. The screams from the helmet took on a wet, bubbling quality as the liquid ate his face down to the bone. It was only when the bone itself dissolved into a thick, frothing mass that the screams grew silent, and he fell, still thrashing, to the ground. When Laskari tore her eyes away there was no sign of Valcrev, but the crater of disturbed earth was writhing with massive centipedes, gleaming beetles and fist-sized white maggots.

'Fall back.' Even the lord castellan was sounding tense now. 'In good order. On my mark–'

Another explosion turned the world scarlet.

Sergeant Major Strahl staggered dead-eyed back from the firing line, blood streaming from the ruin of his right arm to mix with the bloody rain. Whatever had hit him had severed his forearm just below the elbow, leaving the skin hanging in tatters around the two jagged ends of bone. The medicae was on him within seconds. With well-practised efficiency, she drew a bottle of haemostat from her belt, sprayed the wound and dragged him by the underarms away from the enemy.

Strahl looked down at the stump of his arm, and the stunned look on his face was replaced with one of abject horror. He screamed, the sound incongruously high and shrill like an animal caught in the jaws of a trap.

'Shut off his vox, Throne damn you!' the lord castellan shouted. The screaming was appallingly loud, reverberating through Laskari's vox-bead and into her skull, making it impossible to concentrate, impossible to think – until Strahl's vox-bead cut out. The screaming grew muffled, but the deactivated vox continued to broadcast in a rasping whisper that had no origin in a human throat.

*'Embrace the inevitability of your demise. Feel the dissolution of your flesh, the creeping rot moving through muscle and bone.'*

'Shael!' Anka's hand was tugging at her sleeve. 'We're falling back. Come on.'

*'Your place is with your people, daughter of Cadia. Mouldering in the soil that gave you birth. Yield to me, and accept the mercy of decay.'*

Laskari nodded, but fear was freezing her feet to the ground.

The horde were close now, so close that the smell was stifling, and she could see fat maggots writhing in the gaping eye sockets, the pus running in gleaming rivulets from sores in the mould-ering skin.

'Shael, please!' Dully, she registered the desperation in Anka's voice. 'They're coming! Move!'

And then the world exploded again, and Anka was gone.

Just as Ursula had predicted, everything had gone to hell.

They were surrounded on three sides, with three dead Scions – no, make that four – an obliterated sniper and a sergeant major so badly wounded that she could hear him screaming even with-out a vox-link. They were facing a seemingly endless horde of cultists and poxwalkers, with a Heretic Astartes prowling behind the ruins of the martyr's wall, choosing its targets with heavy ordnance and meticulous care. She had the suspicion that it was waiting for something, watching its horde of minions surge forward and fall with dispassionate curiosity.

There was only so long they could hold out like this.

Ursula activated her vox and opened her personal channel to the *Oriflamme*. 'Thysia, this is the lord castellan. We are under heavy assault half a mile north of the landing zone' – was that really all the distance they had covered? – 'on the outside of Kasr Gallan's perimeter wall. We have sustained significant losses and have at least one serious casualty.' By the time help arrived, she was fairly sure that number would be higher. 'Requesting imme-diate air support and evacuation craft on standby.'

The silence stretched out. Ursula raised the bolt pistol and obliterated another mass of cultists. Her heads-up display flashed red: ammunition running low. They were almost out of time.

'*Message received and understood, lord castellan,*' Thysia said, her words rendered partially inaudible by the static on the line. '*We have a Valkyrie en route to you now. Head for the landing zone and await further contact.'*

'Understood.' Ursula returned her vox to the open channel. 'Help is on its way. We are moving back to the landing zone, full retreat in good order. Is that clear?'

There was a chorus of assent.

'Am I to understand we are withdrawing from Cadia entirely, lord castellan?' Van Haast asked. He sounded irritated at the mere idea.

'If you want to stay and die for the sake of a new medal for your collection, colonel, then you have my blessing.' She used one of her precious bolt-shells to destroy a poxwalker that had come too close for comfort. 'But I don't intend to throw any more lives away today chasing down ghosts.'

# XVI

## THE EXECUTIONER

Ossian was back to back with Liga, moving at the rear of the Imperial unit and choosing his shots with care. Their lascarbines had been taken out of their hands in the frantic seconds after Clavie's death, and were strapped unloaded and useless to the side of the big sergeant's pack, but they had been left with a sidearm each and Liga's combat knife. The horrors moved with unexpected speed and stealth, appearing out of the driving blood-rain as if from the warp itself.

'What do we do now?' Liga asked him.

'Follow them to their drop-ship.' Ossian shot out a poxwalker's knees with two quick las-bolts, and it dropped to the ground without showing any sign of pain. It kept moving, dragging itself along with its ruined legs trailing behind it, but it was slower now, and that was all he needed. 'It can't be far.'

'What makes you think they'll take us with them?'

'What makes you think they won't?'

'Seriously, doc?' Liga finished the maimed poxwalker with

a shot that burned off the right side of its skull, and spat a mixture of blood and saliva onto the ground. 'We're nothing to them. You saw what happened to Clavie. Didn't stop to check, just shot her down like she was nothing at all. You think they're going to give us a seat on a Valkyrie, strap us in and take us home for medals?' She shook her head. 'That thing with the scythe is still out there. Unless we're on that bird we haven't got a chance.'

Ossian looked across the torn ground to where the lord castellan and her soldiers were fighting. He and Liga were penal legionnaires, but they were still Imperial, and that had to count for something, didn't it? What sort of an officer would leave soldiers behind on a hell world to die?

The answer came to him with unpleasant clarity. The same officer who'd put them there in the first place.

Another poxwalker lurched, broken-legged towards him, and he blew out its throat with a single shot. Its head lolled to one side, but it kept up a steady shamble, its jaw working furiously, trailing two long streams of pink drool.

One of the Scions – the one with the snake-and-staff of the Astra Militarum Chirurgical Corps stencilled on her pauldrons – broke formation and moved ahead of the main group, the body of an injured soldier over her shoulders. An idea occurred to him, bringing with it a tiny flicker of hope. What he was about to do might not be enough to buy a pair of seats on a Valkyrie, but then again, it might…

He headed for the Scions, his open hands raised in the hope that she might not shoot him before he had a chance to talk. 'Excuse me. I'm a medicae. A chirurgeon. I can help you with that man's injuries.'

Another flash of lightning lit the lowering clouds, bringing another vision of writhing bodies and fang-toothed maws. The clouds were getting thicker, lower, and the wind was rising, stirring the blood-rain into scarlet flurries.

The Scion put her hand in the centre of his chest and pushed him aside. 'I don't need help from you.'

'Maybe not, but he does.' Strahl's screams had taken on a hoarse, desperate quality. His arm was dissolving from the wrist up, only the bones and a few shreds of sinew to hold them together remaining. Even the bones themselves were turning black, softening and rotting in front of his eyes. The wound stank like week-old wound dressings. 'Take the arm at the shoulder. Do it now and you might stop the contagion. Leave it and he's dead.'

'We have no time for that,' she said.

'Then make time. At least let my friend and I help you carry him–'

'Doc!' Liga's howl was deafening, and he turned to see one of the dead clawing at her ankle. Sometime in the battle the poxwalker had been ripped in half – probably by the lord castellan's bolt pistol – and its torso ended at the lower ribcage, trailing off into tatters of bone and intestines. Liga was hacking at it with her combat knife, but the abomination's jaws were gnashing around the ankle-cuff of her boots, its hands clawing at the leg of her jumpsuit as if it was trying to cram her into its gaping mouth in one piece. Ossian aimed his laspistol directly between the gaping eye sockets and pulled the trigger. The horror kept moving, and he fired again, sending shot after shot into its skull until there was nothing but a blackened crater where the head had been.

Liga shook her leg free of the charred remains. 'Shit. I thought I was a goner–'

Another piercing scream came from Ossian's left. A fresh horde had emerged from the rubble to their right and were swarming the medicae, rotting hands clawing at her waist and legs, teeth gnashing inches from her skin. She dropped the wounded man and tried to draw her lasgun, but the poxwalkers were dragging her down by the straps of her armour. She fumbled her sidearm from her hip and took a shot, but for every abomination she killed another three shoved their way into its place.

'Grab the sergeant!' Ossian shouted to Liga, and took a shot. A pox-walker's head exploded, just as another sank its teeth deep into the meat of the medicae's calf. She screamed, and the sound drove the horde into a frenzy. Rotting fingers shoved themselves through the gaps in her armour, yellow teeth ripping at cloth and leaving inch-deep scores through the surface of the cara-pace. Ossian took another shot, but it didn't seem to make a difference, the writhing bodies packed so tight he couldn't tell which one he'd hit.

His stomach tightened with second-hand panic, his feet suddenly feeling as though they were encased in leaden boots. Time slowed to a trickle, viscid as blood. He watched a pair of mouldering hands lock around the Scion's helmet and twist it free, revealing a young woman's face, her wide violet eyes rolling with terror as the tide of decaying limbs dragged her down. She screamed, and two grey fingers hooked themselves around the corner of her mouth and pulled. Fresh blood spilled from her torn cheek, slurring her speech. 'Don't let them take me...'

Too late he realised what she was asking. Hand shaking, he raised the laspistol and aimed for the centre of her forehead, but before he could shoot, her head was tugged to the side with a resonant crack, and vanished into the squirming pile of rotting meat.

'Doc!' Liga was shouting. 'Stop staring and give me a hand, this guy's heavy!'

He knew he had to move, but the sight of the horde was as

hypnotic as it was appalling. Gaping jaws rose and fell, trailing strings of meat and sinew as they tore the medicae to pieces, still screaming as they swallowed her down a mouthful at a time.

Had it been simple cowardice that held him to the spot, he wondered, as the unnatural reverie broke and he turned to join Liga in lifting the wounded man, or had he acted out of self-preservation of a different kind? He couldn't be sure, but one thing was certain. With the Scion's death, the Imperial soldiers would need a medicae – and that might be their only chance to get on whatever extraction method the lord castellan had in mind.

Ursula had lost track of how long they had been running, but the horde of the damned showed no signs of slowing down, slithering down the sloping banks of the dried-up river in a hungry tangle of limbs. Some of the dead were nothing more than skeletons, coated in filth as though they'd just dug themselves out of the ground and dressed in rags so filthy that their original colours were anyone's guess, which was the only good thing about them: she had a fair idea what those corpses would have been wearing when they died, and the less she recognised, the better. Others were grotesque parodies of the human form, covered in blisters and buboes that leaked streams of bloody pus down unnaturally coloured skin, the flesh bloated and overripe, bony horns protruding from shoulders, arms and the stumps of severed limbs.

'Thysia, what's the arrival time on that Valkyrie?'

The vox crackled. '...*storm... signal,*' it squawked.

That level of interference didn't bode well for any part of their extraction: navigation, the emergency beacon, or any hope of making further contact if their ride home went off course. The terrain was more difficult too, every footstep taken over ground rendered slippery with half-clotted blood.

'…*minutes*…' Another blurt of vox-static. '…*storm worsening*… *than expected.*' Another gap. '…*chance to… out.*'

'The line is poor, please repeat.'

This time only a single snippet came through clearly, the rest drowned out by the background noise.

'…*on that Valkyrie, lord castellan. It's your last*…'

The vox went dead, the connection gone.

'Landing zone's up ahead,' Harapa voxed.

'Do you see anything in the sky?' A poxwalker lunged towards her, its right hand replaced by a jagged blade of yellow bone. She stepped to the right, used the hilt of her weapon to punch its blade aside, then took its head from its shoulders with a leisurely backswing. There was no sign of the Heretic Astartes, but she had no doubt that it was still close by. Still watching.

'Can't see. Cloud's thick.' Another purple-white flash lit Harapa's face, followed by a crash of thunder.

'Send up a flare.'

'On it, chief.'

The vivid cherry-red light of a signal flare lit up the landing zone. Less than an hour had passed since they had touched down, and here she was again with nothing achieved and too much lost.

Ursula looked up. The thick layer of cloud was stirring, and this time the flash of light wasn't lightning. 'Throne be praised. Support's here.'

The last of the stragglers – Laskari, Colonel Van Haast and the pair of legionnaires – broke ahead of the horde just before the Valkyrie's guns unleashed a barrage that rendered the poxwalkers and the bloody earth into a shredded pulp. The pilot didn't wait, and the Valkyrie's ferocious downdraught battered at her head and shoulders as the gunship brought itself around.

'Give it room!' she shouted.

The Valkyrie was coming in fast, its guns still clearing row after row of the horde. They weren't all dead, but the gunship was doing a good job of thinning them out. In a few seconds there would be a clear area for it to land – in less than a minute they could be in the air, heading for the *Oriflamme* and some semblance of normality. The plan had been doomed to failure from the start, and she had been a fool ever to agree to it. There would be consequences for her failure, of course, but those could wait until this hellhole was behind them…

And then she saw it. Moving through the storm of bullets with monstrous grace was the hulking figure of the Heretic Astartes, twisted antlers spreading from its visored helm, a scythe in one hand and a wide-barrelled heavy weapon held in the other, pointed not at Ursula or her soldiers, but directly up at the descending Valkyrie.

She opened her mouth to vox a warning, but it was too late. The massive weapon fired, and an explosion tore the sky in half. For a split second the Valkyrie was haloed in a sickly greenish-yellow light, and then it erupted in a thunderclap of light and sound. Black smoke poured from the ruined engines, and shards of metal fell like shooting stars.

Ursula watched the flaming debris rain down. The battlefield fell silent, the bloody earth strewn with the remnants of dead poxwalkers, while those still animate had melted back into the rain. The Heretic Astartes was nowhere to be seen.

'Well,' Harapa said, as the last piece of the Valkyrie crashed to the ground. 'Pardon my Cadian, but what the frekk do we do now?'

# XVII

### THE CANDLE, REVERSED

The longer Ursula looked, the more obvious it became that Sergeant Major Strahl was dying.

The survivors of her squad huddled together like sewer-rats after a flood. They had skirted the outer edge of the martyr's wall at a forced march, fighting the ground for every step, painfully alert for any signs of the Heretic Astartes or his decaying retinue, but they had melted away into the ruins of the kasr as though they had never existed. It had taken the better part of an hour of walking before they had reached another break in the wall, this one below a watchtower that still had three sides and most of its roof, enough to shelter them for an hour or two. The rain had stopped, but the air still stank of freshly butchered meat.

'I think I speak for us all when I say this is an unmitigated disaster,' Van Haast said, dabbing fastidiously at his face with a surprisingly clean kerchief. 'Half the squad is dead – the competent half, I hasten to add. And I'm afraid that our *reinforcements*' – he waved dismissively at the pair of penal troopers in the corner, newly divested of a laspistol, a combat knife and the control module for their bomb collars – 'fail to provide adequate compensation for the loss.'

She didn't disagree.

A trickle of blood made its way through the hole in the roof, down the filthy wall and across the ancient rockcrete floor, half liquid and half clot. She smeared it away with the toe of her sabaton. Van Haast was right. This had been a disaster from start to finish, and it wasn't over yet.

'How's Strahl?' she asked.

'Not good.' Harapa looked up from tending to the sergeant major, laid out in the driest corner of the ruin. The old man's face was even greyer than usual, and his right arm stopped short in a mass of liquefying tissue. His breath was coming in short, quick gasps, and the muscles of his neck stood out like steel cables. 'The medicae got haemostat and antivenin into him before she went down, but he's not looking good. I can dress the wound, but I'm no good for anything fancy.'

'They will send another Valkyrie, won't they?' Argent shot an anxious look towards the heavy cloud. 'They know where we are. If we trigger the emergency beacon and hold position, it should only take them a few minutes to arrive, shouldn't it?'

Ursula pulled the beacon from its pouch and held the little adamantine sphere up to the light. 'I triggered it twenty minutes ago. Given that there's no sign of rescue, and no vox-contact with the other groups of Scions either, I think we can be fairly confident that nothing is getting through that storm.' She turned it over and pressed the little aquila set into its base a second time to deactivate it. The glowing light went dim as the machine-spirit returned to dormancy. 'No point in wearing it out when there's no chance of getting a signal through.'

'I imagine we can't count on supply drops either, then,' said

Van Haast. 'And there I was, dreaming of hot rations and cold lead.' He sniffed, and jerked his head towards the legionnaires. 'We don't have the resources to take those two along with us. My advice to you, lord castellan, is to trigger their bomb collars and have done with it.'

Ursula shook her head. 'They're soldiers, colonel. We're not in the business of killing our own.'

'Really?' Van Haast arched an eyebrow. 'I rather thought their purpose was to die for the Emperor. Matters would have gone considerably better for all of us if they had died with their fellows, rather than leading that abominable horde directly to our position.'

'The enemy would have found us regardless.' A wave of exhaustion passed over her, and she was suddenly glad of the support her armour provided to her aching joints. 'The planet is crawling with hostiles. It was only a matter of time.'

'An inconveniently short matter of time.' Van Haast gestured to the control module for the penal collars, now secured around her gauntlet at the wrist. 'Still, I have said my piece. If you lack the stomach for the deed I would be happy to step in.'

Out of the corner of her eye, Ursula saw the female trooper tense like a cornered animal, ready to spring. The man put a steadying hand on her elbow and gave a near-imperceptible shake of his bloodied head. 'Someone needs to take that arm,' he said.

'I don't reca–' Van Haast began.

Ursula cut him off mid-vowel. 'What do you mean, legionnaire?'

'Your medicae's dead.' The man's voice was full of a professional assurance completely at odds with his dishevelled appearance and shaven head. Level violet eyes stared out from beneath a blood-smeared penal tattoo across his brow. 'Your man there has creeping rot. I've seen it before. The only chance he has is amputation before it spreads.' He shook his head. 'We might already be too late.'

'Excellent,' Van Haast spat. 'Chirurgical advice from a convict. I can hardly believe I didn't think to ask myself.'

'Have you experience as a medicae?' Ursula asked.

The convict nodded. He took a deep breath, clearly deciding how much he was going to tell her, then seemed to come to a decision. 'Ossian. Regimental chirurgeon with the Four-Seventy-Seventh.'

She leaned forward, intrigued despite herself. 'And who was your last commanding officer?'

'That would have been Colonel Brynn.' He spat the name like a curse.

'Fascinating.' Ursula studied the legionnaire's face. 'I received a report that Edric Brynn had been killed in the mess-hall by one of his own soldiers. The culprit was given the choice of death or the legions, and had their name expunged from the military record. I don't suppose you were there at the time, were you?'

The legionnaire stared stonily ahead.

'Lord castellan, diverting though this is, can I remind you of our situation?' Van Haast tapped one manicured nail on the stock of his lasrifle, light glinting on the freshly cleaned band around his ring finger. 'Unless you intend for us to dig our graves here and have done with it, I assume we'll be required to move at some point in the immediate future before we attract the attention of those poxwalkers again.' He shuddered. 'Or something worse.'

'Strahl's not moving anywhere like that, and I'm not leaving him behind.' Ursula pointed at the legionnaire. 'You, do what you can for the sergeant major. The rest of you, I want eyes out. I want us ready to move when I give the command.'

A ripple of sheet lightning passed across the heavy cloud.

Again a vision of the warp seared across her retinas. This time she had the distinct impression that something was looking back.

'And where exactly do you intend we move to?' Van Haast drawled.

'I'm surprised you've forgotten so soon.' If anything, the colonel's resistance made the decision easier. 'We have three more squads out there heading towards the vault, and once we gain access we can potentially use whatever's inside to boost our signal and make contact with the *Oriflamme*.'

When it came down to it, what choice did she have? Stay and die, or head deeper into the kasr towards a slender hope of survival.

Ossian cut open the old man's tunic and inspected the state of his injuries, painfully aware of the eyes on the back of his neck. The arm looked terrible, and even in a fully equipped infirmarium he would only have given Strahl even odds of survival. Operating in a filthy lean-to with a basic field kit lengthened those odds considerably, but it wasn't like either of them had a choice. Something about the way the officer with the ornate heirloom rifle was looking at him suggested that more than one life depended on the application of his surgical skill.

'Have you ever done this before?' he asked Liga.

She shook her head.

'It isn't hard. All you have to do is hold him steady on his side, make sure I can see what I'm doing, and keep your hands out of the wound if you want to keep your fingers.'

The joke fell flat, but what had he expected?

He started by giving Strahl a decent dose of morpholox, then infiltrated nocio-blockers into the nerves of the upper arm to dampen down the pain signals. It would have been considerably quicker to amputate the arm through the elbow, but the grey tendrils of rot had already spread beyond the joint, the veins discoloured like rivulets of contaminated water. The disease was progressing in front of his eyes, inching its way through the old man's bloodstream towards his failing heart.

Strahl's muscles went slack as the morpholox took effect. Ossian wondered for a moment if he had given too large a dose, but then the old man heaved in a deep, slow breath. His eyes opened to reveal an unfocused gaze, the pupils tiny dots of black in their violet circles.

Ossian lifted the flimsy disposable scalpel, weighed it carefully in his hand, and offered up a silent Chirurgeon's Prayer.

*God-Emperor guide my hand.*

One swipe of the blade cut the skin in a lazy downward curve from the tip of Strahl's shoulder to under his arm. A second cut mirrored the first around the back, completing a single circumferential loop that encompassed the shoulder joint. Strahl made a noise that was halfway between a scream and a moan and tried to move, but Liga had him held fast. Blood flooded out of the wound to coat her hands like a pair of slick crimson gloves.

*May my knife flense what is corrupt and leave only purity.*

'Bone cutters.' He asked for the instrument by reflex, then realised that no one was going to provide them. The closest the field kit could provide was a set of snips that looked better suited to fixing heavy machinery than performing precision surgery.

*May my art preserve this mortal flesh.*

Two sharp crunches divided the clavicle a third of the way down its length. As he twisted the short end free, blood and marrow oozed from the truncated bone, but he had a clear view of the vein and artery gleaming through the gap from beneath.

The delicate part was dealing with the blood vessels. This sort of surgery was nothing new to him, but even so his hands shook as he slipped a pair of ties around the vein, tied the knots and snugged them down. Now came the test. A badly tied suture would slip the moment the vessels were divided, and Strahl would exsanguinate in seconds. Ossian hooked the scalpel blade under the vein, held his breath, and cut towards himself.

*That this man may live to serve and praise thy name.*

The knot held. He looped the suture around the artery, tied and cut it, then sliced sharply through the branching plexus of nerves that supplied the arm. The white filaments instantly retracted behind the broken collarbone like tiny glistening serpents retreating to their lair. The wound was oozing sluggishly, but there was no major bleeding. Either everything was going well, or Strahl was so close to death he no longer had a blood pressure to speak of.

The next part was butcher-work, but it was quick: a simple job of severing the tendons that held the ball joint of the arm in place, disconnecting humerus, scapula and the splintered end of the collarbone from the tissues around them, until the whole upper limb and the shoulder girdle came loose in a single piece.

'Press on that,' he said to Liga, and fumbled in the kit for some means of closing the wound. There was no shortage of silks and needles, but stitching by hand would take time they didn't have, not when the horde of the damned might return at any point. His hand closed around the smooth, familiar pistol-shape of an autostapler, and he lifted it, drew the skin edges together and ran it along the length of the wound.

Ossian sat back, pleased despite himself at a job well done. The surviving tissues were livid and bruised beneath the gleaming row of staples, but for the moment it was free of visible contagion. Strahl's whole forequarter was missing, cut off in a smooth diagonal line that ran from the base of his neck to the top of his armpit.

The sense of satisfaction Ossian had felt a moment before bled away. The hasty procedure hadn't been worth the name of chirurgery. It had been simple mutilation.

He placed his fingers on the old man's carotid artery and counted. It was too quick, weak and thready, but the pulse was there. He sat back and stripped off the thin plastek gloves from the field kit, folding them so that the bloody surface was tucked inside.

'That is all I can do for him. Now we wait. We'll know over the next twelve hours if he's going to live.'

The lord castellan was watching him, her pale violet eyes flicking from his face to the injured man then back again. Unlike the rest of the squad, her face had avoided the worst of the rain of blood, and there was only a vague smear at the angle of her jaw where she had brushed it with her gauntlet.

'How long until we can move him?'

*Shit.* He'd said the wrong thing, said that he had done all he could. He should have emphasised the importance of ongoing medical care, in the hope that he would keep his head attached to his shoulders for a few more days.

'In an ideal world I would leave him in a monitoring sarcophagus for at least a week.' He shrugged, and settled for the truth. 'But on balance of risks, the sooner he's inside a properly equipped chirurgical facility the better.'

The lord castellan's gaze didn't move from his face. He had a curious feeling that he was laid bare under those eyes, their colour so close to pale blue that they were barely violet at all. She gave him the curtest of nods.

'Our best chance of finding that is in Creed's bunker. Make him ready to move.'

They had crossed the martyr's wall into the city a quarter of an hour ago, picking their way through the outskirts down narrow streets lined with ruined hab-blocks and carpeted in brittle fragments of bone. The bloody rain had turned to a thick red mist, and tiny droplets were hanging suspended in the air, reducing visibility to a matter of mere yards. Laskari played her flash-lumen across the facade of the nearest building, the beam picking out the stigmata of war, still visible after all these years: shattered windows, sprays of projectile-holes in the masonry, astrogranite melted smooth as glass by the discharge of energy weapons.

'I'm not going to ask if you're all right,' Harapa said. 'Stupid bloody question. But you holding it together?'

Laskari wondered what answer the sergeant was looking for. 'I'm fine,' she lied.

'Glad to hear it. Thought I'd better check.' Harapa didn't sound much like he believed her, but she was grateful that he didn't push the point.

Kasr Gallan had been majestic, once. She had seen pictures of the great Cadian fortress cities, but seeing its remains in the flesh was overwhelming. Even in ruins, its fortifications crumbling and overgrown, there was something magnificent about it, a towering mausoleum to lost glories. She reached out to touch a finger to a mottled red-and-white blossom rooted precariously in the crack of a doorframe, and instantly the fleshy petals snapped shut, catching the edge of her glove with a tiny array of serrated needle teeth.

'Best not to touch anything,' Sergeant Harapa said, not unkindly. 'Rule one of exploring any death world – nothing's friendly. And from what I've seen, this is one short step from classification as a daemon world.'

Laskari wiped her glove on her armour. The needle teeth weren't long enough to pierce her skin, but they were hooked into the fabric of her gauntlet and refused to let her shake them free. She tried to focus on the ground ahead, but her mind was a mess of flashing images – the dead ogryn, the poxwalkers, the massive antlered abomination, the appalling suddenness of Anka's death. She kept imagining him at the edge of her vision, expecting him to be there at her shoulder every time she turned.

'I'm sorry about your friend,' Harapa said, as if he had read her thoughts. 'Least it was quick, not like that poor bastard there.' He jerked his helmet briefly towards Strahl on his make-shift stretcher, a trail of half-clotted blood dribbling in his wake. From time to time the old man's head rolled from one side to the other, his eyes half-open, his face slack. If it weren't for the shallow rise and fall of his chest, she would have sworn he was dead already.

'We weren't close.' A soft scuffling noise on her left caught her attention, and she shone her lumen through an empty window. The floor was covered in what at first she took for a thick green carpet, until the tiny green filaments moved in a wave, the ones in the lumen-beam shrivelling away from its light. The same shuffling noise came again, but the source of it was hidden in the shadows. It made her think of something heavy, something dead dragging itself inch by inch towards the light. She shud-dered, and turned her lumen away.

'Even so. First death you've seen up close?'

Laskari nodded, and swallowed down the lump in her throat. It wasn't grief she felt. Anka had been a source of misery in her life for so long that mourning for him would have felt strange, but she still felt diminished by his loss. The sheer arbitrariness of his death was the worst part. If the shell had landed a few yards to his left, he would have survived. A few to his right, and it would be him walking with Harapa and her fragmented remains churned into the mud.

'Sorry to say it won't be your last. We'll have a drink once we're back at base. You can tell me about what an arsehole he was then.'

That raised a smile. 'I thought we weren't supposed to speak ill of the dead.'

'If you're going to speak ill of anyone, they're the ones to choose. They don't talk back.' It was Harapa's turn to shoot an uneasy glance towards the building and its gaping, dead-eyed windows. 'Even the ones that move don't seem much up for conversation.'

The vox crackled unexpectedly in Laskari's ear, a low burst of static mixed with the whine of a tuning frequency. A man's voice was speaking, though the signal was too distorted to make out the words.

'Is anyone else hearing this?' Major Argent asked. There were nods of assent from the members of the team with vox-beads. The penal legionnaires hadn't been equipped with comms equipment, and the team didn't have any to spare.

'I've got interference on the secure channel,' the lord castellan said. 'Are all of you hearing the same?'

There was another chorus of agreement. Laskari nodded.

'Perhaps the *Oriflamme* is trying to make contact...' Argent began, then fell silent as the sound changed.

Before, the vox whine had risen and fallen seemingly at random; now the broadcast was unmistakably a piece of music. Not just any piece, either. Laskari knew the melody from every parade, festival and ceremony she had attended from the day of her birth, and, if enough of her remains were recovered after her death to allow a military funeral, it would be the song the pipers played when her body was lowered into the ground.

'That's "Flower of Cadia",' Colonel Van Haast said softly. 'How is that...?'

The music faded away. A man's voice spoke over the dying

notes, low and deep and resonant. Laskari recognised it instantly. There wasn't a Cadian alive who hadn't heard recordings of the wartime broadcasts, the ones that had come through the vox every day during the last battle for their home world, one man's message of solidarity and hope.

'*Cadia stands.*'

'Ursula, that's–' Argent began.

'I know who it is,' the lord castellan snapped. 'It's Ursarkar bloody Creed.'

# XVIII

## THE FALLEN ANGEL

Either they were hearing something on the vox-system, Ossian thought, or the other Cadians had all simultaneously started hallucinating. He could see the effect the broadcast was having on them from the speed at which their lumen-beams swung back and forward through the bloody mist, the way they jumped at the slightest sound from the ruined hab-blocks, the quick, jerky movements as they advanced ahead through the rubble. The music they said they were hearing – to say nothing of the dead man's voice – was spooking them, and that made him nervous. Jittery soldiers had a habit of making snap judgements, and he and Liga were close enough to the firing line already.

'Hold up,' he said quietly. Strahl was a dead weight on the hastily assembled stretcher – a tarpaulin from Harapa's pack slung between two rusted vox-antennae – and adjusting his grip on the blood-slick metal was doing nothing to relieve the burning in his arms. The weight didn't seem to bother Liga as much. Maybe she was stronger than he was, or more used to discomfort. 'I need to put him down for a minute.'

'You should have let him die. I could do without carrying all twenty stone of the bastard and his kit.'

'They were going to shoot us. I had to think of something.'

Liga rolled her eyes. 'And what do you think'll happen when he dies *after* you took a knife to him?'

'They're still going to need a medicae as long as they're on-world. I can make myself useful to them.'

'Oh, great. So you're sorted. Me, not so much.' Her voice was bitter. 'Cadians looking after their own. I should have known.'

Ossian felt his temper flare. He propped his end of the stretcher on a twisted lump of metal that might once have been part of a groundcar, and rubbed his aching arm. 'In case you haven't noticed, I'm in the same situation you are. I didn't exactly get an open-armed welcome when we showed up either.'

'No, but they didn't *shoot* you.' Liga leaned over the stretcher and hawked up a thick gobbet of phlegm. 'That little bitch with the long-las shot Clavie without thinking. Did you forget that? That's how much we mean to them. They shot her because she got in the way. Because she didn't matter to them at all.'

Ossian didn't have an answer to that. He bent down to pick up the stretcher again, and Strahl shuddered, sending the helmet balanced between his ankles tumbling to the mud.

'Frekk's sake.' Ossian bent to pick it up, then noticed the flashing light of the vox-bead clipped inside. It was one of the better models, the ones that came with their own inbuilt power supply. He worked it free of its casing, set it to receive but not transmit and placed it in his own ear.

'What are you doing?' Liga asked.

He pointed towards the front of the group. 'They're hearing something through the vox, and it's making them jittery.

If something is about to happen, do you want advance warning or not?'

Liga shrugged. 'It's not like we can get away, anyway, not now you've given them the control module for the collars.'

'Fine.' Ossian shook his head. 'It's all my fault. I should have told them no, except then they'd have shot me and taken it anyway. It may not look like it, but I'm doing my best for us both here.'

He hadn't meant to shout, but his voice had clearly risen loud enough to attract the attention of the big sergeant, who signalled for them to quieten down. Ossian nodded, not meeting the man's eye.

The vox-bead was quiet. Liga stepped forward, pulling at the poles of the stretcher, and Ossian trailed after her through the glistening crimson fog with a growing sense of unease.

There could be a perfectly rational explanation for the broadcast, Ursula told herself, as the squad picked their way past the burned-out ruin of a dead Chimera. If Enginseer Rho was here, they would have had an explanation before the first broadcast had faded: the product of an old transmitter station, perhaps, its dying machine-spirit broadcasting decades-old messages on a vox-channel whose frequency happened to match their own. Even so, hearing the dead lord castellan's voice had been unnerving, as though Creed's soul were still trapped on Cadia, one of millions of nameless dead, eternally condemned to repeat the futile deeds of his final days.

She shoved that thought firmly away. Either the preachers were right and Ursarkar E. Creed was seated in glory at the Emperor's right hand, or he was dead and rotting in the Elysian Fields. There was no third option. He wasn't sending messages from beyond the grave, no matter what she thought she was hearing.

Ursula glanced up at the sky, but the fog was as thick above her as it was to every side. It pressed around her on all sides, muffling her footsteps, giving the world an eerie, disorientating quality, as though notions of up and down, left and right, could be dismissed at any time.

She checked her chrono: six hours since they hit the ground, all of it spent moving except for the brief hiatus for Strahl's amputation. The squad was getting strung out and jittery, and she was starting to feel the strain herself, jumping at shadows in the fog, seeing flickers of movement in the narrow vennels between the hab-blocks that vanished in the beam of her lumen.

The chirurgeon had known his business, she had to grant him that. His hands had moved with a well-practised, deliberate ease that had been a pleasure to watch, flowing through the gruesome act like a musician at an instrument, or an artist painting a divinely inspired masterpiece. He had enjoyed it, too, in a sort of way. She had seen that in his face.

He was also a penal legionnaire and a cold-blooded murderer.

A soft, haunting refrain came through the vox: 'Flower of Cadia' again, played by a lone piper on a distant hill. It was almost soothing. If she closed her eyes and shut out the hell world around her, she could lose herself in the music, let it carry her away–

'On your right!'

Van Haast's shout startled her from her reverie. She swung around, raising the bolt pistol to point at a bombed-out doorway, where something low and grey with a long white-tipped tail was streaking at speed across the rubble. Lumen-light glinted off a pair of amber eyes, and then whatever it was vanished behind a twisted mass of razor wire and rockcrete.

'What was that?' Laskari asked.

'Looked like a wild canid,' Harapa said.

Ursula lowered her bolt pistol. 'Surprised to see anything alive here,' she said.

'It must be corrupted, whatever it is.' Van Haast pointed his lasrifle at where the creature had disappeared as he moved past. 'Nothing pure could survive here for long.'

Laskari's face went pale. Ursula knew how she felt. How long would it be before Cadia's corrupting influence began to affect them? Would she even know when it began?

Harapa fell into step beside her. 'They're getting tired, chief,' he said quietly.

'I know that, sergeant,' she said.

'A meal and a couple of hours' rest would do everyone the world of good.' He nodded towards the penal legionnaires and their burden, stumbling along at the back of the group. 'We're losing formation. That horde catches up with us in this state, it'll roll right over us.'

He was right. She was tiring too, and if the maps were right they had another fifteen solid miles to cover before they reached Creed's bunker. At this pace that distance would take them five hours or more, and that was assuming they didn't blunder into another encounter with the enemy, a risk that rose the more exhausted they became. Her failure to notice the canid was clear evidence she was losing her edge.

'You'll get no disagreement from me, sergeant,' she said. 'I'm open to suggestions as to where we can make camp.'

He nodded thoughtfully. 'Plenty of hab-blocks. We'd get a good view from those windows at the top. Get some advance warning on what's ahead of us on the route.'

'Each of those hab-blocks was built to house three hundred soldiers and their families,' Van Haast put in. 'It would take hours to sweep a building of that size. Which sounds only marginally preferable to trying to rest in a warren infested with the Neverborn.'

'We could set watches,' Laskari said. 'If I kept vigil while you rested–'

'Then I'm sure the sound of your screams would give us precious seconds to contemplate our imminent demise,' Van Haast cut her off.

'Is this merely an objection for its own sake, colonel?' Ursula said. 'Or do you have an alternative in mind?'

The colonel drew himself up to his full height. 'As it happens, lord castellan, I do. I recall a barracks in this general vicinity, a mile or so to our left. The main complex has all the flaws of these hab-units, but there was a penitentium in the grounds.' He shrugged. 'Nothing of significance, you understand, but for security's sake it was built with a single entrance. Once we had it cleared and a guard on the entrance, we would rest in relative comfort.'

It sounded tempting. 'It isn't on the map,' she said.

He shrugged. 'Then of course I defer to the *Oriflamme*'s infallible auspex system, and the omniscience of its operators.'

Ursula took a moment to run through their options: trudge on through the growing gloom, or leave the path to seek out a place to spend the night in the nebulous hope that it might still be standing and defensible. A detour would cost them precious hours, but they were moving slower by the minute. Of course, it meant trusting Van Haast's memory over sensor data, but wasn't that why he was here?

'Very well.' She watched his face carefully, but his expression betrayed nothing at all. She had the feeling that he would have looked exactly the same had she thrown the suggestion back in his face. 'Lead on.'

It was another hour before Van Haast's barracks came into view: first an arched gateway set into a ten-foot-high wall, beyond it a series of squat grey buildings deroofed at the level of the first floor. More than once Ursula had considered ordering a forced march, but any increase in pace would have come at the loss of focus and vigilance. As they moved deeper into the city, sounds of gunfire drifted through the air, the reports becoming clearer as the bloody fog thinned and dispersed into cold, clear air.

Van Haast's cursory description had hardly suggested anything impressive, but she had hoped for more than a few roofless buildings and a rickety-looking watchtower. She signalled the group forward, and paused on the threshold for them to catch up.

'Is this it, colonel?' she asked, trying to keep the disappointment from her voice.

'My apologies for the poor state of repair, lord castellan,' Van Haast said. 'I shall have words with the base commander.'

Under other circumstances she might have welcomed his clumsy attempt at humour, but the joke fell flat. She found herself wondering how the soldiers here had died. Had they fallen in defence of the barracks, or had their lives been thrown away on one of her father's last futile attempts at heroism? They were over a hundred miles from the nearest evacuation site – the one secured by Marda Hellsker's last-ditch heroics at the Delvian Cleave – and it was impossible that anyone so far away would have made it out. Only Strahl might have known the answer to that, but in his present state there was no way he was answering questions.

'Don't trouble yourself, colonel.'

She walked beside him through the empty gateway, past the remains of a sentry-box, the tangled shreds of a metal fence. Whatever gate had once hung here was long gone, but the stone aquila that had surmounted it had fallen to the ground, where it lay headless and wingless, blinded and grounded by time. There was a curious irregularity to the stonework, the surface creased into branching channels that resembled nothing more than bulging veins, spreading in an intricate lattice across every wall.

Laskari was staring at it with fascination, her hand pressed to the side of the archway. 'It's warm, my lord. I can feel it through my glove. It's moving… pulsating.'

'Didn't I warn you about touching things, trooper?' Harapa said, and Laskari jerked her hand away as though the stone were red-hot. Now that she was looking, Ursula could see the stone moving almost imperceptibly, rippling and contracting as if it were a living thing. That, along with the slowly clotting blood adhering to every surface and the low red cloud, gave her the uncomfortable feeling that she was standing inside the walls of some monstrous bodily organ.

'Lord castellan.' The chirurgeon's voice sounded strained. 'Permission to lower the patient to the ground.'

'Granted.'

The pair of them laid the stretcher down with obvious relief. Strahl stayed motionless, his eyes open and staring, his breath coming in shallow irregular gasps. She would have to make a decision about him soon. Recovery or death she could plan for, but this half-living limbo was the worst of both worlds for all of them. Twelve hours, the chirurgeon had said. They would know either way by then.

Of course, in twelve hours they could *all* be dead.

'First thing we search the base,' she said. 'I don't want us bedding down for the night only to discover it's crawling with the damned. Argent, you take Laskari and Harapa and sweep the perimeter.'

'As you command, my lord.' Argent still sounded sharp enough, but Ursula knew him well enough to recognise that he was out of sorts. He'd been unnerved since the Valkyrie had been shot down, and now she thought back, maybe even before that.

'Van Haast, wait here with the sergeant major and watch the gateway.' She pointed to the legionnaires. 'You two, you're coming with me.'

'Lord castellan, I really must–'

She cut Van Haast off mid-sentence. 'Good point. They're better off armed. Colonel, return Troopers Ossian and Yager their laspistols, if you'd be so kind.'

It was a calculated move, and Van Haast clearly knew it. His scowl was evident even in the dim light, his jaw set, teeth gritted. He'd been close to insubordination since before they had landed. It seemed a good time to test if he was willing to cross that line.

No one moved. A few faint strains of music whispered through the vox, then faded to static. The colonel took the confiscated laspistols from his pack, checked them both, and offered them out with a mock-courtly air. Ossian was the first of the two to move, extending a wary hand to take the weapon. Van Haast maintained his grip on the barrel a fraction longer than necessary, meeting the convict's eye with a stare that spoke of centuries of breeding and privilege.

'Do be careful with it, won't you?' Van Haast's voice could have frozen promethium. 'These things can be dangerous in the wrong hands.'

# XIX

## THE HOUND

By the time they had swept the ruins of the barracks, Laskari would have happily laid down to sleep in the rain. Harapa had been his usual unhurried self as they had searched the low, roof-less buildings, but Major Argent had seemed even more nervous than she was, his attention awkwardly split between watching for trouble and checking if the lord castellan was still in sight.

'Perimeter's clear,' Harapa voxed.

*'Acknowledged.'* The lord castellan's armoured outline was just visible through the sleet, the penal legionnaires a pair of indis-tinct blurs to her side. *'We've found the entrance to the penitentium. Converge on my position, all of you. Laskari, you and I will go down first.'*

The entrance to the cells was sunk into the ground, down a worn set of rockcrete steps just wide enough to go two abreast, veined with the same twisting vessels that covered every surface inside the perimeter wall. At the bottom of the stairs, a rusting steel door clung to one of its hinges, but something had pushed the lower part open to make a gap large enough for something human-sized to crawl through.

A noise came from inside, wet crunching sounds interspersed with a series of deep, nasal grunts. Laskari aimed her rifle, visions of the walking dead flooding her mind's eye. The lord castellan stepped forward.

'On my mark.'

A single kick from the powered sabaton sent the door crashing inward. Flashlight beams streaked the darkness, playing over a hulking mound in the centre of the room. Laskari drew a sharp breath, and instantly her mouth was full of the rank and sulphurous taste of rotting eggs.

She choked down a mouthful of vomit. Something enormous was hunched over in the gloom, tearing at a huge corpse pinned beneath its clawed forefeet. The light of her flash-lumen picked out a pair of glowing red eyes, a mouth of gleaming serrated teeth, and a crest of spikes down its leathery hide.

'Throne...'

Its head jerked up, and the glowing eyes fixed on her with malign intensity. A leathery frill erupted open around its neck to frame a long-muzzled face, and it opened its jaws wide to let out an ear-piercing shriek so loud that the vox-bead in her ear overloaded in a scream of static.

That wasn't the only sound. The lord castellan's bolt pistol delivered a volley of shells, the secondary explosions as they hit the wall behind sending reverberations through the floor, through the air, deafening in the confined space.

'Flesh hound!' she bellowed, the sword crackling into blue-white life in her right hand. The creature was still on its feet, bounding with impossible speed towards them as she took a shot, missed and aimed again. 'They hunt in packs!' the lord castellan was shouting, her voice loud enough to send an echo of feedback squealing across the vox-channel. 'I've fought them before. If there's one down here, there's more up–'

'*We have contact!*' Argent's voice was tight with panic as it came through the vox, accompanied by a burst of las-fire. '*Two of them. They must have been stalking us all this time!*'

The beast sprang, hurtling towards Laskari, coming so close that she could smell the rotting meat on its breath. There was a collar around its neck, and she had a split second to wonder what blasphemous hand had fastened it there before the lord castellan shoved her bodily aside and brought the power sword round in a broad crackling arc. The beast shrieked as the energy field bit into the plating on its shoulder, and it sprang backwards, righted itself then lunged forward again. This time the lord castellan reacted a moment too late, and the creature's massive foreclaws slammed into her shoulders, the weight bearing her to the ground. Laskari took a step back, stumbled on the step behind her and almost fell, righting herself with a hand on the pulsating wall. The sound of las-fire overhead was a steady roar, underscored by shrieks and growls from the abomination's pack mates.

'Get… up… there…' the lord castellan grunted. She was sprawled across the bottom steps, the power sword sparking uselessly on the ground beside her, holding the flesh hound's gnashing lower jaw at arm's length while its claws gouged glinting silver streaks across the red enamel of her armour. 'Laskari!'

Until she heard her name, she hadn't realised the lord castellan was talking to her. She aimed at the flesh hound's head, but it was thrashing back and forward so quickly that she couldn't be confident of hitting it rather than the lord castellan.

'My lord, shouldn't I–'

With a twist of her upper body, the lord castellan freed her left arm from the creature's taloned forelimb, and rammed her

183

hand wrist-deep into the gaping mouth. The razor-sharp teeth closed around her wrist, and with a thunderous roar from the bolt pistol, the back of the flesh hound's head blew out in a spray of viscid magenta slime, and the huge body went slack.

Laskari darted forward and shoved the massive corpse to the side. Below it, the lord castellan was prising the huge jaws open with her right hand, the leathery skin already sloughing away from the bone as the entire corpse lost its shape and consistency. By the time she was on her feet there was nothing left but bones, liquefying slowly in an oozing puddle of slime.

'I said get up there,' the lord castellan said. She picked up her power sword and strode up the stairs two at a time. Laskari scuttled after her, but the steps were slick and uneven under her feet, and she arrived just in time to see Ursula Creed step in front of the two legionnaires and the wounded sergeant major, raise her bolt pistol and fire a volley of bolter shells into the only surviving flesh hound. The shells blew it in half, and the two pieces fell to the ground in a spray of gelid matter. Another frill-necked horror lay dissolving on the cracked astrogranite, its lower jaw partially blown off and Harapa's combat knife buried in its eye.

'Anyone injured?' the lord castellan asked.

'All good here, chief.' Harapa's knife came free of the flesh hound's eye socket with a resonant squelch. He inspected the blade, then wiped it clean on the beast's neck-frill.

'Yes, we're quite all right.' Colonel Van Haast wasn't even breathing hard, his elaborate lasrifle cradled loosely in his hands as though he were strolling out to hunt game. 'We're lucky the fog cleared when it did. They almost got the drop on us as it was.'

'We have to assume there are more of them. The same kind, or something else.' The lord castellan took off her helmet, and brushed back the strands of sweat-soaked hair clinging to her face.

She looked weary, Laskari thought, older than she had seemed back on the *Oriflamme*. Locked in combat, wearing the armour with its magnificently plumed helmet, the lord castellan had been an invincible hero summoned from the Imperium's glorious history to lead them to victory. Out of it she was a tired-looking, middle-aged woman with creases at the corners of her eyes and shadows beneath them.

'We can't risk getting caught in there unawares. I want a sentry in that watchtower, ready to identify and intercept anything that comes through the gate before it reaches the entrance to the cells. Laskari, take that long-las of yours and get up there now. Argent, you go with her, the pair of you will take first watch. Everyone else, we sweep those cells and check for any more of the damned things, get some food in us and get our heads down for a few hours. Harapa, you and Colonel Van Haast are on second watch. I'll take dawn shift with Trooper Yager there.'

The female convict looked up sharply at the sound of her name, her hand still clenched white-knuckled around the laspistol. The lord castellan turned to the medicae and fixed him with a gimlet stare.

'And as for you, see to Sergeant Major Strahl, and take what rest you can between your duties.'

The cell designated as their improvised infirmarium hadn't smelled all that great to begin with – mould, damp and a pungent stench of decay that made Ossian think the flesh hound and whatever it had been feeding on in the antechamber hadn't been the only thing to die in here – but the reeking pus soaking through Strahl's dressings was making the stench a hundred times worse. They had found an old combustion lantern in a store cupboard in the guardroom, and while the light it cast was welcome, the acrid smell of burning promethium was not.

A pair of bunk beds and a tarnished metal sink clung tenu-
ously to the wall, and the whitewashed interior was stained with
spreading continents of dark mould that seemed to change their
shape every time his eye was off them. The floor sloped downwards to a point in the centre, where a drain sat, clogged with
a decaying mass of something too far gone to identify.

Liga had helped lay Strahl out on the lower bunk, on a stained
mattress that still bore the imprint of its long-dead inhabit-
ant, then left the room before he could ask her to help again.
He didn't blame her. The mutilation he had subjected Strahl
to earlier would be enough to put anyone normal off witness-
ing chirurgery for life.

The bunks were identical to those in every barrack-room in
the Imperium, not quite enough room to sit up straight without banging your head on the bunk above, and the regulation
gap down the side of the mattress wide enough for a packet of
lho-sticks and whatever suggestive picts might appeal to its user.

Ossian hooked a fingernail under the edge of the sodden
dressing and pulled it free. The wound edges had been pristine when he had left it, but in the intervening hours the
rot had returned just as he had feared. The tissues were an
unhealthy-looking purple, and a thin greenish-grey pus was
oozing from between the staples. He dribbled cleansing
unguent from the field kit onto his hands and twisted one of
the staples free. The skin yielded like wet parchment, and a
gush of foul-smelling exudate flowed out in a thin stream to
soak into the mattress.

Strahl moaned. His eyes opened and he lifted his head, cords
of sinew standing out on his neck as he looked down at the
purulent ruin of his shoulder. How long had it been since the
last dose of morpholox? The nocio-blockers would have worn off
hours ago, but Ossian had taken the man's silence for comfort,

or at least, for the absence of acute distress. The thought that Strahl might have been lying there in mute agony for hours was an unpleasant one.

'Hold still. I'll get you some pain-blockers.'

'No.' Strahl shook his head. 'Not yet.' The words came in quick, broken bursts.

'There's no sense in waiting, it'll only get worse if you–'

'Stimms in that kit?'

Ossian nodded.

'I'll take some, then, and don't give me any "medically inadvisable" groxshit. I want to die with my eyes open.'

Ossian removed the little phial of stimms from the medkit and tipped two into his hand.

'Under the tongue. They're fast-acting–'

'This isn't my first time, medicae.' Strahl took the tablets and tucked them under his tongue, grimacing at the bitterness of the taste. He lifted his remaining arm and ran his hand over the front of his half-open tunic, searching for something tucked in an inside pocket. 'Still rotting. I can feel it.'

Ossian considered a comforting lie, then decided on the truth. 'It is. I can try to debride it again–'

'Not much left to take. I'd rather go to the Throne with what's left of me intact, not filleted away a bit at a time like a messhall roast.' The grey face grimaced. 'I've kept Him waiting long enough.' Strahl lay back and closed his eyes, motionless for so long that Ossian wondered if he had slipped back into unconsciousness. 'Where were you born, lad?' Strahl said at last.

Ossian looked up in surprise. No one had called him 'lad' in a good few decades. 'Cadia.'

'I knew *that*. What kasr?'

'Skalish.'

'Knew you were a northerner. An accent like that, all the drill

187

abbots in the schola wouldn't be enough to beat it out of you. You there when it fell?'

Ossian shook his head. 'I was off-world with the regiment by then.' He held up the autoinjector in the lumen-light, showing it to the dying man. 'I can block the nerves in your shoulder. It'll take the edge off the pain, but it won't sedate you.'

Strahl nodded. Ossian pressed the autoinjector to his neck and activated the mechanism. Too many doses too close together risked permanent nerve damage, but that wasn't something worth worrying about now.

Strahl's pupils went wide as the blockers took effect. With a shaking hand, he reached into his tunic pocket, pulled out a slender package wrapped in brown suedecloth and laid it down on the filthy mattress between them. 'Give this to Creed's daughter,' he said.

'What is it?' Ossian lifted the parcel and peeled back the wrapping. It contained a notebook: a slender, unremarkable volume with a green parchment cover, the sort of nondescript Militarum stationery you'd find on any officer's desk in the Imperium. Three initials had been pencilled in the top right corner, faded to the merest graphite shimmer.

*U.E.C.*

'The old man's journal. One of his last. He gave it to Colonel Hellsker before the Delvian Cleave. Said it was to go to his daughter when she came back to Cadia. A gift. So she has a chance to know something of her old man after all these years.'

'Why didn't you give it to her already?'

'Trust me, lad, I tried.' Strahl shuddered out a breath. 'She wouldn't take it from me, not back then with the pict-caster and the propagandist, all that bloody nonsense. Should have known better. Chosen my moment. You'll make sure she gets it.'

Ossian laughed. 'You have noticed the collar I'm wearing, yes? She's hardly going to listen to me.'

'What are you afraid of?' Strahl made a wheezing gasp that might have been a laugh. 'You're a dead man walking already. If that doesn't make you bold, nothing will.' His remaining hand found Ossian's wrist and squeezed it in a convulsive burst of strength. 'Make it happen.'

'I'll do my best.'

'Good lad.' Strahl lay back and stared up at the rusting bedsprings. 'All those bloody years. All those campaigns we fought, trying to make sense of life after Cadia. None of it mattered, nothing at all. All we were doing was marking time before we came back here to die.'

Ursula watched them through the makeshift infirmarium door: the dying man on the filthy bunk, and the penal legionnaire tending to him. She hadn't thought it was possible to be stealthy in a suit of armour of this size, but from the expression on the medicae's face when he finally looked up and saw her, he had had no idea she'd been standing there. She wasn't sure why she'd decided to trust Ossian with Strahl's life, though his chances were so slim that there seemed little to lose. Besides, the man was so obviously competent that not putting him to work would have seemed a criminal waste of a valuable resource.

As she watched, he stood and anointed his hands with a dribble of cleansing unguent. She approved of that. Attention to detail was important, even in surroundings like these. *Especially* in surroundings like these. She took a step back and beckoned him out of the room into the dank rockcrete corridor that ran the length of the penitentium. The walls were thick with mould, but the veins that streaked the masonry above ground were absent, the stone reassuringly inanimate.

'How is he?' Ursula asked.

Ossian paused before he answered. 'Dying.'

'You're sure?'

'I've seen it often enough to predict the inevitable.'

His words came as a relief. Strahl's death would simplify matters enormously, and while any death was occasion for solemn reflection, the man was a Cadian and a soldier. Survival was a gift, not a promise.

'Is he in pain?'

'I've done what I can.'

'I see.' She watched the medicae carefully. 'You will make sure he doesn't suffer.'

The reaction wasn't what she was expecting. Ossian's tattooed brow furrowed, the well-defined lines of his jaw setting hard. 'If it's taking too long for you, you can give him the Emperor's mercy yourself, lord castellan. I'm not doing that for you.'

'That's not what I was asking.' Ursula kept her voice soft. Clearly something she had said had hit a raw nerve. 'If Strahl is dying, the least we can do is make it easy for him.'

The look of suspicion didn't fade from the medicae's face. 'Like I said. I've done what I can.'

'And you have my thanks for that.'

Ossian held something out to her at arm's length, holding it away from himself as if it were a particularly noxious substance instead of a little green notebook. 'Strahl asked me to give you this. He said he'd tried to give it to you before.'

'That again.' She had thought she was too tired for emotion, but the indignation cut through the long day's weariness. 'What did he say to you?'

Ossian shrugged. He looked as exhausted as she was, which was no surprise, considering that the penal legionnaires had been on their feet longer than any of them. If she wanted any use out of the man she would have to let him rest.

'He said that you needed to have it. That it was important.' The expression that crossed his face was almost a smile. 'That he should have chosen his moment better to give it to you.'

Ursula took the book. Her fingertips brushed against his, his skin unexpectedly warm and dry. She opened the notebook, flicking through page after page of densely scribbled notes, the handwriting so cramped and tightly packed as to be almost illegible. The names Rossvar, Delvia, Elysium and Kasr Myrak appeared over and over again like the words of a litany. Some pages had casualty lists; others troop movements, the names of tanks, key strategic pinch points to hold and keep. Even skim-reading it made her feel giddy, like she was looking through a gate that led not across the galaxy, but back in time.

Scrawled on the inner cover were a few lines of text: a quotation she vaguely remembered from one of the works of Jennit Sulla. *A good soldier must know both their duty, and their place.* To an archivist, the journal would have been priceless. Here, it was worth nothing at all.

'Lord castellan?'

She looked up. Argent was staring down the passageway at her, his shape a dark silhouette against the lantern-lumen. She started guiltily, as though she had been caught doing something forbidden, something unwholesome. She rolled the notebook small enough to fit into the pouch at her waist and tucked it inside.

'What is it, major?'

'There's something you need to see. Outside. Laskari's found something. It's easier if you come.' Argent hesitated. 'Alone.'

# XX

## THE BLIND SEER

'What do you see, trooper?'

Laskari jerked her eye away from her sights, and turned to see the lord castellan and Major Argent scrambling up the broken masonry of the watchtower at speed. There had been an internal staircase once, but time had crumbled the steps into a treacherous rubble-strewn ramp that shifted underfoot as they climbed. At the top, twenty feet in the air, the walls no longer had much resemblance at all to mundane materials, the surface a deep liverish red, the veins prominent and pulsating in a heavy rhythm that shook the entire tower. Laskari swallowed down a faint sense of nausea, and fixed her gaze back through her sights. What she was seeing there wasn't normal either, but at least it was further away.

'Ten o'clock, lord castellan. A quarter of a mile or thereabouts. Three humans and a canid, none of them moving like poxwalkers.'

The lord castellan lifted her field glasses to her eyes and trained them on the group of figures. 'How long have they been there?'

'I called as soon as I saw them, my lord.' They would have been easy to miss, Laskari thought. It was only the flash of white on the canid's tail that had drawn her eye as they moved through the abandoned streets towards the burned-out ruins of a basilica on a low hill. 'A few minutes at most.'

The three humans were wrapped in bulky hostile-environment gear, two of the three with old-fashioned respirator-masks covering their faces. The third was kneeling on the ground, their own glass-eyed mask in front of them, its air-pipe curled in on itself like the trunk of an exotic pachyderm. The canid – not a warped monstrosity like the ones they had fought before, but a lean, sinuous hunting beast of the sort you might see trotting to the hunt at an aristocrat's heels – was moving around the kneeling figure in anxious circles, pausing now and again to nuzzle its snout against a hand or the crook of an elbow.

'Fascinating.' The lord castellan adjusted the focus on her field glasses. 'What are they doing?'

Laskari focused her scope through the gothic arch of a broken window. The deep green marble of the basilica looked better preserved than the rest of the city, the empty window frames for the most part intact, the silver bell tarnished black, but still hanging, silent in its tower. Both of the standing figures were armed, the smaller with a lasgun in their hands – bullpup pattern, all large bore and truncated barrel – while the other had theirs slung over their back, beside a set of folded entrenching tools. The third – the one on their knees – wasn't carrying a rifle, but they weren't unarmed, with the distinctive shape of a laspistol laid across their knees.

The kneeling figure reached out to the canid, scratching the beast behind its ears and smoothing down the rough grey fur at the nape of its neck. The creature's mouth opened wide, its tongue unspooling with evident pleasure. The unmasked human – a woman, Laskari thought – leaned forward, touched their forehead to the top of its head, then waved the animal away.

Slowly, the seated figure raised the laspistol, opened their mouth and slid the barrel inside. The soldier with the lasgun – something about the way they moved made Laskari sure all three were soldiers, or had been before they deserted the Imperium to serve the Ruinous Powers – took aim at the back of their kneeling companion's head.

'Should I stop them?' Laskari asked. The mere thought of it was enough to set her hands shaking, making the image dance wildly in its sights.

'Hold your fire. We can't risk compromising our position.'

'But what if they–'

The laspistol flared and died. The figure fell forward, the canid yelped and sprang to its feet, darting forward to sniff at the corpse. The standing figures remained motionless, heads bowed, their eerie masks giving the scene a solemn, almost eldritch air.

'Cultists,' Major Argent said, lowering his field glasses. 'A sacrifice to their false gods.'

The two remaining cultists bent over the body. Laskari watched them straighten it out until it was lying with its arms folded across its chest, then they doused it in liquid that had to be promethium, and set it alight. Oily black smoke billowed into the air, obscuring all four.

'A remarkably cooperative sacrifice if it was,' the lord castellan said. 'I saw that canid earlier, or one damn like it.'

'We should send someone out to take a closer look,' Argent said. 'Harapa can go–'

The lord castellan shook her head. 'We can't afford to get sidetracked. What cultists of the Ruinous Powers do to their own isn't our concern. Keep a close eye on them and alert me if they're coming this way. Otherwise we'll have to let them carry out whatever profane business they have planned.'

What the cultists had planned turned out to be waiting over an hour for the fire to burn down to ashes, before gathering the scorched remains into a tarpaulin and vanishing from sight. Ursula stayed in the tower until they were gone, then climbed out of the watchtower and headed towards the sunken entrance that led to the penitentium.

It had been a mistake to bring Argent on the mission. The years that had passed since he had been properly in the field had clearly taken their toll on his nerves, and the man was starting to become a liability. It wasn't that his ideas were necessarily bad ones, but he delivered them with such an anxious, hang-dog air that she found herself ready to reject them by reflex, followed by second-guessing the correctness of any course of action on which he had an opinion.

She rubbed at her eyes, trying to make sense of what she had just seen. Three people in hostile-environment gear had walked out into the forest – walked out from where? – only for one to end their life at gunpoint, and the other two to strip the corpse and carry out an otherwise respectful disposal, all the time watched by a well-trained canid. Argent's assumption that they were cultists engaged in ritual sacrifice was all too plausible, but something about it didn't ring true. Why had they chosen the basilica? Why had the victim gone so willingly to their own death? All of them, the canid included, had acted with a discipline rarely found outside the Cadian regiments. They hadn't behaved like cultists, but it was impossible that they could be anything else. No one on Cadia had survived the Fall.

The low note of the hunting horn sounded, far in the distance, sending a chill down her spine and stiffening her resolve. It didn't matter who the masked figures were. Her priority was to reach Creed's last bunker and recover its contents. Allowing sentimentality to send her on a wild grox-chase in the slim hope of finding Cadian survivors would be an unforgivable mistake.

The distant horn sounded again, but this time she realised it was coming through the vox. Ursarkar Creed's voice spoke across it, a tinny, distorted fragment without context or explanation.

'*...the barb that holds the foe...*'

She knew that speech. Creed had delivered it after the fall of Kasr Batrok. A shiver went down her spine, as though time had slipped backwards and she was hearing the words as they were first broadcast. The regiments at Kasr Batrok had spent months in a grinding war of attrition, only to be charged with slowing the enemy advance long after hope had fled. She had thought she had made her peace with her absence during the Fall, but hearing the speech washed that certainty away.

'*Reinforcements are on their way. The High Lords of Terra commend you for your sacrifice. Hold the line.*'

Why was she hearing it now?

Strahl had slipped into unconsciousness, and his breathing was coming in short bursts interspersed with periods of silence that increased in length each time. He had murmured a few words that Ossian thought might have been a name an hour or so before, but there had been nothing after that.

Ossian unscrewed the lid from his water-flask, and dribbled a cautious stream onto the mass of clot and fabric stuck to his shin where he had caught it on the razor wire before. It took more water than he had hoped, but eventually the clot loosened enough for him to roll the fabric gingerly upward, ripping to expose the raw laceration beneath. He wasn't looking forward to what came next.

Most of the nocio-blockers had gone on Strahl, and the sedating effect of the morpholox was something he wasn't willing to accept, not in daemonic territory with a pitched battle less than a mile from their location. Instead he filled a shallow votive receptacle with more of his precious water and added a purification wafer stamped with the sacred blood-droplet of Saint Sanguinius. It dissolved with a hiss, turning the water a rich wine-red. He soaked it up on a square of clean gauze, and rubbed it across the wound on his shin.

It felt like he had poured concentrated acid on his skin. He gritted his teeth against the pain, counting down from a hundred until it faded from appalling to merely agonising. When his hands finally stopped shaking he lifted the gauze. The skin edges were stained a deep red by the purifying salve, but the base of the wound was fresh pink granulation tissue. The relief was enough to make him light-headed. If he had been infected with the same corruption that was killing Strahl, it would have manifested itself by now.

He used the last of the autostapler clips, then bound a sanctified bandage around the wound. Strahl sighed, and Ossian checked the old man's pulse: slow, weak and irregular. He tucked the hand beneath the blankets. There was no point in disturbing the old man any longer. They were just marking time now.

Someone moved behind him, but before he could turn something struck him between the shoulder blades, not hard enough to hurt, but startling all the same. He half turned to see Liga standing there, her hand upraised.

'What the frekk are you playing at?' He scrambled to his feet, the staples tugging at the freshly closed wound as he turned. Liga's face was twisted in disgust, staring not at him but at the floor, where a six-inch-long segmented insectoid with dripping mandibles and too many legs was struggling to right itself. She stamped down hard and it burst with a spray of green ichor.

'What am I playing at?' The expression of disgust on her face didn't fade as she shook the mutilated remains from her foot. 'Well, I don't know exactly what *that* thing had planned, but I figured you probably didn't want it down the back of your neck.' She shrugged. 'What did you think I was doing?'

Ossian rubbed his eyes. 'I don't know. You startled me, that was all.'

'I was looking out for you is what I was doing.' She turned away from him and unrolled her bedroll from the legionnaire's pack in the far corner. 'Except I forgot. You don't need me to do that any more.'

A jolt of irritation cut through the bone-deep weariness. 'Cut out the jealous act, would you? I'm trying to keep us both alive here.'

Liga flopped down on her bedroll, and pulled the blanket up over her head. 'Sure you are.' Her voice was muffled, but the venom in it was clearly audible. 'Just remember you're only alive as long as you're useful to them. The moment the old man dies...' She paused for effect. 'Boom.'

# XXI

## THE REAPER

The lantern was still burning when Ossian woke, sure in the knowledge of two things: firstly, that it was still night, and secondly, that something in the room had changed. He sat up, his joints and muscles rigid, the neglected injuries of the day before making loud demands for payback with interest. His vision was grainy around the edges, in a way that suggested that something had woken him midway through a sleep cycle.

Four o'clock in the morning. The hour of the dead.

He reached over to touch Strahl's hand, and found it motionless and cool. There was no pulse at the wrist. Memories of the night before returned, a creeping sense of guilt along with them. He had intended to keep vigil, but in the end sleep had dragged him down, luring him in with comforting lies. *He would only rest his eyes. He would only sleep for a few minutes. He would wake at the first sign of change.* He had been weak, and Strahl had gone to the Golden Throne alone.

'Ave atque vale,' he murmured.

*Hail and farewell.*

Strahl lay neatly, with none of the usual untidiness of death. He had died with his eyes open, and his corneas were already clouding with a misty white film. His lips were parted and his head was turned a little to one side as if listening to a far-off sound. Ossian pulled the blanket up over the dead man's face. Should he wake Liga? There didn't seem much point in depriving her of the rest they both desperately needed, but to leave the old man's death unmarked until morning felt wrong. He should tell the officer of the watch if nothing else.

Ossian got to his feet and stepped out of the cell. Thin grey light was spilling down from above into the corridor, and he took the steps slowly to spare his aching right knee and the wound in his shin. He had been lucky to walk away from the crash at all.

He still wasn't sure why the God-Emperor had seen fit to spare him when so many others had died. It wasn't for him to redeem himself, that much he knew – death in the penal legion would have been adequate atonement for his crime. Besides, the scriptures were clear on the fact that penitence was a prerequisite for redemption, and he wasn't sorry in the least for what he'd done. Maybe the God-Emperor's all-seeing eye had been elsewhere when the drop-ship had come down, and his survival was a mere act of chance. But despite everything that had followed, he was surprised to find himself clinging to life with both hands. That was the trouble with life, wasn't it? The more you had, the more you wanted to cling to what was left.

He stopped at the top of the stairs, and waited for his eyes to adjust to the light. The sky was still covered with a thick layer of cloud, the rain – actual rain this time, not the blood of the night before – falling in a steady grey drizzle. The colonel of Hussars – Van Haast, that was the man's name – was a little distance from the entrance, gazing out across the perimeter wall, while Sergeant Harapa was up in the watchtower, facing the gate and the kasr beyond.

It took Ossian's sleep-deprived brain a moment to work out what was wrong with the scene. The colonel was stripped to his waist, his uniform jacket and shirt neatly folded on the ground beside him, and his back streaked with blood that ran from a series of thin vertical lacerations. Ossian took a step closer, skirting the perimeter so that he could get a better look at the man's face. His eyes were unfocused, staring out into the wasteland, lips moving in a continual silent whisper. Ossian recognised the silvery cord in his hand as a flagellum sanctus, a fine braid of barbed adamantine fibres, designed to inflict a precise and consistent jolt of agony with every lash. From the look of the skin of Van Haast's back – scarred, leathery and torn – the flagellum had seen good use over the years.

'What exactly do you think you are doing?' Van Haast snapped.

Ossian realised he had been staring. The colonel's exquisitely sculpted features were contorted with rage, his eyes wide, lips drawn back in a snarl. Ossian took a startled step away, forcing himself to calm down. What was he afraid of? He was a dead man walking. There was nothing the colonel could do to him that he hadn't threatened him with already.

Ossian shrugged. 'From a chirurgical perspective, I would advise against any unnecessary breakage of the skin on a world like this. You never know what foul miasmas are in the air. At the very least you should let me cleanse it for you.'

Van Haast's glare stayed locked on him a moment longer, then suddenly the impassive mask returned. He retrieved his shirt and pulled it over his head, and fresh blood instantly soaked through at the shoulders. 'Remember your place, legionnaire,' he sneered. 'Medicae you may have been, but what you are now is… disposable.'

Ossian suppressed his rising irritation. He knew Van Haast's sort: old blood, old privilege, old money; aristocrats for whom everyone else was automatically lesser, their only value coming from how grovelingly they served and how hard they tugged their forelock when doing it. His last commanding officer had worn the same expression when he'd seen him last, cold-eyed and sneering as he had explained exactly why it had been necessary that those shells had landed precisely where they did to achieve his grand strategy.

'You can grate yourself to shreds for all I care, colonel. But given that we find ourselves another man down, you might want to consider keeping yourself in fighting condition.'

'Sergeant Major Strahl has gone to his just reward, then?' The colonel slipped his jacket over the bloody shirt, seemingly completely unconcerned by Strahl's death or by the state of his own shoulders. Typical arrogant aristocrat, obsessing over the mortification of his own precious flesh while the world was going to shit around him. 'Wake your... friend. Deal with the body before the contagion spreads any further. I want it disposed of by dawn watch.'

Ossian stared at him, then managed a nod. 'As you order.'

Van Haast yawned. 'And one more thing, legionnaire. If I hear so much as a syllable that makes me think you have mentioned what you just saw to the lord castellan, or any of the others...' His words dripped loathing. 'I will personally ensure that your death is so agonising and protracted that you will beg me to trigger that collar before your end comes.'

Rain ran down the inside of Laskari's collar as she watched the penal legionnaires lay out Sergeant Major Strahl's remains on a hastily gathered pile of rubble beneath the watchtower and douse his body in what was left of the lamp oil. They had wrapped him in a mouldering prison bedsheet, but the peaks and hollows of the old man's profile were still clearly visible through the flimsy cloth. In this weather she'd be surprised if anything burned at all.

Another death.

At least this one hadn't been her fault.

There had been so much slaughter in the last day that she should be getting used to it by now, but each time it was hitting her harder than the last. Cadians didn't fear death – that was something she had been taught along with her catechisms, the litanies of courage learned by rote as soon as she could lisp them out through milk teeth – but the sight of the corpse lying in the filthy trench brought what had been an abstract concept into leaden clarity.

Major Argent cleared his throat. 'God-Emperor, we commend the soul of Sergeant Major Domnik Strahl into thy hands, in the hope that you may find his sacrifice acceptable in thy sight.'

The words hung in the empty air, hollow and meaningless.

No one had said the litanies for Lainn Anka. There would be no headstone for him, no place in the garden of memory for his body to lie until time robbed the living of recollection. No one would exhume his bones to lay them in the ossuary with his forgotten kin. He was gone, as if he had never existed, and the world was diminished by his loss.

She hadn't even *liked* him.

'Would anyone like to say a few words?' Argent asked. Laskari kept her silence. The sooner the funeral was over the better.

Sergeant Harapa lit a taper and touched it to the oil-soaked sheet, and a thin flame caught, guttered, then spread until oily black smoke was billowing from the makeshift pyre. The thick scent of roasting meat filled the air, and Laskari's mouth flooded painfully with saliva.

'He did his duty for Cadia.' The lord castellan sounded more relieved than saddened. 'No one could ask for more. Now. Unless anyone has anything more to add, get yourselves ready to move. We're less than eight miles from Creed's vault, and I want us in there by noon.'

# XXII

## TEMPTATION

The message that came through the vox had been so quiet that Ursula had barely heard it.

'Very glad to hear your voice, Tempestor. What's your status?'

'One moment, lord castellan. We have contact.'

A burst of las-fire in her earpiece gave her a fair indication of why Tempestor Sulien needed to take a brief pause. She fixed her eyes on the dark road ahead, alert for any moment that might bring her squad to a firefight of their own. Just because they'd made contact with their allies on this Throne-forsaken hell world didn't mean the danger was over. If anything, attempting a rendezvous was going to lead them into direct contact with the enemy.

'Still with us, Tempestor?'

Sulien didn't answer, and Ursula's heart sank. It would be entirely in keeping with how the mission was going to achieve vox-contact just in time for them to be cut down by enemy action. Her worries were absurd, she told herself. Sulien and his soldiers were Tempestus Scions, the finest troopers the schola progenium provided. They were capable of looking after themselves.

They had made heavy work of moving deeper into the city, winding their way through branching streets that no longer made sense. Every kasr she had ever visited had been built with the roads running north to south or east to west in well-regimented grids, but here streets twisted and connected in new combinations never intended by its architects. The buildings, too, were changing. On the outskirts the grey astrogranite facades had been torn and cracked, but their construction was still recognisable as Imperial. Here they had taken on a dull red sheen, their surfaces smooth and glassy as if touched by intense heat. The proportions of the doors and windows were wrong, too, their apertures stretched into elaborate filigreed arches, while bulbous turrets and twisting spires sprouted from walls and roofs like malign growths. The kasr had been built as a fortress, but now it was a castle from a childhood nightmare, the fevered imaginings of a diseased mind.

'*Still with you, lord castellan.*' The las-fire on the vox-link died away.

'What's your current status?'

'*I have the target location in my sights. Demolitions Specialist Irada and I have a vantage point overlooking the building we believe holds the vault.*'

'How many of you are there?' Ursula was fairly sure she knew the answer already, but the question had to be asked.

'*Two, my lord. We lost the others in an ambush close to the dropsite.*'

'Any sign of the other Scion squads?'

'*None, my lord. Our attempt at vox-contact went unanswered.*'

Ursula signalled her own squad to move on, and they resumed their cautious prowl forward. Something moved in the corner of her vision, and she looked up to see a fresh window open on the side of the building, the masonry parting like the opening of an eye. Mercifully there was no eyeball staring back at her, but the longer she looked, the more she started to imagine the aperture lined with a ring of needle-sharp teeth. She looked away, and kept walking. The kasr was changing around them. The less time they spent here the better.

'Have you made contact with the *Oriflamme*?'

'*No, my lord, despite several attempts. Our vox-operator's conclusion was that unusual atmospheric conditions were interfering with the signal.*'

'No contact here either. What can you tell me about the vault?'

'*The building is surrounded by the enemy, as intelligence suggested. There are multiple hostiles, engaged in combat with each other. Those nearest to the building are monstrous canids. The others–*'

'Others?'

The Tempestor paused before he answered. '*They are hard to describe, my lord. A swarm of flying beasts – like a pair of wings with a mouth underneath – that attack by swooping down through the air. Some of them leave a trail of fire. The rest...*' She heard him swallow. '*My lord, there are all manner of blasphemies here. I can describe each in turn for you, but it will take time–*'

'No need.' She would see them with her own eyes soon enough, and graphic details could only harm the unit's morale, her own included. She had fought the enemies of humanity from one side of the Imperium to the other, but facing a daemonic incursion of this nature was unheard of since the Fall itself. This was work for the Astartes, or the Sisters of Battle – except for the fact that it was taking place on Cadian soil. That made the duty fall to her, no matter how fearful the prospect of the battle to come. 'Good work, Tempestor. I'll vox again when we're getting close. From what you've described, I expect the place will be hard to miss.'

\* \* \*

'When do we do it?' Liga asked. The two legionnaires had fallen to the back of the group, watching the street receding behind them into the fog, searching for any sign they were being followed. Ossian was developing the uncomfortable feeling that the road was not merely fading from sight, but from reality, and that any attempt to retrace their steps would lead into a blank grey nothingness. He focused on his feet instead. At least he could be sure they were real.

'Do what?'

Liga pointed to a narrow side street between two buildings leaning so close together that they had fused at the top. 'Make a run for it. The old man's dead. Now he's gone, what use have they got for us?'

Ossian wanted to laugh. 'Throne's sake, Liga. I can't think of a worse place to end up on our own. You remember what it was like when we landed, don't you? At least with them...' He gestured to the front of the group, to the lord castellan in her magnificent armour and her entourage, half obscured already by the creeping fog. 'At least with them we stand a chance.'

'Oh, yeah, obviously. Remind me who it was sent us here again?' She shook her head ruefully. 'You're kidding yourself, doc. The only reason we're still breathing is because they don't have ammunition to waste. First chance they get, they'll throw us to the wolves.'

'Whereas you're proposing running straight into the wolf's mouth. And then there's the matter of the collars to take into account – have you forgotten about those?'

That made her pause. 'All right. So we need to get that control module back. That's the key to getting out of here.'

'And how exactly do you plan to get off-world? Or are you planning to spend the rest of your days here?'

'One step at a time, doc.'

'Our chances are better with them than on our own.'

Liga raised an eyebrow. 'You're a trusting soul, aren't you?'

He wanted to tell her that it wasn't trust that was stopping him from running, but he had no enthusiasm for prolonging an argument that was rapidly becoming circular. Liga might have had a rough life as a ganger on Brythok, but his time in the Astra Militarum had taught him that there were far worse fates than the one that waited for them around their necks. The things in the mists – and he was in no doubt there were things out there, watching them from just beyond the limit of his vision – wouldn't just destroy their bodies. They would rip their souls to shreds and laugh while they did it.

'At least there's no sign of our friend with the scythe,' he said instead, and a chill ran down his spine at the thought. Nothing he had seen on the planet so far, not even the flesh hounds with their slavering jaws and quivering, lizard-like frills, had come close to the sheer dread the Heretic Astartes had inspired in him. At least there had been no sign of him or his poxwalkers since they had entered the kasr proper: a small mercy but a welcome one. He had made the decision sometime the night before that he would blow his own brains out if ever that abomination got within arm's reach.

Liga didn't answer. She pointed up ahead, at a pair of armoured figures coalescing out of the mist. The vox-bead in Ossian's ear crackled, and the Tempestor he had heard before came through.

'Specialist Irada and I are straight ahead of you, my lord. The situation at the bunker is escalating. I thought it better I spoke to you directly.'

Ossian motioned to Liga and began a steady jog-trot towards the main body of the group. The little sniper – Laskari – still looked jittery as all hell, but the addition of two Scions to their complement felt like a development that would increase their chances of survival considerably. The lord castellan stepped into the shadow of a side street with the smaller of the two newcomers, clearly having decided to take the conversation off the vox, while the other Scion joined Harapa and Van Haast in covering the street in all directions. Ossian strained his ears, and tried to make out what they were saying, but the sound was muffled by distance and the fog. Instead he found his ear tuning in on the sounds of combat – high-pitched shrieks, a howl that he recognised as belonging to the flesh hounds, and a melodic sound like a woman's laughter.

'When we get to the vault,' Liga was saying. 'She's bound to be distracted then. First opportunity we get, we take that module and we run. Right?'

Ossian nodded absently. He was fairly sure that by the time they reached the vault they'd have other things on their minds.

Laskari stole a sidelong look at Colonel Van Haast's face, trying to read his expression. The lord castellan was still deep in conversation with the newly arrived Tempestor, but they had started moving again, presumably towards a vantage point from which they could plan their next move.

'How are we going to get in, sir?' she asked. 'The vault, I mean. If it's surrounded by the Neverborn.'

The colonel didn't look around, all his attention on the fog ahead. 'I imagine the lord castellan will inform us shortly, trooper.'

'Yes, sir.' She accepted the rebuke meekly. 'Only your family holdings were here, weren't they, sir?'

Van Haast fixed her with his piercing violet gaze. 'Go on, trooper?'

Suddenly she regretted her staggering misjudgement in asking the question. Under normal circumstances she wouldn't have raised her eyes to a full colonel, let alone spoken. She swallowed. 'I wondered if the lord castellan had made use of your expert knowledge of the local area yet, sir, that was all.'

'Should she deign to ask me for my advice, I would of course be delighted to provide it.' His gaze slid away from Laskari, and her muscles fractionally relaxed as his attention returned elsewhere. 'Though I must confess I spent more time in Kasr Arroch than on this side of the Rossvars. My family home...'

His voice trailed off. He looked up, and Laskari followed the direction of his gaze to see a shadow unfolding in the sky behind a layer of cloud. Its wingspan was easily thirty feet across, a long barbed tail whipping the air behind it. It turned sharply to the right, to plunge towards some distant land-locked target. A second identical shadow followed in its wake, letting out an ear-piercing shriek that echoed through the misshapen streets and drew a chorus of howls from the city around them. Something lithe and sinuous bounded across the street ahead, gleaming teeth bared, and lost itself in the shadow. Thunder rumbled overhead, and rain began to fall again in heavy droplets that reeked of sulphur and hissed when they touched the ground.

'Regrettably, Trooper Laskari, I rather fear the rest of our conversation will have to wait.'

'Of course, sir.' She took up a position at his left shoulder, then froze as a familiar silhouette caught her eye. When she turned it was gone, but for a fraction of a second she had thought she saw Lainn Anka, his long-las over his shoulder and a familiar mocking smile on his face.

# XXIII

## THE DAEMON

Ursula lay flat on her belly, and trained her field glasses on the battle unfolding below. The hab-unit that was serving them as a vantage point was on the tenth storey of a ruined hab-block, featureless and empty, its front wall torn away to leave a sheer hundred-foot drop straight down.

If the *Oriflamme*'s auspex system was to be believed – and she had no choice but to trust it – the vault was secured beneath a squat grey bunker in the middle of a wide square. Every inch of space around it was swarming with creatures of Chaos, from the horrors capering on the ground to the shrieking ray-creatures that swooped and dived through the misty air. Lightning was playing across the clouds with a crackle audible from the ground, its light casting the unearthly scene in shades of red and violet. There was a humming in the air that made the skin on the nape of her neck stand on end.

The temperature had risen steadily from the moment they had entered the kasr, and a thin trickle of sweat was making its way down her back. The thought of stifling herself under her helmet again was a thoroughly unwelcome one, but only idiots like Pyoter Valk fought with their hair flowing in the breeze, inviting headshots from any opportunist who might happen to find them in their sights.

'Did you see another entrance?' she asked Tempestor Sulien, who shook his head.

'No, my lord. As I understand it, this pattern of bunker has a single entrance for maximal security.'

She focused in on the doorway. Two flesh hounds were facing a swarm of tiny abominations that attacked in waves of flaming yellow, sickly pink and a blue so intense it hurt her eyes if she looked at it too long. The third flesh hound was pawing at the bunker door, its talons scraping fruitlessly off the adamantine surface without leaving a mark.

'How has it kept them out for so long?' she murmured, more to herself than the others.

'Has to be warded,' Harapa said. 'No way that could have stayed sealed otherwise all these years, right?'

'You may well be correct.'

Ursula turned her head and focused her field glasses towards the ruined basilica, but the spire had been swallowed up by the fog. The Blessed Sisters of the Adepta Sororitas had fought in Cadia's defence, but whether or not they had been present at the last defence of Kasr Gallan she didn't know. Thick adamantine-plated walls would only hold so long, but if there was faith involved – true faith, the kind that slew daemons and raised the martyred – then that might explain why the vault's seals had protected its precious contents when so much else had failed.

'Regardless, we need to get inside. And unless anyone has the key to that door, we're going to be making an entrance ourselves.'

The other Scion, a big woman with a spool of detonation cord dangling like a lasso from her backpack, leaned forward from where she was sitting on the floor. 'Ready to serve, lord castellan.'

'What do you have in that pack of yours, Specialist Irada?'

Irada patted her rucksack affectionately. 'Aside from the usual, my lord, I'm carrying six high-potency fyceline charges, wired and remote detonators, and a selection of grenades.'

Argent gave a soft laugh. 'Walk carefully, please. Ideally a good distance away from me.'

Irada ignored him. 'And a melta bomb, my lord.' The smooth metal object in her fist was a little larger than a standard grenade, a shallow flat-backed dome with a handle on one side.

'Excellent news.' As Ursula watched, one of the shrieking winged beasts swooped down and folded its massive wings around one of the flesh hounds in the attempt to raise it into the air. The hound erupted in an explosion of talons and teeth, and the pair of them became indistinguishable as they ripped and tore at each other. 'That's our way in then. The real trick is going to be clearing a gap long enough to get there, then stopping them following us in once the walls are breached.'

'I'm going to assume that a frontal assault doesn't feature in your plan,' Argent said.

'Only partially,' she said. The flesh hound had its teeth in the shrieking thing's wing now, and was tearing away chunks of silvery-blue meat that dissolved into glittering smoke between its teeth. 'An explosion of moderate size a little distance from the bunker would be guaranteed to draw the Neverborn's attention.'

Sulien nodded. 'We've observed their behaviour several times now. When one of the larger ones gets badly wounded, the smaller ones flock towards it to rip it apart.'

'Which is when we set off a second, larger charge, designed to kill and cripple as many as we can. Meanwhile our second group forces a breach in the bunker wall and moves inside, opens the vault and takes the contents. With the sort of materiel Indomitus Command is hoping we find in there, clearing a path out again shouldn't be too difficult.'

'Why not send the penal legionnaires with the explosives, lord castellan?' Van Haast said. He was leaning elegantly against the wall with his arms folded and eyes half-closed. 'If two explosions are required then we have the correct number of bodies to deploy them.'

Ursula glanced over at the two figures sitting unobtrusively in the corner of the bombed-out room. Van Haast's suggestion was straight out of the Tactica Imperialis – the legionnaires could solve a problem for her, and redeem themselves at the same time – but sending them to certain death was needlessly wasteful, especially when one of them was the squad's only chirurgeon.

She shook her head. 'Demolitions is work for experts. Specialist Irada, you and the Tempestor stand the best chance of laying those charges and setting them off on time. Once the explosions go off, your orders are to retreat to a defensible position, ideally here if you can do so without drawing enemy attention. Trooper Laskari will remain here in our vantage point, picking off any enemies that get too close. Major Argent, I'll need you here with Laskari, providing support and maintaining vox-contact with the other two groups.'

Argent didn't look like he thought much of that plan, but he said nothing.

'Van Haast, Harapa and I will enter the bunker. You two' – she motioned to the legionnaires – 'are with me, putting those carbines to use.'

Ursula had briefly considered leaving the legionnaires and the control module with Argent, but had discounted that plan after a few seconds' thought. She was starting to think she might be able to trust the medicae – for no reason other than the obvious care that he had shown Strahl, kindness that had gone beyond mere self-preservation – but the woman was an unknown quantity, her trustworthiness yet to be demonstrated. She could imagine all too easily how the woman might over-power Argent and Laskari, take the module and run. The device was safest around her wrist, and the legionnaires where she could see them.

'If we lose each other, the rendezvous point will be the basilica, two miles back the way we came, close to the martyr's wall. You'll know it by the spire. Questions?'

She glared around the room, daring Van Haast to criticise. To her surprise he shrugged a languid shoulder and said nothing. Trooper Laskari was staring blankly into space, her lips moving in what Ursula assumed was silent prayer.

'Trooper? Any questions about what we're about to do?'

Laskari jerked away. 'No, my lord.'

'And you're clear on your part in this?'

'Yes, lord castellan. I'll be...' Laskari paused, swallowed, then spoke again. 'Providing fire support to the demolitions team from here, along with Major Argent.'

The medicae had his hand in the air. Ursula nodded to him. 'Go ahead.'

'Correct me if I'm wrong, but I'm assuming you want me inside the bunker for my medical expertise rather than my combat skills.' He waved a vague hand towards the lascarbines, still strapped carefully to Harapa's backpack. 'I think it would be worth considering the professional skills of my colleague here. She has relevant knowledge when it comes to...' He stopped and looked down at the floor, stifling what she thought might have been half a smile. 'When it comes to this sort of breaking and entering. She'd be happy to volunteer those skills to help once we're inside.'

Ursula looked round at the other trooper, who was glaring at Ossian in outrage. He was definitely smiling now, and Ursula had the sense that some score between the two was being settled. Her instinct was to dismiss the offer outright – the woman had clearly been a ganger in her former life and could hardly be trusted – but the medicae had a point. Someone who knew their way around a security system might be an asset they could use once they were inside.

'And what do you say to that, Trooper Yager?'

The woman shrugged. 'If you like,' she said.

The hab-block that had been designated as their snipers' nest looked more like a ribcage, but the central stairwell was solid, the spine that held the building's skeletal remains together. It was a dark, windowless space, with shadows that danced in the squad's lumen-beams as they made their way from the tenth floor to the ground, taking the stairs at speed. Liga hung back at the rear of the group, and Ossian slowed down until she came alongside him. Her expression was sullen, and when she saw him there she looked away.

'I thought you'd be pleased,' he said.

She managed to ignore him for a few more steps, and then clearly the effort of biting her tongue became too much. 'Did you? Thanks so much. Just when I was planning on getting away, you drew her attention right back to me. Now she thinks I'm a thief, she'll be watching everything I do.'

'You were a thief, weren't you?'

Liga glared at him. 'You don't know anything about me.'

He held up a placating hand. 'Look. I'm sorry if I got it wrong. But you said you were worried you weren't useful to them.'

Ossian shot a quick look over his shoulder, but the other three were further ahead, safely out of earshot. 'So I made sure they knew how useful you are.'

'This is payback, isn't it?' Liga was checking her lascarbine, newly returned to her possession by Sergeant Harapa. 'Because I volunteered you for this mess.'

'In part.' He shrugged. 'But it's mostly what I said. Surviving those monsters won't matter at all if they're not willing to take us with them when extraction comes, and the more use to them we are before then, the better. Besides, isn't there any part of you that wants to bring the fight to the enemy?'

'You're forgetting, doc. I'm not Cadian.' She still didn't meet his gaze, but she sounded fractionally less sullen than before. 'If it was Brythok we were fighting for...' She paused. 'If I'm honest, I wouldn't care much there, either. I lived enough of my life trying to follow the rules and do the right thing, and look where it got me.'

'Move up, you two.' Harapa waved them forward. 'We don't want to get strung out.'

Ossian clutched his carbine a little tighter. The front lines were somewhere he'd always done his best to avoid, but once again he was out of options. The carbine was a dead weight in his hands, and he tried to remember the last time he'd fired a weapon in anger – barring the las-bolt he'd put through Edric Brynn's forehead, naturally. That one didn't count.

They pulled to a halt behind the wall of a vehicle deposit-ium, the rusting remains scattered across the patch of ground like long-fossilised skeletons. The rain had stopped, now, and though the ever-present cloud hadn't lifted, he had a sense of the brightness of the burning sun behind it, the air heating like an oven.

'Specialist Irada, are you in position?' The lord castellan's voice was calm. She could have been ordering manoeuvres on the parade ground, not leading a potentially suicidal mission into the midst of a pitched battle with the denizens of the warp.

*'Affirmative, my lord. Setting the charges now.'*

The lord castellan turned to face the tightly packed squad, and seemed to be scrutinising each of their faces in turn. Her gaze met his own, and he stared back at her, trying to read the expression in those pale violet eyes. Finally satisfied – though satisfied by what? – she gave him the curtest of nods, and lifted the heavy gilded helmet back onto her head.

'Stay close to me,' she said. 'I'll do what I can to put this ridiculous armour between all of you and the enemy. If we get swarmed, run for the bunker and I'll make a way in.' She held up the melta charge, the dull metal gleaming with an oily sheen. 'And we'll hope that whatever's inside will get us back out again.'

*'The primary and secondary charges are laid, lord castellan,'* Irada voxed. *'I've rigged the primary explosives to take out the remains of the auspex shrine overlooking the bunker. When it falls, it should injure enough of them to draw the attention of the rest. I'll use the time to get clear then detonate the second charge remotely.'*

Sergeant Harapa gave a nod of approval. From the way he had helped Irada prepare the charges in the snipers' nest, he had more than a passing acquaintance with demolition charges.

*'On my mark.'* A pause.

'Get ready to move,' the lord castellan said.

*'Five. Four. Three–'*

Argent's voice cut across the vox-link. *'Demolitions team, I have multiple hostiles converging on your position. I count two airborne and numerous land-based from multiple directions.'*

'Irada, Sulien, time you got out of there.' The lord castellan still sounded calm, but a hint of urgency was creeping into her voice.

*'We're surrounded, sir.'* Something on the other end of the

vox-link shrieked. *'I'm setting off the first charge now.'* A barrage of fire from the Scions' hotshot lasguns cut across the cacophony of the damned. *'I'll give you as much time as I can before I detonate the second.'*

The lord castellan shook her helmeted head. 'Irada, get–'

The first charge detonated.

# XXIV

## SACRIFICE

From her sniper's nest on the tenth floor, Laskari watched the horrors converge on the pair of Scions, the narrow alleyway lighting up with bright bursts of cherry-red las-fire. Argent was issuing orders down the vox, a note of panic in his voice that was making it increasingly difficult to maintain her own composure. She aimed her long-las and put a bolt through the wing of one of the flying abominations, but the creature didn't react. She tried again, this time catching it just above the viciously barbed tail, but the second shot made as little difference as the first. The daemons were converging from all sides now, the Scions obscured by hideous blue-grey wingspans – and then the alleyway became an explosion of fire and astrogranite.

Even at this distance, the shockwave was enough to set her ears ringing, muffling Argent's voice as he kept up the attempt to contact the teams on the ground.

'Tempestor, specialist, what's your status?'

The vox gave a crackle. Irada drew a sharp breath on the other end of the link, but any other reply was cut off by a second, louder crash as the ruined auspex shrine at the end of the alley-way toppled to the ground, pinning a flesh hound beneath its dish and crushing an uncountable number of the capering, brightly coloured creatures. A thick red liquid began to ooze out from below it, trickling from its severed base. It wasn't the daemons it had crushed that were bleeding. It was the tower itself.

'Lord castellan, I've lost contact with the demolitions team.'

*'So have we, major. What can you see?'*

'The auspex shrine's gone down.' He swallowed. 'The dust hasn't settled, but the explosion seems to be having the desired effect in drawing the daemons. The second charge should take out a good number of them.'

Laskari focused her scope on the tide of daemonic creatures surging towards the shattered auspex shrine. A group of six or seven abominations that resembled elongated, purple-skinned women were running after them, some with barbed whips waving in their claw-like hands. Laskari watched them leap on an oozing green snail the size of a bull-grox, ripping chunks of its rubbery flesh free with their needle teeth and cracking the shell to pull out handfuls of grey, stringy guts. Her stomach lurched, flooding her mouth with a mixture of acid and half-digested corpse-starch, and she fought it down with an effort of will. The scene unfolding through her scope didn't seem real. She was Cadian by birth, which meant that she knew of the existence of the Neverborn in a way that members of lesser regiments did not, but being confronted with them was a different matter entirely. Their mere existence was an affront to reality, something that shook her to the core.

If this is what the final battle for Cadia had been like, no wonder it had ended in slaughter and devastation.

'We can't wait for the second charge,' the lord castellan voxed. 'If the two of them are dead, there's no chance of it going off at all.'

'In which case we should retreat, regroup and re-evaluate–'

'I know my Primer as well as you do, Gideon, but we're in position. I have a clear line of sight to the bunker. We won't get another opportunity like this one.'

'My lord, I must counsel you against this… this recklessness.'

'Your objection is noted.'

It was clear from the lord castellan's tone of voice that she had no intention whatsoever of stopping.

The air was thick with dust from the explosion, mixed with a heady cocktail of sulphur and iron, ozone, rotting meat and a sickly floral perfume that put Ursula incongruously in mind of her mother. Through the gap in the depositium wall, she could see that the majority of the daemons had taken the bait: a good two-thirds of them had headed for the carnage promised by Irada's explosion. She tapped an armoured finger to the melta charge mag-locked on to her hip, and tried to assess the threat that was left. A group of elongated scarlet daemons with backswept horns and serpentine tongues were hacking with bloodthirsty enthusiasm at sinuous purple-skinned daemons with crustacean claws in place of hands, which writhed and shrieked and danced out of the way of their enemies' heavy iron swords.

'I make that six,' Harapa said quietly. He had shouldered his lasgun and drawn his combat knife and an autopistol that looked old enough to have known Solar Macharius. 'We can deal with six.'

Ursula raised an eyebrow. 'Does that statement come from a position of expertise?'

He shook his head. 'More a position of blind optimism, if I'm honest.'

'We shall have to hope that optimism is not misplaced.' She raised her left arm, and aimed her bolt pistol. She could feel the pressure of her soldiers' eyes on the back of her neck, a sense of expectation. What were they expecting? A heroic speech? There was no place for bombastic nonsense at a time like this.

'Eighth Regiment, with me. Now!'

They were going in.

The second explosion came just as they hit the first wave of the enemy, the Neverborn striking with such indiscriminate hatred that they seemed as likely to strike their fellows as their adversaries. Ursula aimed her bolt pistol and sprayed a volley of shells at waist height, eviscerating the nearest crimson creature and cutting a pair of lilac-skinned daemons almost in half. They fell with a look of utter ecstasy on their almost-human faces.

'*Second detonation has taken effect.*' She was only half listening to the quick-fire of Argent's words through the vox, focusing on pushing forward step by step as daemonic figures pressed in from all sides. One strike with the power sword severed a wiry scarlet arm from its shoulder, and the daemon's mouth opened impossibly wide, its tongue lashing like an extra limb. It brought its heavy iron blade up with impossible quickness, and she twisted her wrist just in time to raise her own weapon in a parry. Blue-white sparks met infernal radiance as the daemon's blade blackened and corroded, finally snapping into a shower of brittle shards. She didn't stop to admire the look of disgust on its grotesque face. A clumsy backhanded swing took it below the ribs, opening a deep gash in its flank.

A las-bolt struck it in the throat, and it toppled backwards, ichor streaming from its open wounds. Ursula stepped over its remains as it discorporated and took the violet-coloured legs from one of the two daemons locked in combat with

Harapa before finishing it with a bolt through the skull. He stabbed his combat knife into the remaining daemon's lower abdomen, gutting it like a freshly slaughtered prey-beast, then stepped back, wiping a mixture of dried blood and sweat from his forehead. A livid bruise was blossoming across his jaw, and he paused to spit out a mouthful of blood and broken teeth.

A capering pink fiend lunged out of the melee. Harapa discharged his autopistol into its misshapen head and the thing fell in shreds of magenta flesh, only to coalesce into new, smaller creatures, these ones a bright blue with gnashing oversized teeth. The smell of ozone they left in their wake was strong enough to override even the sickly sweetness of the dissolving violet daemons.

'*I can report multiple hostiles slain in the second explosion,*' Argent was saying. '*But you're starting to draw attention.*'

'Anything from Sulien and Irada?' A volley of shots streaked past her right ear to strike a flaming blue-robed daemon with too many mouths, its hand wreathed in flame, ready to strike.

'*Nothing.*'

The daemon in the robe recoiled, and she lunged forward to pierce it through the place where its chest should have been. It lost its substance completely, nothing but an azure robe drifting to the ground where it had been a moment before. The sheer chaos of the situation was working to their advantage, the mass of daemonkind striking at each other in their frenzy to reach the hated human enemy first.

'How close are we to the bunker?' The daemons were packed so close it was hard to see past them.

'*Almost there, lord castellan. About five yards.*'

'Excellent news. Laskari, clear me a path.'

It took a moment for the sniper to respond, but when she did it was with las-fire instead of words. The last of the scarlet daemons fell, a perfectly placed las-bolt piercing its skull just above one glowing amber eye, then with relentless and uncharacteristic efficiency green las-fire rained down on its surviving companions. They scattered, turning faces monstrous with outrage to the sky, fleeing the vivid green rain of death from above.

*'That's cleared the way, my lord!'*

'Good work!' The bunker door was visible now, the ground and the adamantine door streaked with dissolving daemonic remains. 'All of you, move up, I want clear ground between us and them while the charge does its work.'

Harapa unslung his lasgun, and joined Ossian and Van Haast in laying down an arc of fire as she closed the distance and raised the melta charge to the door.

'Wait!'

An unarmoured hand tugged at her arm, and she turned with a sense of building outrage to see Liga Yager staring up at her.

'What?'

'You brought me because I'm useful, right? If you blow that door, we can't close it again. Those things will surge in and overwhelm us before you can get whatever's in the vault.' The legionnaire raised her right hand and twisted off the tip of her index finger, revealing a fine metal augmetic ending in a series of equally fine adamantine tools. 'I know that pattern of door. Six seconds and I can have it open. That's quicker than a melta charge, plus you can close it behind you.'

Ursula shot a quick look at the advancing horde, drew her laspistol and took a shot at the creature in the lead. 'Six seconds. Do it.'

Yager nodded and dropped into a low crouch, a soft whirring rising from the thieves' tools as she slotted them into the lock.

Van Haast blew away one of the blue fiends. 'Allow me to express my surprise' – he followed up with a pair of shots that took out the fiery daemons that appeared in its wake – 'that you expect a bunker which has kept out all the horrors of post-Fall Cadia to yield to a set of thieves' tools.'

Another violet-skinned daemon sprang towards them, huge crab-claws extended. Ossian stepped forward, jammed his las-carbine under its chin and pulled the trigger, showering the rank behind in ichor. The horde was closing in again.

'Progress, Trooper Yager?'

'Bear... with me...'

There was a loud click, and the bunker door swung open. Yager let out a triumphant yowl and scrambled inside.

'You three, in!' Ursula discharged another volley in a broad arc, buying seconds of time for the unit to retreat through the door. She went through last and slammed it behind her. 'Can you lock it?'

Liga shook her head. 'Shouldn't need to. Bolt should go home the moment it's closed.'

Something huge threw itself against the door, shaking the walls of the bunker, but the door held. Ursula pulled off her helmet and activated her flash-lumen, moving the beam across the bunker's walls.

'Well done, legionnaire. That was quick work...'

She broke off. They were standing in a fortified antechamber, a large inner door that looked every bit as substantial as the outer one leading to what she assumed was the vault proper beyond. The walls were covered in close-packed script up to a foot or two above eye height, while kneeling in front of the door was a figure in glossy black power armour.

Ursula took a step closer. The figure was a woman, her head bowed forward so that her sharply bobbed hair fell over her face.

'Van Haast, have a look at that script and tell me what it says.'

Now she was close, Ursula recognised the black-and-scarlet

robes beneath the armour, and the symbol of the Order of Our Martyred Lady embroidered in gleaming white silks. The Sister's face was pristine, a smooth porcelain only a shade darker than her hair, but her skin was cold to the touch, her eyes glassy and unseeing.

Inside the inner door, something moved.

'High Gothic,' Van Haast said. 'It's one of the litanies of warding.'

'That doesn't make sense.' Ursula removed her gauntlet, and put a hand to the inner door. 'Why would Creed–'

A tremor shook the walls of the bunker. 'Look at the walls,' Van Haast said, an unfamiliar note of urgency in his voice. 'The script. It's changing.'

Radiating outwards from the door they had first passed through, the script was smudging and blackening as though being wiped away with a solvent-soaked cloth. The woman's face was changing, too, the eyes falling in and the skin desiccating from the bone, as though decades of decay were occurring all at once. Behind the inner door, something gave a deep, bellowing howl, the inhuman voice joined first by one and then two more.

'This place wasn't sealed to keep those things out,' Ursula said, a sick sense of realisation washing over her. 'Those wards are to keep something in. Something that Sister gave her life to contain.'

'Am I to take it this is the wrong vault?' Van Haast began, sounding more disappointed than angry.

'I fear it must be.'

Ursula closed her eyes. The disappointment descended on her shoulders like a physical weight, bringing with it a crushing sense of shame. She had taken intelligence at face value, allowing herself to be blinded by its source. In a green lieutenant that might have been understandable, but for her it was a catastrophic, unforgivable error. Like her father, she had let her ego get in the way of her good judgement and wasted the lives of good soldiers in pursuit of an unattainable goal. If the fabled lost vault of Ursarkar Creed did exist – and she was starting to doubt that, too – then it could be anywhere on Cadia, and with no contact to the *Oriflamme* she had no way of choosing the next likely location.

'How are we getting out?' Trooper Yager's staring face flashed into the lumen-beam. Something huge thudded against the inner door.

'The way we came in, legionnaire.' Harapa had his hand on the door's inner mechanism. 'Clear a way through and make a run for it. Unless you've got another plan, chief?'

Ursula shook her head. 'An excellent strategy, sergeant.' There was no time for self-pity, not when the others were relying on her.

The walls were dribbling with black ink now, spreading like corrosion to the door to the inner vault and trickling through the cracks in the doorframe. There was another thunderous impact from the other side, and this time the inner door buckled outwards, and a huge taloned paw shoved itself through the gap.

'Now!' she shouted.

Harapa threw the door open, and Ursula sprayed bolt-shells blindly into the gap then stepped out of the bunker, clearing space with a second volley. Her visor's heads-up display registered her diminishing ammunition reserves, but she ignored it. There was enough for now, and anything after that was something she could worry about later, assuming there was a later.

Monstrous bodies closed in on her, and she forced herself forward into the press, slashing and shooting without much care for her targets. Something vast swooped overhead, and she brought her bolt pistol up a split second before a vast set of blue-white wings closed around her. She fired, and the muzzle flare illuminated a huge transverse mouth lined with glittering knives, before the creature's underbelly tore apart and it fell.

'Keep moving!' she shouted. Now that the others were through, they moved into close formation, Van Haast and the two legionnaires covering their rear and both flanks, while she and Harapa pushed forward. 'Laskari, clear me some space!'

*'I'm trying, my lord! They're reinforcing as fast as I can deal with them.'*

Metal shrieked behind them, followed by another chorus of howls from the vault's occupant. The flesh hound in front of her answered the roar with a gibbering shriek of its own, and she took its head at the shoulder, and risked a glance behind her.

A three-headed canid the size of a Chimera was pulling itself free of the building, shaking the body of one of the violet daemons between one set of its jaws like a hunting hound with vermin. Its companions – some mounted on two-legged creatures halfway between reptiles and avians – charged towards it. With a triumphant roar it ripped through the bunker door and bounded forward, rending and tearing with joyful abandon.

Even with the distraction the beast provided, there were too many daemons. Ursula cut down something with rotting green flesh that looked mostly mouth, but it bought her a foot of progress at most. She unclipped a grenade from her belt and threw it into the press, rewarded a moment later by an explosion that sent chunks of meat spattering into the air, but the daemons were pressed as closely as ever.

'Argent, we're getting swarmed here. I need to know which direction they're thinnest.'

*'They're all around you. I'm trying to find you a route, but I'm not seeing it. You're going to have to cut your way through.'*

'Doing my best, Gideon.' The irony of the situation wasn't

lost on her. The best intelligence the Imperium had to offer had sent her to Cadia in search of something designed to defeat the horrors that had claimed it, only for her to unleash yet another. It would have been funny if the consequences hadn't been so dire.

'Let's see how many of them we can take with us,' she said quietly, and Harapa nodded.

'*Lord castellan!*' Laskari was shouting down the vox, near hysterical. '*I can see something… Someone moving towards the daemons. They're heading towards you. I think… I think it's one of the Scions…*'

The world erupted. A wave of heat and light washed over her, and the tide of daemons parted, ripped into brightly coloured shreds. Smoke billowed from a shallow crater, and a figure stood at the other side, one hand held up in greeting.

'Go!' Ursula didn't waste time on trying to make out who it was. They sprinted over the broken ground, ignoring the roars and shrieks from behind her, the impact of huge paws thudding against the earth. Was it her imagination, or were the daemons thinning out? Beyond the figure – it was Irada, her armour scuffed and scorched and her helmet missing, but she was alive – she could see the depositium walls, and beyond it the narrow twisting alleyways through which they had come. If the presence of the monstrous canid was enough to slow down its enemies and rally its allies against them, then she and her soldiers could lose themselves in those streets.

Irada drew back her arm and threw a grenade. The Scion had a throw like a professional scrumball player: it soared over Ursula's head to land thirty feet behind her, and a gust of warm air buffeted Ursula forward as she ran.

'*Clear path ahead of you, my lord!*' Laskari was shouting. '*Don't look back! Keep running!*'

They were almost at Irada now, reaching her just as the special-ist primed and threw another grenade.

'I thought you were dead!' Ursula gasped out between strides, and the specialist's face lit up in a broad grin.

'Tempestus Scions, my lord. We're hard to–'

Her mouth opened, and a gush of blood surged down her chin, spattering the ornate chestplate of her armour. A knife-shaped barb was protruding from her throat, and before Ursula could react a pair of vivid blue talons locked around Irada's shoulders and hoisted her vertically upward. Something with a long yellow beak beat the air with feathery blue wings, and then it and Irada were gone into the cloud without a trace.

Ursula looked behind her. The air was still cloudy from Irada's grenades, but from the sounds of mortal battle the daemons had more pressing concerns than chasing them. She counted heads. Four, not counting her own, all of them human.

'Anyone who can hear me, we are withdrawing. Rendezvous at the basilica. We'll regroup and plan our next move from there.'

There would be time enough to take stock of her failures later.

# ACT THREE

*'Lost are we, and are only so far punished*
*That without hope we live on in desire.'*

– Fragment from an ancient text,
kept in the Great Library of Terra

# XXV

## THE OSSUARY

The God-Emperor's face said it all.

The basilica was an overgrown ruin of slabs and spires, the narthex and nave completely obliterated, the apse and transept open to the misty air. Windows that had depicted the lives of the saints or the war for Terra were shattered and empty, but the statue of the God-Emperor still stood, the once pristine metal tarnished and pockmarked by time. From the look of judgement on His face, He knew exactly how badly they had failed.

No, that wasn't right, Ursula thought. They hadn't failed. *She* had.

'You should eat.' Argent sat down next to her on the soggy ground and offered her a ration bar.

She shook her head. 'I'm not hungry.'

'You still need food.' He dropped the bar into her lap and left it there. 'Unless your plan is to lie down and die here, of course, in which case feel free to starve yourself.'

'I may as well.' Ursula removed her gauntlets to unwrap the

unappetising-looking block of corpse-starch, bit off the end and swallowed it down before she could taste it. 'We're finished here, Gideon. The best we can hope for is that the sky clears long enough for the beacon signal to reach the *Oriflamme*, and I have my doubts that will happen any time within our lifespans.'

Argent nodded thoughtfully. 'Quite right. Situation desperate, all hope lost, defeat inevitable. You might as well wallow in self-pity and have done with it.'

'That is not what I am…' She stopped. Argent was right. That was *exactly* what she was doing. She sighed. 'Point taken. I got you all into this. How am I going to get you all out of it?'

'You're the great strategist. You work it out. But finding the vault would seem like a good start. There can only be so many of them, after all.'

'And how exactly do we do that?'

'I don't think you brought Colonel Van Haast along for his winning personality. He must have some idea of the nearest likely location.'

The thought of going begging to Van Haast was about as appealing as finishing the rest of the corpse-starch, but clearly she was going to be forced to swallow both down.

'Come on then.' She took another bite, winced and got to her feet. 'Let's see what the colonel has to say.'

They found Van Haast in a small stone alcove, at the top of a flight of worn stone steps that looked older than the God-Emperor Himself. He had managed to clean the blood and filth from his armour, and with his hair neatly combed he looked as close to presentable as any of them were likely to get.

'Colonel, I need your expert knowledge of this area–'

'There's something unsettling about this place,' he said before she could finish. When she didn't reply, he gave an angry huff, as if she were being deliberately obtuse. 'The cultists we saw here, the ones who burned their companion. They left the bones here.'

'Go on.'

He pointed over his shoulder, down the dark steps into the crypt beneath. 'They left them in the ossuary. Unless someone else has been burning bodies in this general vicinity.'

'Show me.'

The space beneath the basilica stretched out into darkness, the air reeking of damp. The low, vaulted ceiling was separated by simple stone columns, and the walls were lined with columbaria, shallow alcoves that held the bones of the dead. There was an ossuary like this in every kasr in Cadia. Bodies were buried twice: first in the corpse fields with a headstone to mark their resting place, and the second time when their name had worn from their headstone and they had passed from memory. The bones would be exhumed, wrapped and laid to rest in the kasr's ossuary, to take their final repose with generations of their people.

'Where did they put the bones?' she asked.

Van Haast pointed to one of the alcoves. As her eyes adjusted to the darkness, she could make out the dark shape of burned human remains.

'There's more than one skeleton,' he said. 'Looks like they've been burning their own and putting the bones here for a while.'

Ursula lifted the blackened skull and turned it in the lumen-light. The back of the skull was missing where the las-bolt had pierced it, but the whole of the skull was distorted by an irregular series of growths that covered the entire dome of the cranium. Light glinted on metal, and she hooked a finger behind a fine silver chain and pulled it free. Hanging on the end was a set of ident-tags marked with a name, rank and an Imperial aquila, hand-stamped on a roughly cut metal oblong. They were a passable imitation of standard issue, as though someone had copied the usual Mechanicus-produced tags with homemade tools.

If the tags were correct, the skull had belonged to a Captain Sarya Krozer. There was no Munitorum number.

Ursula weighed the tags thoughtfully in her hand, considered tucking them into a pouch, then returned them to the pile of bones.

'Get the medicae down here. I want someone who knows what they're looking at to examine these bones.'

She used the time until Ossian arrived to count the remains. There were at least twenty skulls, some of them so freshly interred that traces of charred skin and hair still clung to the surface of the bone, others older and crumbling around the orbits and jaws. Some of them had met violent deaths, and most had some evidence of the distortions she had seen on the first skull, though the older the bones were, the more subtle those changes became.

'You summoned me, lord castellan?'

The medicae was at her shoulder before she noticed, his tone anything but servile. She held the skull out towards him. 'Take a look at this and tell me what you think.'

He held her gaze a fraction of a second longer than necessary, then took the skull from her hand, turning it thoughtfully back and forward.

'I'll start with the obvious. It's a human skull. The teeth are fully erupted, so it's an adult. I'd say it belonged to a woman, but that is mostly a guess.'

'The name on the ident-tags would substantiate that. What about these lesions on the brow?'

'Malign growths. You see them occasionally in factorum labourers, or voidfarers who work close to the reactors. But this is *much* worse. I've never seen anything like it.'

'And those other bones?' She lifted a femur and handed it to him hip first. He took it, rotated it to bring the many-lobed growth at the hip into the light, and handed it back with a nod.

'Similar. I'd want to see it with the meat on to be sure, but it looks like the same corrupting process.'

'Would it have been fatal?'

Ossian turned the skull in his hands and poked a finger through the bullet hole in the temple. 'It wasn't the cause of death.'

'That is not what I asked you.'

The man lifted his head and stared at her again. Throne, he was infuriating. She had seen his sort before: the sort of obstinate idiot who'd dig in his heels a hundred times before he'd show a moment's weakness. It was a common personality trait in chirurgeons: grox-headed stubbornness that would have been inexcusable in anyone less skilled. In his former life he must have been a devil to command, which probably explained why his career had ended the way it had.

'Then yes. It would have easily been fatal. Within a day or two, maybe a few days longer if they cauterised and amputated each lesion at the first sign of corruption. Whoever put the round into their skull was doing them a favour.'

The pieces of the puzzle were falling into place. The death she had witnessed had been a suicide, supervised with dignity, perhaps even kindness. The bones had been laid to rest here with generations of Cadian dead, not to desecrate the place, but to honour its sanctity. The Sister of Battle's faith had held the daemon at bay in Kasr Gallan's vault for decades; who was to say that faith of a different kind had not endured beneath the once-holy basilica?

'The question is how they got here,' Ossian asked. 'Another mission before yours?'

'Rather an omission on the part of the lord regent were that to be true,' Van Haast said. He was silhouetted in the doorway, his posture rigid and unforgiving.

'What's the alternative?' Ossian said. 'That they've been here since the Fall? That we've found survivors?'

Van Haast shook his head. 'Anyone that remained after the Fall would be corrupted beyond recognition. You've seen the horrors out there. The mere fact that they ape the old rituals is no assurance of purity.'

Ursula took the skull and returned it to its alcove. 'You may be correct, colonel. But I find myself eager to meet them – either to destroy the abominations they have become...'

A thrill of anticipation shot through her.

'Or to acquaint myself with new allies.'

# XXVI

### LOST SOULS

'Should we wait?' Trooper Laskari asked, as the squad formed up, ready to move out of the basilica. 'For the Tempestor? Or leave a message for him?'

Ursula considered the options. 'If he was coming, trooper, I think he would be here by now.' Most likely he had perished in the first explosion, or died like Irada in the talons of some airborne abomination. 'And leaving a message risks telling the enemy which direction we have taken.'

'I don't imagine they will need many clues to follow us,' Van Haast said, slipping a fresh charge-pack into his lasrifle. 'Not the way we move.'

'Then Tempestor Sulien should be able to follow our trail.' Ursula put a hand on Laskari's shoulder, and gave it a reassuring squeeze. 'If he is alive, then he will have the skills to find us. And if he is dead, then he died as a Cadian should – in defence of his allies, and striking a blow at the heart of his enemy. We should all be grateful for such an end.'

Laskari stood a little straighter. 'Yes, my lord.'

'Excellent. Colonel, you're our local expert. Which way are we most likely to pick up their trail?'

Van Haast shrugged. 'I think we can safely rule out back into the city. The foothills of the Rossvars are immediately to our north. The intervening ground was cleared before the Fall to allow mining machinery access to the mountains, but there seems to have been considerable regrowth. If these *Cadians*' – he laced the word with scorn – 'are eking out an existence here... If, Throne be praised, they are carrying on a war against the old enemy, then some sort of cover would be a prerequisite.'

'Are there caves in this part of the Rossvars?' Ursula tried to remember what she had learned in the schola, more years ago than she cared to count.

'I believe so. Some of them formed the basis of your father's plan to excavate the rock to connect the two kasrs on either side of the mountain. It might have served as a refuge during the Thirteenth Black Crusade, if it had been started ten years earlier.'

'Then that's another possibility.' She focused her field glasses on the thick forest in the middle distance. It didn't look like it had grown there in the last few decades. It looked as ancient as Cadia itself. Still, nothing else here played by the normal rules; why should the trees?

The atmosphere had been peaceful in the basilica, but as soon as they left the hallowed ground Ursula's old sense of unease returned, in no small part due to the alarm-rune on her visor display informing her that the armour's power reserves had dropped below fifty per cent.

That was another bad sign.

Rho had assured her that the power pack's machine-spirit should have been capable of sustaining five days of full combat activity – more if she was careful – but something about this place was burning through its reserves at a punishing rate.

She dismissed the warning, and fixed her attention on the treeline ahead. The intervening ground was hard and barren, littered with relics of Cadia's final war. The twisted remains of a Leman Russ lay upturned and gutted near a ruined hab-block, and the ground was littered with shell casings and spent charge-packs. Once she saw a ruptured plasma pistol far too large for a human hand, its coil melted in a final discharge of energy. She left the remains where they lay. To move them would have felt like disturbing the dead.

'Good thick forest,' Harapa said approvingly, as they approached the trees. 'A place like that, you could hide in for months.'

'What are they *eating?*' Van Haast asked. 'I can't imagine anything here is edible. Not without subjecting themselves to even *more* of the planet's corrupting influence.'

They paused on the edge of the forest. The boundary felt unnatural: hard earth underfoot on one step, spongy green loam on the second. Ursula cast a final look back over her shoulder at the twisted kasr behind. The path lay ahead. If only it were clearer. The thick moss muffled her steps, the air unnaturally opaque beneath the thick green canopy. She had the urge to lift off her helmet again, but resisted, though the fact it made good sense didn't mean she had to like it. The armour's air-scrubbers were doing their best, but the sour sweat accumulating in her body-glove was proving too much for them.

'Fan out. Maintain vox and visual contact with the soldier on either side of you. If you see something, tell me.'

'And if they see us first?' On her left, Van Haast was moving between thick trunks overgrown with creepers, the Cadian drab of his armour blending seamlessly into his surroundings.

'If they're friendly, that will not be a problem.'

'And if they are not?'

'Then at least you can say you were right all along.'

Laskari had hated the kasr, but the forest was worse. Stepping inside had been like stepping into another world, somewhere that smelled thick and green and fecund. Thick strings of phosphorescent fungus dangled from gnarled branches, lighting the misty air an eerie iridescent green. A soft whisper drifted from leaves stirred in the wind.

It took her almost a minute before she realised that there *was* no wind.

There had been no more strange interference on the vox since Kasr Gallan, but she took the vox-bead out of her ear anyway to make sure the noise was coming from the physical world around her, not through the comms channel. The whisper continued unchanged, coming from no particular direction, drifting through the strange, dead air.

'Anyone else hearing whispering?' the medicae said.

'I hear it,' Laskari said. It felt like confessing a sin, a heavy weight lifting from her shoulders. She wasn't hallucinating. Not this time, anyway.

'Throne…'

The strangled syllable came from Yager. Laskari squinted through the trees to her right, and caught a flash of orange jumpsuit. The legionnaire was standing in front of a tree, ramrod straight.

'There's a face in the tree. It's… I think it's trying to speak.'

With the sound of tearing cloth, the tree closest to Laskari opened vertically along its trunk, revealing a mouth filled with razor teeth and a long fleshy tongue.

*'Help us,'* it whispered in a chorus of voices, words overlapping each other in pleas born of desperation. *'We were promised escape. The children… Where are the children? Why did he leave us to die?'*

An eye opened on its surface, the glistening orb beneath bleeding scarlet tears that dried like sap as soon as they touched the bark below.

Laskari backed away, directly into the trunk of another tree. Something rustled close to her ear, but before she could turn, something whipped around her throat and locked tight. She aimed her long-las over her shoulder and pulled the trigger, but a second filament – long, thin and barbed along its length with wicked black thorns – pinned her arms to her torso, squeezing the breath from her lungs. She tried to speak, but managed only a terrified squawk. Her blood was thundering in her ears, her lungs screaming for air as the murderous branches hauled her into the air.

A shuddering impact shot through the tree. Gravity reversed itself, and she fell, thudding a second later into spongy loam that stank of rotting meat. She drew a wheezing breath through her bruised throat and pushed herself upright. Sergeant Harapa was standing over her, his combat knife severing flailing branches with systematic efficiency, the tree shrieking and recoiling.

'Remember what I told you. Nothing here is friendly.'

Laskari stepped away from the tree, careful this time to avoid backing into the others. The one with the mouth gave a cough, and she moved out of reach just quickly enough to avoid the cloud of spores that billowed from between the knife-like teeth. She jogged forward, heading for a patch of open ground, ringed with mercifully normal-looking trees, and breathed a shuddering sigh of relief.

When she looked back, the mouth and the eyes were gone. The horror she had seen a moment before could have been any one of the trees behind her.

It could have been *all* of them.

\* \* \*

It wasn't until the second volley that Ursula recognised the distant flash of light ahead as las-fire. The first had been a mere flicker, so subtle that she almost missed it, but the second was unmistakable. She adjusted the focus on her helmet-lenses, magnifying the image and panning back and forth until she saw a dark shape moving between the trees.

'Hold up. Something's happening up ahead.'

*'Want me to scout it out, chief?'* Harapa could have been anywhere, a disembodied voice in the forest.

'Get closer. Stay out of sight if you can. The rest of you, converge on me and maintain a steady advance.'

As they moved up, it became clear that the fight was little more than a skirmish, a few dozen walking corpses facing off against a smaller group of soldiers in the same outdated hostile-environment gear they had seen the night before. Whoever they were, they were good, moving in practised formation with well-defined arcs of fire, every shot finding its mark in a rotting skull.

*'I make that ten soldiers,'* Harapa said.

'My lord!' The excitable note was back in Laskari's voice. 'I saw one of the Scions!'

'Fighting or observing?' Ursula tried not to get her hopes up. Sulien might have escaped the kasr – or the newcomer might be a survivor from one of the other hitherto unaccounted-for fire-teams.

'Forgive me, my lord. I only got a glimpse.'

Ursula scanned the treeline again. The fight was moving more quickly now, the masked soldiers allowing the poxwalkers to gain ground. She tried the vox.

'This is the lord castellan, do you hear me?'

There was no reply, nothing except the infuriating low crackle that was becoming the soundtrack to her life. That didn't mean much. Their communication system had been demonstrated to be unpredictable enough that the other team's vox-system might have failed entirely by now. Ursula got to her feet.

'I think it's time to take a closer look.'

*'What d'you reckon, chief? Want me to get involved?'* She could hear the eagerness in Harapa's voice.

'Hold your bloody position.' Van Haast sniffed. 'Just because they're fighting those poxwalkers it does not mean they are on our side.'

A sonorous note echoed through the woods. Ursula felt her muscles lock rigid.

'That damn horn again,' Argent said.

'They're Cadians, lord castellan.' Laskari's voice was shaking. Ursula looked her up and down. The trooper flinched, but she stood her ground.

'Your point, trooper?'

'Shouldn't we be helping them?'

'Rushing in blindly will not help anyone.' The words came out sharper than she had meant, but too late to change that now.

'Yes, lord castellan.' Laskari's eyes were downcast, her moment of courage seemingly fled. If her deference had been designed to defuse Ursula's temper, it was having exactly the opposite effect. The girl needed to grow a spine. Cadia was no place for cowards.

The horn sounded again. Branches cracked, sharp as gunshots.

*'More of them,'* Harapa said. *'Chief, I'm seeing movement behind us.'*

'Throne-on-Terra.' Ursula cursed the forest, the poxwalkers and her own stupidity. She had been so focused on making progress through the forest, so fixated on the battle unfolding in the trees that she had committed the unforgivable sin of losing her situational awareness.

'Keep moving,' she said. 'If we're going to fight them, I want a say in choosing the battleground.'

The woods were alive with movement now, silhouettes moving forward in the thick grey light, the stench of decay so strong she could smell it through the vents in her armour, closing in like a blanket pulled up over the face of a corpse.

*'I've got poxwalkers on three sides,'* Harapa said. *'Only clear route is towards that fight.'*

The hunting horn sounded again, and Ursula's stomach dropped into her boots. 'The Heretic Astartes... He's herding us. He must have known the moment we stepped into the woods. What does he want?'

'You can't understand something like that.' Van Haast brought his rifle up to his shoulder. 'You can only fight it or run from it.'

A vast silhouette moved behind the monstrous horde, the gnarled antlers spreading from the helmet and the scythe it carried leaving no doubt as to its identity. A tattered robe hung from the rotting green armour, and as it moved through a patch of light she saw that its visor was pushed up, but what lay beneath was obscured by shadow.

A poxwalker staggered into the clearing ahead of the rest of the horde. Ursula raised her bolt pistol to obliterate it, then stopped at the sight of what it was wearing. It was dressed differently to the others, still wearing the suit of armour it had died in: a suit of black-and-gold carapace, the helmet staved in like a cracked egg to expose cratered bone and spattered brain matter beneath.

'Scions,' Argent said, sounding like he might be about to vomit. 'It's one of our Scions.'

His shot took the walking corpse squarely in the faceplate, vivid green las-fire illuminating the helmet's skull-like features even as it scorched them black. The poxwalker didn't stop.

'Correction. It's not *one* of our Scions.' Van Haast took aim down the sights of his lasrifle. 'By my count it's at least fifteen.'

\* \* \*

'We're going.' Liga's hand bit into Ossian's arm, her voice a hiss in his ear. 'Now. We're out of time.'

'We're what?' Ossian jerked his arm free.

'We're going. Look.' She stabbed the muzzle of her laspistol towards the oncoming horde. The poxwalkers were closing around them like the tightening of a noose. Something had changed in the air, the visibility down to a few yards, the gaps between the trees filled with a thick, acrid fog. Someone shrieked, then other voices joined one after another in a panicked cacophony.

The trees were screaming.

'He's set the damn forest on fire.'

'Then we use the smoke for cover,' Liga said. 'We hang back. Wait till that lot are engaged, then we make a run for it.'

Ossian almost laughed. 'Make a run for it where?'

'Anywhere. Anywhere but here.'

'Liga…' He held out a checking hand, but she knocked it aside.

'No. I'm done. Done waiting for them to decide they're sick of us. I can't live with this… this sword hanging over my head.'

'You made a difference back in that vault. We'd be dead if you hadn't been there to pick the lock–'

'And look where that got us!' Her voice was almost a scream. 'She's got no idea what she's doing, and the longer we spend blundering about in the dark, the worse this gets!'

Ossian tapped the collar around his neck. 'And you are remembering this? The distance trigger?'

'Like I said before, I'll take my chances.' Her voice fell, and her face softened, just a fraction. 'Final offer, doc. You coming or not?'

The woods were thick with smoke. The lord castellan and her soldiers were already moving through the trees towards the other firefight. While they were distracted, he had no doubt that he could slip away unnoticed. He might even escape the attention of the shambling horde and their monstrous shepherd. But what then? Wait for oblivion in the form of an explosive charge? To his surprise, he realised that wasn't what was holding him back. Death was one thing, but infinitely worse would be proving to that bastard Van Haast that he was nothing more than worthless convict scum after all.

'I knew it.' Liga smiled ruefully. 'You Cadians stick to your own. Do me one last favour, would you? Tell them I'm dead. Killed in the fighting. Make it sound good, yeah?'

There was no changing her mind. A stab of grief caught Ossian below the breastbone. Liga was a ganger, a criminal and a thief, but he had grown to like her in the days they had spent together.

'I'll do my best.'

She offered him a hand. 'Good luck, doc. Be seeing you.'

'God-Emperor protect you, Liga Yager.'

'Pretty sure He's dropped the ball on that one already,' she said, and then she was sprinting through the fog, firing wildly at nowhere in particular, until even the flare and crackle of her laspistol was swallowed up by the smoke.

It only took an instant for everything to go wrong.

One moment Ursula was watching the dead soldiers move between the trees, and the next the forest was thick with them, the air reeking of smoke and rotting meat, the shriek of the trees underscored by a low, unsettling moan coming from all sides. One of the dead still bore a Tempestor's insignia on his armour, though his helmet was gone and his dead face was slack and expressionless. It wasn't Sulien. She had met this man on the *Oriflamme*, a veteran with more decorations than a governor's palace, but his name wouldn't come to mind.

The corpse turned its head to look at her. Half of its face had been torn away. Broken white teeth shone through the tatters of its cheek, the right eye a mess of jelly in a ruined orbit. There was nothing left of the man he had been, just a broken-limbed puppet dancing to an infernal tune. She fired one precious bolt-shell, and finished the performance.

A las-bolt streaked past her shoulder, missing the head of another pox-walker by inches and setting a tree alight, followed by a second shot that went equally wide. Laskari's aim was off, which meant the little trooper was starting to panic – the last thing they needed. Panic was infectious, and it would spread through an untried squad like this one in seconds.

'Laskari, I need numbers,' she voxed. Giving the trooper something to focus on was the oldest trick in the book. It didn't matter what, anything to get her mind off how badly the situation was spiralling out of control. 'How many dead Scions, how many other walking dead, get me a count of the soldiers in the masks. Quick as you can.'

'Yes, lord castellan.'

She switched the bolt pistol to single shot and drew her sword. 'Rest of you, headshots where you can. If they still have helmets, shoot to disable instead. You'll need to take both legs.'

'Nineteen Scions, my lord.' Laskari sounded a little calmer. Her next shot seared through a rotting eye socket, and the poxwalker fell.

'At least two squads, then.' Argent was at Ursula's right hand, firing with reliable precision at first one target, then the next.

One of the undead lunged forward with an unexpected burst of speed. Ursula sidestepped, power sword crackling, and took its head from its shoulders in one easy swipe. Maybe the lack of ammunition wasn't going to be a problem after all.

'At least twenty other poxwalkers.' Laskari's voice was still shaking, but her aim was improving. 'The soldiers keep moving. It's hard to keep count.'

'Good enough.'

Ahead, a pair of the masked soldiers were back to back, laying down complementary arcs of fire with form that would have been a credit to any drill abbot. Maybe Laskari was right. Maybe they were friendly. But if that were true, where had they come from?

Ursula triggered her helmet's laud-hailers. 'Unidentified combatants, this is Lord Castellan Ursula Creed. Identify yourselves or we will assume hostile intent.'

Another dead Scion lurched towards her with arms outstretched, one hand bare, the other still wearing an armoured gauntlet. She punched her powerblade through the centre of its ribcage and ripped it out through the shoulder before turning the blade to sever the head. A shape flashed in her peripheral vision. She turned to see Harapa, his combat knife slicing efficiently through rotting flesh as he danced between the clawing dead.

'You good, chief?' He flashed a brief grin.

'Never better, sergeant.' Another slash. Another dead horror. They had almost reached the other soldiers now, though if they had answered her laud-hail the reply had been lost in the melee.

'At least they're not firing at us,' Argent voxed. He sounded breathless, the note of panic back in his voice. She had been right. He was out of practice, out of condition. She should never have agreed to bring him. Too late now.

'Unidentified combatants, this is your final warning,' she voxed.

Still no answer.

'We're surrounded by poxwalkers, lord castellan.' Van Haast seemed barely concerned by the fact, his sabre flicking out with contemptuous ease to dispatch one rotting enemy after another. 'Not that they pose much of a challenge individually, but I'm given to understand that' – another flick of the wrist – 'weight of numbers is usually the problem in this sort of situation.'

'Fine. They've had their chance.' Ursula calculated the distance between their position and the masked soldiers. 'Horde's thinnest at ten o'clock. Don't target the soldiers, but at the first sign of trouble...' She paused to cleave a poxwalker's skull from crown to jaw, its brain so desiccated that it crumbled to dust at the touch of the blade. 'Don't hesitate to take them down.'

They moved forward, and the horde pressed in thicker on all sides. Half of the dead Scions were in the dirt where they belonged, but the rest were still scattered amongst the older poxwalkers, their dull-eyed helmets almost more unsettling than the dead faces around them. The ranks of the dead were changing, too. While the first waves had been nothing but bone and sinew, those behind were stronger and faster, their bodies thickly corded with muscle and sprouting new growths: horns, talons, extra mouths. Some of them were carrying clubs and knives, others wielded rusty bayonets strapped to ancient autoguns. None of the weapons were likely to breach her armour, but a lucky stab could easily penetrate the Guard flak the others were wearing. Her armour was more robust, but it contributed a different problem to the equation: when its power supply failed, it would become a very ornate, custom-fitted sarcophagus.

The smoke was getting thicker, flames licking from tree to tree. With a wet crackle, first one trunk and then its neighbour exploded in a gush of spores that hung in the air, glistening and green.

'Fix respirators!' Ursula closed her helmet vents and checked her seals: intact. Another tree erupted, sending emerald motes dancing upward in the scalding air. 'If you haven't got one, stay as clear as you can, we'll get out of the trees as–'

'Yager's dead,' Ossian voxed from somewhere. 'I saw her dragged down by the horde.'

'My condolences.' Van Haast didn't sound sorry at all. 'We'll leave the conversation about how you got a vox-bead for later, shall we?'

'Stop bickering, damn you!' The warning rune was flickering in the corner of her vision again in a rapid, infuriating pulse of light. The armour had under an hour's use left and the bolt pistol barely enough ammunition for a single decent burst of fire. 'We have better things to do than–'

She stopped. The tide of corpses parted like a sea, and the vast, antlered figure of the Heretic Astartes stepped between them, green eyes glowing beneath the raised visor of its helm. Las-bolts spattered off its armour, scorching the surface but having no effect on the pitted ceramite beneath. The abomination drew back its scythe and sickly purple lightning crackled down the blade, its edge running with yellow pus.

'Fall back!' Ursula voxed.

No time to think, only time to act – and maybe not enough time for that. She stepped forward and unleashed the bolt pistol's final volley, the explosive shells raising craters in the grey-green armour. The Heretic Astartes didn't slow, striding through the barrage of explosive rounds as if they didn't exist, bringing the scythe down in a great reaping arc. She brought up her power sword to parry, then at the last possible instant changed the angle of her blade to turn the scythe instead of meeting its unstoppable force head-on. The power field raised a shower of sparks on the scythe's tarnished metal haft, and the blade missed her head by inches. Purple lightning arced from the scythe down her right arm and across her armour, the heat impossibly intense despite the layers of protection covering her. Her visor display lit up in red, the machine-spirit expending the last of its energy to issue its final, desperate warning.

*Power reserves exhausted. System failure imminent. Vents opening in three seconds…*

'Creed's daughter,' the heretic said. 'Come to claim your birthright?'

Ursula tried to bring up her sword, but the joints of her armour were locked rigid, all systems unresponsive. She was going to die, she thought, and felt almost calm. If it was time to die she would meet her fate with open eyes, but what she wasn't willing to do was die without a fight. There were pistols on her belt, and a grenade. If she could get a hand to one of them then she could still strike at it, still go down spitting in the heretic's face. The dead armour resisted her with all its force, but her hand was moving, one impossible inch at a time.

'To hell with my birthright.'

The armour's vents opened, flooding her mouth with the taste of rotting meat. Bile welled up in her throat, and she forced herself to swallow it down. Her hand was so close to the grenade that her fingertips were almost touching it.

*All I need is one more second…*

The thing threw back its head and laughed, the sound full-bodied and loathsome, a carrion-bird's screech mixed with the buzz of a thousand corpse-flies. Her index finger touched the grenade.

'Perhaps you do not desire your father's legacy,' it said. 'But I do.'

The scythe came down.

# XXVII

## THE SILVER DOOR

Ossian was watching at the precise moment the scythe hit the lord castellan. The force of the blow was tremendous, sending her armoured body flying thirty feet through the air into the gnarled trunk of an ancient tree and smashing it to splinters. The bolt pistol flew free from her hand and landed separately, vanishing into a thicket of writhing thorns.

'Lord castellan?' Major Argent's voice cut over the vox, sharp-edged and urgent. 'Are you hearing me?'

The gilded figure lay motionless.

'Colonel, your orders?' Harapa was already moving forward. 'I've got a clear line of sight, I can get her out of there.'

The young trooper with the long-las – another one young enough to be his granddaughter – was shooting too quickly, though the horde was dense enough that her shots were still finding their mark. There was a conspicuous silence from Van Haast. A fresh wave of unease clenched its hand around Ossian's gut. If the lord castellan was dead, that would leave the Hussar colonel in charge, and at that point Ossian's life expectancy would drop off a sharp cliff.

A series of explosions ripped through the forest, and the Heretic Astartes vanished behind a wall of smoke and debris. Ossian spared a glance to look for their source, and saw one of the soldiers in hostile-environment gear ducking back out of sight. He was under no illusions that the grenades would stop the monstrous abomination, but it might be enough to slow him down.

Ossian looked over at the big Catachan and raised a hand. 'I'm with you. That armour's heavy. You might need a hand.'

A brisk nod, even though the Catachan looked like he was easily capable of dragging the lord castellan's body on his own. 'Sure thing. We grab her and run, got it?' He removed his hand from his lasgun just long enough to tap the bandolier of grenades over his chest. 'Couple of these'll clear us some space. Laskari, you cover us, got it?'

'Got it, sarge.'

The ground was treacherous underfoot, branches and roots catching at Ossian's ankles as he fought to keep pace with the bigger man. The smoke around the Space Marine was clearing, the huge mould-green figure moving forward with slow, heavy footsteps, as if it had all the time in the world. The lord castellan was trying to rise, her gauntlets already tossed to the ground, bare hands at the locked joints of her armour. There was a huge dent in the chestplate of her suit where the scythe had struck her under her right arm, deep enough to promise broken ribs if not major internal injuries.

Ossian stuck close to the Catachan's heels, picking off the occasional poxwalker that lurched out of reach of the flashing combat knife. Why didn't the damned thing shoot? One blast of its oversized gun would wipe them out, but instead it was holding the scythe two-handed, weighing it with a thoughtful, almost playful air.

Another grenade tore the air in half. This time the explosion had its epicentre a little to the Space Marine's right, shredding the trunk of a monstrous tree to splinters of green wood. The tree's crown of branches slipped sideways, then, with an unpleasantly human shriek, thudded into the ground in front of the heretic, obscuring him entirely.

'Quickly!' Harapa shouted. The Catachan was already on the lord castellan, grabbing one of her arms and dragging her upwards. Her voice came from below her visor, muffled and thick with pain.

'Armour's dead. Shorted out.' The knowledge that she was alive and conscious should have come as a relief, but with the abomination already tearing its way through the tree's remains, and the horde closing in on all sides, it was quite possible that all he and Harapa had achieved was increasing the body count from one to three. He grabbed the lord castellan's other shoulder, the rolled edge of her pauldron smooth and cool beneath his bare hands. From what he'd seen of her unarmoured, the lord castellan herself wasn't a slight woman, but the armour had to be easily tripling her weight.

'If you can't get me out of the armour, you're going to leave me. Understand?' She coughed, an ugly wet rattle that she followed with a muffled curse.

'Struggling to hear you there, chief.' Even the unflappable Sergeant Harapa was starting to sound strained. 'Legionnaire, take the weight a minute.'

'What?' Ossian looked up sharply as the full mass of the lord castellan came down on his arms and almost took him to the ground with it. The Catachan was already moving, his motions quick and purposeful as he pulled a grenade from his bandolier, primed it, and threw it into the densely packed horde.

'Frag grenade!' The earth exploded, scattering body parts in all directions, and Harapa let out a whoop of delight. 'Few more of those'll see us clear!'

Lightning pierced the air. When Ossian opened his eyes, the Heretic Astartes had closed the distance to a half of what it had been before. It moved the scythe to its left hand, and pointed with its right, squarely at the centre of Harapa's chest. For a moment the Catachan stood stock-still, then he shrugged out of his bandolier at breathtaking speed, hurling it overarm into the tangle of thornbushes to their left.

'What the frekk…?'

Harapa was shaking, his eyes two wide white circles, a sheen of sweat on his top lip. 'It was… I saw…' He swallowed. 'They were serpents.'

'Sorcery.' Ossian heaved the lord castellan another step. 'Give me a hand with this.'

'Throne damn it.' Harapa put his weight behind the armour again and heaved. The gilded heels of the sabatons caught every thorn, vine and root of the undergrowth. 'Could have used those frekking grenades right now.'

Ossian risked a look behind him. The rest of the unit were closer than he had thought, pushed together by an ever-growing circle of poxwalkers. The Heretic Astartes had stepped back again, watching the scene from behind its featureless helmet, smoke billowing through its robes in a malign cloud.

'Go. Leave me and go.' The lord castellan's voice was tight with pain, but her tone was resolute. 'Find the bunker – that's your best chance.'

'Hate to interrupt, chief, but we're surrounded. Couldn't leave you even if we wanted to.'

Strahl had been right, Ossian thought. All these years Cadia had cast its shadow over them, waiting for them to return so it could claim its own. There were probably worse places in the Imperium to die, but he couldn't think of any right now.

'Blessed Emperor.' Laskari's voice was shaking. 'In my hour of death, call to me and bid me come.'

A barrage of las-bolts ripped through the air, punching through the massed ranks of poxwalkers. Vivid crimson after-images danced in front of Ossian's eyes, while shadowy figures materialised from between the trees, light glinting from the oversized eye-shields of their respirator-masks.

One of the masked soldiers raised a grenade launcher and unleashed a volley into the horde of the undead. A grenade struck the undergrowth where Harapa had tossed his bandolier, and the forest erupted in a chain reaction of explosions.

The barrage ended, and slowly the air cleared, revealing a hellscape of jagged tree stumps and twitching, severed limbs. Of the Heretic Astartes, there was no sign.

One of the masked figures stepped forward.

'Lord castellan.' Their voice was muffled by the hostile-environment mask, but the accent was unmistakably Cadian. 'Captain Ari Tethys of the Twelfth Cadian Sappers. My apologies for the delay. We had to be certain you could be trusted before we could intervene.'

An awkward silence fell.

'My lord?' Laskari said at last, her voice hesitant. 'What do we do?'

There was a strangled laugh from inside the helmet, followed by a painful burst of coughing.

'You could start by getting me out of this frekking armour.'

# XXVIII

## TEMPTATION

When Ursula remembered it afterwards, the journey out of the forest passed in a haze of pain. Sometime in the immediate aftermath of the fight, expert hands had removed her useless armour one piece at a time, but Ossian had insisted that the breast and backplates remained in position over her bodyglove, motivated, she was fairly sure, by the suspicion that it might be all that was holding her together. She had protested at first, frustrated by his intrusive concern, but when she tried to stand unsupported, black stars swam in front of her eyes and an invisible knife stabbed between her ribs with every breath she took. After that she had focused on staying upright, albeit with most of her weight on Sergeant Harapa's shoulders. She'd led them into that particular battle, and she'd be damned if she'd let them carry her out of it.

Time blurred around the edges. The light changed from the bioluminescent green of the forest to a colder, sharper light as they left the trees, heading towards a pair of huge cylindrical structures made of metal girders that sat in the shadow of the Rossvars. They were easily fifty yards high and twice that in diameter, the kind that had been used to store liquid promethium before the planet's every resource had been devoured by war. A circular metal hatch set into the side led into a tunnel with cool plascrete walls, and then they were descending through a warren of passageways that went on for miles, interspersed with heavy bulkhead doors that put her in mind of the ones on a voidship.

Her pride had been buckling under the pain by the time Tethys called a halt, and she leaned against the wall, giddy with relief.

'Welcome to New Gallan, lord castellan.' Tethys still hadn't removed their mask.

They were standing in a roughly hewn stone cavern, a heavy adamantine door sealing them off from the access tunnels they had used. Lumen cylinders bolted to the walls with heavy wrought-iron brackets provided a brilliant white light that hurt to look at. Everything was clean and crisp, and after the horrors of the surface, blessedly normal.

'My thanks for your assistance,' Ursula said. The pain that shot through her with every breath was making it hard to concentrate, but curiosity was enough to keep her on her feet. 'How long have you been here?' She wanted so much to believe that they were survivors of the time before, but there were other possibilities – survivors of a previous attempt to return to Cadia, or escorts for the *Oriflamme*'s explorers left behind during a hasty evacuation.

There was a long silence before Tethys spoke. 'Since the Fall, my lord.'

Tethys removed their respirator, revealing a hairless scalp and a triangular vox-grille that covered their lower face from the bridge of the nose to the jawline, held in place with straps gouged in so tight that the blanched skin had grown around them. Two deep-set violet eyes gazed out from blanched white flesh, deeply scored with lines of age. Tethys wasn't the oldest-looking soldier Ursula had seen, but they were certainly the oldest one she'd seen in the field.

'We have been waiting all this time. For you.'

'Waiting for *me*?' The surprise was enough to set off another paroxysm of coughing. She steadied herself with an outstretched hand to the wall.

'This conversation needs to wait until the lord castellan has received chirurgical attention.' Ossian stepped in front of her, moving with effortless authority. 'I assume you have an infirmarium?'

'We do,' Tethys began. Ursula drew a sharp breath to register her objection in the strongest possible terms, but the inhalation sent a bolt of pain through her ribs sharp enough to buckle her at the knees.

'Excellent. Then the lord castellan will be ready to speak with you after I've dealt with her injuries.'

'My lord, I must protest–' Argent was already puffing himself up, leaping like a well-trained canid to her defence. She waved a hand. Ossian might be so far over the line it wouldn't have been visible even with an auspex, but the thought of a few minutes' peace and a decent analgesic was alluring to the point of being irresistible.

'No protest required, thank you. Captain Tethys, if what you say is true then I imagine you'll want a little time to prepare a report on the state of Cadia since the Fall.' It was wild improvisation, but it had the desired effect on Tethys, who saluted smartly.

'Of course, my lord.'

'Excellent. Then I shall accede to the chirurgeon's advice in the mean-time.'

She allowed herself to be guided into a small, spartan room with a bed, a chair, a desk and the same over-bright lighting as the tunnels, bracing herself against the pain.

Ossian was speaking as the door swung closed, leaving the pair of them alone inside. 'If you're going to blow my head off for gross insubordination, can we get that over with before I start? I prefer not to leave a job half-finished.'

'That would seem ungrateful, considering I owe you and Sergeant Harapa my life.'

The chirurgeon's mouth quirked in a half-smile, a fine spider web of lines crinkling around his bright violet eyes. 'All self-preservation, you understand. I was fairly sure if you were killed then Colonel Van Haast would take about a minute to get rid of me.'

'You're rapidly becoming a useful man to have around, Mister Ossian.' She lowered herself carefully to the edge of the bed, and began unfastening the side-locks that held the now woefully dented breastplate closed. 'Let's see how long we can keep that head on your shoulders, shall we?'

As soon as the words left her mouth she regretted them: both for the stupidity of the statement itself, and for the abruptness with which the smile vanished from the legionnaire's face. The joke was crass. Ossian wasn't her friend, her squad mate or anything like it. He was a convict under sentence of death, and that wasn't going to change even if they both managed to survive this mess.

He raised an eyebrow, but said nothing. Taking a seat beside her, he moved her hands aside and unfastened the armour. As he lifted it free her lower ribs grated together, and she struggled to hold back a yelp of pain, turning it into a strangled hiss instead.

He unfastened her bodyglove at the waist and rolled the close-fitting cloth upwards, exposing the skin over her right flank and ribs. The broken ends of bone moved painfully under his fingertips, and on reflex she brought up her hand to catch his wrist before he could probe more deeply.

'Enough.'

He turned away to lift a bottle of morpholox from his pack, holding it up for her approval. 'A small dose will take the edge off the pain. I'm making the assumption that you want to stay clear-headed for what's ahead, but I'm open to correction. Assuming you trust me to deliver it.'

She pushed her hair to one side, exposing her neck. The drug deployed with a sting and an audible hiss, and instantly she felt her muscles relax, a pleasing languor spreading through her limbs. Her pulverised ribs still ached like she'd been run over by a Rhino, but she found she no longer particularly cared.

'Better?' Ossian asked.

She nodded. In some dispassionate part of her brain, she wondered what the hell she was doing, letting a disgraced chirurgeon from the penal legion medicate and examine her without the supervision of the rest of her squad. It came down to two things: one, that she had no particular desire for the rest of them to see her exposed and vulnerable, and two, that despite everything, she trusted the man. Ridiculous, really, given the circumstances and the brevity of their acquaintanceship, but her gut rarely served her wrong, and he had demonstrated practicality, compassion and a pleasing streak of bloody-mindedness that made him impossible to dislike. She leaned back against the wall and suffered the rest of his examination with stoic endurance, thinking of how bright the stars had looked from Guilliman's observatorium, and how far away they were now.

'You were lucky,' he said at last.

She looked down and inspected the injury for the first time. A livid weal the width of her forearm stretched horizontally across her right flank, a vivid purple-red bruise haloed around it from hip to armpit, the skin torn along its length where it had been pinched beneath the dented metal of the breastplate. The morpholox would wear off soon enough, but for now she could treat it as a curiosity instead of a painful inconvenience.

'Lucky?'

He nodded. 'Three broken ribs. From the blood on your teeth I'm guessing a lung contusion as well, but without proper facilities it's impossible to tell how bad. If not for your armour, I expect that blow would have cut you in half. Even breaking the skin with that scythe should have been a death sentence.'

She thought back to the hellish forest, to the towering figure of the Heretic Astartes, the scythe blade dripping bitter yellow pus, and shuddered.

'And what would be your recommendation for treatment?' she asked.

He shrugged. 'With proper facilities, surgical fixation. With time, rest and analgesics until the bone-ends fuse.'

'And with neither?'

'Precious little. The cut's too shallow to stitch. A layer of synthskin to cover it, and strapping for the fractures should help. I would tell you to avoid vigorous activity for four to six weeks, but I think we both know how successful that would be.'

'Do what you can, then.' She turned her face away, and winced as the aerosolised sealant hit the wound on her side. Ossian's hands were deft and quick as he applied the adhesive bindings to her broken ribs, and she felt a wash of gratitude for his care. How long had it been since she had felt the touch of a hand in anything but anger?

Before she could thank him he rose, dropped the empty spray back into his kitbag and opened the door.

'I'll have them bring you some fresh clothes.'

The door closed again, leaving the memory of his touch – warm, dry and skilful, so entirely at odds with the crude tattoo etched across his forehead – lingering on her skin long after he had left the room.

Laskari slung her kitbag on the ground and sat on it, laid her long-las across her knees and began the ritual of cleansing. The process was calming, as though the litanies were designed to soothe her own restless spirit every bit as much as the firearm's.

'Are you a tech-priest?'

The voice belonged to one of Tethys' soldiers. She couldn't have been more than thirteen or fourteen, her head shaven and her skin with the same deathly grey pallor as her commanding officer. Laskari blurted out a laugh before she could stop herself.

'Throne, no. Speaking the litanies, that's all. I'm not even a lay preacher.' She pointed at Harapa, who had the base's antiquated vox-system gutted on a workbench on the far side of the little cavern. 'The sarge is probably the closest we have, but he's not ordained.'

The girl nodded thoughtfully. 'We had a tech-priest once. Captain Tethys says we got lazy with the litanies since she died.' She shrugged. 'Doesn't seem to make much difference to how the guns shoot, if you ask me.'

Laskari blinked, startled by the casual blasphemy. 'The last thing you need is an angry machine-spirit in your weapon.'

'That sounds convincing, but I'm yet to see the difference.' Her eyes – dark purple, one shade short of black – met Laskari's with a challenge. 'It's a good job you're *not* a priest. If you were, you'd probably have me burned alive for heresy.'

Laskari turned her attention back to her litanies. 'Fortunately that's all above my stipend-grade.'

That got a laugh. 'Mine too.' The girl wiped a hand on her fatigues and offered it to Laskari to shake. 'Amyt Meraq.'

Laskari put down her long-las and took the offered hand. 'Shael Laskari.'

'I like your long-las. I can't shoot straight to save my life.' Meraq's hand tapped on the hilt of the combat knife on her belt. 'Decent with this though.'

'Was there something you wanted?' Laskari said, and was startled by her own rudeness.

Meraq pulled an apologetic face. 'Sorry. I don't mean to be a nuisance.' She shifted her weight from one foot to the other. 'I just… It's the first time I've ever met anyone from' – she gestured vaguely around herself – 'outside.'

'What do you mean?'

'I mean outside. Anywhere that's not here. I've met about forty people in my entire life. Unless you count the walking dead and cultists, which I don't.'

It was almost unbelievable. In the barracks on Shukret-Dhruv, Laskari had shared a bunkroom with thirty-nine other White-shields. She tried to imagine what it would be like to have never known anyone other than her fellow recruits – no parents or sister, no sprawling multigenerational family crammed together under a single roof. No wonder Meraq was jumping at the chance to talk to someone new.

'That must have been very difficult for you.'

'I don't know, it was easy enough until I knew there was an alternative.' Meraq threw her hands wide. 'I'm second generation. The captain and a couple of the sergeants are all that's left of the original soldiers left behind. Most of the others were orphans, the ones left behind in the evacuation. They remember *before*, a little. And then some of us were born *after*.' Meraq flashed a quick, nervous smile. 'Not as many as you'd think, though. We've got enough contraceptives in stores to last a whole army a couple of hundred years. Zhata, my half-sister, she says they only started breeding when they realised it might take more than one generation before anyone came.'

Laskari shook her head, drowning in the torrent of words. 'Slow down. Before anyone came for what?'

'For us. And what Lord Castellan Creed left here with us.' Meraq spoke the name as though she were speaking of an Imperial saint, her hands making the aquila across her chest. 'Is she really his daughter? The big woman, I mean?'

'I think so.'

'Amazing. I bet she's just like him. I've seen picts, the old recruiting posters. "Cadia Needs You."'

'I'm sorry.' Laskari got to her feet and propped her long-las carefully down against the wall. 'This is a lot to take in all at once. We weren't expecting to find anyone here at all.'

'You weren't?' Meraq's mouth dropped open with surprise. 'I thought you were here to take us away.'

It was Argent who opened the infirmarium door a few minutes after Ossian had left, a fresh set of fatigues tucked under one arm, a mug of recaff in his hand and her sword and laspistols hanging from a belt looped over his shoulder.

'The God-Emperor has blessed us with a miracle.' She accepted the mug, swigged down a mouthful so hot that it burned the back of her mouth, then took another. After two days of abstinence, the taste was sublime, the stimulant dancing through her synapses like captive lightning.

Argent turned his back, and she exchanged her sweat-soaked bodyglove for a fresh shirt and combat-trousers. 'How is everyone else?' She wrapped the belt around her waist and settled the weapons into position on her hip, the weight an instant comfort.

'They're fine. And Captain Tethys is waiting for you, when you're ready.'

She swigged down the last of the recaff and instantly wanted more. 'No time like the present.'

They walked through the door, down the passageway back to the chamber with the heavy door through which they had entered the complex. Tunnels led in all directions, the widest of which was guarded by a pair of soldiers in the same hostile-environment gear. Both saluted crisply as she approached.

'Where can I find Captain Tethys?' she asked.

'The captain is waiting for you, my lord.' The soldier on the left turned smartly on his heel. 'Please, follow me.'

Tethys was waiting in another small room, equipped with furniture in a passable imitation of a base-commander's office from a few decades ago. Simple metal chairs sat to either side of a broad steel desk, a rusty autoquill to one side and a small pile of ancient hidebound volumes pushed to the corner. Tethys sprang to their feet as the door opened, standing stiffly to attention as Ursula and her adjutant walked in.

'Lord castellan. It is my honour to welcome you here.'

Ursula considered sitting, but the chair looked considerably less comfortable than staying on her feet. Instead she folded her arms over her aching ribs and leaned back against the wall.

'Well, captain. You may as well start the stubber firing. What do I need to know about this place, and your soldiers?'

'As you command, my lord.' Tethys' voice came through the vox-grille in a tinny buzz. 'I had the privilege to serve with your father during the Fall of Cadia. Before he left for the Elysian Fields he charged my sappers – the Mole Rats – to hold this bunker and its contents against all enemies until such time as he or his successor returned to claim it. I am honoured to say I have done so.'

Ursula watched the officer's face carefully. The vox-grille made their expression difficult to read, but pride was shining from the sunken eyes as clearly as if a lamp had been lit inside their skull. She felt a momentary stab of guilt. This moment was the culmination of a life's work for Tethys, and here she was letting it pass without ceremony.

'A tremendous achievement. My congratulations, and my thanks for your faithful endeavours. We were sent here by...' She paused. Mentioning the lord regent would no doubt take them down another avenue of questions and answers, one that could wait until she had had a meal and a few unbroken hours of sleep. 'By high command to recover Lord Castellan Creed's final plans for Cadia. The weapons he intended to use against the enemy but never had the chance. We'll also need access to your vox-equipment in order to contact our ship in orbit and arrange retrieval.'

'All that we have is at your disposal, lord castellan.' Tethys shook their head. 'But I regret that much of our equipment has ceased to function over the years, vox-casters included.'

'That wasn't you, then?' Argent shot the captain a quizzical look. 'Those broadcasts. The music? The last speeches of Lord Castellan Creed?'

'No, major.' A frown wrinkled Tethys' brow. 'I would counsel caution. Cadia is not as it was. Malign forces hold domain here. Corruption is in the very air.'

'Do you know what the contents of the bunker are?'

'No, lord castellan. Your father's orders were explicit. It was to remain undisturbed.'

'And you never doubted someone would return for it?'

'No, lord. Never.'

'Remarkable.'

A flicker of excitement shot through her. What weapons from the world before were held beneath the mine? Fighting their way across Cadia would be a less daunting proposition with some heavy ordnance in hand. There might be vehicles, broadcast equipment, any number of hoarded treasures. It must have taken a supreme effort of will for Tethys not to investigate and put its contents to use in all the long years of their exile.

'I see why my predecessor entrusted you with this.'

Tethys stood even straighter. 'I am proud to serve, lord castellan.'

Ursula's excitement faded. The captain's blind obedience was yet another example of the sheer servility that her father managed to instil in everyone he met; the sort of mindless loyalty that led soldiers to spend their lives in pursuit of a cause long after the war was lost.

'We saw some of your people yesterday. An execution, in the woods.'

'Yes, lord. We spend our lives in duty, but our faith is not strong enough for our bodies to withstand this place forever. Prolonged exposure to the environment has corrupting effects. We serve as long as we can, as long as our bodies and minds are securely under our own control, and when that is no longer the case, we give Cadia our deaths as we have given our lives.' Tethys spoke as though they were giving a sermon, as though the words had been spoken a hundred times before.

'And the burning?'

'We do not wish to see our dead returned to us in service to the enemy.' Tethys moved towards the door, clearly uncomfortable with the direction the conversation had taken. 'With your permission, lord castellan, I will go and make sure your father's inner sanctum is ready for you. You must be eager to see inside.'

'Very kind of you, captain.' Argent stepped smoothly in before she had a chance to speak. 'And perhaps you could arrange for a suit of armour and another flask of recaff for the lord castellan.'

She waited until Tethys had gone before kicking the door shut and glaring at Argent. 'Is that really the priority right now?'

'You can't tell me more recaff wouldn't be welcome. And you're looking thoroughly under-equipped.'

She snorted. 'Stupid idea, that power armour. I should have insisted on a suit of carapace. Something that doesn't come with a power pack.'

'I imagine there'll be something here to fit you. There should be enough for a whole damned army down here, if your father's other caches are anything to go by.'

'If he had put them to use fighting rather than holding them in endless reserve then things might have gone differently.' She rolled her eyes. 'Isaiah Bendikt used to go on for hours about that bloody mountain stronghold, the one where he spent half the war. A whole army sitting on its hands for months when they could have been out there actually making a difference.' She stopped. 'Anyway. That's not important.'

'No?'

'No.' She let her gaze settle on the great hollowed-out cavern below. 'Tethys and their soldiers are far more interesting. Living here all these years, generations of them. Following a dead man's orders, waiting here for... for what?'

'For you, I suppose.'

She glared at him. 'And you're trying to tell me that Creed saw this coming, did he? Guilliman sending me here? Adding prophecy to all those other gifts of his, are we?'

'I don't know, Ursula.' Argent sat down in one of the uncomfortable-looking chairs, and ran a hand through his sandy hair. There was more grey in it than she remembered. He was starting to look middle-aged, the ghost of the old man he would someday be shining through his skin like a skull. When had that happened? That thought brought a pang of regret with it. She was being selfish. She wasn't the only one exhausted by the last few days. Fighting like this, with everything up close and personal, was a young soldier's game. That description didn't fit either of them any more.

'He must have meant to return,' she said. 'After the Delvian Cleave. Before the Elysian Fields. Whatever he left down there…'

'Whatever he left down there,' Argent said into the silence that followed, 'must have been something he thought would turn the tide of the war. Something he was saving until the very end.'

# XXIX

## THE HUNTSMAN

After he had finished strapping up the lord castellan's broken ribs, Ossian had found himself walking aimlessly around the corridors of the sub-terranean base. Eventually a soldier had taken pity on him, and guided him to the chamber where the others were waiting. Laskari was in conversation with a soldier who looked even younger than she did, while Colonel Van Haast was lounging with a book, freshly shaven and in a clean uniform looking as though he had just gone for a stroll in a Volpone pleasure garden. He opted to sit with Harapa instead, who looked the least likely to mind his company.

Harapa looked up from the disassembled vox-unit, and motioned to Ossian to sit down. 'You any good with this stuff?' Harapa asked.

Ossian shook his head. 'I'm better with organic components, if I'm honest with you.'

'Pity.' The big sergeant turned his attention back to the ancient vox-caster, its contents lying exposed like a half-dissected corpse. 'Could have used someone who knows what they're doing.'

'You seem to be making a decent stab at it.'

Harapa pinched one long, red wire between thumb and fore-finger, and attempted to connect it to something inside the casing. 'Shows how much you know. I'm making this up as I go along. Still, I know enough to know that we're not going to get a decent broadcast out through those rocks overhead, but maybe if I get it working we can take it outs–'

There was a bang and a bright flash of light. Harapa cursed, shook the fingers of his right hand, then held them up for inspection. Two tiny circles were burned into the pads of his index finger and thumb, haloed in red.

'All right, all right.' He rolled his eyes. 'The machine-spirit doesn't want to be disturbed.'

'Is it fixable?'

'Might be.' Harapa touched his burned fingers to his tongue, then returned to the vox-caster. 'I'm not seeing a way off-world if it isn't. Don't know about you, but I'm not desperate keen to live out my days with this lot.'

'I can think of worse places to end up.'

'Guess so.' The wires sparked again, but this time Harapa kept his hands steady. 'How come you're here, then?'

'I was going to ask you the same.'

Harapa raised his eyebrows. 'You mean I don't look like a proper Cadian yet? And there I was, thinking I was doing well at fitting in.' He pointed one hand at an open toolbox on the far end of the desk. 'Pass those pliers, would you? Yeah. So the Munitorum comes sniffing around the regiments, asking for volunteers for a special mission. And you know what that means, right?'

'Do I?'

'Death worlds. It's always death worlds. When someone comes round the Catachan regiments looking for volunteers, you can guarantee it's because someone's decided they're going into the worst shitholes the galaxy has to offer, and they want someone to keep their arse out of the fire as long as possible. And it's made clear that if someone doesn't step up, they're just going to start choosing at random. And I put a lot of work into my squad. I figured either I watch one of them get sent to certain death on their own, or I go instead.' Harapa spoke completely without sentimentality, a simple, factual statement of events. 'Taking a while to feel welcome, if I'm honest.'

'I would have thought they'd be glad of your expertise.'

'Mm.' Harapa sounded unconvinced. 'Transplants. That's what they're calling us. You'll know better than I do, but as I understand it, what defines a transplant is that it gets rejected.' He shrugged. 'Anyway. It's not like I had a choice. What about you?'

'Turns out when the penal legions decide to send you some place, you don't get a choice either.' Ossian unpacked the medkit from his kitbag, and laid the instruments out on the workbench. Might as well take inventory of what they had left.

'Not exactly what I meant. How did you end up in the legions in the first place?'

'I shot my commanding officer.' Ossian kept his eyes on the medkit. He was out of nocio-blockers and the counterbiotics were running low. 'Apparently they take a dim view of that.'

'Can't say I've never been tempted.' Harapa sat back, scanning the rewired vox-system critically. 'Never done it though. Don't fancy a bomb collar much. Why'd you let them put it on you?'

An unexpected blurt of laughter forced itself from Ossian's mouth. 'Like I said, I wasn't presented with much of a choice.'

'Sure you were. Even if they were running low on bullets they'd have hanged you if you asked. All I'm saying is there are easier ways out than the penal legions, that's all.'

'Why does anyone choose the legions? I didn't want to die.' Ossian rubbed a hand across the stubble on his chin. 'It seemed pointless. And my soul isn't ready for the Golden Throne.'

'You were a chirurgeon, right? If the God-Emperor's keeping score, you're probably still ahead on lives saved against lives taken. Wouldn't be too worried about the state of your soul if I were you.'

'It's not…' Ossian stopped. The conversation was dredging up memories he preferred to keep buried. The flames. The screaming. The things he had done when first the morpholox ran out, and then the ammunition. Now wasn't the time to dredge that particular swamp. 'It doesn't matter.'

'Your call.' Harapa connected a final pair of wires. 'Flip that switch for me, would you?'

Ossian clicked the little brass level. Something imploded inside the vox-unit, and the air filled with the smell of burning circuitry.

'Frekk it,' Harapa said. 'This isn't sending any messages any time soon.'

'What's it like?' Meraq asked. 'Serving under the lord castellan?'

'I don't know.' Laskari finished stripping and reassembling her long-las, and turned her attention to the rest of her kit, unfolding her spare clothes and checking them for damp. The laser targeter sat at the bottom of the bag, eight pounds of useless metal and reinforced glass. 'No, I mean, it's an honour.'

'I bet. All those stories about the great Lord Castellan Creed, and you're getting to serve with his daughter. One of her own personal squad. All the Cadians in the galaxy, and you got picked. That must feel good.'

'I suppose so.'

'Is she like him? Lord Castellan Creed, I mean. I've read everything we have of his, all the tactics and strategies. Captain Tethys is always saying that Creed's defeats were still better than anyone else's victories.'

Laskari looked up from her kitbag, trying to think of what to say and how to say it. 'I don't know. She's different to what I expected. I suppose I was expecting a hero, someone who'd be… more inspiring.' She shook her head. 'I don't know. I've only been in the squad for…' She thought back. 'Two days.' It seemed simultaneously like no time at all, and much, much longer.

'She must have picked you for a reason.'

Laskari shook her head. 'I don't think it was a good reason. The whole thing's been a bit of a disaster from the start.'

Meraq pulled a face. 'It has?'

'In a way.' Laskari dropped her gaze back to her feet. 'We were ambushed just after we landed. We took heavy casualties. The Valkyrie sent to retrieve us got shot down. And I… There was a friendly fire incident. I… ah… I killed an ogryn.'

'An ogryn? Nice shooting.'

Laskari nodded miserably. 'Except she was one of ours. She was a penal legionnaire. She came running out of the trees and I thought…'

'What did the lord castellan have to say about it?'

'Not much.' Laskari tried to swallow down her shame. 'If I'm honest, I don't even think she was surprised. I'm only here because they wanted a New Cadian for the propaganda picts.'

'Honestly?' Meraq shook her head, as if she couldn't quite believe what she was hearing. 'You've travelled off-world, through the void – the warp, even – and *that's* what's bothering you? I'd give my right arm for all that.' Her purple eyes were glittering. 'Other worlds. Fighting xenos, not just endless poxwalkers. Have you ever seen a Space Marine? A loyal one, I mean.'

'I'd never even been in a battle until yesterday. Life in the Guard hasn't been all that exciting, at least not so far.'

From Meraq's expression, it was clear she didn't believe Laskari for a second. 'Well, then I'll look forward to being bored out of my mind anywhere but here once we're off-world.'

The armoury door opened. Standing there was another one of the sappers, her respirator in one hand and her lasgun on a strap over her shoulder. A grey-and-black canid was at her heels, staring past her knees with intelligent amber eyes. The soldier looked only a few years older than Meraq, but the right side of her face was mottled with an uneven growth of scarlet pustules. Her gaze fell on Laskari, and she turned her blemished cheek away.

'Amyt, get your gear. You're needed upstairs.'

'Poxwalkers again?'

The soldier gave Meraq a withering look. 'No, it's Goge Vandire. *Obviously* it's poxwalkers.'

'They get close sometimes,' Meraq explained. 'If there are too many of them they make noise, draw others in. No one wants a horde nearby. That's the sort of thing that makes the Huntsman take notice.'

'The Huntsman?' A chill ran down Laskari's spine.

'The Heretic Astartes. With the horn.'

'You've seen it?'

Meraq nodded. 'It's been here for as long as anyone can remember. We have to be careful it doesn't follow us back. If it found us here, everything would be over.'

'I saw you,' Laskari said, turning to the newcomer. 'In the woods. Your canid, anyway, and some other people.'

'Last rites,' the soldier said briskly. 'Meraq, you're needed. Come on.'

Meraq got to her feet. 'You should come too, with Zhata and

me. You can bring your long-las. We can always use another good shot on the parapet.'

Laskari cast a quick look around the armoury. Harapa and the penal legionnaire were sitting in quiet conversation, their attempts at fixing the vox-equipment abandoned. The lord castellan had vanished with Captain Tethys not long after they had arrived, and Colonel Van Haast was immersed in a heavy leatherbound book of maps. Everything was quiet.

'Colonel?'

Van Haast looked up. 'Trooper.'

'Permission to assist our allies in defence of their home, sir?'

Van Haast regarded her thoughtfully, then nodded, his attention back on his book almost immediately. 'Granted.'

'Thank you, sir.'

Zhata led them back into the passageway and up a narrow stairway. The canid darted past her, claws clattering on stone. The paint on the walls had yellowed with time, the flaking remains of a series of large numbers marking off each floor as they passed.

'Ventilation chimneys cut into the rock,' Meraq explained. 'The whole place is full of tunnels. There are maps in the captain's office, but I don't need them. I know about twenty ways to get to the surface.'

'None of which you are supposed to use,' Zhata said.

'They can't watch us all the time.' Meraq grinned. Her teeth were remarkably white for someone who'd lived her entire life without the benefit of dental care. 'There were plans for this place, you know. It would have been a fortress city in its own right, protected from the Eye of Terror by the mountains.'

The muscles of Laskari's legs were burning, her breath coming quickly as she hurried to keep up. 'How many more stairs are there?'

'Keep climbing!' Meraq called cheerfully, and Laskari gritted her teeth and committed herself wholly to the task of putting one foot in front of the other. The numbers stencilled on the walls rose steadily until she was sure that no building in all of Cadia could be so high – and then the light changed from the steady yellow glow of the lumen-rods to something harsh and grey, and a gust of sour-smelling wind buffeted her face.

Meraq took the last few steps at a run, stopping a split second before her momentum would have carried her directly into her sister's back. The stairway opened onto a tiny circular chamber with a waist-height stone parapet. The canid was already resting its forelegs on the edge, leaning its head into the wind with its mouth hanging open. Another freezing gust of wind blew shards of half-frozen rain into Laskari's face. She steadied herself with one hand against the stone wall and squinted out at the view unfolding below.

She was looking down a rocky mountainside, the whole expanse of Cadia unfurling before her. The miles they had travelled through the tunnels had taken them deep beneath the foothills of the Rossvars, and the endless staircase had taken them to a vantage point at the top of a cliff-face. There were the huge promethium containers, now no larger than a child's toy; beside them the unnatural forest that had seemed so dark and threatening when they had been in its midst, much diminished by distance.

Beyond it, Cadia Secundus stretched out like an ocean of steel and astrogranite: once proud kasrs reduced to rubble or warped beyond recognition, every inch of land a battlefield hard fought for and bitterly yielded. Misshapen figures flickered in and out of existence between the hulks of the great war machines, once majestic engines of destruction, now crippled and rusting in the ground. The wind made a high, keening wail as it blew through the crags, a ghostly voice mourning for the lost world.

A shrieking flock of huge scaled creatures wheeled through the air below them on leathery wings, their long toothed beaks snapping at each other as they flew. Somewhere in the distance, a vast explosion threw up a plume of fire and smoke.

'The land to the south is crawling with Heretic Astartes,' Meraq said, as if the concept of a fallen angel were something commonplace. 'Like the Huntsman. We think he was one of them once, before they cast him out, but who knows what goes on in the mind of something like that?'

'You shouldn't talk about them,' Zhata said, raising her lasgun and looking through the sights. 'Even *thinking* about them corrupts the soul.'

Meraq scoffed. 'They want dominion over what's left of Cadia. They're all fighting over it, all the time – the ones that look like the Huntsman, and all the others. The captain says there are even more of them laying siege to Kasr Arroch.' A shrug. 'No one goes there.'

'Why not?'

Zhata raised a finger to silence her sister. 'Kasr Arroch is a place of ill omen. Nothing good comes from there. Enough chatter, Meraq. *Look.*'

Laskari put her scope to her eye and followed the direction of Zhata's pointing finger. Something was moving between the forest and the promethium towers – a poxwalker, shambling jerkily across the open ground. She focused in on its face. Its one remaining eye was dangling from the socket on a shred of tissue.

'I have a clear shot. Shall I take it?'

'If you like,' Meraq said. 'But I think it's the rest of them she's worrying about.'

Laskari jerked her eye back from the scope. Tiny figures were lurching from the woods; she set her scope to a lower magnification and scanned the area. There were poxwalkers, dozens

of them, but interspersed between them were horrifying creatures so warped and twisted by the Ruinous Powers that they
no longer remotely resembled humans. Some had too many
limbs, while others had not enough. Naked two-headed beasts
with brightly coloured skin and mouths on their abdomens
loped forward, their twinned maws snapping at each other in
futile acts of self-destruction. One-eyed monstrosities draped
in rotting green skin walked with tiny green daemons capering
around their feet, while something holding what looked like a
bagpipe made of meat was dancing with frantic abandon to a
melody of its own, too far away for her to hear the tune.

But the horn was loud enough.

'He's here,' Meraq said. Her eyes were wide. 'And he's brought
an army.'

# XXX

## THE DAMNED

The Guard flak fit well enough, though there was a pervasive smell of damp to the armour that made Ursula think it had spent more than a few years in storage. Rockcrete walls gave way to roughly hewn stone as Tethys led them deeper beneath the mountains, as though the excavation of this part had been performed with greater speed than care. Wall-mounted lumens flickered into unsteady life at their approach, casting dancing shadows across the ground, the uneven walls, and the great adamantine doors at the end of the tunnel.

'Your father's inner sanctum, lord castellan,' Tethys said.

Ursula laid a hand on the cool metal, tracing the aquila etched on its surface with an outstretched fingertip. With a sound like a terminal breath, a panel in the doorframe slid back, revealing a red-eyed servo-skull, a horizontal rod and a steel control panel etched with glowing green runes.

'Primary genomic authorisation required,' the skull rasped

through a rusty circular vox-caster hanging below its upper teeth. The lower jaw was missing.

'It can't just be a gene-lock, can it?' She thought of the command baton on the *Wrath of Olympus*, the mental image accompanied by a vivid sense-memory of the lancet piercing the skin of her palm. 'If it is, why the runes? There must be something else to it.'

The sense of frustration that had been bubbling beneath her skin since she had left Tectora was rising again. Once again she was dancing to her father's tune, following the steps of some pointless riddle the old fool had left for her, exerting his control over her life from beyond the grave. 'Did he leave instructions with you?'

'No, my lord. He told me they were on his person. That he would leave them with his successor.'

She shook her head. 'He was killed on the Elysian Fields. His body was never recovered. Whatever he was carrying was lost with him.'

Ursula racked her brain, trying to think like the father she had never known. Her mind was blank. Had they really come all this way only to be turned back at a locked door?

'Can we break the damn thing down?'

Tethys shook their head. 'I would advise against the attempt, my lord. Your father was quite clear that any attempt to breach the inner sanctum would result in the destruction of its contents.'

She leant forward and rested her head against the cool metal of the doors.

'Primary genomic authorisation required,' the skull said again.

'What am I missing here?' She looked at Argent, and saw her own frustration mirrored in his face. 'What did Creed expect me to know?'

'Where's the lord castellan?'

Ossian looked up from the dismembered vox-caster to see

Trooper Laskari bursting into the chamber, flanked by two of Tethys' soldiers and their canid.

'Still off with Tethys and the major.' Harapa leaned forward in his chair. 'What is it?'

'There's a problem, sarge. Outside.' Laskari's top teeth raked at her lower lip. 'An army of hell spawn. Converging on our position.'

'How many are we talking?'

Laskari and the taller of the two troopers – the girl with the blistered face – exchanged a quick glance. 'Upwards of five hundred,' Laskari said. 'Meraq and Zhata took me up to one of the vantage points. You can see the whole valley from up there. Hundreds. Maybe more, and more joining them all the time. Some shambling up from the south, others... others coming out of the earth.'

'We heard its horn,' Meraq added.

'Did you see him?' Van Haast's book closed with a snap, and he rose to his feet.

Zhata shook her head. 'But that doesn't mean he isn't there.'

'Has this ever happened before?'

'No, sir. Only ever down on the plains or in the kasr. We knew that if they found this place everything would be lost.'

Harapa got to his feet and swept his equipment into his kitbag. 'Good work, kid. Colonel, I think the lord castellan's going to want to know about this.'

The vox-caster crackled, loud enough to startle everyone in the room.

'I thought...' Ossian said, then stopped. The 'caster was making a low, continuous hissing noise, a faint up-and-down whine just audible over the top. 'I thought you said that damn thing was beyond repair?'

Harapa's attention was back on the half-eviscerated machine. 'I certainly thought so.' He held up a small square object, a pair of disconnected wires trailing from one surface. 'Either way, it shouldn't be working with the power pack taken out.'

Someone was talking through the vox-caster, the words still too quiet to make out, but getting closer with every second. Louder, Ossian corrected himself, not closer, but the mental description still felt correct, as if something were approaching from a long distance. Something powerful.

'Bloody thing's back at its tricks,' Harapa said.

'*Hope*,' a faint voice said.

'That's Lord Castellan Creed again,' Laskari said, her voice full of wonder. 'Sergeant, you don't think that's really him, do you? That he's somehow–'

'Giving us orders from beyond the grave? Through the vox-system? No, trooper, I'm pretty sure the priests would have views on something like that.'

'There were miracles on Cadia.' A note of stubbornness had entered Laskari's voice. Her eyes were bright with fervour. 'The blessed Saint Celestine appeared, even when all hope seemed lost. The Angels of Death fought beside us–'

'*Us*, trooper?' Van Haast's voice was sharp. 'You must be considerably older than you look to have fought in Cadia's last defence.'

'Yes, sir, but the God-Emperor's eye was on Cadia, even as it fell. And we know... we know that those who were lost can rise again. The lord regent returned from the grave to lead the Imperium to victory. What if... What if Lord Castellan Creed has done the same?' Laskari's hands were shaking as she made the aquila across her chest. 'What if it's a miracle?'

Music cut across the static. 'Flower of Cadia' again, though this time the notes were subtly distorted, out of tune as though the melody were being played underwater and a long distance away. Hair prickled along the nape of Ossian's neck, though the air in the chamber was perfectly still.

'*Hope,*' the voice said again, as the music swelled and died, '*is the first step…*'

'You see, sarge?' Laskari said. 'He's telling us to keep the faith, not to give up!'

Except that wasn't what Creed had said. Ossian shook his head. 'Keep listening.'

'*…on the road to disappointment.*'

It took a moment for Laskari's face to fall. 'I don't understand. What's he trying to tell us–'

Another deafening burst of static blared through the vox-caster's speaker. This time, the voice was distorted, polyphonic, simultaneously the buzzing of a cloud of flies and the scream-ing of the damned.

'**Cadia is fallen. Creed is dead. All is lost.**'

Harapa drew his knife and punched it casually through the speaker. Silence fell.

'No miracles,' Harapa said. 'Anything we do here, we do on our own. Now. Didn't we have somewhere to be?'

'Primary genomic authorisation required.'

Ursula considered putting her fist through the skull's leering face. She turned away instead, her frustration bubbling over like a pot of over-brewed recaff. Being asked to solve a puzzle set by her father was aggravating enough, but being asked to solve a puzzle where all the pieces were missing was positively perverse.

'I need some time to think about this.' Maybe walking would help her thoughts fall into place. The gene-lock was one part of the access requirements. The other was something to be entered on the runic keys, but what? A date of birth? A service number? A musical phrase? What if Creed had set it up to allow only a limited number of attempts before destroying the vault's contents? The more she thought about that, the more likely it seemed.

Hurried footsteps echoed down the passageway, followed a moment later by Laskari, two of Tethys' troopers, and then at a more sedate pace Harapa and Ossian. Van Haast was in the rear, striding along with his spurs jingling.

'Lord castellan!' The young trooper was red-faced as she skidded to a halt.

'What is it, trooper?'

'A horde is on the approach. Poxwalkers. The damned. Neverborn of all kinds.'

'Collect yourself. Now, where are they?'

'Converging on the entryway below the old promethium tanks.' The older of Tethys' two troopers snapped a quick salute. 'Hundreds already, and the Huntsman with them.'

'How does one escape from this place?' Van Haast was immaculate, his uniform freshly pressed. How had he found a hot pressing iron in this of all places?

'We have several, colonel.'

'My recommendation would be to head north. Through the mountains if necessary, and head for Kasr Arroch. There are hot springs beneath the earth, and the majority of its power supply was geothermal. There may well be surviving infrastructure and equipment there which we can use to boost our beacon's signal.'

A shudder passed through the passage, shaking a snowfall of dust from the ceiling.

'Is this place prone to earthquakes, captain?'

'No, my lord.'

Ursula looked back at the double doors and the skull standing sentinel over its locking mechanism. They were running out of time.

'I'd advise we withdraw immediately,' Van Haast said.

Harapa nodded. 'If that abomination gets inside, things are going to get extremely messy in short order. I agree with the colonel. We can head towards the city. There's bound to be kit there, we can use it to make contact with the *Oriflamme*–'

'We're at the Throne-damned bunker,' Argent said sharply. 'You're seriously telling me you want us to move on when we're this close?'

'As an alternative to being consumed in the dark by hungry abominations?' Van Haast snapped back. 'Yes. I rather think I am. We can return another day. This place looks well-enough sealed. If high command want its contents that much, they can return with excavators–'

'That won't be possible.' It was Tethys' turn to interrupt. 'We have our orders, to be enacted *sine questione.*' Without question. 'Under no circumstances are we to abandon the inner sanctum to the enemy. Were that to be necessary, I would be compelled to release the fuel-air mixture from the tanks beneath the mine, in order to destroy the facility entirely in an uncontrolled explosion.'

'And if the lord castellan were to give you an order countermanding that?' Argent said.

'I would, regrettably, be obliged to refuse. As would the soldiers under my command.'

'Quiet.' Ursula raised her hand. 'Can you all just be quiet for a moment.'

Her choice was clear: forget the mission and leave the bunker and its contents to be destroyed, or waste time in what might prove a futile attempt to open it.

*What would Lord Castellan Creed do?*

It wasn't the first time she had thought that when faced with a difficult decision, but usually her answer was to do the exact opposite. If she wanted to get into the bunker, she would have to think like the old general. Always he'd been one step ahead with a plan up his sleeve, always ready to step sideways away from defeat… until the end, when he'd made his last stand and gone to his death like so many thousands before him.

A siren wailed through the tunnel. Tethys inclined their head, touching the antiquated vox-bead in their right ear. 'I have reports of poxwalkers massing at the southern entrances, lord castellan. If we wait much longer we run the risk of letting them surround us.'

They were running out of time.

*'Not exactly her father's daughter, is she?'*

The rogue trader's voice was so clear in her mind that it might have been coming through her vox-bead. She could imagine vividly how it would feel to return empty-handed, to present herself to Guilliman and his shadow council and admit failure, to confirm all of their expectations that she would always fall short of her father's heroic example.

'Captain Tethys. You said my father intended to pass the instructions to his successor, correct?'

'Yes, my lord.'

'When did you see him last?'

'Not long before his death on the Elysian Fields, my lord. He took one of the mountain passes–'

'The Delvian Cleave?'

Tethys blinked, surprised by her interruption.

Ursula repeated herself, more slowly. 'Did he leave to travel through the mountains via the Delvian Cleave?'

'Yes, my lord. I believe he did.'

The first piece of the puzzle clicked into place. Creed *had* left instructions for his successor, and they had been placed in her hands the moment she stepped off the Valkyrie.

'It's in that bloody journal, isn't it?'

# XXXI

### THE TOME OF SECRETS

'Primary genomic authorisation required,' the skull rasped again.

'What journal?' Argent was staring at her, open-mouthed. Of all of them, she realised, only Ossian would have the faintest idea of what she was talking about.

Ursula fumbled in the pouch on her belt, convinced for one stomach-lurching moment that she had lost the damned thing somewhere in the fighting, until her fingers found the crumpled parchment cover. She pulled it out into the light and smoothed it flat.

'One of his war journals. Strahl gave it to Ossian before he died, and he passed it on to me.'

'Have you read it?'

She shook her head. 'Why would I have wanted to?'

'Why didn't you tell me?'

'Frankly, Gideon, I didn't think it was any of your business.'

'Very good, lord castellan.'

She chose to ignore his wounded hero act. 'I thought it was

some stupid sentimental gesture for the picts, and for all we know it might still be.'

'Or it might be the key to getting into that vault. That you didn't think I needed to know about.' His voice was stiff. Throne's sake, why did the man have to be so overly sensitive about everything?

'You know now.' She opened the journal at a random page. Dates, troop numbers, isolated words that must have made sense when they were written, now rendered meaningless by time. One of the later pages was all but blank, nothing but a date written at the top and a few scrawled words beneath.

*Jarran Kell killed in action today.*

*He was the best of us.*

The writing was heavy on the page, as though the letters had been scored deep by the weight of grief. Kell had been Ursarkar Creed's colour sergeant for decades, as much a Cadian legend as Creed himself, but she had always assumed their friendship to be an inspirational fiction cooked up for the propaganda broadcasts. But this sparse and leaden grief had been recorded in Ursarkar Creed's own hand, for his eyes alone.

She had no doubt that it had been real.

Kell had died at the hands of the Despoiler himself, or so the story went. In a last-ditch moment of heroism, the colour sergeant had shoved Creed onto a Valkyrie, spitting defiance in the enemy's face to his last breath. Tales of his sacrifice had rallied troops, kindled the fires of vengeance in weary hearts, but not in her father's. She had held his legend in such contempt that she had never imagined the man behind it, never imagined him burdened with regret, or weighed down with the same guilt that sat heavier on her shoulders with every death. For the first time, she thought there might be something to him that she recognised in herself. The thought was an uncomfortable one.

The passageway shook again.

'That Huntsman's a sorcerer,' Ossian said quietly. 'If he's trying to get in it's only a matter of time before the defences crumble.'

She closed the book and handed it to Argent. 'Keep looking. There must be something in there we're missing.' Then, with her right hand, she seized the control rod set into the doorframe.

The lancet hurt more than she was expecting. The barb on the *Wrath*'s gene lock was so sharp it slid painlessly through the skin, but this needle was blunted by corrosion and time.

'Primary genomic authorisation acquired,' the skull wheezed. 'Welcome, Ursula Creed.'

It *knew* her.

The needle was still lodged in her palm.

'What now, chief?' Harapa said.

She looked up at the glowing red eyes. The ancient bellows rasped, and the skull wheezed out a series of numbers, pausing, then concluding with 'M41'. The rune panel beneath flickered invitingly.

'Secondary numeric authorisation required.'

'It's a date.' Ursula turned to look at Argent, her hand still locked tight around the command sceptre. 'Check if it's referenced in the journal.'

'It's not... I don't...'

'That date was the Battle of Kasr Kraf,' Laskari said. 'Lord Castellan Creed fought the armies of the Despoiler.'

'Secondary numeric authorisation required,' the skull reminded them. 'Obliteration will commence in one minute.'

'Anything in the journal for that date?'

Argent flicked through the journal. 'I don't see anything.'

'What are the coordinates for Kasr Kraf?' It seemed like a long shot, but what else could it be?

Laskari rattled off a series of numbers, so quick that Ursula, typing left-handed, could barely keep up.

'Secondary numeric authorisation denied. Obliteration will commence in thirty seconds.'

'Are you sure those are right, trooper?'

'Yes, lord castellan.'

'What else happened that day? Elsewhere on Cadia?'

'There were hundreds of battles!' Argent snapped. 'How can we possibly know which one?'

Ursula closed her eyes and tried to find a shred of focus. The fleeting kinship she had felt for her father was gone, eradicated by yet another example of his ludicrous overconfidence, the sleight of mind that had kept him one step ahead of his enemies before he had tripped over his own cleverness and taken a fatal fall.

The skull had given her a date. *He* had given her a date. What numbers did it expect in return?

'Tell me, captain, how far will we get if we start running now?'

'Not far enough, my lord.'

'Secondary numeric authorisation required. Obliteration will commence in fifteen seconds.'

*Think. Think like your father.*

Argent was flicking frantically through the book, skimming each page as if the answer might miraculously appear where nothing had been before.

The idea hit her like a shell.

'Gideon. The front of the book. The quotation. What did it say?'

The paper rustled as he turned the pages.

'Just show me it, for Throne's sake!'

'Obliteration will be activated in five...'

There was the answer.

'You devious old bastard.'

Now that she had the solution, she felt almost fond of the old man. She typed the digits of the answer as fast as she could, praying for accuracy and a small dose of luck, as the skull continued its wheezing countdown: four, then three, then two...

'Come on!'

The skull's eyes flashed green. 'Secondary numeric authorisation acquired.' The needle in her palm retracted with another painful rasp. Ursula let out a long, slow, controlled breath, and the doors to the vault swung open.

'What was in the book?' Ossian asked. Of all of them, he looked the least shaken and the most curious.

Ursula took the book from Argent and showed him the inner cover. 'It's a quotation. From General Sulla's memoirs. "A good soldier must know both their duty, and their place."'

'I thought the coordinates for Kasr Kraf didn't work.'

'They didn't. It wasn't looking for *his* location on that date.' She permitted herself the luxury of a smile. 'It was looking for *mine*.'

# XXXII

## THE VAULT

Ursula had been expecting tanks. Imperial Knights, heavy ordnance, the relics of a war fought to a standstill, a war that had consumed the resources of an entire subsector. Instead, Lord Castellan Ursarkar E. Creed's Sanctum Interioris was all but empty.

'I don't understand,' Laskari said into the silence. 'I thought there were weapons here.'

'Looks like your father had the last laugh after all,' Van Haast said dryly. 'All this way for nothing. Still, I imagine anyone left here to guard an empty room for decades feels even more foolish.'

Ursula stepped into the empty chamber, her footsteps echoing off the bare rockcrete walls, as one after another the long-dormant lumens came to life. The chamber was smaller than she had been expecting, an unadorned rockcrete box with lumens set into the walls.

'Captain, were you here when he made this place?' Her voice

echoed back at her – *this place, this place* – before dying to nothingness.

'No, lord castellan. We were given our orders after its construction. None of us saw inside.'

There were only two pieces of furniture in the centre of the room: a simple ironwood table with a foot-long metal ammunition case in its centre and a metal chair beside it.

'That's all that's in here?' She walked towards it, stirring the thick layer of dust on the ground into eddies around her ankles. 'That box?'

'It looks large enough for a laspistol or two.' Van Haast was making no secret of his contempt. 'Hardly the fabled weapon that could have turned the tide of history.'

She opened the case. A curious collection of objects stared back at her: a compact hololithic projector, an old stylus, an empty bottle with a shot's worth of sticky brown residue at its base, and a faceted blue crystal the length of her index finger, hanging on a long silver chain. She lifted them one at a time and laid them on the table. Why had he gone to so much effort to store such a paltry collection of junk?

More puzzles.

Ursula hooked her finger through the silver chain and held the crystal up to the light. Tiny spiralling runes were trapped inside it like flaws in a piece of quartz.

It was a data-crystal.

She slotted it into the holo-projector, and pulled the brass lever set into its side. The projector whirred into motion and sent a beam of light into the crystal spinning in its centre. A flickering human shape came to life, full-sized, seated at the same desk as the one in front of her. She drew a sharp, involuntary breath, wincing as pain shot through her broken ribs.

It was him.

'*Hello, Ursula,*' her long-dead father said.

The projection was grainy and tinted grey-blue, but his features were unmistakable. He looked older than her mental image of him, smaller too, with lines of care scored deep in his face. A cigar drowsed in his hand, a plume of smoke in the air so clear that she could almost smell the aroma of burning leaves.

'*It can't have been easy, fighting your way here after everything that has happened. I'm glad I won't live to see what the Despoiler makes of Cadia. I want my last sight of it to be something I recognise.*'

Creed tucked the cigar into the corner of his mouth. '*I chose this location because of the Rossvars. Even if Abaddon hits us with cyclonic warheads, this place has the best chance of surviving intact. And I chose you to find it because you are every bit the daughter I hoped you would be.*'

All she could do was stare. Ursarkar E. Creed was talking to her, father to daughter, for the first time in her life. It didn't matter that he was long dead, or that the words had crossed decades on their journey from his lips to her ears. He was speaking to her. He had known who she was. Suddenly she wanted to know what his next words would be more than anything in the world.

'Dim the lumens.' Ursula waved a hand impatiently at the door. 'Do it!' Mind racing, she lowered herself into the chair until she was sitting at her father's desk, a perfect mirror of the one in the projection. The lights died, and the hololith grew brighter and more substantial. She could almost imagine he was physically present in the room.

'*What I'm about to tell you won't make up for all those lost years. Your mother and I never agreed on much.*' He looked down at his hands and gave his head a rueful shake. '*Least of all what would be best for you. I let her convince me I had no place in your life. Who needs an old soldier always on campaign for a father, anyway?*

But there's not a day gone by since then that I haven't thought of you, or been proud of what you've made of yourself. I've followed your career with interest, captain.' He laughed. 'I expect that rank will be wrong by the time you get this.'

Creed poured himself a shot of amasec, and rolled the liquid back and forward in the glass. 'The war for Cadia is over. No matter what we send against them, they double their efforts and throw it back in our faces. Every soldier in the Imperium could descend on Cadia, and it wouldn't be enough. All we're doing now is buying time for Holy Terra to prepare for what's coming, and to get as many of our people off-world as we can. And this.'

He pulled a chain from around his neck, and deposited the glittering image of the little crystal on the table in front of him. 'We've always known that one day the enemy would be strong enough to take what's ours. Cadia has been home to our people since before recorded history, but that doesn't mean they have to die with it. There are other worlds out there ripe for the taking. Not for the God-Emperor or the High Lords of Terra, but for us. I'm talking about a New Cadia.'

Ursula realised she had been holding her breath. What Creed was talking about was better than any weapon. He hadn't built his vault to contain something that could save Cadia. It was something that could save Cadia's *people*.

He tapped a stubby finger to the crystal. 'Kell and I worked for years on the contents of this data-crystal. There's a list of systems on it, all with habitable planets not yet brought into the God-Emperor's light. Each location is of key strategic importance to the wider Imperium, where a Cadian defence could make all the difference. Our people will need time to mourn this place once it's gone, but they need a home. They need somewhere to defend, somewhere that's not a voidship or space on someone else's world.'

He leaned forward, and rubbed at his eyes with thumb and

forefinger, a gesture so weary and so humble that she felt a wave of pity for the man, sitting alone on the eve of a crushing defeat that would destroy his life's work and everything he had fought to protect.

'I've made so many mistakes over the years. We all have. It's hard to see what good could come out of the loss of our world, but you can learn from the mistakes that we made. I've watched you doing it, over and over. You can rebuild for them, stronger and better. You are their future, Ursula. I've never doubted you for a moment.'

A shiver went down her spine.

'Everything I could give you to make it possible – navigation charts, the names of allies who will help you, favours owed for you to call in.' The bulldog face creased in a smile. 'Please accept this as my gift to you. Something to make up for all those missed name-days. It's up to you what you do with it. From everything I know of you, you'll make the right choice.'

He lifted his amasec, closed his eyes as if savouring the aroma, and knocked it back in one gulp.

'Cadia stands. And it can stand again. Emperor protect you, my daughter. Goodbye.'

The image blinked out, and she was sitting alone in the centre of a featureless rockcrete box, an afterimage of his outline lingering in her vision. She looked down, and realised that her hands were shaking, her throat tight with a sudden sense of loss. The others were standing in silence.

She lifted the data-crystal from the projection cradle, looped the adamantine chain around her neck, and tucked it beneath the collar of her borrowed fatigues. It was heavier than she expected, a cool, sharp-edged weight against her skin. Everything they had endured on Cadia – and a sizeable amount of endurance on Creed's own part, judging by the look of exhaustion he had worn – had been for this.

'Well.' She cleared her throat, her mouth dry. 'We have what we came for.'

'It's a miracle,' Laskari whispered.

Ursula pushed back her chair and stood, her thoughts swirling. Where were the worlds her father had selected? What resources did they hold, and how exactly would she muster the resources to find them, let alone conquer them? Her fingers itched at the thought of loading the crystal into a data-loom and exploring its contents.

'Miracle it may be,' Ursula said. 'But we still need to get it off-world.'

'And what's your plan for that, lord castellan?' Van Haast shrugged a languid shoulder. 'Wait here for the storm to break?'

'We start by getting out of these tunnels. Like you said before, we head for Kasr Arroch, to the space port. That gives us our best chance at finding high-powered vox-equipment, something that'll get a message out through that storm.'

'No.'

'What do you mean, no?'

'I mean I have a better idea. Which you are of course at liberty to refuse, my lord.' The man actually sounded enthusiastic. 'My family holdings are in the heart of Kasr Arroch. We were charged by the regional governor with control of the raw materials mined from this part of the Rossvars, and coordinating their distribution through the entirety of Cadia Secundus and a sizeable proportion of Primus. You can imagine the extent and complexity of the communications equipment at our disposal.'

'Except according to Captain Tethys, Kasr Arroch has been fought over by warring bands of heretics since the Fall. What makes you think there's anything left?'

'The fact that it was less a home and more a fortress, lord castellan. Hightower was built to withstand a siege, by the same engineers that constructed your father's vault. If anything remains intact in Kasr Arroch, we will find it there.'

For the first time, Ursula had the sense that Van Haast actually cared about the plan he was proposing. Maybe it was the data-crystal and its contents, or perhaps he was simply eager to get out of this warren of tunnels. Either way, the change was a welcome development.

'How far until we reach the kasr walls?'

Van Haast glanced at Tethys, then back. 'As the crow flies, thirty miles. Another two to Hightower. Of course, none of us have wings. I imagine the route from here through the mountains will add a little more.'

Tethys nodded. 'The going is hard. Two days, three if the weather is against us. The route takes us through the high passes before we descend into Kasr Arroch.'

Another tremor shook the cavern walls, showering them in a fine dusting of rock powder. Tethys put a hand to their vox, their brows furrowing with concern. 'I'm getting a report of the rock changing at the main entrance to the mine. Liquefying. Like it's rotting away.'

'Tell your people to secure what they can and fall back, Tethys. Do you have an exit route from here into the mountains?'

'Several, my lord.'

'Excellent. Choose the most defensible. We have to consider the likelihood of a fighting retreat.'

Now that the enemy was the main problem facing them – rather than the implications of everything she had just heard in her dead father's message – she felt curiously calm. All they had to do was survive. The difficult decisions could come later.

'I want everything ready to blow this mountain to rubble. Let's see how well that heretic bastard can play that horn when he's under a few hundred tons of granite.'

# XXXIII

## THE GREAT HOSTE

'You see why we're called the Mole Rats now?'

Meraq flashed a smile at Laskari as they joined the tide of bodies in the narrow passageways. The sappers were moving with purpose, handing out weapons, backpacks, grenades and combat knives, and carrying spiked wooden barricades to block the tunnels behind them as they went.

'It looks like you've been planning this for a while.'

'We've had a long time to get ready.' Meraq's eyes were sparkling with excitement. 'The captain had us rehearse the evacuation plan once a month for as long as I can remember. We always knew it would come to this in the end.'

'How many of you are there?'

'Thirty-six. Thirty-one in the base right now. Jylda and her team are out on patrol.' A soldier handing out charge-packs shoved two into Meraq's free hand, and offered the same to Laskari. She took them and tucked them into her belt. 'Jylda's smart,' Meraq continued. 'She'll work out a route through the mountains. Meet us where we're going.'

The lord castellan's plan was a simple one. They would retreat in good order through the tunnels, trusting the barricades to slow down the horde for the first few miles and buying time for the promethium fuel-air mixture to build up in the tunnel system. After a winding three-mile hike through increasingly narrow passageways, once they were clear of the tunnels Tethys would activate a remote detonator, igniting the mixture and immolating anyone caught inside. The blast wave would be enough to collapse the tunnels, destroying the mine and the vault beneath.

They had a head start. They had a decent plan.

If it hadn't been for the events of the past few days, Laskari might have found that reassuring.

'Get to your positions. Meraq, lead us out.' Captain Tethys waved the two of them past, along with Zhata, her canid and another pair of young soldiers. Meraq was the youngest-looking Mole Rat of any of them, which was a massive relief. If there had been children in the base, the whole mission would have taken on a fresh level of complexity.

'No one's been born for ten years,' Meraq had said, when Laskari had asked her about it. The numbers didn't quite add up, but whatever had happened to make it that way was something Laskari didn't want to know.

'You're sure you remember the way?' she asked.

'I've lived my whole life here. I could do it with my eyes closed.'

A thunderclap echoed through the cavern, followed by a gust of warm, foetid air. The Huntsman's horn sounded behind them.

'He's inside,' the lord castellan said. 'Time to move.'

'How long will it take?' Laskari whispered into Meraq's ear.

'An hour. There are a couple of bottlenecks that'll slow us down while everyone gets through, but it isn't far.'

Laskari looked behind her at the cluster of soldiers. Tethys' platoon were bare-headed, their respirators slung over one shoulder, moving with quick, easy confidence. She envied them their cohesion.

They turned left off the main passageway into a lateral mining gallery just as the path began to slope upward, the walls glittering with dull grey ore.

'Watch your footing,' Meraq said. 'The ground's loose here.'

The canid streaked ahead, a grey blur in the darkness.

'Have you got canids where you're from?' Zhata asked.

The question caught Laskari by surprise. Zhata had been silent for most of the time since they had met, her half-sister doing the talking for both of them.

'I suppose so, yes.' Laskari thought back to the scrawny yellow-brown creatures that had come snuffling around the barracks on Shukret-Dhruv, raking through the midden heaps for scraps of food. They had become such a nuisance that the drill abbots had tried to start a competition between the Whiteshields to see who could shoot the most, until the major had got wind of the plan and put a stop to it before it could begin. 'A bit different to yours. Thinner. Less fur.'

The canid looked back, its head cocked to one side.

'How did you get that one?'

'Used to be lots of them.' Zhata gestured back over her shoulder. 'Wild canids. When the war started they put an order out that everyone needed to get rid of their animals, unless they were needed for food or fighting. Some people turned theirs loose rather than kill them.'

'Was it you that found it? Out there, I mean?'

Zhata shook her head. 'The captain had two breeding pairs. When Amyt and I were small, there were… six? Seven?'

'Eight at one point,' Meraq said.

'Is it the only one left?'

Zhata nodded. 'They don't live as long as they used to. You used to get one or two strong ones out of each litter, but not any more. The last female died in the winter. I've been looking for another one, but none of the wild ones are… right.'

Meraq shot her a warning look. She met it without flinching.

'They end up wrong. Corrupted.' She touched her fingers to the tumorous growth on her face in a quick, unconscious gesture. 'More of them than not, now. Not this one, though.'

'It's all right,' Meraq said. 'We'll find other canids off-world, maybe even a mate for him.'

'Has he got a name?'

'The captain says we're not allowed to name them. That means you get attached.'

From the way the sisters were acting, it looked like that void-ship had already sailed.

The path forked again. Meraq and Zhata conferred, then took the left path, which almost immediately dog-legged to the right up a worn flight of steps cut into the rock. The wall to her right had a curious polished look to it, and she ran a finger along it, surprised to find the surface smoothed as if by the touch of countless other hands.

Meraq noticed her interest. 'They're old, these tunnels. There were people living in these caves all the way back to the Great Heresy. Maybe even before. Weird to think we could be the last.'

Laskari hurried to catch up. 'Have you ever seen anyone else here? Any other survivors?'

'Cultists, yes. Real people? No.' Meraq shook her head. 'I used to wonder if there were other vaults like ours, but if there are, they're dead now. They would have made contact otherwise.'

The lumen-light played across the surface, picking out patches of colour that resolved into crude, stick-like figures dancing across the wall, their arms raised in worship or in war. Animals had been painted there, too: an aurox, a horned feline predator crouched to spring, birds and fish and a loping hound like Zhata's. The images were simple, but the art with which they were painted made them elegant in their simplicity instead of crude.

'Are these…?' Laskari whispered.

'Good, aren't they?' Meraq flashed another of her lightning smiles.

'Keep moving.' Zhata's hand pressed against the small of Laskari's back and pushed her forward. 'We're not here for sight-seeing.'

It was hard for Laskari to tear her eyes away. Someone at the very birth of the Imperium had marked these pictures on the wall with brushes and fingers, telling stories never to be forgotten.

One last illustration caught her eye. A swirling maelstrom of faded violet lines, hanging in the air above the dancing figures. The Eye of Terror. The painter and their – their what? Their family? Their tribe? – had lived beneath the Eye. There had been Cadians, even then.

'They're going to be destroyed,' Laskari said.

Zhata glared at her. 'What are?'

'The pictures. We'll be the last to see them.' The thought was unbearable. In less than an hour the ancient images would be entirely obliterated, the last trace of that artist and their people lost forever. It would have been enough to make an archivist weep.

'Yes.' Zhata shot an uneasy look over her shoulder, to where the rest of the soldiers were following in close formation. 'And unless you want them to be the last thing *you* see, I suggest you don't linger.'

'How far now?' Ursula asked.

They had been climbing through vaulted stone tunnels for almost an hour, and there was still no end in sight.

'Half a mile, lord castellan.' Tethys was at the rear of the group, their lasgun slung over their back. 'Promethium levels are rising. I'd be wary of anything that might raise a spark.'

'You heard the captain,' Ursula voxed the squad. 'Keep the lho-sticks for the surface. No las-fire until I give the word, and someone might want to help Colonel Van Haast take off his spurs. Those are the devil for kicking up sparks.'

'One step ahead of you there, lord castellan.' Van Haast tapped his pouch, which jingled softly. 'Strange though it may sound, I have no particular desire to be immolated in a dingy stone labyrinth.'

A low buzz sounded in the depths of the tunnel, the echo making it hard to pinpoint exactly where it was coming from. It could have been half a mile down in the depths, or around the next corner.

'They're catching up,' Harapa said. 'Say what you like about those bastards, they're fast.'

'A commendable trait.' Van Haast drew his sabre. 'You'll forgive me if I don't express my admiration in person.'

'Look. Could we keep the witty banter to a minimum please, gentlemen?' Argent said, shooting Ursula a pleading look. She shrugged and kept her mouth shut. The last thing she was going to do was scold them for expressing the first shred of camaraderie she'd had out of them.

'Laskari, what's your progress?' she asked instead. The trooper was at the front of the group, leading the way along with Tethys' scouts, both of whom handled a lasgun like they'd been doing it from birth. You know you're getting old when the soldiers start to look like children, she thought. Except these really were children.

There was a moment before the trooper voxed back. *'Entering a gallery now, lord castellan. Trooper Meraq says about a third of a mile to go.'*

'Capital. What are we expecting between here and the surface?'

*'I'll ask her, my lord.'* A few quiet words were exchanged. *'She says the tunnels get narrow near the surface. There's a series of fissures before the Bone Cave–'*

'And what, dare I ask, is in the Bone Cave?'

*'Mostly bone, apparently, my lord.'* There was an awkward pause. *'It's close to the surface. Apparently beasts get trapped inside and die.'*

'There's a comforting thought,' Van Haast muttered.

The hunting horn sounded. Its brassy note was full and rich, with an edge to it that put Ursula incongruously in mind of spoiled meat. Everything about the sorcerer was wrong, loathsome, rotting, corrupt. As the last of the horn died away, an answering sound came from the tunnels: a soft clattering, like dry bones over rock. A low moan joined it, followed a few seconds later by the sound of hundreds of skeletal feet moving in unison. The Huntsman was calling the dead, and the dead were answering.

Nothing that some cleansing fire wouldn't fix.

'Movement to the right.' It was one of Tethys' soldiers, featureless behind his respirator.

'What do you see?' Ursula closed her hand around the hilt of her power sword, her thumb brushing against the activation stud before she realised what a catastrophic mistake sparking the power field would be. Instead she checked the safety catch was securely in place and drew it cold. The adamantine blade alone was little more than a metal bar, but the weight of it was a comfort in her hand.

'Lord castellan, we've got movement up ahead, too.' Laskari's voice was tight.

'Keep it together, trooper.' Ursula fought to keep her own breathing under control. Even the broader tunnels were claustrophobic enough. The thought of them swarming with the spawn of Chaos was something she didn't want to consider. *Not yet.* She closed her eyes, offered a quick, wordless prayer to the God-Emperor, then opened them again.

'Not poxwalkers, my lord.' Tethys' soldier took half a step into the darkness and unfastened his respirator to get a better look. A heavy hum was building in the air, the air vibrating with the beating of massive membranous wings.

'Hold your fire!' Ursula shouted. 'Unpowered weapons only!'

A huge bulbous shape flew around the corner, a human-sized shape with rotting green flesh straddling its back, leaning forward like a cavalry officer at the charge. She waited until it was so close she could see the mucus glistening on the stinger curled below its abdomen, then brought the sword round two-handed, upward into its segmented underbelly. It was lighter than she had expected, and the blow sent it careering off course to slam into the wall. The rider's single eye went wide, and it lashed out with the heavy iron cleaver clutched in its taloned hand, but by then she had closed the distance and hit it again, raining down blows until the bile-green carapace cracked and a viscid brown liquid oozed out. The necrotic wings beat out a frantic tattoo on the stone walls, while its abominable rider tried to free itself from beneath the thrashing bulk of its mount. Ursula brought her power sword around underhand and knocked the cleaver from its grip, reversed the blade and crushed its skull on the downstroke.

From the heavy buzz of wings filling the air behind her, there were plenty more of them. She turned and saw Harapa with his left hand locked around the throat of one of the rotting humanoids as he pinned it into the wall, his knife flashing silver as it rose and fell. Two of Tethys' soldiers were hacking at one of the insects, its viciously barbed proboscis lashing back and forward in the attempt to bury itself in human flesh.

'How many?' she shouted.

'I count seven still in the air,' Argent said. She caught a glimpse of him ducking between chitinous bodies, sticky green liquid clotting on the blade of his bayonet.

She chose the nearest drone as her next target – one without its rider – and swung her edgeless sword into its many-jointed foreleg, which splintered sideways with a sickening crack. It curled in on itself like a wriggling maggot, the stinger flashing towards her so quickly it scored across the chestplate of her armour. She clubbed at it again with her sword, and the insect riposted with another lunge of its stinger. Every movement was sending a stab of pain through her ribs, and the urge to draw her laspistol and press the muzzle into its eye socket was overwhelming.

She renewed her assault, driving it back with heavy-handed blows to its head until one of its smooth, jewel-like eyes ruptured with a wet squelch. The other two eyes fixed her with a look of inhuman hatred. It was slowing now, but so was she. Fighting with the sword unpowered required brute force. She raised it overhead and slammed it down on the creature's exo-skull, and was rewarded with a loud crunch.

An insect the size of Ursula's thumb flew directly into her face. Its razor-sharp mouthparts found the skin of her cheek and it bit down. She wrenched it off, leaving its mandibles lodged in her flesh, and swatted at the gathering cloud around her face. They were swarming so thickly that it was becoming difficult to see, but at her best guess there were two of the larger drones still in the air, one with its rider and the other without.

'We have to push on,' she voxed. 'Tethys, how long to the surface?'

'Less than a mile.' Tethys grunted, stabbed their bayonet upwards into a segmented underbelly and twisted. Ichor spilled out from the wound, and Tethys stabbed again, darting nimbly out of reach of the creature's thrashing legs.

'One left. Take it down.'

Ursula pressed her back to the wall and watched the soldiers efficiently dismember the final drone. The ground was slick with ooze, and one of Tethys' soldiers lay slumped by the wall, a fist-sized hole punched through the centre of his chestplate, leaking black blood. Another was limping heavily, but her own squad – when had she started to think of them as hers? – were on their feet, breathing heavily but with no visible injuries.

'Fix respirators.' She flicked a crawling insect from inside her mask, stamped on it underfoot and locked her respirator into place. When she inhaled, the stale smell of the filters was a vast improvement over the thick scent of rot rising from the ruptured arthropods. 'We keep going towards the surface, and we do not slow down until we reach it.'

One of the larger insects broke off from the swarm, rising into the air like an ornithopter. It hovered for a split second, turning one glittering green eye towards her as if committing her image to memory, then vanished into the darkness again.

There had been something looking through that multifaceted eye. Something that now knew exactly where they were.

They were close to the exit now. Laskari could tell from the feel of the air against her face, laced with the sharp, cold smell of sulphur. The canid knew it too, running back and forward in excited little sprints, eager for Meraq and Zhata to follow it out into the open air.

'Another left turn,' Meraq said as Laskari gulped down the cool air like fresh water. 'A couple of tight squeezes, then the Bone Cave.'

'And then we're out?'

'And then we're out.'

The horn blew behind them again, this time a low note followed by a higher one that put her uncomfortably in mind of a klaxon. The Huntsman was doing it to unsettle them, Laskari told herself. To let them know it was there and that it was following them. She was a soldier of Cadia, and she was not afraid, or at least she was going to do her best not to show it.

'This way.'

Meraq slipped sideways through a crack in the wall and vanished into the cave beyond. Laskari squeezed through, wondering exactly how Sergeant Harapa was going to fit himself through a gap of that size, and headed down a long, narrow passageway towards a pool of natural light. The tunnel roof dropped sharply, and as she stooped to duck beneath it she nearly missed a similarly sized step down underfoot.

'Should have warned you,' Meraq said. 'Fracture lines in the rock. When the Fortress hit the whole Rossvar range shifted. We're lucky we're at this end. The western end erupted.'

'Volcanos?'

'Volcanos, earthquakes, the works.'

Laskari took a step, and her foot crunched on something brittle that sent a puff of ivory dust into the air. She had partially crushed the skull of a small mammal, but as she tried to make out the shape of the skeleton she realised that the whole cavern was carpeted in bones of all shapes and sizes. Some of the remains looked truly ancient, while others were still shrouded in moist skin and rotting flesh.

'Lord castellan,' she voxed. 'We've reached the Bone Cave.'

'*Good news. Keep going.*' Ursula Creed was breathing hard, and there was a strained note to her voice that suggested she might be squeezing herself through one of the narrower parts of the passageway. Something on the other end of the vox-link moaned, and the Huntsman's horn blew again. '*We're facing poxwalkers.*' A wet, cracking sound reverberated unpleasantly through her earpiece. '*Plenty of them.*'

The canid let out a sharp bark and flattened its ears to its head. One lip curled back, revealing mottled pink-and-black gums and one long ivory fang.

'Laskari. Look,' Meraq whispered.

The light in the chamber changed. Something was moving towards them, coalescing out of the shadows into a hulking armoured figure, the antlers spreading out from the open-visored helmet. A nauseating sense of recognition swept over Laskari as it raised the horn to its lips, and blew.

'Lord castellan!' Laskari voxed. 'The enemy is blocking our exit route.'

The canid was barking so loudly she could hear it over the booming of the horn, caught between an evident desire to sink its teeth into the mouldering green armour and whatever sense of self-preservation the beast still had.

'Laskari!' Meraq shouted. 'Look! We need to go!'

'How do we get out?' Her thoughts felt slow, stupid, like the horn was scrambling her brain. The remains on the floor were moving, squelching wetly towards each other into a heap from which something vast and profane raised a shapeless head. Lips the colour of mould drew back in a hideous leering rictus, the mouth beneath lined with shards of jagged bone in place of teeth.

Laskari's paralysis broke, and she ran. The canid gave one more furious volley of barks, then darted ahead of her back the way they had come. Laskari didn't dare look back at the shapeless nightmare behind her. Something that was all mouth and teeth lunged for her, and she stabbed her bayonet directly into the back of its throat. Its oversized jaws clamped down on the stock of her long-las, and she shoved the blade in deeper, twisting it until it emerged from the back of the daemon's head. She shook it free, stepped over the liquefying body and kept running. Compared to what was behind her, whatever was in the tunnel was the least of any number of evils.

'Where do we go now?' she gasped. She raised her long-las and took aim at a poxwalker as it lurched open-handed towards her.

'No!' A hand slapped the muzzle of her long-las towards the ground, so sharply that her finger almost pulled the trigger by reflex. It was the penal legionnaire, Ossian, his eyes wide above the rubberised respirator covering the lower half of his face. He stabbed a curved knife into the poxwalker's throat and sawed it back and forward until the head fell to one side and the mouldering carcass toppled to the ground. 'Pull that trigger and all of this goes up, us along with it. The gas, remember?'

She managed a nod. 'There's something in the Bone Cave, something blocking our way to the surface.'

The lord castellan dispatched the nearest poxwalker with her unpowered sword, smashing in the dome of its skull. 'Another route. We need another exit.'

She was breathing heavily, clearly unaccustomed to the force needed to hack an unpowered blade into bone, but each blow was still economical, practised and well placed. Nearby, Harapa was in his element, his combat knife glinting as he took heads and limbs with consummate expertise, Colonel Van Haast moving like a duellist at his side.

'What did you see, Laskari?' asked the lord castellan.

'I don't know what it was.' The monstrous mound of flesh and bone she had seen defied description. 'A huge mound of rotting meat. Teeth. It had a face–'

'Let's hope we don't get a second look,' the lord castellan said. 'Trooper Meraq. Nearest clear exit. Now.'

'Yes, lord.' Meraq glanced at Zhata. 'Martyr's Rock?'

Zhata nodded. 'Martyr's Rock.'

'We will hold them here, lord castellan.' Tethys was unbuckling the straps that held the vox-grille over the lower half of their face.

'Like frekk you will.' The lord castellan dispatched another pair of pox-walkers with two heavy blows, then took another step back. 'Controlled retreat. All of us. Besides, you have got the remote detonator.'

'Forgive me the deception, my lord.' Tethys' metallic voice was perfectly calm. 'There is no detonator. These rocks are ancient and strong, too thick to permit a signal to pass through them. Someone must stay to ensure these abominations are destroyed.'

Tethys raised a hand and unfastened the vox-grille. The face beneath was a cavernous ruin, the lips eroded to raw flesh, a gaping, livid-edged hole where some canker had eaten the captain's nose away. The pain must have been appalling, but the violet eyes were calm and clear.

'Lord castellan, I would take it as a personal favour if you would allow Amyt and Zhata to go with you. Amyt is young enough that she may yet have a future away from this place.'

Bone clattered against rock, getting closer by the second. One by one, each of the surviving sappers removed respirators, hoods and masks, rolling up sleeves, pulling aside collars to reveal tumours, ulcers, and patches of necrotic skin.

'We have lived our lives for Cadia,' Tethys said. 'Allow us to die for it.'

The lord castellan stepped back out of the battle-line and

moved her sword to her left hand, reaching out to take Tethys' with her right. 'It has been an honour, captain.'

'The honour has been mine, my lord.'

Dust erupted from the side passage as an enormous fleshy hand shoved itself through the narrow gap, dripping pus as it locked foot-long talons into the rock.

'Eighth Regiment,' Ursula Creed snapped. 'We are moving. Now. Captain Tethys and their soldiers are staying to buy us time to escape. Let us make good use of it.'

Colonel Van Haast took a moment to neatly skewer a poxwalker through the eye, then joined the lord castellan. The sappers closed the gap in the line, standing shoulder to shoulder as the warp-spawned army advanced. Another vast mouldering hand forced itself through the fissure in the rock, and a deep bubbling laugh echoed from the depths of the cavern. Laskari didn't want to see what was coming next.

'Did you hear me?' The lord castellan grabbed Laskari's shoulder and turned her away from the poxwalkers, from the horror tearing itself through the rock, from the sight of Tethys and their soldiers moving into formation for one last stand. 'You have your orders, trooper. Run!'

By the third turn Laskari had lost all sense of direction, all the world condensed down to two narrow rock walls and the ever-descending roof. Her legs were burning, her throat raw from gasping in air full of dust and promethium vapour. The monster's demented laughter echoed through the tunnels behind them, the horde's advance heralded by the moaning of poxwalkers, the buzzing of wings, the low boom of the Huntsman's horn. Tethys and their soldiers were fighting in silence.

'How long... now?' the lord castellan gasped out between breaths. She was keeping pace with Meraq despite the difference in their ages, but she was scarlet in the face with the effort.

It was Zhata who answered. 'Nearly there, my lord.'

'How long until Tethys lights the gas?' Ossian said, casting a wary look back over his shoulder.

'They'll hold as long as they can. When we reach the surface I'll give the signal.' The lord castellan tapped the laspistol on her belt. 'If they hold that long.'

'They'll hold,' Meraq said. 'They have to.'

A deafening crash came from the tunnels behind them. Laskari didn't look back, focusing instead on the circle of light ahead.

'Come on, kid.' Harapa was a reassuring presence at her side, his voice steady despite the effort of propelling two hundred and fifty pounds of bone and muscle at speed. 'Nearly there. Think how good it's going to feel to breathe fresh air.'

'Cadia stands!' someone shouted from the tunnel behind them, and the rest of the sappers answered the call.

'Cadia stands,' she whispered, and ran.

The cave-mouth opened beside a massive promontory covered in snow, one thick spire of rock jutting upwards like a martyr tied to the stake. The sky overhead was a dull orange, the freezing sleet sharp against her skin, but they were out of the caves, free and alive.

'See, you made it!' Harapa grinned and slapped Laskari on the back, sending her forward so quickly that she almost fell.

'Keep going, you fools,' Van Haast said. He still hadn't slowed, his long legs eating up the ground as he moved away from the cavern mouth. 'Any minute now it's going to–'

The ground rumbled, shook, and then a blast of fire blew the mountainside apart.

# XXXIV

### THE UNNAMED DEAD

'Up! Get up!'

Laskari opened her eyes. She was sure she hadn't lost consciousness, but the world didn't make sense. She was lying on her back, staring up at a blank white ceiling that reflected the light in a thousand glittering particles. Something sharp was digging into the small of her back, and her head was aching as though she'd just fallen down a flight of stairs.

A pair of hands grabbed her shoulders and pulled her unexpectedly upright. The horizon spun wildly around her, and she found herself standing on a mist-covered world, its horizon tilted to the right at a dizzying angle. The ground underfoot was dusted with fine powder snow, but when she scuffed it aside with her foot the thick layer of translucent ice beneath came into view. It was unnaturally clear, like looking down into deep coastal waters, but the shadows moving within it were something more terrible than fish. As she watched, a human face turned slowly away from her, ragged flesh trailing behind it as it moved through what should have been solid ice. Severed hands blossomed open like flowers, drifting to the surface then back into the depths as though pulled by an invisible current.

'Look up,' Colonel Van Haast said. 'Not at your feet.'

She stumbled, righted herself, and focused on the figure in front of her. Colonel Van Haast glared back, the snow dusted through his hair and eyebrows making him look like he had aged twenty years in the space of a minute. Major Argent was sitting in the snow a little distance away, his chin resting on his cupped hands, shocked but seemingly uninjured. There was a curious optical illusion to the mist where it shrouded the neighbouring peaks, as though they were drifting in a sea of cloud-coloured vapour. The movement was nauseating.

'Trooper, are you hurt?' the colonel asked.

'No, sir.' She answered by reflex, but on checking realised she probably hadn't lied. She looked up the hill to where they had emerged onto the hillside, and saw only a mass of bare rock and shattered ice where the cavern mouth had been.

'Holy Throne!' The figure of the lord castellan shot up from the ground in a shower of bloodstained snow and expletives. She looked around herself. 'Where is everyone else?'

'The explosion took care of the tunnels, and anything inside.' Van Haast wiped fastidiously at the front of his uniform, seemingly more concerned by the state of his clothing than their buried companions. 'I suppose we should have considered the possibility it would set off an avalanche. We're fortunate it only took us this far down the hill.'

Heavy boots crunched over the ice. Laskari turned towards the sound, and saw Harapa moving effortlessly towards them.

'Any sign of the rest?' the lord castellan asked.

'Two of Tethys' soldiers made it out, the youngest ones. They're further down the slope. I think one's injured at least.'

'And the medicae?'

'No sign as yet.'

The lord castellan got to her feet. 'Harapa, Argent, get looking for Ossian. I'll see to the other two.'

Van Haast raised a hand. 'My lord, must we waste–'

'Yes.' Ursula Creed didn't raise her voice, but the edge in it was razor sharp. 'We must.' Laskari hurried down the hill after her, and saw Meraq kneeling beside her sister, the snow-covered canid huddled between them making soft whines of distress.

Even knowing what had happened, it took Laskari a moment to make visual sense of what she was seeing. Zhata was *broken*. That was the only word that fitted the shattered body lying on the snow. The good side of her face was crumpled in on itself, reducing her brow, cheekbone and eye socket to a wet red pulp. Her right arm had been snapped above the elbow, and her pelvis had been twisted through a full ninety-degree arc to the left.

'All right.' The lord castellan knelt down and lifted Zhata's good hand, rubbing at the freezing fingers with a gentle, abstracted air. 'We have you. All is well.'

Zhata didn't move, but the single wide eye swivelled to lock on to the lord castellan's face. Laskari felt tears well in her own eyes, freezing as soon as they touched her cheeks. Zhata's mouth opened, and blood spilled across her jaw in a sudden wave. The growth on her face was a dusky purple, her mangled features putting Laskari in mind of the dreadful drifting remains beneath the ice.

'I'm here,' Meraq said.

Zhata's head made a tiny vertical movement that might have been a nod.

'I give you my word I will protect her,' the lord castellan said softly. 'We will see her safely off-world.'

The canid pressed its muzzle into the crook of Zhata's neck.

She coughed once, but this time the blood from her mouth was only a trickle. Her breathing slowed, then stopped. Meraq's silent tears turned to howls of grief, tears and snot running down her face in glistening streams. Laskari turned her face away to spare both Meraq's shame and her own.

The lord castellan stood.

'Will… we bury her here?' Laskari asked.

'No.' The bluntness of the reply caught Laskari like a physical blow. 'There's no time. Not while we've got the living still to find.'

'The legionnaire?' Van Haast's expression left no doubt about what he thought of that particular idea. 'And where exactly do you propose to start? He could be anywhere under the snow. Down a crevasse, for all we know.'

'Except he isn't.' The lord castellan tapped the control module on her wrist, which was flashing with an insistent green light. 'Because if he was, the collar would have detonated already.'

Ossian was dead. He knew that from the bodies on the floor, from the overturned beds, from the light shining in through the shattered wall of the infirmarium. He knew it from the screams.

He had been here before.

The second shell landed with an explosion that turned the world white. When his vision returned the air was full of smoke, the rasp of his own choked breathing mixing with the desperate screams rising from around him. He had been frightened the first time he had lived these moments, but what he was feeling now went beyond fear into outright dread.

The force of the explosion had brought the roof down on half the room. Anyone at the far end had been killed outright by the falling rubble, but from the screaming there were plenty of survivors in various states of injury. They had all been in a bad way to begin with – anyone who could be moved had been shipped out the moment the order to evacuate had come. The rest were the ones that Colonel Brynn had told him to 'deal with'.

Someone moaned. He turned to his right, where a soldier lay with her leg torn off, hands clutching at the ragged stump in a vain attempt to stem the gushing blood. Another's skull had been crushed above the brow-line, the dead man's face otherwise intact, his eyes still open as if surprised by the arbitrary nature of his death. A twisted knot of adamantine limbs and red robes lay crumpled in the corner: Thermet Chi-Six. They had stayed with him when the majority of the staff had left, in a curious display of what he could only assume was loyalty to the patients, an emotional state firmly at odds with the medicae's wholly augmetic appearance. Look where that choice had got them. Blood and sacred machine oil pooled from around the crumpled remains. Ossian didn't look closer. If any fleeting spark of life remained in that wreckage of metal and flesh, he wouldn't even have known where to start.

A hand tugged at his ankle. 'Help me. Please.'

Another shell whistled overhead, landing mere yards from the infirmarium. He had to move. If he stayed he'd be every bit as dead as the rest of them.

'I…' He looked down into a pleading face, one more amidst the dead and dying. The ones that couldn't be moved. Couldn't be saved. All he could do was carry out the orders he'd refused that morning. 'All right. Hold still, I'll do what I can for the pain.'

'Morpholox, wasn't it?' a familiar voice said.

The scene around him froze, a still frame in a malfunctioning pict-show. Liga was standing behind him, her penal collar gone, dressed in a long, grey-green robe with the hood draped loosely around her shoulders.

'Am I dead?'

She smiled. 'No, doc. These poor bastards are, though, aren't they? You saw to that in the end.' Her cheeks were flushed, her eyes bright, as if she were in the throes of a fever. She looked happier than he had ever seen her.

'What's going on?'

'You're dreaming. Sort of.' She waved a hand vaguely round the room. 'All this suffering. The priests'll tell you that it all means something. That the God-Emperor heeds the fall of every sparrow, all that groxshit. *Someone* remembers, but I can tell you for sure it isn't Him.'

'What do you want?'

'I want you to see sense.' Liga picked her way through the rubble to an overturned surgical tray. She lifted a pre-filled syringe of morpholox and held it up to the light between thumb and forefinger. 'The Huntsman wants to make a deal. In exchange, he'll see you right, like he's done with me.'

'No.' He shook his head, nausea washing over him at the atrocity of what she was offering. 'Liga, do you understand the payment he'll take for that is your soul?'

She shrugged. 'I wasn't using it. He's taken the collar off me. That's more than your boss ever did. And he'll do the same for you, if you'll do him a favour.'

'A favour?'

'That's right. And in return, you get your freedom.'

'Freedom to do what? To serve the enemy?'

Liga raised an eyebrow. 'You're not exactly over-endowed with choices, doc.'

Ossian put a hand to his neck. The collar was still there, chafing against his skin, heavy as lead. He sighed. 'What does he want?'

She smiled. Had her teeth always been sharpened to points? 'The lord castellan,' she said.

Ossian's stomach lurched. 'What does he want her for?'

'Beats me, doc. But he's got something planned. Something big. You don't want to be on the wrong side when it happens, believe me.'

'I'm confident which side is the wrong one.'

'That's your loss, doc.' Another insouciant shrug. 'But don't make any hasty decisions, that's all I'm saying. There's another life waiting for you when you're ready to take it.'

'And how exactly am I–'

Liga vanished, and time crashed back like a tidal wave. The injector of morpholox fell to the ground; the dying man clawed at his ankle, screaming filling the air like the howl of the warp itself. He stooped down to retrieve the syringe just as the third bomb hit.

Ossian opened his eyes to a darkness that burned his corneas, the pain etching itself onto his consciousness with every blink. His head was a throbbing mess, his ears thick and dull as if they had been stuffed with wadding. Something thick, sticky and metallic was running into the corner of his mouth. The world pressed in on all sides, tight as a vice, cold as death.

Memory returned in flashes. The tunnel mouth, the feel of fresh, cold air against his face. The look of triumph on the lord castellan's face changing to horror as the shockwave erupted from the tunnel mouth in an explosion of rock and fire and thick, choking smoke. Rising into the air as though propelled by a giant fist, the snow-capped mountains spinning around him like the spokes of a wheel, and then…

And then darkness, and the dream.

Liga had wanted to make a deal. It didn't seem possible that she was appearing to his unconscious mind, but then none of this was possible. She had sold herself to darkness, enslaved herself to the Huntsman in exchange for her freedom. And she was offering him the same. A simple trade. His soul in exchange for his life.

Neither of which would be worth much unless he could dig his way out from under the avalanche.

He turned his head and tried to take stock of his situation. The merest hint of bluish light was seeping through the snow around him, but there was no way of knowing from which direction it was coming. His head was pounding with such ferocity that it dislodged any thought before it could develop, making even the simple process of working out which way was up impossible. He pushed out with his bleeding left hand, and almost immediately his wrist touched something soft and cold.

Something at his left hand twitched and let out a feeble moan close to his ear. Frekk. From the sound, it wasn't only the living that had been caught up in the avalanche. His stomach twisted, his mouth filling with acid. He was buried under Throne knew how many tons of snow, with only a rotting corpse for a companion. The poxwalker convulsed again, and he jerked his hand away with revulsion. He was covered in grazes. One drop of the poxwalker's body fluids would be enough to infect him with any number of pestilences.

*Think.*

Light was coming through the snow. That meant two things: that the snow was lightly enough packed to allow the light to shine through, and that he had to be close to the surface. That was good. All he had to do was work out which way to go, and the rest would be easy.

He laughed, his mouth instantly filling with snow. Easy. Like any of this was easy.

What had they said about surviving an avalanche during basic training? He had spent three weeks with the other Whiteshields training in the Rossvars, a couple of hundred miles to the east, all of them more concerned with drinking and trying to bed the objects of their respective affections than anything they were there to learn. The face of his drill abbot flashed into his mind for the first time in thirty years: a martinet of a woman composed of equal parts leather and spite, perpetually hawking gobbets of pungent spit, her teeth stained brown by the wad of cotin she kept tucked into her cheek.

That was it. *Spit.* With one hand he compressed the snow into a miniature cavern around his nose and mouth, opened his mouth, and spat a mixture of snow, blood and saliva, trying to make out which way it fell.

*Down.*

He was facing down. If he'd dug the way he had landed he would have succeeded only in burying himself deeper, wasting his energy on a pointless journey towards inevitable death. He heaved himself over, caught between the fear of touching the poxwalker buried beside him and the need to escape his icy prison. Snow filled his eyes and nose, and he wiped it away with a panicked hand, brushing against something that felt uncomfortably like icy skin. Was that it? Was he facing the right way now?

The poxwalker moaned again. It was on his right now. That meant he had managed a full one-hundred-and-eighty-degree turn. He put a hand to his ear to check for his vox-bead, but the little device was missing, torn away during the fall.

He shoved his arms out above his head and pulled them down like a swimmer, kicking his legs in the attempt to propel himself upwards. The snow shifted around him, and there was a sudden moment of weightlessness as the world slid sideways then juddered to a stop. A second, more cautious kick bought him a few precious inches of upward movement with no repeat of the sideways motion, but that didn't mean much. If the snow was unstable enough that he could move it with a few kicks, that meant that gravity was already exacting its force on the drift where he was buried. For all he knew he was hanging over a precipice, one wrong move away from a drop into oblivion. If he fell far enough, maybe the explosive collar would trigger before he hit the ground, sparing him the bone-splintering agony of impact and a slow and torturous demise.

Ossian breathed out slowly, partly to calm himself, partly to direct what little warmth remained of his breath upward in the hope of melting the snow obscuring his vision. He was being an idiot. His head was still attached to his shoulders. That meant that the lord castellan – or, more likely, her corpse – was close enough that the collar hadn't yet triggered. He managed a few more upward pulls through the snow. Was it his imagination, or was the light getting brighter, softening to a dirty yellow where it had been the merest bluish glow before? If there was anyone alive up there, he might even be close enough for them to hear him.

He was running out of time.

'Hey!' His voice was deadened by his icy prison. It was hard to imagine that any sound waves had reached the surface. 'I'm down here! Can you hear me?'

The buried poxwalker moaned again, the sound building with hungry intensity. Ossian had thought his efforts might have brought him a few yards closer to the surface, but the poxwalker sounded as close as ever. He kicked out in its general direction, and his boot made contact with something that yielded like rotting fruit. Fingers scrabbled at his ankle, and he kicked again, pulling his boot away, but the movement had inspired the poxwalker to a frenzy.

'I'm here! Please!'

The reply from above wasn't a voice, but it was familiar all the same: a sharp, metallic, repetitive bark, followed by the heavy scrabbling of claws on ice.

'Still…' someone said, and the scratching noise grew louder. If he was lucky, rescue might only be minutes away. *If* he was lucky.

'Hey!' He thrashed his arms wildly, the snow moving beneath his feet as the poxwalker grabbed for him again. 'I'm down here! Dig me out! Hurry!'

'Hold still, damn you!' The lord castellan's voice was close, now, as though she had her face pressed to the surface of the snow. 'Keep that up and you'll have us all over the edge!'

He had been right, then. The cornice was shifting towards a crevasse. He swallowed, forcing himself to keep his voice calm.

'Doing my best, lord castellan. Can't promise the poxwalker down here with me is listening.'

The snow shifted around his right boot. With an act of super-human will he kept his legs motionless as a hand locked around the ankle of his boot, sharp fingernails probing at the cuff, trailing their way across the skin beneath, then his nerve broke, and he pulled his foot away, risking another pull towards the brightening light above his head. It hadn't been his imagination. He was almost there.

'Hold still, I said!'

The snow shuddered around him, but falling was suddenly less of a concern than the thought of a jaw full of rotting teeth piercing his skin. His right hand broke the surface, the air impossibly cold and dry.

'Here! I'm here!'

The ice around him cracked. The world shifted abruptly to his left, and a rumble like a collapsing building built until the whole mountain was shaking around him. A hand locked around his wrist, and he almost pulled his arm away before he realised that the skin was warm instead of cold – strong, vital, indisputably alive. He reached up with his left hand and grabbed the wrist holding his, clinging on for his life as the snow thundered past, carrying rocks and bloody chunks of ice with it down the crevasse. A screaming human face swam towards him out of the rocks; he turned his own face away as a torrent of dismembered human remains swept through the snow towards him: heads, hands, racks of ribs still trailing meat and muscle, the appalling force of the avalanche threatening to tear his arm from its socket. Every part of him was screaming to let go, to yield to the irresistible force that promised to dash him to a painless end, but the hand on his wrist refused to give him up...

And then it was over.

Light spilled into his eyes. He looked around him. He was dangling over a precipice, the lord castellan lying flat on her belly on the cliff edge with her outstretched hand tight around his wrist. There was a rope around her waist, and a cluster of figures a little further up the slope were holding tight to the other end. Zhata's canid was crouching next to her, its breath rising as vapour into the freezing air.

'What's your condition?' The lord castellan's voice was strained.

'Alive.'

'Thank the Throne for that. Are you bitten?'

He risked another look down, taking in the bloodied remains of his jumpsuit and the scrapes that covered his legs. 'Not as far as I can tell.'

She grunted. 'Under the circumstances, that will do. Sergeant, pull us up.'

# XXXV

## THE PSYKER, REVERSED

From his vantage point at the top of the mountain, Livor Opilionis watched the band of survivors pick their way across the snow. Their thoughts were a delectable maelstrom: fear, mistrust, hatred and treacherous hope all blending into a resentful codependency. He understood what it was to be part of such a unit. To serve under an unworthy leader. To feel himself scorned and belittled at every turn. His own brothers had cast him out, dismissing him as a mere sorcerer, as though any of the Pestilent Lord's gifts could be other than miraculous.

When his ascension was complete, they would learn their mistake.

He had borne many names in his life, though the first were lost in the distant morass of memory. The name Opilionis had been given to him on his rebirth, when he had emerged from the warp reborn in Grandfather Nurgle's image, his once frail flesh fused into the rotting ceramite of his armour, a mouth across his belly through which he might draw sustenance, his

341

scythe blessed with the gift of a thousand virulent plagues. He had long considered it a joke on the Pestilent Lord's part that his helmet was the one part of his armour he could still remove. No one who had known him in the time before would recognise the once beautiful battle-brother in the blanched and leprous features beneath his visor, but the gifts he had received in return were more than adequate compensation for his loss.

'The Huntsman', the cave-dwellers had called him. They were little more than insects, the last dying remains of a banished people, eking out a half-life on a shattered world, but in the naming of him they had shown remarkable perspicacity. Even now, his quarry ran before him, ignorant of their place in his grand scheme. The battle in the tunnels had cost him dearly in minions and the materials with which to re-form them, but the sacrifice had been worth it.

Creed's daughter was his, now. She bore his mark upon her flesh. He had tasted her thoughts, felt her dearest hopes and deepest shames. In her veins ran the blood of a slaughtered people, her mere existence a potent symbol of the hope that Cadia might yet rise again.

And when he spilled that blood, all of its power would be his.

# XXXVI

## THE WASTELAND

The blizzard blew up an hour later. Ossian had found it difficult enough before, as they picked their way down the frozen mountainside towards the shallow pass between two peaks, but now thick, ash-grey snow filled the sky. Visibility dropped to yards, and the drifts lay deep across the treacherous ground beneath. They covered the frozen body parts in the ice, but the thought of the disembodied heads turning beneath them to witness their passage with dead eyes was somehow worse than having them in plain sight. The enemy was always more terrifying when you couldn't see them.

He was fairly confident the mountaintops were moving, too. The compasses were useless, but trying to take a bearing from the peaks swimming out of the fog had become impossible as they flickered in and out of existence. The faint crimson glow of Kasr Arroch was the one constant ahead of them, though what was making the light invited fresh and uncomfortable questions of its own.

'Take this.' Sergeant Harapa appeared out of the snow, dangling an oversized tunic in front of Ossian's face. 'Put it over your jumpsuit. Don't get cold if you can help it.'

'Too late for that, I'm afraid.' Ossian took it anyway, took off his pack and slipped the extra layer over his shoulders before they walked on. His teeth were chattering, and he was starting to lose the feeling in his fingertips as well as his freezing feet. Frostbite would be an unwelcome addition to his list of complaints. From the look of it, he wasn't the only one suffering. Trooper Laskari was shivering so hard she looked like she might fall over at any time, trudging along at the back of the column at a snail's pace along with Meraq and the tireless canid at her heel. If she fell any further behind, they would lose her completely.

'We can't go on like this much longer.' Harapa's voice was quiet. 'We need to find somewhere to stop. Somewhere we can wait for the storm to blow over.'

'It isn't me you have to convince.' Ossian pointed up ahead, to where the lord castellan was trudging doggedly forward into the blizzard.

'She's not for stopping. Wants us off the high ground first.' Harapa grimaced. 'I get her point, but if we carry on in this we'll get strung out.' He jerked his head towards Laskari. 'Someone is going to fall over and get left behind, or drop off a precipice. We're not equipped for this. Safer to hunker down here, dig snow-holes and wait out the worst of it.'

A gust of wind brought Ossian another stinging face full of snow, the flakes now closer to tiny shards of ice. 'And what makes you think the storm will end any time soon?'

'This place is all about change. I wouldn't trust anything to stay the same for long.' Harapa shook a flurry of snow from his shoulders. 'Look. Go and give her your medical opinion. She won't listen to me.'

'She won't listen to me either.'

'Don't know till you try, do you?'

Ossian shook his head, but he picked up his pace anyway, closing the distance between himself and the lord castellan on feet frozen solid with cold. She turned her head as he approached, and acknowledged his presence with a brief nod.

'Should have brought that bloody ice-climbing champion after all,' she said.

'How much further are you planning to carry on with this?'

She scowled. 'Until we come out of the blizzard.'

'Harapa thinks we should stop. He's our death worlder–'

'I understand that, but his expertise is chiefly in jungle death worlds, not the Rossvars. We need to get off this mountain. Digging in and waiting is a gamble. At least by moving we're making ground.'

The lord castellan turned to face the rear of the group, and he turned with her. Laskari's snow-covered outline stumbled, fell, then picked herself up again.

'I'm in no doubt that you can carry on,' Ossian said, as gently as he could. 'But your soldiers will walk themselves to death before they tell you they need to stop. Give them a few hours. If the storm doesn't blow over, at least we can carry on fed and rested.'

She glared at him. 'Is that your chirurgical opinion, Mister Ossian?'

'Will you take my advice if it is?'

'Very well.' She lifted her hand and signalled the halt. 'Sergeant Harapa, we will stop and rest here. I look to you to coordinate our efforts in making camp–'

'Wait!' Van Haast had been on point, and was running back towards them, waving his rifle above his head. Ossian swung his carbine around on its strap. If they were attacked in this visibility, they would be overrun in moments.

'What is it, colonel?' Argent asked.

'I've found something. A building.' He pointed into the blizzard. If Ossian squinted, he could just make out a shadow, where the sky behind the snow looked imperceptibly darker than its surroundings. 'One of the old beacon towers, I think. There was a string of them across this section of the Rossvars.'

Harapa broke into an easy jog. 'Looks like a bed for the night to me.'

The beacon tower might once have been tall enough for its light to be visible from the two kasrs, but now it stood a mere two storeys high, with what had been the upper floors scattered around it as a pile of rockcrete rubble, covering over most of the lower floor and concealing the doorway completely. Harapa scrambled deftly up the uneven masonry and swung himself in through an upper window, emerging back into sight a few minutes later with a smile on his face.

'Building's clear. It's not spacious, but once we get a few bodies inside it'll warm up in no time.'

It was only once he was inside that Ossian realised just how cold he had been. The room was circular, no larger than a moderate-sized field tent, its floor covered in a thick slurry of ice, decomposing plant matter and mud, but as a shelter it was more welcome than the Imperial Palace on Holy Terra. Harapa was busying himself piling the rusted remains of furniture into one corner, issuing brisk instructions over one shoulder as he worked.

'Wet clothes off. Officers too. None of us have the privilege of modesty in here, not unless you want to freeze to death. You got dry clothes, put them on. If not, find someplace to hang them up and get in your bedrolls. We'll get a fire lit, dry out as much as we can before we head on in the morning.'

Laskari was huddling in the corner next to Meraq, her arms wrapped tightly around herself. The canid had curled into a tight furry ball at her feet.

'Boots off too, kid,' said Harapa. 'Soon warm you all up.'

'What if the fire alerts the enemy to our position?' Argent was standing against the wall, his fair hair plastered to his scalp with melting snow.

It was the lord castellan who answered. 'The enemy we can fight. You can't shoot hypothermia.'

'Not without a flamer, anyway,' Harapa said. 'You Cadians are tougher than I thought. I was figuring you all for frozen corpses by now.'

'For *what*?' Van Haast said imperiously, the effect only slightly spoiled by the fact that he had already stripped down to his long johns.

'Nothing, sir. Just admiring your remarkable fortitude and resilience.'

'See that it stays that way.'

'Throne-on-Terra.' The lord castellan rolled her eyes. 'Stop arguing and get yourselves warm. Ossian and I will take first watch. Yes?'

'Yes, my lord.' He tried to keep the crushing disappointment from his voice, and followed her back up the stairs to the remains of the second storey. The ceiling had mostly fallen in, but enough of it remained to give partial shelter from the falling snow, and the empty window frames gave a decent view of the frozen landscape beyond. She was sitting by the window, rummaging through her pack, producing in turn a carefully wrapped block of fyceline, a box of powdered recaff, a metal cup, a water canister and a small packet of lucifers. She broke off a thumb-sized piece of explosive, lit it and balanced the tin mug above the fiercely fizzing flame.

347

'I wonder how many years it's been since I've done this.' She looked up at him, the fire glow and her expression of eager satisfaction making her look twenty years younger. 'Explosives add flavour, that was what they used to tell us.'

She tipped the recaff powder into the mug, turning the water the colour and consistency of sacred machine oil, stirred it and brought it steaming to her lips to take a sip.

'Good?' Ossian asked.

She swallowed. 'Utterly disgusting.' She gulped down another mouthful and held out the mug. 'Have some.'

He took the tin mug by the handle, his fingertips brushing across her own. The drink was sour with more than a hint of fyceline, but the scalding heat down his gullet was more than welcome.

'You might as well finish it.' She flashed a quick smile. 'I expect Harapa is carrying a container we can use to brew up for everyone. I wanted to see if I remembered how before I started making promises of hot recaff for all.'

'I'll go and ask him.' Ossian handed the mug back to her and rose to his feet, but she put out a hand to stop him.

'Wait. I wanted to ask you something.' With no apparent shame, she stripped off the borrowed Guard flak and the tunic underneath it, down to the cropped black compression vest beneath. The strapping on her ribs was starting to peel at the edges, and the livid bruising had spread like a cuirass around her entire torso.

'Is it giving you trouble?'

A troubled expression crossed her face. 'I want you to take the strapping off and check the wound.'

'It's too early for any healing to have—'

'I know *that*.' She shook her head irritably. 'I need you to check it for corruption. This place is making me doubt myself.

I need to know the–' She winced as he tugged on the adhesive dressing, but didn't pull away. 'I need to know the things I am hearing and seeing are outside my head, not in it.'

'What sort of things do you mean?'

He lifted the dressing and squinted at the wound beneath. The synthskin had peeled off with the strapping, but the surrounding skin looked healthy enough despite the bruises. There was no suppuration, or anything to suggest ingress of a corrupting force.

'Voices through the vox. Shadows moving through the snowstorm. When we were in the vault, I grabbed that control rod on impulse.' She shook her head. 'Not my usual behaviour in any way.'

'Have you expressed this concern to any of the others?'

'Of course not. I barely have their trust as it is.'

Ossian studied the lord castellan's face. Her pale eyes were grey in the half-light, her lips chapped scarlet by the weather. For a moment he wanted to tell her about his dream, about the offer Liga had made in the hope that her own experiences might make her understand – then something in her expression closed off, like the visor of a helmet snapping back into place.

'You're going to tell me I'm imagining it, aren't you?'

He unpeeled the last of the strapping, inspected the skin beneath then took a fresh roll from his medkit. 'What I can tell you is that it appears healthy, insofar as you can apply that term to someone who looks like they were hit by a cargo hauler.'

That got a laugh from her, followed by another wince of pain. She leaned forward to let him work, wrapping her hands back around the cooling metal of the recaff mug. 'Why did you do it?' she said.

'Do what?'

'Kill him. Edric Brynn, I mean. I'm assuming you had your reasons.'

He froze, startled by the question. 'They seemed like good ones at the time,' he said eventually.

'What were they?'

Ossian paused again to gather his thoughts, which had been scattered by her sheer bluntness. She had been honest with him. The least he could do was return the favour, even if it was the last thing in the world he wanted to talk about.

'We were fighting on Brythok. A bloody mess from start to finish, a meat-grinder of a war. Push after push into heretic territory, and any ground we made one day they took back the next. I was running the field infirmarium, not far from the front. Occasionally the enemy got close, but never enough for concern.'

He risked a look at the lord castellan's face. Her head was cocked slightly to one side, her brows furrowed with interest.

'Brynn got it into his head that he could set a trap for the enemy. Pull back in one part of the line, lure them in, then hit them with artillery followed by a flanking assault. All sound tactics, except when it came to evacuating a field infirmarium in a single day. I told him I had wounded there, soldiers not fit to be moved. He ordered me to transfer the ones I could, and give the Emperor's mercy to the rest. I told him I wouldn't be leaving until there was a proper evacuation plan in place.'

'How did he take that?'

'About as well as you would expect. He gave the order for the air strikes that levelled the infirmarium that night. I still don't know how I survived. I was picked up by a convoy and made my way back to headquarters, and there he was, drinking down amasec with all his cronies slapping him on the back. Thousands of enemy casualties, and all it cost was a few dozen wounded soldiers. So I shot the bastard between the eyes, right there in the officer's mess.' He sat back. 'That's your ribs strapped up again.'

Silence fell. The lord castellan set the empty mug down at her feet and pulled her fatigues back over her head, tucking them into her trousers at the waist.

'That seems reasonable enough, all things considered. You have a first name, I take it?'

Whatever reaction he'd been expecting from the lord castellan, it wasn't this calm acceptance. Her approval wouldn't be enough to get the collar off his neck, but it felt good to be treated like a fellow soldier instead of the scum on the bottom of her boot.

'Mac,' he said.

'Short for?'

'Macharius.'

She raised an eyebrow. 'Your parents expected great things, did they?'

'After the tank, not the Lord Solar. My mothers served in the Fifty-Eighth Armoured. It could have been worse. I have a brother called Astraeus.'

'Any sisters?'

'Basilisk.'

The lord castellan snorted, clearly not quite sure if he was joking. 'Poor woman. Still, I'm hardly one to talk when it comes to namesakes. Half the children born since the Fall were named Ursarkar or some variant of it.'

That smile again. The fyceline's dying glow was enough to soften the harsh planes of her face, turning her forbidding mask into something more welcoming. Unexpected warmth stirred in the pit of his belly, so utterly absurd given everything that had happened that he wanted to laugh. He allowed himself a single moment to wonder what she would do if he leaned forward and brushed his lips against hers.

Shoot him in the head, most likely.

'Thank you,' he blurted.

Her brow furrowed. 'What for?'

'For dragging me out of the snow.'

'I was hardly going to leave you there, was I?' She scowled at him, as if gratitude was something she had learned to mistrust. 'It was easy enough to find you. The diode on that control module that runs your collar started to flash whenever I got too far away from where you were buried. All we had to do was wait for it to get unhappy and we could triangulate your location.'

'A step too far in the wrong direction and you could find yourself digging up a headless corpse.'

She shook her head. 'We were careful. Medicae don't grow on trees.'

He felt a hint of disappointment at her off-hand remark. *Idiot.* It wasn't like he'd done anything to deserve her good opinion, much less her regard. She'd trusted him to see to Strahl's wounds, and look where *he'd* ended up: rotting in a shallow grave that was more mud than earth.

'I suppose not.'

Her scowl intensified. 'Oh, for Throne's sake. You're so damned prickly, the lot of you.' She pushed up the sleeve of her tunic, unfastened the control unit from around her left wrist and held it out to him. 'There.'

'What are you doing?' What was he supposed to do? Refuse the damn thing, or accept it and risk overstepping some as yet unknown boundary that applied to penal legionnaires? The briefing he'd been given hadn't covered what to do if your *de facto* commanding officer tried to give you the means to blow your own head off.

'What does it look like? I'm giving the damn thing to you.'

'Why?'

'Because I am not in the business of keeping slaves. And because another avalanche like the last one could see us strung out from here to Kasr Arroch. One decent downhill slide and it could take your head off your shoulders.' She shoved it into his hand. 'If I had the means to deactivate it I would, but until I do, the safest place for it is on your arm, not mine.'

He took the device, still warm from her skin, and buckled it around his wrist.

'I do not intend to leave anyone here to die,' she said. 'Not Meraq. Not even you.'

'And what if you're making a terrible mistake, and I make a run for it the first chance I get?'

She snorted. 'Feel free to try. If you do, I'll shoot you myself.'

'Am I to assume you have taken leave of your senses?' Argent was red-faced, his waving hand sending hot recaff slopping down his sleeve. When he had asked for a quiet word, Ursula had invited him to join her on their improvised watch-platform, but from the volume at which he was speaking she was starting to think they should have moved away from the building entirely.

'Quite the assumption.' She was cold, tired and in no mood for any more of his petulance. 'Which particular action are you critiquing right now?'

'Giving the legionnaire that... that...' Argent stopped, closed his eyes and lowered his voice. 'You trust too easily, Ursula, that was always your problem. What on earth makes you think you can rely on him to do anything other than run the first chance he gets?'

'Because whatever the man may be, he is not a fool.' She fixed Argent with an icy stare. 'He is competent, a good medicae, and by this stage, I consider him as much a part of the team as any of the rest of you. Does that answer your question?'

Argent's face screwed up, as if he were in physical pain. 'Throne-on-Terra, Ursula, listen to yourself! Comparing soldiers with *years* of loyal service, highly decorated veterans, the cream of the scholam to… to… that!'

'Ossian is Cadian.'

'Oh, is that what it is? A *Cadian*, so that makes him special, not like those thousands of other legionnaires on the *Oriflamme* who you quite cheerfully sent off to die.'

'Enough.' Ursula was so tired she could hardly keep her eyes open, but she wasn't going to let Argent's insubordination slide, not when the others could hear. He might think their years of shared service had earned him the right to challenge her in public, but this was neither the place nor the time. 'I'm not asking you to like the man, merely to accept that I've extended him the same courtesy as I have to the rest of you.'

'Which is?'

'Which is the right to live and die on his own terms, assuming he does what he's damn well ordered. Is that clear, major?'

There was a long, uncomfortable silence.

'Yes, lord castellan.' Argent's lips were pressed into a tight, colourless line. 'Will that be all?'

'I don't know.' Her own cheeks were burning, adrenaline flooding her system. Sleep was suddenly very far away. 'Do you have any more insubordinate questions for me?'

'No, lord castellan.'

'Then take the rest of your Throne-damned watch, Gideon, and think twice before you come to me with this groxshit again.'

Laskari looked hurriedly away as Ursula Creed thundered down the stairs into the shelter, trying to look as if she had been staring vacantly at the wall instead of listening intently to the shouting match between the lord castellan and her adjutant.

'Well,' Sergeant Harapa said, pulling his jacket over his shoulders. 'I should take my watch with the major.' He tapped a hand on the room's thick astrogranite wall. 'Cadian construction. Nothing like it in the Imperium. You could fire an autogun up there and you wouldn't hear anything down here, would you?' He nodded to Laskari and Meraq, huddled for warmth in the corner. 'You get some sleep.'

'I don't like this,' Laskari whispered.

Meraq stared back at her, her eyes wide and empty. She'd barely spoken since they'd left her sister's corpse on the mountainside. 'What don't you like?' she said.

'Any of this. All of it. The officers arguing. Everyone is exhausted, and we don't even know where we're going, or if we're going to get off-world at all.' Giving words to her nagging thoughts brought a certain sense of relief, but Meraq didn't react. 'I'm sorry about Zhata,' she added.

Meraq lay down on her bedroll and turned her face away, her voice thick and wet. Laskari felt sick with misery.

'I haven't seen my sister in three years,' she said quietly. 'I look at all of this, and I think how grateful I am that it's me here, not her.' Laskari looked down at her hands. She didn't know exactly what she was trying to get Meraq to understand – maybe just that older siblings looked out for younger ones, and that if one of them had to die then it was better this way round than the other. 'And if we fail here, maybe next time it will be her that they send.'

'I'm supposed to be glad she's gone to the Emperor,' Meraq said, her voice muffled by her bedroll. 'But I'm not.' Her voice choked. 'It's not fair.'

'It doesn't seem that way,' Laskari said. 'But it's all part of the God-Emperor's plan. We have to hold to that.'

'The God-Emperor gave up on Cadia.' Meraq spat out the shocking blasphemy. 'He doesn't care what happens here, not to us, not to anyone.'

Laskari's mouth fell open. 'You should sleep,' she said at last. 'You'll think differently when you've rested.'

She pulled her own bedroll tightly around herself, and turned her face to the wall. Meraq wasn't a heretic or a blasphemer, she was worn out and grieving, that was all. The thought nagged at Laskari as she tried to sleep, racing around her head like an out-of-control grox.

What if the God-Emperor *had* turned His back on Cadia? What hope would there be for any of them then?

# ACT FOUR

*'Of my own house, I made myself a gibbet.'*

– Fragment from an ancient text,
kept in the Great Library of Terra

# XXXVII

## THE WARP

The snow had stopped falling by the time Ursula woke, her hair frozen to her bedroll. Sometime in the night an unseen hand had rearranged her bones into a new and ill-fitting configuration, the muscles of her shoulders and hips objecting in the strongest possible terms to the overuse of the day before. She knew she had dreamed, but the memory returned only in fragments: the caverns reeking of promethium and death, the Mole Rats and their martyrdom, Zhata lying like a discarded toy soldier in the snow. And woven through it, a faint, unsettling sense of being followed by something with too many heads and glowing red eyes.

The data-crystal was still hanging around her neck. She lifted it into the light and gazed at the tiny runes trapped inside it, as if she could read its secrets without the benefit of a cogitator array. Such a tiny thing, so easy to lose or destroy, and yet it carried within it a series of vast and daunting possibilities. Creed's plan for a New Cadia could change the fate of her people: a future in which they could rebuild what was lost instead of continuing their steady death march to oblivion. But at what cost? Would Guilliman even allow her to withdraw so many soldiers from his great crusade to commit to yet another battle-front?

She got to her feet and peeled away her bedroll, and wriggled into her freezing fatigues before the last of her body heat could dissipate. Laskari and Meraq were still asleep in the corner, huddled together like sleeping children. Argent was already awake and dressed, kneeling in silent prayer with his face turned to the far wall. She considered disturbing him, but his expression was sufficiently tormented that she decided against it. Added to that, the smell of brewing recaff was drifting down the ruin's stairs, and any continuation of the argument of the night before would be easier to endure with a dose of that in her belly.

Outside, the sky was a dull grey, flickering with distant lightning and heavy with the promise of yet more snow. Harapa looked up from the fire and flicked her an informal salute before returning his attention to the jerrycan of boiling water and the metal ration-pack set in the fire to heat. Van Haast had left the tower and was standing a little distance to the north-west, staring out towards a series of great iron spires in the valley below. Before the Fall, another range of mountains had risen behind it, the city cradled in a bowl between the mighty peaks. Now they were gone, ripped apart and lost in the void.

Kasr Arroch. The end of the world.

Ursula threw a ration-pack of her own into the fire, and handed her mug over for Harapa to fill. His recaff tasted considerably better than her own attempts of the night before, unless it was simply that she was getting used to field brew again. She gulped it down, and held out her mug for a refill.

'You want me to get the others up, chief?'

She shook her head. 'Let them sleep a bit longer. Big day ahead.'

'*Another* big day? You're spoiling us.'

Ursula had served with soldiers like the sergeant before. She recognised the pattern of his behaviour – that curious combination of deference and humour, all of it delivered without the remotest hint of sincerity. As long as he kept doing his job, she had no objection to the manner in which he did it.

'How are you finding Cadia, sergeant?'

The big man shrugged. 'It's no Catachan, but it'll do.'

'I'm sorry to disappoint.' She sipped at her refilled mug, letting the welcome warmth spread through her. 'If you're looking for yet more hostile conditions, I think we should have some for you before the end of the day.'

He lifted his mug in an informal salute. 'I'll hold you to that.'

Van Haast left his vantage point and crossed the fresh snow back to the tower. He was moving stiffly, flinching at each step as though his back was paining him. She could sympathise with that.

'Everything all right, colonel?'

He climbed the rubble and took up a place near the fire, rubbing warmth back into his hands. 'As well as can be expected, lord castellan. I make it twenty miles to the walls of Kasr Arroch.'

'You have a route for us in mind?'

'Several. Most of them vertical, and directly fatal.'

Ursula studied his face, wondering how serious the man was being, and decided he was mocking her as usual. She let it slide. It wasn't ill-natured, and lacked the sting of Argent's petulant rebuke of the night before.

Van Haast accepted a cup of recaff from the sergeant, sipped it and grimaced, the taste clearly an affront to his refined palate. 'On an unrelated note, I see our chirurgeon has decided not to desert after all.'

Ursula followed the line of his pointing finger to where Ossian was trudging towards them across the snow. She hadn't even noticed he was missing; if he had decided to desert then he could have been miles away by now. Her lack of vigilance was a marker of how shaken the message in the bunker had left her; that and the painful trudge through the bone-gnawing cold of the night before.

A whisper came through the vox-bead in her ear, so soft that for a moment she thought it must have been a crossed signal, until the absurdity of that notion struck home. There was no crossed signal on this planet. There was barely a signal at all. The now familiar notes of 'Flower of Cadia' played in her ear, fading out, then replaced with her father's voice.

'One of them is a traitor,' he said. The impression was so realistic it would have been easy to believe it really was the old lord castellan dispensing wisdom from beyond the grave, if that hadn't been idiocy as well as heresy. 'Ask me and I will tell you before they put the knife to your throat.'

'The damn thing is speaking through the vox again,' she said, keeping her voice deliberately light. She took the bead from her ear and tucked it into her breast pocket, trying not to notice the way her hand was shaking. 'Are the rest of you hearing that?'

Harapa shook his head. 'Not this time, chief.'

'Just as well.'

Van Haast had frozen in place, his aquiline features a rigid mask.

'Is it talking to you?' she said. He didn't react. She waved a hand in front of his face. 'Colonel, if it's bothering you, take the damned vox-bead out of your ear.'

That seemed to break his paralysis. His hand shaking, Van Haast removed the micro-bead from his ear, dropped it to the ground and crushed it beneath his boot-heel.

'What was it saying to you?' she asked.

Van Haast shook his head. 'A private matter.'

Ursula accepted the last of the recaff from Harapa's jerrycan, trying to keep her own hand from shaking. Why was this latest broadcast bothering her so much? Part of it was the accuracy of the mimicry. Less than twelve hours ago she had heard that same voice speaking her name. She could understand Van Haast's urge not to speak about what he had heard. Silence made it easier to pretend it wasn't real, but secrets would demolish a squad's morale faster than a ratling would a ration bar.

'It's mimicking Ursarkar Creed for me. Making up nonsense about how one of you is a traitor. Sowing dissent. Classic psi-ops.' She gulped down the last bitter mouthful of recaff, but the taste had lost its savour. 'The sort of thing he would probably have done himself, assuming he was alive and on the side of the enemy.'

'You don't think that is true, do you, lord castellan?' Laskari's hesitant voice came from the top of the broken staircase. 'That he's still alive?' Her hands made a spindly aquila across her chest. 'Corrupted, somehow?'

'Don't be ridiculous, Laskari. Even if the incorruptible Lord Castellan Creed had chosen to throw his lot in with the enemy, do you really think they would have let him live after the sheer number of them he killed?' The flippancy was for her benefit as much as the trooper's. It kept her from worrying about what the message had said. 'Defection is strictly for the second-rankers. The big names don't get a chance to change sides.'

The sniper nodded. 'Yes, lord castellan. Of course.'

'Any particular reason you hate the man so much?' That was Ossian. He had joined them on the watchtower, his voice full of idle curiosity as he stoked the dwindling fire with scraps of crackling green wood. The smoke smelled heady, floral, not quite wholesome.

Her first instinct was to deflect the question, or to outright refuse to answer it, but on second thoughts, there was no reason not to. The squad had fought their way through Cadia without pause or question. What would it cost her to repay a little of their trust? If nothing else, the story would buy a little time for Colonel Van Haast to regain his composure before they moved on.

'Did you ever meet my father, Mister Ossian?'

The medicae shook his head. 'I saw him once on a parade ground. Wouldn't call that a meeting, though.'

'A similar experience to my own, then. The first time I remember meeting him was when I was in the Whiteshields. The great general was visiting the troops. You have no conception of the extent of the preparations required for his visit. The drill abbots had us scrubbing every surface for weeks, everything was gleaming. The bunks were made so tightly you could have bounced a Throne-piece off them and it would have hit the bunk above. And there I was, all of fourteen years old in my pressed dress tunic and breeches, desperate to finally meet my father.'

Laskari was leaning forward, her eyes wide. The canid had joined her on the ground, and was leaning against her as she absently scratched its wiry neck-fur.

'Front and centre, first rank, standing to attention like a good little toy soldier.' Ursula had replayed the day in her mind too many times for the memory to retain any sting, but it was still crystal-clear. The dust of the parade ground. The way the light had glinted on the gold fittings of the lord general's ground-car as it had drawn to a halt. The fawning sycophants around him at every step.

'I don't know what I was expecting. Acknowledgement, I think. That he would look at me, recognise me, I suppose. Even just a nod, to let me know that he knew I was his.'

'What happened, lord?' Laskari asked.

'Nothing at all.' Ursula delivered the words like the punchline to a particularly unfunny joke. 'He walked straight past me like I wasn't even there, asked the trooper three down their name, what kasr they came from, how they liked life in the Guard. And you could see that every idiot on that parade ground was hanging on every platitude that came from his mouth, grovelling over him like he was the greatest thing to happen to Cadia since the conquest. And I realised I didn't want anything to do with him after all. I was still going to be the best soldier the Guard had ever seen, but I was going to do it myself, so not one of those bastards could ever say I'd only got there because of who my father was.'

She shrugged. 'I dropped his name from mine, and never missed it. Took the first posting I could get off-world, made a half-decent career out of avoiding the man.' Wet wood crackled in the fire. 'Until the lord regent had other ideas.'

'You really think that he – Creed – wasn't a real hero, then?' Laskari asked hesitantly.

'That depends on what you mean. The Imperium decided that Lord Castellan Ursarkar Creed was a great hero, the man who was almost the Saviour of Cadia. And he might have been, if things had gone differently. But when it comes down to it, what I think of him doesn't matter. Heroes aren't born that way, and it's not always your deeds that make you one.'

'Well, that's an answer and a half, lord castellan.' Ossian poked the fire. 'Did you ever see him again?'

Ursula shrugged. 'Twice, I think, both times in passing. Luckily his heroic exploits kept him busy, and by the time the Black Crusade was underway I was with the Seventeenth on Hakeldama. I thought for years he didn't even know I existed, or if he did he certainly didn't want anything to do with me.'

'What about your mother?' Laskari asked. 'Did she... Does she ever speak about him?'

'Occasionally. I made my lack of interest clear to her. Besides, she's busy with her own affairs. She's Chamberlain-Sacrosanct to the planetary governor on Theta Sykan. She hardly has time for family reunions.'

'But he did know, didn't he?' The little trooper was leaning forward again, all eager anticipation, so keen to prove that her hero had feet of gold after all. 'He said so. In the vault. He knew where you were, even when he was fighting at Kasr Kraf. He must have followed your career, all those years.'

'You'll forgive me if I don't find that a particularly comforting thought.'

Ursula scooped up a cupful of snow in her mug and let the meltwater rinse away the last of the tarry residue. If only the past could be washed away so easily. It had been effortless to cut all ties to her father when she had thought he had done the same to her, but from what he had said, the long years of silence had not been of his own volition. She wondered what it might have been like to grow up with a father made of flesh and blood instead of a distant hero. Would she have achieved so much with her life without his image to despise?

'Anyway. That's enough storytelling. Get yourselves ready to move.' She looked at Van Haast, whose face had resumed its usual sneer. 'Are you with us, colonel?'

'Certainly, lord castellan.' His voice was perfectly calm. His momentary disquiet was gone, vanished into the thin morning light like a warp ghost. There was no evidence it had ever happened at all, except for the shards of his broken vox-bead glinting like obsidian on the snow-covered stone.

# XXXVIII

## THE WATCHER

'Do you want me to have a look at your back, colonel?' Ossian asked.

They were picking their way along the mountain pass that led to Kasr Arroch, past the rusting remains of what must have been a motorised convoy: Chimeras, Rhinos and the occasional Baneblade jutting from the snow like ships wrecked on a frozen sea. The light had returned to an unnatural red, dyeing the snow the colour of blood. Van Haast had fallen to the back of the group, ostensibly as a rearguard, but from the way he had stopped, bent forward and drawn a series of sharp breaths, it was clear to Ossian that the man was in considerable pain.

'Why in the Emperor's name would I want that?'

'To see if that wound on your back is suppurating. Rotting from the inside out. Any wound on a world like this can provide ingress for corruption.'

Van Haast turned a cold-eyed glare on the medicae. 'I remind you that I am not wounded, a fact you should take care to remember.'

'And you would be fine with a hearty slap on the back right now, would you?'

The colonel's hand dropped to the hilt of his sword. 'Careful, legionnaire. I've killed for less.'

'I don't doubt it.' Ossian raised his hands in a gesture of placation. He was getting overconfident. Pushing Van Haast too far would be a mistake he would only briefly regret. 'Be careful. Very little is required for the corruption to get in, and before you know it you find yourself thinking things with a mind that isn't your own.'

'Rest assured I will put a round through my own skull the moment I feel the presence of any malign influences.'

'Except by then it will be too late.' Ossian fell into step beside the aristocrat. It was hard not to admire the poise and elegance with which the colonel moved, as though he were stepping across the polished floor of a ballroom and not trudging through ankle-deep slurry. It made his intermittent winces all the more noticeable.

'Enough of this.'

Van Haast unslung his backpack from his shoulders. He unfastened it, glanced forward to make sure that the rest of the group was far enough ahead, and withdrew a long, thin object wrapped in flaxcloth that smelled of incense and oil.

'Will this satisfy you? It was blessed by Mother Adalind of the Little Sisters of the Holy Ossuary.' He flicked the cloth aside to show the gleaming filaments of his electro-scourge, lying smoothly together like strands of silver hair. 'It is sanctified both by prayer and by cleansing heat. You need have no fear of contagion afflicting any wound it inflicts.' Van Haast flicked the cloth back across the flail and returned it to his pack.

'I saw that before. Good you took the time to clean it. Mother Adalind would be proud. Did she bless that cilice on your leg as well? Good thinking, hiding the jingle with the spurs, but it spoils the line of your breeches.'

'Once again, legionnaire, you overstep the mark.' Van Haast picked up the pace, striding smoothly across the ice. Whatever the barbed chain was doing to his leg didn't seem to bother him.

'Listen to me,' Ossian said. 'That thing talking through the vox. The Huntsman, or whoever it has working for it…' A vivid image of Liga flashed into his mind, her cheeks flushed with feverish heat. 'It knows our weaknesses. It will exploit them. If something is eating away at you… Throne's sake, you don't need to tell me, you need to tell *her* before it wedges itself in the cracks and tears you open.'

'That would be an indication to continue with the mortification of the flesh, not to cease it.'

'You weren't hearing Ursarkar Creed through that vox-bead, were you?' Ossian made one last attempt to get the aristocrat to listen. 'Who was talking to you? What were they saying?'

But Van Haast was already striding ahead, and if he answered, the words were lost in the empty air.

It was almost dusk again by the time they came off the mountain, the icy upper slopes receding behind them as the ground underfoot was replaced first by hard-packed basalt, then loose scree, then the ferrocrete of an ancient road, cracked and uneven where tufts of acid-green foliage had pushed at it from below. Ursula's knees were aching, her muscles trembling whenever the little party drew to a halt. If they stopped to take a proper rest she wasn't sure she'd be able to get moving again.

Kasr Arroch was a prophet's vision of the warp. The storm that had hung overhead like a sentence of death from the moment they had set foot on the planet had its epicentre there, swirling in the form of a scarlet maelstrom. Even on a world famed for its fortress cities, the kasr was a testament to its architects' tenacity and ambition. Its wall was a hundred feet of blackened adamantine, beyond which the spires and turrets of the city rose out of the looming red granite peak. The governor's citadel still lowered from the top, the great skull-face carved into its topmost tower glaring down in eyeless accusation.

A barrage of artillery thundered on the city's northern side, where a corrupted Knight was locked in combat with a force of daemons surging across a section of shattered wall. Other encampments were dotted around its perimeter, some flying tattered banners lit by clusters of flickering braziers, others silent, dark and malevolent. After the isolation of the mountains, to see so many other signs of life only added to the jarring sense of unreality she felt.

'I see we have company,' Ursula said. 'Colonel Van Haast, how do we get inside without attracting any more unwelcome attention?'

Van Haast had been quiet during the descent. Other than a brief conversation with Ossian, he had hardly uttered a single word. The lack of his vox-bead wasn't helping, but there was nothing to be done about that now. If what he was saying about his home and its supplies held true, then there might be the chance to re-equip him then. If there was surviving communications technology there sufficient to get a broadcast off-world, then they might not even need to.

'The kasr's foundations run deep,' he said. 'The city you see is built on at least three, if not four previous kasrs of the same name. It's been levelled and rebuilt with each Black Crusade.'

'Which means tunnels?' Ursula asked.

'Which means *sewers*. The kasr's sanitation facilities were without equal.'

'Must be why every frekker wants to get in,' Ossian muttered.

'You're proposing we go through the sewer pipes?' Argent said. It was the first time Ursula had heard him speak since their argument of the night before. Good. He was a grown man, and he could come out of his sulk in his own time.

'It's a shit-pipe adventure,' Harapa said under his breath.

Ursula stifled a laugh. 'What are we likely to find in there?'

Van Haast's lip curled with distaste. 'All manner of horrors. But close quarters will give us an advantage against superior numbers.'

The thought of more close-quarters fighting in the dark banished her good humour.

'Why do those warbands at the walls want this place so much?' Laskari asked.

Van Haast turned his hands palm upward, deflecting the question. 'How anyone can understand the motivations of the forces of Chaos is anyone's guess.'

'They do have motivations.' The levity was gone from Harapa's voice. 'It may be difficult to understand them, but that doesn't mean they don't have a plan.'

'How fortunate we have an expert amongst us.'

'Wouldn't say I'm an expert, sir.' Harapa shrugged one shoulder. 'Fought Chaos cultists plenty of times, though. You start to think they're acting on a whim, and that's when you get into trouble.' He hooked a thumb over his shoulder. 'It might look like it's just about the death and destruction, but all of this is part of a plan. Got to be. Trick comes in figuring it out before it's too late.'

'I don't believe I was given any details on your former deployments, Sergeant Harapa,' Van Haast said.

'Sorry to hear that, colonel. I'm sure it'll all be waiting for you back on the *Oriflamme*.'

Laskari cleared her throat, breaking the awkward silence with awkwardness of her own. 'Where will the sewers bring us out, colonel? Inside the kasr, I mean?'

'The upper city. Close to my family's holdings.'

'And you believe it'll still be standing?' said Ursula.

'I don't need to believe, lord castellan.' Van Haast extended a hand to point at the city's jagged silhouette, backlit against the crimson storm. 'I can see it from here.'

Another hour of walking brought them almost to the kasr walls. The grey adamantine rose up like a cliff face, stark and forbidding. Its surface was scarred from a thousand assaults, but most of it was still intact, broken watchtowers and sentry posts clinging to its summit. The Black Crusade had broken the kasr, but what remained refused to bow its head to time.

A hundred yards to the right, the hulking shape of a heretic siege engine loomed into view. It was roughly humanoid in shape, with a skull-like head hanging down below the shoulders, one arm ending in a macrocannon and the other in a giant buzz-saw.

'Down,' she hissed, and dropped to lie flat on her belly. She peered through a twisted coil of razor wire, the engine close enough that she could make out the black-and-yellow hazard stripes on its shoulders, hear the soft growl from its vox-units. It stamped restlessly from foot to foot, its head turning from side to side, probing the massive wall for any points of weakness that it might exploit, then retraced its massive footsteps in the direction it had come.

What did it want in there?

'Prepare yourselves to move,' Van Haast said, his voice low. 'The ditch immediately by the wall contains access to the sewer pipe, fenestrated at intervals to allow venting of volatile gases.'

'And presumably our ingress.'

'Yes, lord castellan.' He glanced ahead of him, then to the hulking back of the heretic engine. 'At your command.'

She gave the signal, and the seven of them scurried across open ground. She waited until the last member of the squad was moving before she followed, skidding the final six feet like a scrumball player heading for the touchline. Van Haast was already prising a rusting grate from the top of a sewer pipe with his entrenching tool, flakes of rust showering into the darkness below. When the hole was large enough, he swung his legs through the hole and vanished into the pipe, landing with an audible splash.

'Do come in, won't you?'

Inside, the pipe was a little over six feet in diameter, high enough that no one except for Harapa would have to stoop as long as they moved in single file through the ankle-deep slurry. The walls were coated in the same thick green liquid, dripping from smaller pipes overhead and dribbling down the walls in viscid, iridescent streams. The smell of human waste and decaying meat was strong enough that Ursula dry-heaved as soon as she took her first breath.

Eyes watering, she fixed her respirator, grateful for what remained of the stale tanked air. She checked the tank's pressure gauge. Barely a quarter remaining. Another supply running short, to add to their dwindling reserves of food and water.

The sounds of her breath rasped in her ears, loud enough even to drown out the sloshing footsteps of the soldiers behind her. Trooper Meraq was on her right, the girl's face already hidden by her own respirator. What they were going to do with Meraq was another worry. Zhata's death had been a mercy. There would have been no chance of taking her off-world, not with her face already blossoming with corruption, but Meraq was a different matter. To all outward appearances she was unaffected by her life on Cadia, though whether or not the Ecclesiarchy would take that at face value was a different matter. What mattered was that she had given her word that she would see Meraq safely off-world. What happened then was a problem for another day.

A pair of red eyes flashed in the darkness. Meraq's canid lunged forward, its feet splashing through the filth as it bounded towards a small green shape. A lumen-beam flared into life, lighting green skin slick with filth, a leering mouth stuffed with rows of teeth, a pair of horns stretching wide from the sides of its misshapen head. It made no effort to defend itself as the canid seized it by one leg and shook it vigorously back and forth, its shrieks more like laughter than screams of pain. It grabbed the dog's ears with its misshapen hands, wrenched its head to one side and bit down on the soft flesh of the dog's face. The dog yelped and recoiled, thrashing its head until the rotting imp flew free and struck the wall with a moist squelch. Ursula dispatched it with a headshot from her laspistol, but the laughing continued, echoing down the tunnel from every direction.

'Which way, colonel?'

Van Haast pointed in the direction from which the creature had come. The walls were moving, mounds of the same gibbering daemons climbing over each other in their haste to sink their teeth into living flesh. They were too close for a grenade, and in the absence of a flamer – an omission she was starting to regret with depressing regularity – they would have to take them out one at a time.

'Keep moving.'

She killed another, then a third as it leaped towards her, an appallingly childlike giggle emanating from its overstretched mouth. How many were there? Individually they were no challenge at all, rupturing like balloons with a single shot, but like all of these abominations their threat came in numbers.

Las-bolts peppered the sewer walls around her, and she shifted her pistol to her left hand and drew her power sword, severing horns, limbs and rotting intestines. One grabbed on to her ankle, giggling even as she skewered it through the top of its grotesquely distorted skull. Another hung from an overhead pipe, swinging back and forth until a las-bolt burst it like a balloon. When the last one dissolved into the same sludge that filled the pipe she turned to the others, breathing hard.

'Anyone wounded?'

'All fine, chief,' Harapa said. 'For now.'

The canid was whining, blood dripping from the wound in its cheek. Meraq was standing protectively in front of it, her lasgun pointed into the darkness.

'Move on.'

Ursula took point, the sloshing of the thick liquid against her ankles almost enough to drown out the faint sounds of laughter drifting through the feculent air. The tunnel was coming to an end, opening up into a large empty space that swallowed the lumen-beam like a monstrous throat, divided by huge marble pillars encrusted in algae, the floor dropping away into a deep cistern of filth. She moved forward, unease prickling at her skin, and paused on the threshold.

'Is this where we're–'

The chamber erupted in a frenzy of thrashing tentacles, spraying filth in all directions as they lashed towards her. Las-bolts tore the first tentacle into tatters, but three more whipped forward into the space, tearing away the stonework and ripping the mouth of the chamber wide. She brought the power sword down, its energy field crackling as it met the rubbery meat. The blade bit deep, but not deep enough to sever the tentacle entirely, and as she tugged it free a second writhing limb wrapped itself around her ankle and tugged her from her feet.

She aimed her laspistol at the base of the tentacle and pulled the trigger, but her shot went wide, its sizzling beam illuminating a dozen ropes of rubbery green flesh, their pallid underside covered in palm-sized suckers…

And the sewer-water hit her like a tidal wave, ripping the respirator from her face, and everything turned to panic and darkness.

# XXXIX

## THE DROWNED MAN

Ancient sewage flooded Ursula's mouth, her nose, her ears, muffling all traces of the world above. The filthy water was churned into a froth, the tentacle around her ankle tugging her downward as others lunged at her like striking snakes. Her hand was still locked around the grip of her power sword, effluent flash-boiling furiously around its sparking field, the light barely penetrating the gloom. She hacked at the tentacle around her ankle, but another found its way around her waist and squeezed, sending pain shooting through her ribcage as she fought to keep her precious lungful of breath.

Energy discharges from above cut through the water, their green beams lighting up the murky depths. She brought her sword up in a clumsy backhand, severing the tentacle around her waist, but two more wrapped around her legs. They seemed to be limitless in number, which left her with two options: reassess her strategy, or drown.

Her lungs were burning. She killed her sword's power field

and let her body drift aimlessly in the water as though all the fight had left her. The tentacle around her ankle gave her an experimental tug, then her downward momentum continued. She forced herself to wait. Act too soon, and her deception would gain nothing. Of course, waiting too long would have the same effect.

Her diaphragm spasmed, her lungs desperate to release the used-up air. Her heart was thudding in her ears, her chest burning. How long did she have? The water surged beneath her, sucking her down like an undertow.

Enough waiting. The power sword fizzed into life, casting sufficient light to reveal a warp-spawned atrocity fused with the bottom of the cistern. A ring of tentacles thrashed around what might once have been a drainage pipe, now open like a monstrous throat lined with row after row of jagged teeth and surrounded by a circle of fist-sized milky eyes.

Twisting her body through the murk, she lunged for the nearest eye. The relentless downward current sucked at her legs, pulling her into the gaping maw. She kicked her legs furiously, reaching out with the power sword for purchase to slow her movement, and the tip caught in one of the giant eyes. She shoved it deeper, piercing its pulpy substance until it met resistance. A resounding belch came from the huge throat; it spasmed open, then shut. The tentacles lashed towards her, but the viscid liquid was slowing them down.

She drew her sword back and slammed it wrist-deep into the empty socket, and this time the resistance yielded. The tentacle around her waist went slack. That was all she needed. She kicked upwards, desperate for light and air, then she broke the surface like a breaching ice-whale, drawing in lungful after lungful of air and gasping like she had sprinted the length of the *Chamberlain Tarasha*.

'Is it dead?'

Her brain caught up with her reflexes a second before she lashed out. Ossian was treading water mere inches away from her, then Harapa surfaced a little distance to her right, combat knife held in his teeth.

'What are the pair of you doing?' she gasped.

'We came in after you.'

She blinked filth from her eyes. Van Haast, Argent and the two troopers were standing on the ledge, lasguns aimed at the water. She pointed at the knife in Ossian's hand.

'Were you planning on stabbing it to death? With a knife?'

He looked affronted. 'I was, as it happens.'

'I had the matter perfectly in hand.' She kicked her legs to propel herself a few inches higher in the murky filth. 'Which way, colonel? Across or back?'

Van Haast looked down at the pool of filth. 'Straight across, lord castellan.' He sighed. 'Give us a moment. We will be right behind you.'

With the exception of Sergeant Harapa – was there nothing the man wasn't good at? – none of them were particularly adept swimmers, but it was still only the work of minutes to cross the rancid liquid to the cistern's far side. The water was swirling in unsettling eddies that gave the tentacles an uneasy appearance of life as they slowly dissolved, but whatever else was lurking in the deep had decided to keep its own company for now.

Ursula dragged herself up onto the far side and looked down at her filthy clothes, considered trying to clean them, and gave up on the idea. She reached over the side and hauled Meraq over by the collar of her fatigues, the girl in turn bringing her canid up by its scruff. The beast looked terrible, the wound in its face leaking pus, its eye swollen shut. It gave a feeble whine, shook itself with no particular enthusiasm and lay down at Meraq's feet. Ursula met the girl's eye, and knew they were thinking the same thing.

'Not yet,' Meraq said quietly, and Ursula nodded.

'Not yet.'

But soon.

They followed the narrow ledge of the right-hand tunnel deeper beneath the kasr, faint tremors from the rock below answered from above by the thrumming of monstrous engines.

'Iron Warriors,' Argent said softly. 'Remember the fortresses they built across Secundus?'

A growl echoed down the tunnel, its origin somewhere behind them, and Ursula picked up her pace by reflex. It was the same growl she had heard in her dream.

'It followed us, didn't it?' she said. 'That damned beast from Kasr Gallan.'

Meraq's canid whined again, and an answering chorus of yips and barks joined the bass growl that had preceded them. The three-headed daemon, it seemed, did not hunt alone.

'Pick up the pace.' Ursula tried not to let the panic enter her voice, but the idea of fighting flesh hounds again made her guts twist with panic. 'How far do these tunnels go?'

'Another mile.' Van Haast glanced at her. 'At a guess.'

The tunnel ended at an iron grate, its metal bars thick with rust, but set tight into the stone above and below. To its left, a well-worn set of steps led to an upper level, their surface thick with dribbling green slime. The stench of the sewer followed the group as they climbed, deeply ingrained into every set of clothing, to say nothing of the workings of Ursula's lasweapons. Whether or not the heirloom pistols had survived submersion would only be known once she had a proper chance to field-strip and clean them. Until then, she would have to make do with the power sword alone.

The first flesh hound reached them as they approached the top of the steps, the scent of brimstone charring the air. These tunnels looked older than the sewers, carved out of red Rossvar granite and set with empty iron wall sconces, but there was no time to admire the intricacies of their construction. They were in full retreat, now, the lasguns laying down a field of covering fire, Ursula and Van Haast taking turns to use their powerblades against any snapping jaws that got too close. The growls and whines of the beasts reverberated off the stone, underscored by the deeper growls from their leader's three throats.

A sharp right turn took them along another passageway, a quick sprint that bought them a few moments' respite from the hounds at their heels. The ground under Ursula's feet felt different, and she looked down to see cobbles instead of stone. To either side, low doorways led to a honeycomb of chambers beyond. Van Haast was staring at them with a pensive air.

'These tunnels were Kasr Arroch, once,' he said. 'A city of the living, now a city of the dead.'

She thought of her father's words, when he had spoken of building a better future. He had been right. The past was a shackle that bound Cadia's people to this shattered ground. If there was to be any future for them, she would need to break those chains.

The first step in that was surviving long enough to make it out.

Another turn took them to the foot of a spiral staircase, the steps narrow wedges of foot-polished stone. A slip here would mean a broken wrist or a broken ankle, followed by a hasty and painful dismemberment if the clatter of claws on cobblestones was anything to go by.

'There's our exit. Quickly!' Van Haast was already reaching overhead, cutting at a metal hatch set into the roof with his power sword. Sparks fell like glowing rain, the metal hissing and sizzling as it yielded to the ancient blade.

Argent drew his chainsword and took up a position at Ursula's shoulder. She waited for the onslaught of teeth and claws.

'Ready?'

Argent nodded. 'Ready.'

With a howl, a monstrous hound bounded up the stairs, its neck-frill wide around the gaping jaws, claws reaching out to rend and tear. She stepped forward and ripped the power sword up through its underbelly, rewarded with a scalding gush of blood on the bare skin of her hand. She hissed and stabbed again, and the daemon hound sprang forward, one massive taloned paw striking her squarely in the chest. She stumbled backwards, tripped and fell, and it sprang forward, its full weight slamming onto her shoulders, sulphurous breath gusting into her face.

The gears of Argent's chainsword screamed as the blade found its home in the abomination's flank, and another gush of scalding blood sprayed into the air. The razor claws lashed out again to scrape across the chestplate of her flak; she turned her head away and locked one hand in its leathery ruff, braced against the irresistible force of its monstrous strength. Was it her imagination, or was it weakening?

The chainsword shrieked again, and she shoved its head back to expose the bulging throat. Argent sawed back and forth until the skin yielded with a crackle of vaporising blood.

Somewhere behind her, the ceiling hatch gave way with a shriek of metal. She scrambled to her feet and shoved the flesh hound's twitching carcass away, pushing it down the stairs just in time to block the progress of a second daemonic beast. Glowing eyes flashed in rage as it tore at its dying companion's flesh. They had seconds at most.

The others had moved quickly. Only Harapa was still standing below the hatch, passing Meraq's canid through the aperture overhead towards reaching arms.

'Major, care for a boost?'

Argent nodded, and used Harapa as a human stepladder to lift himself through the hole in the roof.

'After you, my lord,' Harapa said.

'Just get up there.' The snarling at the foot of the stairs was getting louder, accompanied by the crashing of falling stone. Harapa jumped, locked his hands on the edge of the hole and pulled himself through without apparent effort.

With a crash that shook the tunnel to its foundations, the staircase exploded in a shower of dust and rubble. The daemonic canid's three monstrous heads burst into the upper passageway, one mouth holding the still-twitching carcass of a lesser daemon hound impaled on its oversized teeth. Only the narrowness of the passageway was keeping her from those appalling jaws, but the sheer bulk of it was ripping the stonework apart. She jumped for the aperture in the ceiling, grabbed the edge and tried to pull herself over, but her broken ribs registered an irresistible objection to further movement. She kicked her legs in empty air, wondering if this was how she would finally go to the Golden Throne: devoured feet first from below.

Hot, sulphurous breath gusted around her legs. She risked a glance down, and saw the beast was cramming its dominant head into the tunnel, jaws turned on their side, tongue extended to reach for her. She kicked her legs again, scrabbling with her fingertips for purchase on the still-warm metal, just as too many hands to count grabbed at her wrists, her shoulders, the straps of her armour, and dragged her upwards through the hole like a freshly caught eel.

The beast below gave a shriek of frustration. Ursula lay sprawled on the dusty earth long enough to catch her breath, then accepted Ossian's outstretched hand and pulled herself to her feet, the daemon hound thrashing in rage below.

'Where are we now, colonel?'

'The Ossuary of the Blessed Martyrs,' Van Haast said, shining his lumen-beam over the walls. Hundreds of skulls stared back from eyeless sockets, inlaid in an intricate mosaic of human bones. 'Exactly where we need to be.'

# XL

## THE GOD-EMPEROR, REVERSED

Laskari trailed her fingers along the brow ridge of the skull set into the wall, and wondered who it had belonged to in life. What dreams and hopes had dwelled within those nameless bones, now extinguished like the flame of a candle?

'Wake up.' Harapa nudged her forward. 'Time to move.'

'Sorry, sarge.'

'Big thing on Cadia, these ossuaries, are they?'

How could she explain the importance of ossuaries in Cadian culture? How bodies were laid in the corpse-gardens, their graves tended until their names were lost to memory. How when the headstones were scored and worn and overgrown with moss, the nameless bones beneath were tenderly disinterred and placed in the ossuaries with their kin, remade together into something greater than they had been.

Cadia had stood on the bones of the dead. A Catachan could never understand that.

'My lord?' Meraq's voice was shaking. 'It's time.'

Laskari looked round and saw Meraq crouching beside her canid in the centre of the room. The beast looked terrible. The infected wound in its face had spread, eating the cheek down to the bone. Half of its teeth were gone; those that remained, visible through the hole in its cheek, were loose at the root, blood and pus oozing from the swollen gums. Its one remaining eye was fixed on Meraq with perfect trust. The girl was crying, but her hands were steady as she stroked the fur around its neck. The beast whined.

The lord castellan drew her laspistol, inspected it critically, then returned it to its holster. She extended a hand to Van Haast, who placed the grip of his laspistol in her hand without saying a word.

There should have been something to say. Laskari watched in silence as Ursula Creed crouched beside the canid and put the pistol to the back of its head. The beast didn't react, all of its attention fixed on Meraq's face, on the low murmur of her voice.

'Good dog. There's my good dog.'

The lord castellan fired a single shot, and the canid's lithe body went slack.

Meraq lowered the body to the dusty ground, and rose to her feet.

'Thank you, my lord.' Her voice cracked.

Laskari swallowed down the lump in her throat. It was only a canid – hardly something to grieve for when they had already lost so much – but she knew it was more than that. The creature had followed its mistress unquestioningly to its death. There was an uncomfortable parallel there that she didn't want to think too much about.

A curving flight of stairs took them to another crypt, and from there up into the roofless ruin of a once magnificent chapel. Traces of gilding still clung to the pillars and statues, where a bloody-eyed angel kept wingless vigil over the broken altar. It would have been magnificent in its day. She could imagine it in its glory, the air thick with incense, light spilling through the glassaic windows, the robed and hooded Holy Sisters filling the air with song.

'Look upon my works, ye mighty, and despair,' the lord castellan said softly. She paused on the threshold, staring through the open doorway into the streets of the kasr beyond. Laskari had the uneasy sense that leaving the chapel would be crossing another threshold, stepping past another point of no return, but there was nothing for it but to press on. Certain death lay behind. At least ahead left room for the possibility of survival.

Laskari had been expecting signs of life in the city outside – birdsong, or the squeaking and scuttling of rats – but there was a breathless hush to the streets that was more startling than any hubbub. The air was thick and cloying beneath the heavy clouds overhead, the broad boulevards lit with a sickly blood-red light. Every towering building was pockmarked with las-blasts and bullet holes, the ground strewn with tarnished caltrops, spent shell-casings, rusting groundcars still wedged into choke points where they had served as barricades.

'Where are the people?' Laskari asked. 'The remains?'

No one answered. She watched Colonel Van Haast out of the corner of her eye. The muscle beneath his right eye was twitching, his gaze roving nervously from building to building. This place had been his home, she reminded herself. It was no surprise it was making him jittery.

'What is it, trooper?'

Damn it. He must have caught her staring.

'Nothing, sir. Just wondering where we're going.'

'There.' He pointed down a wide boulevard to an open square. In the centre, two Cadian soldiers cast in bronze were standing in triumph atop a mound of brazen corpses. The surface of the statue had turned blue-green with verdigris and time, giving the faces of the heroes of Cadia an unpleasantly decayed appearance.

Someone laughed, close to her ear. Laskari turned, but there was no one there. It had been a child's laughter, she was sure of it, but that was impossible, wasn't it? With a flush of shame she remembered what the others had been hearing through the micro-beads. It looked like her turn had finally come around.

'My lord, I'm hearing voices through the vox.'

The lord castellan nodded. 'At it again, is it? What is it this time?'

'Laughter, my lord. Someone young. A child.'

'Anyone you recognise?'

'No, lord.'

'Anyone else hearing it?'

There was an uneasy silence. 'Not laughter, no.' Argent sounded almost as much on edge as the colonel had been a moment before. 'Voices. Can't make out what they're saying.'

'Turn it off if it's bothering you.' The lord castellan fiddled with her own micro-bead, the lines of her face drawn tight with unease. 'We don't need comms when we're this close, and if we're ambushed I don't want you all distracted.'

Laskari deactivated her own micro-bead. The laughter died, but she had a sense that something was still there, whispering profane secrets just on the edge of her hearing. She was starting to think the micro-bead was just a smokescreen. Whatever was talking to them didn't need technology to get into their heads. It was playing with them, probing at the edges of their sanity to see what would yield first.

Lightning flashed. Laskari braced herself for the split-second vision of the warp that she felt sure would follow, but this time it was different. She was still in the streets of Kasr Arroch, but the walls were running with gore, and a blood-soaked figure stood in front of her. She blinked, and the blood vanished from the walls, but the figure was still there, a flickering haze at the edge of her vision that vanished when she tried to look at it straight on.

It was Anka.

Her heart sped up, thudding in her chest like the beat of a funeral drum. Was she seeing his ghost? Was it a warp-image conjured by the Huntsman, or worse, had her mind finally given way under the strain? She looked away, but the pressure of his gaze was a physical thing. Every time she checked behind her he was standing there, in the darkened shadow of a doorway, or leaning against a broken wall.

'Fan out,' the lord castellan ordered, and the squad moved forward. Laskari focused on the sound of her commander's voice, a single point of sanity in a shifting world. 'Colonel, what's the quickest route to your family's holdings?'

'Straight across the square and behind that chapel.'

They were almost at the square now. Lightning flashed again, illuminating not one statue, but hundreds arrayed around the edges of the square.

The statues moved, and Laskari realised her mistake. The slack jaws and empty eyes of the human figures she had taken for statues weren't immortalised in bronze – their immortality was of a different and darker kind. Hundreds of them, ancient and decayed, held together with scraps of sinew and little more.

Every decaying head turned simultaneously to face them. There was a single intelligence in those glowing green eyes that Laskari recognised. The Huntsman might not be physically present, but he was here all the same.

The lord castellan drew her sword. 'You all heard the colonel. Other side of the square. Don't stop.'

The chorus of assent was missing one voice. Van Haast was staring in silence at the rows of the dead, as if searching for someone he recognised. These people would have been his neighbours. His servants. Perhaps even his family.

'Colonel, are you with us?' the lord castellan said sharply.

He managed a tense nod.

'Then come with me. Now.'

Her power sword crackled into life, and the damned surged towards them like a rotting tide.

# XLI

## THE HULK

Harapa's frag grenade took out the first rank of poxwalkers, sending razor-sharp flechettes tearing through the rotting corpses. The closest were obliterated entirely, while those nearby were simply torn to twitching pieces. Others suffered wounds that would have killed a living human, but they kept coming all the same. The more durable ones were larger, their mortal remains twisted by the touch of Chaos into new and blasphemous forms. Every inch of their skin was covered in weeping sores, their abdomens open and spilling rotting entrails. One carried a brace of severed heads in its outstretched hand. The head of another had been twisted backwards, grotesquely elongated vertebrae growing from its open mouth like strange fungus. All of them held swords made of some dark organic matter, dripping with glistening liquid.

Ursula was under no illusions about her own prowess with a blade. Her inadequacies were becoming all the more glaring as she tired, thrown into harsh contrast with Van Haast's consummate skill. The colonel was a duellist, dispatching one daemon after another with well-placed strikes to the eye socket or throat. She felt like a butcher dismembering an aurox, grunting and sweating with effort as the ancient crackling blade took limbs and heads. The rest of the squad were laying down broad arcs of las-fire, the skulls of the damned exploding in bursts of vivid light.

A shrill melody filled the air. Capering on the edge of the battle was a stunted figure in a scarlet cap, a set of unpleasantly organic-looking bagpipes tucked under its bony arm and a staff covered in bells in the other hand. The melody rose and fell, maddening in its jollity, tearing at the edges of her sanity. A horrible sense of serenity washed over her. The fight was futile. Defeat was inevitable. She should lay down her weapons and join the dance, take her part in the endless spiral of entropy and decay...

*Not yet.*

She fought for control of her thoughts long enough to bark a hasty command. 'Someone shut that thing up!'

A las-bolt streaked through the air and struck the bagpipes, which deflated with a sorrowful wheeze. The musician's hideous face twisted, and it shook the jingling stick in its hand over its head, dancing in impotent rage. Laskari's second shot caught it in the belly, and it exploded in a wet shower of meat and bile.

The music was over, but the dead were still flooding the square. They dragged themselves out of alleyways and clawed through the shattered remains of hab-block doors as if the kasr itself were coming to life. One shambling horror was draped in tattered velvet cloth that might once have been red, now faded to a mottled pinkish brown. Others had been children when they died. Ursula tried not to think about that as she cut them down.

*They're already dead. Nothing left but puppeted flesh.*

The thought didn't make the act any easier.

They were surrounded. The Van Haast citadel was mere yards away, but with the legion of the dead standing in their way it might as well have been miles. A set of broken-toothed jaws slammed shut an inch from her left hand. She spun on her right foot and brought the crackling blade diagonally into the base of the poxwalker's neck, cutting its torso nearly in half. The thing's teeth were still gnashing as she pulled the blade free. Two more took its place.

Argent was at her shoulder, carving into the horde with his chainsword, breathing hard. She hacked a poxwalker's grasping hand off at the wrist, following up with a lunge through its gaping mouth.

'The dead.' Van Haast was a whirlwind, his face a death-mask. 'Look at them.'

'I'm looking at nothing else!' Ossian said. The muzzle of his lascarbine was glowing a bright cherry red as he delivered shot after shot into the horde.

'All of them. They're all the same.'

Ursula finally realised what Van Haast meant. Unlike the dead they had fought before, these had something in common beyond their unnatural state of being.

How they had died.

The corpse at her feet still had a noose around its neck, the silkweave cord bitten deeply into the desiccated flesh. Some had poison-stains around their mouths, others had deeply gouged wounds across their throats or wrists. The kasr's fate was painfully clear. When the promised rescue had failed to arrive, the people of Kasr Arroch had made their escape in the only way left to them.

They were more pitiful than horrifying, Ursula thought, more to be mourned than feared. She took the nearest head with an emotion that was almost tenderness, searching for the human features behind the leering rictus as it fell.

'Clear a path.' She stepped forward over a carpet of twitching limbs. The severed heads were the worst, their eyes still glowing with hatred and – was it her imagination? – horror. She had heard once that the sorcery that animated poxwalkers kept the soul trapped inside, a helpless prisoner in a rotting suit of meat. If that was true then the only mercy she had to offer was a second and final death.

'Holy Throne,' Ossian murmured, his voice so full of horrified surprise that she felt her gut tighten before she turned. She snapped her head to follow the line of his vision, across the pile of corpses to one corner of the square, a little emptier than the rest.

Empty of poxwalkers. Full of something else.

The apparition bearing down on them stood easily twelve feet tall. Its lower half was human, but the torso was grotesquely enlarged and distorted, a pair of thrashing sucker-covered tentacles where the arms should have been. It was naked, dripping pus from open sores in its bile-green flesh; a hideous vertical maw opened deep into the creature's chest between headless shoulders. One tentacle lashed out, sending the nearest poxwalker smashing into a wall to burst like a rotten fruit. The tentacles flailed exuberantly, and it let out a gibbering, ululating howl.

'What is that thing?' Argent put a las-bolt through its shoulder, and the vertical mouth opened wide in a shriek of pain. The noise drew more of its kind from the shadows, many-limbed, many-mouthed, shrieking and laughing as they approached at a loping run.

'Volley fire!' Ursula shouted. 'Take them down!'

Las-bolts splattered the closest of the spawn with vivid green light. The mouth between its shoulders split wide, a long grey-green tongue lashing at the air in a frenzy. It continued its lurching advance, bearing down on them like a juggernaut.

'They're surrounding us.'

Argent was concentrating on the poxwalkers, each shot finding its mark and removing another from the now dwindling horde. If not for the newcomers the battle would be almost over by now. She should have known nothing was ever that easy. She cast a quick look around the square. Three of the new abominations and a handful of poxwalkers. They'd faced worse odds.

'Gideon, you're in charge of the gunners,' she said. 'Take out the poxwalkers first. Van Haast, time for you and me to earn our keep.' She held up her power sword, feeling the heat of the blade on her face. The first of the Chaos spawn was almost on them, its lashing tentacles casting wild shadows in the sickly crimson light.

She lunged forward, power sword outstretched, and the energy field bit deep into the spawn's lashing tentacle. It gave another ear-shattering howl, but the tentacle didn't pull away, snaking forward instead to lock around the hilt of her sword. The power field was burning through its skin, cooking the meat beneath, but the damned thing wouldn't let go, pulling her in closer towards the waiting jaws. She drew one of her laspistols left-handed and pulled the trigger, but nothing happened. Clearly its machine-spirit had suffered from its recent immersion. She fumbled for the second holster on her belt, wondering how long it would be before she was forced to drop the sword.

A power field arced through the air, cleaving the tentacle with perfect precision. The tendril around her wrist tightened like a dying serpent; she jerked her arm away and the severed limb went flying to the ground.

Van Haast was at her shoulder, bringing his sword down again.

She hacked her own blade through the abomination's open mouth, sawed back and forward until it fell in two screaming halves and a gush of olive-green pus.

She paused for breath. 'Lovely.'

Van Haast wasn't listening. He was already running to the next Chaos spawn. This one had two heads where the other had had none, both facing in opposite directions, mouths open and howling out blasphemies. Its skin was covered in patches of grey-green scales that sloughed off in a continual stream, re-forming over raw red meat beneath. The colonel's first blow took one of its four hands, but it lashed out with the other three, claws snapping shut an inch from his chest. He dodged, his footwork still exquisite, but Ursula had the growing suspicion that he was fighting more recklessly with every passing minute.

'Go left!' There was no time to check if he had heard her, but she took one of the spawn's right hands anyway.

*'You will die screaming!'* its left head began, gobbets of spit flying into the air from the open mouth. *'Your teeth will rot from your head, your flesh slough from your bones, your eyes turn to pus and run from their sockets. You will pray for Grandfather's mercy, but he will not hear you!'*

'Shut your' – another slash of the blade, another hand gone – 'mouths!'

Van Haast took the left head. She leaned forward far enough that the tip of her sword scored across the throat of its other head, searing through windpipe and arteries.

*'You cannot!'* it screamed, the words abruptly truncated. With its remaining hand it clutched at its open throat, then it toppled sideways, its mutated form liquefying before it hit the ground.

The square was silent again. The pounding of blood in her ears slowed, and she looked around to see a city square heaped high with the nameless dead. Mummified corpses in all stages of dismemberment littered the cobblestones, heaped against the walls of buildings and the statue commemorating the victory of Annike Muhr's 28th at Korun. The third Chaos spawn was lying dead, its body scorched and punctured by las-bolts: a literal death of a thousand cuts. She hoped it had felt every one of them.

Argent was braced against a wall, breathing hard. Blood was trickling from a wound in his scalp, his sandy hair already matted with clots, and Ossian sported a fresh gash across his left cheekbone, as if he had been fighting an honour duel instead of for his life. Another fight like that and the risk of serious damage would rise exponentially.

'More of them coming,' Trooper Meraq said, pointing a skinny hand down the alleyway to their right.

'Time to move, then. Van Haast, the citadel. Where?'

'Down the alley. That doorway there.'

'Surprised you're taking us through the servant's entrance,' Ossian said, one eyebrow raised.

'Not my usual mode of ingress, I hasten to add. But the gene-locks will recognise me all the same.'

'I hope you have an alternative exit in mind,' Ossian said, pausing as they ran to put a las-bolt through the skull of a twitching poxwalker. 'The number of them out here, they'll have the building surrounded in minutes.'

They crowded into the little portico, lasguns pointed out. A servo-skull was pinned to the wall, its eyes empty, the lower jaw long since torn away. Van Haast pressed his palm to the gene-lock. A motor whined, but the door stayed shut.

'Broken?' Ursula asked.

Van Haast drew back his hand and shook his head. 'The needle is too blunt to pierce the skin.' He drew a rank-pin from his collar, drove the point into his fingertip and raised the jewel-bright bead of blood towards the sensor.

'Wait!' Ursula caught his wrist, his fingertip an inch from the tip of the needle. 'What if it's tainted? You could be inviting corruption in.'

Van Haast smiled. 'If you have another idea, I'm willing to hear it.'

'What if we break the door down?'

'With respect, lord castellan, my family's defences were built to withstand the Black Crusades. I doubt even your indomitable will is sufficient to overcome them.' He turned his hand, so that the pierced fingertip and the trickle of blood pointed directly towards her face. 'With your permission.'

The air smelled of copper, sharp and metallic, heralding the fall of bloody rain. A street away, something shrieked.

Ursula nodded. 'Do it.'

Van Haast touched his fingertip to the rusty needle. For a moment nothing happened, then, with a hiss of ancient hydraulics, the needle retracted and the door slid upwards.

'Inside. Now.'

The door slid down behind them. Lumen-globes blinked into life one after the other, illuminating a narrow passageway that led deeper into the citadel. The air was quiet and still, the remnants of a long-forgotten perfume mingling with dry dust.

Ursula let out a long, slow breath, and scabbarded her sword. 'All well?'

'All well,' Argent said. 'How many was that? Forty poxwalkers? We're getting better at this. Perhaps it's like riding a ground-bike.'

'Uncomfortable over the age of forty?'

Argent grinned, and she felt a sudden rush of affection for her old friend.

'I still think we did all right,' he said.

'Except we are not bloody all right, are we?' The edge in Ossian's voice instantly banished all of Ursula's mirth. The medicae was standing against the wall, inspecting a wound on Laskari's hand that dripped blood in a thick, half-clotted stream. Ursula's own blood ran a fraction colder.

The wound was shallow, trivial almost, if not for its shape. A series of puncture wounds arranged in a perfect semicircle, the flesh around them already swollen and purple with rot. Ursula knew what that meant without having to ask.

Laskari had been bitten.

# XLII

### THE LORD OF DECAY

Triumph was so close he could taste it.

Livor Opilionis stood at the highest point of Kasr Arroch beneath the raging storm and surveyed his army. The dead were dormant, the tatters of their flesh remade into new and pleasing forms that soon would rise to blasphemous life to enact his will. The suffering they had endured in the last moments of their lives – the desolation and despair that had made an entire city choose death in a single day – was what granted this place its power. Let the other warlords of this shattered world gather at the city walls, each of them eager to take what was his by right. They had been too slow. He had seen the power of Kasr Arroch first, and by the time they reached him to challenge his dominance, they would be too late. The thought was enough to stir his rotting hearts, to quicken the coagulated blood in his veins.

When his quarry arrived, the dead would not hunt alone. Between their silent ranks, the Neverborn writhed in an endless state of change, eager to unshackle themselves from the Huntsman's will and enact their furious rage on his enemies. He had done what the God-Emperor had not: he had returned life to a dead city. Soon that would be the least of his accomplishments.

The traitor stood beside him, her thoughts washing over him in an intoxicating brew. Her hatred for Creed's daughter was unmistakable, but there were other, subtler emotions intermingled with it: concern for her friend, hope, the burning desire for freedom. There was pride there, too, in the fact that she had found her place in the service to a greater lord, though he had no doubt that her loyalty to him would last precisely as long as it suited her purposes.

'Why don't you just go and fetch her?' the traitor said. 'Power like yours, you could be in the middle of them right now. Grab her, drag her here, get it done. There's no way they can stop you.'

Opilionis tilted his head down to regard her. She was nothing, of no more importance to him than any of the other rotting human waste with which he had surrounded himself. She existed under his sufferance, and his alone. She might yet have her uses, but when she had served her purpose he would obliterate her fragile hopes and discard her like the eviscerated poxwalker in whose entrails he had seen the future.

'The key is volition,' Opilionis said.

The traitor stared back at him in vacant incomprehension.

'Creed's blood alone is not enough. His daughter has come willingly to this shattered world. She must come willingly to the field of blood that hers may be spilled.'

'What about the others?'

'Soon they will turn on each other.' He shrugged one armoured shoulder to express his indifference. 'They are of no importance.'

'But they *could* be. For you, I mean. You need cultists, don't you? Useful people to help with your work?'

Opilionis could feel the thoughts behind the traitor's words.

This vermin thought to manipulate him, to coerce him to serve her own ends. One swing of his scythe and the irritation of her presence would end in two equal-sized parts. Instead, he decided to indulge her a little longer. The more hope he allowed her now, the sweeter her despair would taste when the time came to crush that hope beneath his heel.

'And what do you propose, little daughter?'

He read her thoughts before she articulated them, but he left her to speak regardless, his own mind turning to the implications of what she had suggested. He had no intention of granting her request for its own sake, but her plan might yet contribute to his own, add a little savour to the hunt. When she had finished, he waited as though considering her words, then tilted his head in agreement. The blossoming of hope across her pathetic mind was delightful, a welcome aperitif to the despair that would follow.

'Very well, little daughter. I grant you this, as my gift.'

Her pitiful thanks washed over him. He ignored her, his thoughts already turning to the glory that was to come.

# XLIII

## THE TRAITOR

Laskari sat cradling her injured hand against her chest, listening to the shouting in the chamber next door. Even inside the citadel the moaning of the dead outside was clearly audible, their rotting bodies pressed close to the thick granite walls. She should have been searching for the comms equipment that would allow them to contact the *Oriflamme* and get them off this thrice-damned hell world. Instead, she was watching lines of corruption spread up her wrist from the wound in her hand, while the officers and the medicae argued noisily in the next room over.

'...know is how the frekk it happened? How did the damn thing get close enough to get its jaws into her?'

Two days ago, Laskari might almost have felt touched by the lord castellan's concern, but it was small comfort now. When she thought back, the moments leading up to the bite – even the bite itself – had a curiously unreal quality. She might have imagined them if not for the throbbing pain in her hand.

She had been so stupid.

She had been delivering fire into the third and final Chaos spawn, watching its skin blacken and singe, a thrill running through her at how well the squad was working together. The spawn had shrieked and ruptured in a shower of bile, and she had turned to grin at Meraq, only to see the other trooper's expression change from grim triumph to horror. Something caught Laskari's ankle, and as she reached down on reflex to knock it away, a set of jaws snapped shut around her hand. A second later the already half-dismembered poxwalker had exploded into a mess of brain and bones, but by then the damage was done.

A wave of nausea passed over her, mortality a lead weight in her stomach. It was one thing to be brave about death in the abstract, but quite another when the sand in the hourglass was down to hours instead of years.

'It doesn't matter how it happened.' The medicae's voice was quiet and calm. 'The fact is that it *did* happen, and we can stand here arguing about it, or you can let me fix it.'

'Like you did with Strahl?' The lord castellan's voice was getting louder. 'We all know how that frekking turned out. You might as well offer her this, it'd get the job done quicker!'

Laskari didn't need to see the lord castellan's laspistol to know what was being offered. She closed her eyes. If she was offered a sidearm, would she have the courage to end it? A sudden memory of the near-execution in the woods played in her mind's eye. It had seemed such a cruel and arbitrary act when she had seen it at first. She knew better now.

'We were too slow to act with Strahl.' Ossian sounded perfectly reasonable, but she could hear the strain creeping into his voice. 'Laskari's younger, better placed to fight off the corruption. If I take the arm at the shoulder now she might have a chance–'

'Oh, a chance,' the lord castellan said, her voice dripping with contempt. 'Well in that case go right ahead. What chance will she have with one bloody arm in this place? She's barely competent with two hands. What makes you think she'll be any use at all with one?'

A door slammed, hard enough to shake a shower of plaster-dust from the walls. Laskari's face burned. Everything was falling apart. She should never have talked herself onto the mission. Anka had known she was useless. The drill sergeant had known, too, which was why he had tried to hold her back for her own good. Instead she had been stupid, arrogant, careless, and cost the mission not only an ogryn but the chance to bring a competent soldier in her place.

'Trooper?' Sergeant Harapa was standing in the arched doorway, leaning against what had once been a magnificent carved wooden doorframe, now warped with time and moisture. 'The doc wants a word with you.'

'He's sharpening his knives, you mean.'

Harapa nodded. 'Yep. But at least he's quick.'

Laskari got to her feet, then stopped at the thought of the flensing knife biting into her flesh. 'I don't want this,' she said, her voice small.

'You know what happens if you don't.'

'I don't care.' Laskari turned away so that he wouldn't see the angry tears welling up in her eyes. 'I'm not going to be dead weight on this mission any more than I've been already.'

'You're not... Ah, hell!' Harapa shook his head. 'You need a minute? Before we go?'

Laskari nodded, not trusting herself to speak.

'No worries, kid. We can wait till you're ready.'

They were idiots, all of them, and Ursula knew she was the worst of the lot. Laskari would never have been bitten if she had been there keeping an eye on her, but instead she'd been off on the same sort of glory-seeking quest that she'd always despised in others. Cadia was getting to her, that was the only explanation, and now the hopeless little sniper was paying the price for Ursula's mistakes. They all knew it, even though Argent was donning his usual hair shirt to take the blame. If she stayed a minute longer in their company she was going to say yet another thing she would regret later.

She stalked down the narrow passageway, heading for the staircase that led to the first floor. The servants' quarters alone could have housed an entire regiment, and Van Haast had vanished into the warren of chambers and passages as soon as the door had closed behind him. From the glimpse she had caught of his face, the homecoming was a bitter one.

'Colonel?' She took the narrow stairway two steps at a time, and emerged through a small door onto a first-floor balcony. She was overlooking a splendid hallway, lit by dull red light shining through a crystalflex dome far above.

The floor below was decorated with a mosaic of a winged aurox rampant, a huge crack gouged across its centre. A series of galleries four storeys high ran around the central stairwell, more signs of brutal combat scarred into the Rossvar granite pillars and punched into the plaster walls. Here a door had been barricaded by an antique gnarlwood table, there an ancient scorch-mark bore witness to an improvised explosive. Stains that might have been blood had soaked into the stone steps, the balustrades cracked and broken, the velvet drapes in tatters. It must have been splendid in its day. Now it had the air of an ancient battlefield, the ground sanctified by blood and sacrifice beneath a heavy shroud of dust.

Of who had fired the shots, and at what they had fired them, there was no sign.

One door leading off the balcony was open, the passageway beyond leading into the depths of the citadel. The soft sound of respiration echoed towards her. It didn't sound particularly like the colonel, but it wasn't as if she knew the man well – at least, not well enough to identify the sound of his breathing. Correction: it wasn't as if she'd known him well *before* they had come here. She was starting to think she had the measure of him quite accurately by now.

Maybe it wasn't him. It couldn't be any of the others, locked in a tight knot of misery around Laskari and her corrupted wound, but that didn't mean it had to be Van Haast. The building had seemed secure, but it was well within the realms of possibility that something had crawled its way inside to die like the animals in Tethys' Bone Cave.

Or something worse.

Ursula pushed the door further open. The passageway beyond was lined in panels of deep brown wood that swallowed any light that touched them. She flicked on her flash-lumen and shone the beam over bas-relief carvings of eagles and aurox snared in thickets of blood-roses. Portraits of Cadian aristocracy in uniform lined the walls to either side, five hundred years of history passing as she followed the passageway to the double doors at its end.

'*One of them's a traitor,*' her father's voice whispered. She took the vox-bead out of her ear, but it made no difference.

'I'm not interested.'

'*Ask me, and I'll tell you which one.*'

Nothing the enemy said could be believed, and to entertain it for a single moment risked the corruption of her soul.

'*You're almost out of time.*'

But what if what it was saying was true? What if one of them wasn't to be trusted? By her refusal to even entertain the idea at all, was she blinding herself to the signs of betrayal until it was too late?

The double doors opened into an antechamber, a twelve by twelve foot marble-floored cube with another set of doors on the far side. The ancient sculpture of a gilded eagle mantled a lectern that might once have supported a book of scripture, while on the other side of the door a huge bronze vase held the desiccated remains of flowers. She was standing in the antechamber of a chapel, and she wasn't alone.

Van Haast sat slumped against the doorway, bent forward with his head in his hands. He could have been dead if not for the soft animal sounds escaping from his throat.

'Colonel?'

She shone her flash-lumen over the man. There were no visible signs of injury, but the man looked crumpled, broken, a puppet with the strings cut.

'They're in there.' His voice was a hoarse rasp.

'They're what?'

He lifted his face. His eyes were empty.

She tried again. 'Who's in there?'

'All of them.' He turned his face to the doors, listening intently through the wood and adamantine. 'I can hear them. Telling me to join them. I've been hearing them for days, ever since we hit the ground.' A sharp, shuddering intake of breath. 'I should have been with them. When it happened.'

'Your household?'

'My *children*.'

Something moved behind the door, and Van Haast flinched. Carefully, as if he were a skittish cavalry beast, Ursula lowered herself to the floor beside him, putting her back against the ironwood beside his. It was warm to the touch, smooth and soothing against her aching muscles. The last few days had taken their toll. It would take time and probably a good few cycles of juvenat to repair the damage done, but neither of those were looking like something her future might hold.

'There's no vox-equipment here, is there?'

Van Haast shook his head without meeting her eye. She should have been angry, but they were past that now. The dead and the damned were massing outside the walls, and the storm was still raging overhead. Even if there had been a fully working comms-system in the citadel, their chance of escape would still have been slim.

'For what it's worth, I am genuinely sorry for the deception.' His voice was thick with misery. 'We were dead the moment we set foot on Cadia. But I had to know what happened to them. And now I do. I left my family in hell.' He drew his laspistol, handed it to her grip first, then tapped his own fore-head between the eyes. 'Do it out here. I don't want to see what they've become.'

She looked at the grip of the offered laspistol. Her duty was clear: she was Van Haast's commanding officer, and in the face of this betrayal, his judge, his jury and his executioner. The smooth ebonwood curves of the weapon invited her hand to slip around it, to place her finger on the trigger and end his misery. How many of the dead Van Haasts whose portraits adorned the walls had held this over the centuries? And now she was to use it to kill the last of them, to put the ancient bloodline to an end in a burst of green fire.

'I'm not doing it.'

His eyes closed, and he nodded. 'Fine. I should have done it myself a long time ago.'

'No.' She got to her feet and offered him her hand. 'We have come all this way, Hadrian. We will not stop now.' His expression changed at the use of his given name, the old look of

411

incredulous contempt ironing out the crumpled lines of misery. 'If your children are in there – if that abomination out there is puppeting their corpses – then we put an end to it, do you understand? That much we can do for them.' She stuffed his pistol back into the holster on his belt.

Van Haast's mouth opened, then closed. He pushed himself upright, sheathed his pistol, and nodded. 'You're right. I owe them that.'

Ursula put her hand to the chapel door, ready to open it and face whatever lay beyond.

For the first time in years, Ossian's hands were shaking. It wasn't the thought of the upcoming procedure – after all, he had recent practice, a healthy patient and a more-or-less-clean indoor environment for the first time in weeks – but the shakes wouldn't go. They weren't the result of the lord castellan's anger, either; he could see clearly enough that most of that was directed inward. Nor was it the unsettling awareness that the whole building was surrounded by the walking dead. It was something else.

The smell of rotting meat was everywhere. A corpse-fly buzzed in the corner of the room, its drone surprisingly loud for such a tiny creature. As he watched, it was joined by another, and then another, materialising out of nowhere, until a huge oily blue-black swarm was buzzing between him and the door.

'All right there, doc?'

Liga stepped out of the swarm, the flies melting away behind her as if they had never existed. *Sorcery*, he thought. Clearly Liga was a fast learner.

'Is this another dream?'

'Not this time.' Liga had changed since he had seen her last. Her face was rounder, and the gaunt, starved look in her eyes had been replaced with a knowing satisfaction. 'Don't go raising the alarm. I'll be gone before anyone gets here. We need to have a little talk, you and me.'

Her hair had grown back to a soft, downy golden fuzz, tiny tendrils of fine fractal moss sprouting through it and following the lines of the veins down her face. That alone should have made her look appallingly unhealthy, but instead she was glowing with life and vigour. She looked younger than he remembered, almost childlike, despite the rusting bayonet in her hand.

'What do you want, Liga?'

'I don't want anything.' A fat black fly crawled out of her robe, up her neck and disappeared into the corner of her mouth. 'It's like I said before. I'm just running errands between the two of you. Have you made up your mind to join us yet?'

'No.' His medkit was already out on the table, the autoinjector full of fast-acting sedatives less than a yard away.

'No you haven't made up your mind, or no you're not going to join us?'

If Liga attacked him he would have to lunge for the injector and hope the drug would kick in fast enough to drop her. A moment's consideration drew that particular avenue of speculation to a close. The most he would do was present a moving target to her, and make any potentially fatal strike into a painful overture to his subsequent murder.

'It's not too late for you,' he said, knowing in his heart he was lying.

'Too late for what?' Liga's glittering green eyes – had they been green before? – sparkled with interest.

'To come back.'

'And why exactly would I want to do that?' She sounded amused.

'To save your soul. That... that *thing* you're serving, it doesn't have your best interests at heart.'

413

'And the God-Emperor does?' Liga frowned. 'Let's get this bit out of the way, then, shall we? No. Not now, not in a week, not in a million Throne-damned years. Your God-Emperor – your *corpse-god* – had His chance with me. The Imperium blew it when they left me to die on Brythok.'

'What exactly did you expect would happen?' Ossian forced himself not to look at the door. Any moment now Harapa would be back with Laskari, dragging the little trooper like a sacrifice to the altar. If he could keep Liga talking for a few minutes, he might stand a chance. Then again, he might just bring a world of trouble down on all their heads as well as his own. 'You were a criminal.'

'Except I wasn't, though.' Liga smiled. 'Enforcer Sergeant Liga Yager, Officio Custos, Brythok Port Authority. Nice to meet you, doc. I was in deep cover with the gangs, trying to get the information we needed to cut the head off the whole damn operation. And I was good at it. Got myself right in deep, no one suspected a thing. Too deep, as it happened.' She produced a packet of lho-sticks from her pocket, the wrapping squashed and torn, lit one and put it to her lips. 'You want one? Turns out these things don't go off, not even after a few decades in a dead guy's pocket. Anyway.' She drew a lungful of smoke, and blew it out tinged with green. 'I fed back everything I learned like a good little soldier, and when the time came to wrap up the whole cartel, it went like a dream. All except for one tiny detail. Me.'

Ossian opened his mouth, but she held up the hand with the knife to stop him.

'I got arrested just like the rest of the gangers. Dragged off in chains, given my choice of the pyre or the legions. And I made the same choice you did. To live. And that's the same choice I'm making now.' Her expression was earnest and genuine. 'You're a decent man, doc. You deserve better than this. But the Imperium... it'll spit you up and chew you out without even noticing.'

'And your Huntsman has promised you better, has he?' Ossian shook his head. 'That's not freedom he's offering.'

'I'm not the one with the collar round my neck.' She sucked another lungful of smoke from the lho-stick. 'I bet she's promised to keep you alive. You know she's lying, don't you? They all lie as easy as drawing breath.'

'I believe her.'

He thought for a moment of how the lord castellan – how *Ursula* – had looked in the light from the smouldering fyce-line, her violet eyes glittering, lips twisted in that infuriating half-smile, her hiss of frustration as she had shoved the collar's control module into his hands. He hadn't imagined it. There had been something between them. Not intimacy, not exactly, but a sense that if things had been different there might have been. She had trusted him, despite the numbers tattooed on his forehead. That was a trust he wasn't willing to betray.

'Come on, Liga. If you're here to kill me, get it over with.'

'There's no helping you, is there?' Liga shook her head. She placed the bayonet against his lips in a grotesque parody of a hushing finger. 'They're waiting for you, doc. He's shown me all those people you killed, ready to settle the score for all eternity. Want to hear them?'

The whispers were soft at first, building until the sound of voices filled the room. They weren't screaming now, but they sounded just as desperate. Just as hungry. Faces were resolving out of the shadows at the corners of the room, features he'd last seen with a las-bolt hole through the forehead, or pleading for life as they vanished beneath a suffocating pillow.

'Remember them?'

'I remember.' He tried to force the images out of his mind,

but they refused to go. He braced himself, ready for the knife. What would it be: throat or chest? At least he could trust Liga to get the job done with a minimum of fuss.

Liga Yager smiled and shook her head. Flies were swarming from the shadows, so thick they blotted out the lumen-light as they closed in around him.

'The Huntsman says it's time. The Imperials are turning on each other. And if I leave you here you're done for. I'm not here to kill you, doc. I'm here to *rescue* you.'

# XLIV

## THE HAND OF MERCY

The chapel doors opened, and instantly scraped to a halt. Ursula shone her light inside and saw that the door had snagged on a fallen beam. She shoved at it clumsily, and it yielded ground a foot at a time, until there was a gap wide enough for them to walk through. Electro-sconces glimmered softly, their light as steady as though they had never been extinguished in all the long years since the Fall. Something scurried away into the darkness – rats, Ursula thought, or perhaps a small felid – but nothing else moved. The chapel smelled of dust and incense and long-forgotten bones. She shone her flash-lumen down the rows of pews, the beam playing over cobwebs so thick that the shapes they shrouded were almost unrecognisable.

*Almost.*

The benches were filled with seated corpses, side by side in death. Ursula's footsteps echoed as she walked down the aisle towards the altar, taking in the rows of the seated dead, staring directly ahead as though paying rapt attention to a sermon only they could hear. Some had slumped forwards, others to the floor. Some were still sitting as they had died, skeletal fingers intertwined or bony arms draped around each other's shoulders, or a smaller skeleton nestled in the lap of a larger one. Each skull had a small hole precisely punched out between the eyes. There were no signs that any of them had resisted in any way.

There was a larger, grander pew close to the front, the sides raised to allow the nobility to worship in privacy, away from commoners' prying eyes. She stopped before the altar, which still bore a gilded chalice with a dark, dry crust of what might once have been wine at its base, and turned. From here she could see that the beams in front of the door had been placed as a barricade, though time had taken its toll on the wood, just as it had on everything else.

The gilded pew in the front row held only three corpses. One was the size of an adult – a man, at a guess – but the other two were far, far smaller. Ursula was no expert in assessing the age of children, but she would have guessed one was a toddler two or three years of age, the other bigger, perhaps as old as seven. All three were nestled closely together, the cobwebs woven around them in a single shroud.

Van Haast dropped to his knees, the thud startling in the tomb-like silence. Ursula sat down on the edge of the dais, and watched as he leaned forward, touched his lips to the finger-tips of each mummified corpse in turn, then tenderly moved the cobwebs away from the three dead faces. Scraps of skin still clung to the bones of the skulls, though the eyes were long gone.

'Their names were Esta and Fynn,' the colonel said. 'My husband was Markus...' He choked on the name.

A gold ring glinted on the dead man's finger, a perfect match to the band on Van Haast's own. His skull was unique amongst them all: the las-bolt that had taken his life had entered not between his eyes, but through the hard palate of his mouth, blowing a crater out through the back of his head. The pistol that had fired the fatal shot – and, if her theory was correct, every fatal shot in the room – lay where it had fallen on the floor, below the fingers of his outstretched hand.

'I'm sorry,' Van Haast whispered. Tears were flooding from his eyes, running like rivers over his high cheekbones and into the corners of his mouth, but he made no effort to wipe them away. Ursula had the sense that she had faded from existence, that nothing in the room was real except for the grieving man and his long-dead family.

Something on the floor caught her eye, and she leaned beneath the pew, careful not to disturb the fragile relics of bone and sinew. It was a tiny vox-recorder, the kind where the data-crystal sat clearly visible between the adamantine cogs and wires. They were far too expensive for military use, but she had known high-ranking members of the Administratum to use them to take notes when an autoquill would be too cumbersome to transport. She picked it up, and the cogs began to turn, the light glowing with an eerie blue iridescence.

*'There's not much time left,'* a young man's voice said.

Van Haast's head snapped around. Ursula held up the little recorder, offering it to him, but he continued to stare at it, as though the man with the light, pleasant voice were standing in front of him instead of speaking through a vox-caster down the years.

*'I'm leaving this for you, Hadrian. I know you're going to hear this one day, because you promised you'd come back for us, and you always keep your promises.'* There was a hint of a smile in the voice. *'I'm only sorry we couldn't wait. We've fought them back and sealed the building, but we're surrounded. It's only a matter of time before they break through and come for us again. We've thrown*

*everything we have at them, but...'* A short, dry laugh. *'There's nothing left to fight with. We're out of ammunition, out of supplies, out of time. The storm has been raging for days, and it's blocking all our attempts at communication. The governor's citadel fell a week ago. We think they have a witch up there controlling the weather as well as the dead.'* The speaker paused. *'Before the vox-receiver went down we heard the reports from Kasr Halig and the Beacons. What the enemy did there. There's no way out.'* Another pause. *'No way out except for one.'*

Van Haast's gaze was back on the man's long-dead corpse. He was crying: not in silence, as might be acceptable at a memorial to a fallen Cadian hero, but in great, slow, racking sobs that shook him like an earthquake. Ursula looked away to spare his shame, and wondered how many messages like this had been left during the Fall, how many final broadcasts of love and grief sent out into the night.

*'We took the decision that no one should be alive when they reach us.'* The man's voice hitched, then steadied again. *'We came here, and we prayed that the God-Emperor would protect us from rising again. And I did my duty for them all.'*

How had that duty felt? she wondered. Had the man prayed or sung, or had the deed been completed in silence, broken only by the crack and sizzle of the laspistol. How had he felt when it was over, when he had gathered the bodies of his dead children into his arms, recorded a final message, and put the still-warm muzzle in his own mouth? The act must have taken extraordinary courage in the face of extraordinary despair.

*'Creed is dead. The last ships have gone. For all I know I'm the last one alive on Cadia. Only one more shot to fire. My final duty, and then I can rest.'* The pause stretched out into silence before he spoke again. *'I need you to know that our children were brave, that they weren't frightened at the end. They died with their eyes open.*

*They died as Cadians.'* Another pause. *'Remember us, my best one. Remember we did our duty, and you must do yours.'*

A soft click. The tiny cogs slowed to a halt. The blue glow dimmed.

'Might I be permitted a moment alone?' Van Haast said quietly, without looking up.

'You're not going to…?'

He shook his head. 'I need a moment, that's all.'

'I'll wait for you outside.'

The little vox-recorder was playing again as she stepped through the door and closed it as much as she could. The least she could grant him was a few minutes of privacy while she worked out what on Terra they were going to do next.

Something shifted in the air behind her. She half turned as something struck the back of her head, light flaring in front of her eyes. A shape moved in the corner of her vision, and then something cold and sharp plunged into her neck with a loud hiss. A snake, she thought stupidly, her thoughts already slowing.

*No. An autoinjector.*

She reached up to swat it away, but her hands felt cold and clumsy. The walls spun, then the darkness closed around her like the slamming of a coffin lid.

# XLV

## THE DESPOILER

'Where's the lord castellan?' Argent said. He was standing in the passageway as Laskari and Harapa emerged through the doorway, so close that the door almost hit him as it opened.

'Sorry, sir,' Harapa said. 'Thought she was with you.'

'She's not with me.' Major Argent ran a hand through his greying sandy hair. 'Not in the infirmarium, either, and neither is Ossian.'

'What's the problem, sir?'

'I heard something upstairs. She's not answering her vox.'

'Any idea what's happened?' Harapa was already heading for the stairs, his long legs eating up the ground.

'Like I said. I heard *something*. It could have been nothing, but...' The major shrugged. 'This damn city has us all on edge.'

The grand hallway was lit in a curious dull shade of red, the light of the storm filtered through the thick layer of pumice-dust that covered the crystalflex cupola. Someone was moving at the end of a passageway through an open door, and Laskari broke into a run, her injured hand throbbing painfully with every jolting step.

'Sergeant!' Colonel Van Haast was shouting from the far end of the passageway, his voice loud and urgent. Argent was right. Something had happened. Laskari followed Harapa and the colonel through the door, Meraq trailing listlessly behind, until the passageway widened out at a pair of chapel doors where the colonel was kneeling on the ground by the lord castellan's unmoving body.

Argent raised his lasgun, not quite pointing it at Van Haast, but not exactly pointing it away. 'What happened here, colonel?'

'I do not know, *major*.' The colonel's eyes narrowed. 'I was praying in the chapel. The lord castellan was waiting for me outside. I heard a scuffle and I came out to find her like this.'

'Any sign of an assailant?' Harapa bent over the fallen woman and pressed his fingers to the side of her neck.

'No.'

'She's alive.' Harapa looked relieved. 'Head wound looks nasty, but that's not what knocked her out.'

'Shall I fetch the medicae?' Laskari offered, but Harapa shook his head.

'Maybe not yet.' He lifted a gleaming object from the ground, turning it back and forward in the light. It was an autoinjector.

'You think…' Major Argent was hesitant, as if the act of articulating the words would give form to an unwelcome realisation. 'You think Ossian is responsible for this?'

'Wouldn't like to speculate, sir.'

'Frekk. I *told* her they were getting too close. He could be miles away by now.' Argent pinched the bridge of his nose between his fingers. 'All right. Harapa, carry her down to the room with the medicae equipment, we'll see if we can revive her. Do any of you have field medicae training?'

Laskari and Meraq shook their heads.

'Not formally, no.' Harapa lifted the lord castellan, not a small woman by any stretch of the imagination, as though she weighed nothing more than a child. Her head fell back, the long ash-brown hair matted to her scalp with blood, her face terrifyingly pale. 'But I know enough to get by.'

'It'll have to do. Meraq, Laskari, you're with me. We'll go and find whatever comms equipment this place has and get it set up to broadcast. Even if it's just a modar dish, we can use that to set up a high-frequency signal, enough to get through the storm–'

'Forgive me, major.' Van Haast raised a languid hand, though there was something strange about his face, Laskari thought. His eyes were red-rimmed, his features puffy. 'I rather thought I was next in the chain of command, while the lord castellan is indisposed.'

Argent's freckled face flushed an ugly, liverish red. 'And once we have a full understanding of the events that led you to be standing over her unconscious body I will be more than happy for you to assume that command, colonel. I'm sure you'll forgive my hesitancy in the meantime.'

'Then perhaps until such time you're convinced of my innocence,' Van Haast said, rolling his eyes, 'bearing in mind that I'm armed with a power sword and could have killed her some minutes ago were I so inclined, we should ensure that *no one* is left alone with the lord castellan.'

The pain came back first. It always did.

At first it was hard for Ursula to tell exactly where it was coming from, but as she slowly swam her way to the surface of consciousness, the pain concentrated itself on the back of her skull, radiating down her neck and into her shoulders. That wasn't good. If she was head-shot then there was no coming back from that, not with her mind and personality intact. Better to slip back into the comfort of oblivion and let someone else make the decisions for a change. She'd done her duty. No one could ask any more of her than that.

Except she hadn't been shot.

Ursula shoved herself upright. She was still wearing her flak armour, which probably meant she hadn't been unconscious for long. Either that, or whoever had brought her here had simply dumped her on the flimsy metal table and headed off to attend to more pressing matters.

She swung her legs over the side and cautiously tested out their ability to hold her weight. The muscles grudgingly responded, but her balance was badly off. A wave of nausea crashed against her, black spots dancing in front of her eyes. When she was sure she wasn't going to fall, she touched one tentative hand to the back of her head, probing the tender crust of dried blood covering her torn scalp. Impossible to know what real damage had been done, but she took the fact that she was up and moving as a good sign.

*Focus on one thing at a time.*

She was in one of the rooms of the Van Haast citadel, in the servants' quarters, close to where they had entered. The room had been set up as a makeshift operating theatre, but the gleaming chirurgical instruments set out on their olive-green cloth had been for Laskari, not for her. Where was everyone?

Trying to think clearly was like swimming through machine oil. Where had she been when it had happened? The memories of the chapel flashed into her mind, the vivid image of the ranks of the quiet dead. The dead children in their dead father's arms. A wedding ring on a skeletal hand.

It hadn't happened in there. She had been outside, waiting for Van Haast to say his last goodbyes. There had been a noise from behind her, and then something had hit the back of her skull like a Taurox, followed by the hiss of an autoinjector. If whoever had done it had wanted her dead, they'd have had ample opportunity to finish her off. That was the strange thing. Whoever had done this could easily have killed her, but they hadn't. Which meant they had wanted something else.

Her hand flew to the base of her neck, fingers scrabbling in a panic for the data-crystal on its chain and finding nothing. The crystal was gone.

Panic rose up in her throat. She forced it down, clinging to the last shreds of hope. It wasn't impossible that one of the others might have taken it for safekeeping while she was unconscious, but she had to know right away.

Ungainly as a newborn aurox-calf, she staggered her way to the door and pulled it open. Voices were coming from another room across the passageway, the floor and walls shifting and rising like they were in the throes of a warp transit. She took a deep breath, steadied herself, and walked through the open door.

The conversation stopped. Five faces swivelled towards her, all wearing such similar expressions of surprise that she would have laughed if that wasn't likely to set off an explosion in her skull. Argent scrambled to his feet.

'You're awake!'

'Who has the data-crystal?' Ursula resisted the urge to probe at the aching wound on the back of her head. For the first time, it occurred to her that whoever had struck the blow could be sitting in the room. At least it wasn't *all* of them. If this was an outright mutiny, she'd already be dead. 'And for that matter, where's Ossian?'

Argent frowned. 'You don't remember?'

'Don't remember what?' She shook her head to clear it, and instantly regretted the movement as a bayonet of pain shot up

427

through the base of her skull. 'I remember everything up until someone cracked me over the back of the head.'

'We think...' Argent ran his tongue across his chapped upper lip. 'We think Ossian attacked you.'

'He *what?*' The whole notion was ridiculous. Ossian might be a penal legionnaire, but there was no way he was responsible. 'Because of the autoinjector, is that it? Why on earth would he do something like that? What would he want with the data-crystal? It's no use to anyone unless we can get it off-world.'

'I don't begin to understand the man's motivations. It could be as simple as an act of revenge for his dead companions. Or if he could find a way off-world, the information on that crystal could buy him anything he wanted. A life in comfort. A place in a rogue trader's retinue.'

'Because of course this place is positively crawling with warrant-bearers.' She rolled her eyes, then regretted it as the room kept spinning. 'Your personal dislike for the man is clouding your judgement, Gideon. Try to approach this with a little objectivity.'

'That is exactly what I'm trying to do. I appreciate you enjoy the man's company, but I need you to put that to one side for now.'

Ursula's face flushed red. Argent looked down at his own hands, his own face reddening in turn.

'Would you care to elaborate on that last point, major?'

'He attacked his last commanding officer. He's been doing everything he can to worm himself into your trust since the moment we found him, but he's a traitor and a murderer. Why is it a surprise that he's done the same thing again?'

'He had his reasons for that.' Her mouth flooded with the sense-memory of cheap recaff brewed over fyceline. 'Under the circumstances, you or I might have done the same.'

Van Haast shook his head sorrowfully. 'Lord castellan, I appreciate you want to believe the best of the man. But he's shown no sign of changing his ways. Meraq, tell the lord castellan what you told the rest of us.'

The girl looked down at her hands, a picture of misery. 'I saw him, lord. Him and the other legionnaire. We were out on patrol, Zhata and I. We saw the drop-ship come down, the one carrying the legionnaires.' Meraq's voice was barely audible. 'Zhata and I watched them search the wreckage. They went into the cockpit, and came out with weapons. When we went in after the Huntsman had moved on, we found the corpses of the pilots. One had died in the crash. The other... had been shot in the head with a lascarbine at point-blank range.'

A fresh wave of nausea rolled over her. 'How do you know it was him?'

'It was *one* of them,' Argent said. 'Either way he was complicit. Remember the laspistols they were carrying when they showed up? Aeronautica standard issue.'

The world tilted suddenly, and Ursula put out a hand to steady herself. Why was she trying to give Ossian the benefit of the doubt? Because she *liked* him? The evidence was staring her in the face.

'Ursula. He's gone, and so has the crystal. The citadel's surrounded, we've got no hope of going after it. All we can do is try to get the comms equipment working here and get a message out to the *Oriflamme*.'

She laughed, careful not to look at Van Haast. 'There's no comms equipment here. Hadrian and I searched the place. It must have been removed or destroyed after he left.'

Argent's face went pale. 'Then we try the beacon again.'

'No point.' She pulled the little sphere out of her pocket, and held it up, glinting in the last of the light. 'The signal's not getting out through that storm.'

'Then what exactly are you saying? That we sit here and wait to be rescued? Because that storm doesn't seem to be going anywhere.'

Ursula closed her eyes. Another choice to make. The data-crystal and the future it had held was gone beyond hope of recovery. The loss was devastating, misery lying like a ton weight on her chest. A week ago she had been perfectly content to oversee the Cadian regiments through their final years, everything that they had been slowly whittled away by time and attrition. But her father's final plan had promised something else. The dream of New Cadia had been an uncertain thing, a tiny flickering candle of possibility, but for a few hours it had taken root in her mind and blossomed there.

And it was gone.

*'From everything I know of you, you'll make the right choice.'*

Her father had been so certain.

What would be so wrong with taking the easy path, for once in her life? Wait here for the defences to be overwhelmed; lie down and die like the families in the chapel. Cadia was a dead world, its people a spent force, the last dying lights of a once great culture flickering out one after the other. A few more corpses wouldn't mean much in the grand scheme of things.

But the Cadians in the chapel hadn't lain down and died, at least not until the last possible moment. They had fought a desperate retreat long after hope and the war were lost, even their deaths an act of defiance. Like Tethys and their soldiers, stalwart to the last, clinging to the dream of Cadia long after it should have been dead and gone.

'Well, if there is nothing more to say, then I think that's settled,' Van Haast said, rising to his feet. 'With your permission, lord castellan, I think I'd like to attend to my prayers in the family chapel.'

'Permission denied, colonel.' She didn't raise her voice. 'The storm is blocking our signal. Your husband said the same thing happened during the Fall – that they had a sorcerer on the highest part of Kasr Arroch calling down the storm. If there's any chance to put a stop to what they're doing, then that's where we need to be.'

She looked around the little group of faces. Her squad. Her mismatched, squabbling, untried, hopeless squad, who had followed her into hell and trusted her to see them home again. Time to find out if they were the Cadians they were meant to be.

Time to find out if she was.

'Cadia is our birthright,' she said. 'I told you that on the *Oriflamme*, before I understood what those words truly meant. A broken world, a slaughtered people, a shattered piece of rock half-fallen into the warp. Who would want that for a birthright? No one. But it is ours all the same – not a right, but an obligation. It falls to us to fight as long as we draw breath, to bear witness to all that we have seen, to tell the Imperium of the last days of Cadia. Of the devastation, but also the courage, unbroken in the face of overwhelming odds. Tethys and their soldiers. The Sister of Battle whose remains we found in Kasr Gallan. Your family, colonel. Each of them embodied the spirit of Cadia, the courage to fight to the last, to demand that the enemy pay for every last inch of ground in blood, to spit defiance with their final breath.' She paused and met each pair of eyes in turn. 'And that is all that I ask of you now.'

Silence.

Laskari got to her feet. 'I'm with you, lord castellan.'

Harapa was next, then Argent, then Meraq.

Van Haast was the last to rise to his feet. 'A speech almost worthy of your father.' He clipped his heels together, and gave a smart little bow. 'I am with you to the end, my lord. And may the God-Emperor have mercy on anything that stands in our way.'

# XLVI

**JUDGEMENT**

The corpse-flies were in Ossian's eyes, his mouth, his nostrils: fat, hairy bodies packed into his earholes so tightly that his entire skull was filled with their wretched droning buzz. At first, he had tried to keep them off by swatting and crushing, all four limbs flailing in a furious dance, but the torrent that had poured from Liga's open mouth had been too thick. The last thing he had seen before they swarmed over his eyelids had been the opening of the infirmarium door, but by then it had been too late.

He had thought – not for the first time over the last few days – that this time his death was a certainty. Wrong again.

It was much worse than that.

He opened his eyes. It didn't make much difference. Every muscle in his body hurt – not the now familiar ache of overuse, but a gnawing pain between every joint, as if he had been disassembled and put back together again in the space of ten seconds. He had a lingering sense of having travelled impossibly fast, down paths best left untrodden.

The cloud of flies parted at last. A fat, buzzing corpse-fly landed on his forearm, where it crawled indolently across the skin. He swatted it away, but it was so large his clumsy blow managed only to crush its lower half into a purulent green smear, leaving the multifaceted eyes to glare balefully at him as it died. He shook his arm to dislodge the mangled corpse, and another instantly took its place, its proboscis extended to suck up its predecessor's juices.

The Huntsman was standing so close that Ossian could have reached out and touched the mould-slick ceramite armour. One of the heretic's hands was raised upward to the sky, the other wrapped tightly around the grip of the murderous-looking scythe. Lightning arced from the cloud to the tip of the blade to earth through the monstrous figure, while around them, rows of kneeling cultists bowed their heads in supplication: old men and women in tattered uniforms, children and teenagers with the lines of corruption already deep into their faces. Fungating tumours dangled from eye sockets, pus ran from open sores, tattered skin sloughed away from flesh so blanched and bloated it seemed impossible that the bodies they covered could even be alive. Every face was filled with the same hideous devotion.

He was standing in an astrogranite courtyard, the city stretching away to the plains below and mountains beyond. The shattered remains of a tower loomed above his head, a great eyeless skull gazing down at him from the stone facade. The long-rusted wreckage of a gun-cutter lay a little distance down the hill. This had been an impressive building once, a testament to the power and might of the local governor.

Now it was a temple of the damned.

The helmeted head moved, the eye slit turning towards Ossian. The Huntsman lifted a hand and brought it sharply downwards, and an unseen pressure drove Ossian to his knees. Liga was already kneeling, her face upturned in reverence. Ossian gathered a mouthful of foul-tasting spit, and hawked it at the heretic's breastplate.

The Huntsman regarded him thoughtfully, removed the gauntlet from his right hand, and dipped his scabbed and rotting index finger into the smear of spittle. He offered the hand to Liga. She rose up on her knees and licked the digit clean with rapturous intensity. He turned his palm upward, and she fixed her mouth against it, suckling at the pus from the open sores like a child drinking from the breast. Soft sounds of satisfaction rose from her throat. Ossian's gut heaved, but he was too empty to bring anything up.

The Huntsman jerked his hand away from Liga's face. Her lips and mouth had taken on an unhealthy purple tinge, her skin slick and gleaming with pus as she licked the last traces of the heretic's fluids from her lips.

'What have you brought me, little daughter?' The voice was impossibly deep, the sounds thick, wet and bubbling as though the heretic were speaking through a cut and bleeding throat.

'The chirurgeon, my lord,' Liga said, the words sounding stilted and formal compared to her usual quick bursts of slang. 'Come to offer his fealty to you, as you asked.'

Liga bowed her head. The heretic placed his seeping palm against Ossian's forehead, and something that had no physical form forced itself into his mind. Tendrils of thought probed the spaces between his synapses, pulling memories and emotions forward to examine them with indolent curiosity, his soul laid bare despite his futile resistance. Then the pressure was gone as quickly as it had come.

'This one is not here to bend the knee,' the Huntsman said, his voice dripping with amusement. 'He is here to serve another end.'

'Go frekk yourself.' Ossian tried to gather enough saliva to spit again, but his mouth was dry. This close, the sheer scale of the Heretic Astartes had him by the hindbrain and refused to let go. Even if the relentless sorcerous pressure on his shoulders eased, he doubted he could force his legs into motion to run. And if he ran, where would he go? The cultists would tear him to shreds in seconds, or if he managed to get past them he'd meet the silent rows of the dead, and the horrors beyond.

'What have I done to earn such hatred?' The Huntsman sounded amused, even playful. 'You are the ones who have invaded my domain. Slaughtered my followers. Disturbed my sanctum. Cadia no longer belongs to your Corpse-Emperor. It belongs to the true gods now.'

A ragged cheer rose from the tattered heretics. He raised a hand, and they fell instantly silent.

'Here I hold domain. Here is the place of the hunt.'

'And what do all those other heretics at the city walls have to say about that?' If all Ossian could move were his lips then he was going to make the most of it, and if the heretic tried to make him drink pus the way that Liga had done, the Astartes would have to break his neck to get his mouth into position. 'Hundreds of them and one of you. I don't rate those chances.'

A bubbling snort of derision came from the helmet. 'They are drawn to the sacred place, but they cannot hold it. No one can. The power... the despair is too great. But I will make that power mine.'

A rustling rose from the serried ranks of the damned. The Huntsman beckoned to the nearest poxwalker, and it lumbered towards him, the tattered remains of a noose hanging from its mummified neck. The Huntsman closed his massive hand around the rope, and hoisted the unresisting poxwalker into the air.

'A whole city, in the throes of despair. When their precious lord castellan's promises rang hollow, when they knew that all hope was lost, each one of them took their own lives rather than see the glory of what was to come. Such horror, such despair that the very warp sang with it. It sings with it still.' The heretic jerked his wrist, and the poxwalker's neck broke with an audible crack. 'And I will take that power, offer it up to the Grandfather of Despair and receive such a boon in return that none will deny me again.'

He opened his hand and dropped the broken poxwalker to the ground, where it lay twitching, despite its dislocated vertebrae.

'So what are you waiting for?'

'Such fools, you Cadians, to live with collars around your necks. It matters not whether they are made of metal or of shame. You live as slaves and die as slaves, never once reaching your hand for the freedom already in your grasp.'

'You're not going to convince me.' Ossian swallowed. His tongue felt swollen against the roof of his mouth, and the blood was thudding in his ears like the beat of a marching drum. 'Just get on with it, would you?'

A bubbling laugh rippled out from beneath the helmet. 'But where would be the sport in that?'

*They're going to hunt me*, Ossian thought wildly. *He's going to set me running for his cultists to hunt like a pack of canids.*

'I'm not playing your game. You want them to tear me apart?' He gestured to the ragged mass of humanity. 'They can do it right here.'

The heretic drew a deep, wheezing breath, and let it out in another purulent cackle. 'Take the device from his wrist, little daughter.'

Liga leaned over and unbuckled the control module from Ossian's wrist. He tried to pull his arm away, but the Huntsman's

437

will was locked tight around his own. Liga placed the device in the enormous hand. The Huntsman lifted it to his helmet, turned it around, then nodded in satisfaction.

'Excellent.' The heretic threw it to one of the capering cultists, who snatched it from the air and scuttled away into the crowd. The great antlered helmet turned its face back to Ossian. 'No, little mortal. You are neither the hunter nor the quarry in the great hunt that is to come. You are the *bait*.'

It was night, and the blood-rain was falling again. The dead were gone, but the storm was in full spate now, lightning striking at the centre of the city in a quick, irregular rhythm like the beat of a failing heart.

How long did they have left?

The answer was obvious. Not long enough. Ursula knew that from the look on Laskari's face. The little trooper's features were pinched tight with pain and fear, her hands shaking as she held the long-las. The rot was spreading up Laskari's arm, no matter how hard she tried to conceal it. From the pace the decay was progressing, without medical attention her life would be measured in hours, though in all probability the same could be said for the rest of them. Ursula had made her peace with that.

They passed what had once been a barracks, its empty windows staring down at them in accusation, the past trapped inside like an insect in amber. An eerie silence clung to the kasr, muffling each step they took.

'Where did the hell spawn go?' Argent whispered.

Lightning struck ahead of them again, close enough that Ursula could smell the sharp scent of ozone.

She shook her head. 'I don't know. Take advantage of the respite. It won't last.'

'And where exactly are we going?' Argent asked.

'The governor's fortress,' Van Haast said. The ground shook again, sending the slates slipping off the barrack-room roof to shatter on the cobblestones. 'An auspicious place to meet our end.'

'No one's going to die except that heretic,' she said. As lies went, it was a good one. 'And that bastard legionnaire if I get my hands on him.'

Ossian's betrayal smarted like an open wound, but she had managed to transform the pain into a jagged ball of hatred in her chest. She had wasted an hour searching through everyone's clothing and belongings in one last attempt to prove Argent wrong, but there was no sign of the data-crystal anywhere. The only explanation was the obvious one: Ossian had taken the crystal and fled. If the God-Emperor was kind, she'd have the chance to repay him for his treachery before she died.

'What makes you think Ossian will be there?' Van Haast asked.

'Where else could he possibly be?' Ursula forced herself to shrug with an indifference she didn't feel. 'There's no way off this Throne-damned world until that storm ends. He's thrown his lot in with the Huntsman in exchange for getting that collar off his neck. It's the only thing that makes sense.'

'Insofar as anything makes sense on Cadia,' Van Haast said.

'How do we kill the Huntsman, lord castellan?' Laskari was doing a good job of staying upright, but her voice was shaking.

'Overwhelming firepower, carefully aimed.' Ursula tried to sound more confident than she felt. 'Hit them in the right place and they die like everything else.'

An explosion ruptured the air behind them, sending a cloud of dust and ash rising from the perimeter wall. An engine screamed, the earth shook again, and a hab-block to the west collapsed. Something the height of a Sentinel walker but easily twice its bulk strode through the dust cloud, moving at speed.

Another lightning strike turned the sky to violet, the veil that held reality intact growing thin. The Huntsman's horn boomed somewhere in the city, and daemon engines answered with a howling shriek no blessed machine-spirit had ever made.

'Quickest route to the governor's palace?' Ursula asked.

Van Haast scanned the streets. A fissure in the ground opened under his feet, and he stepped aside as skeletal fingers pushed up from beneath like impossibly fast-growing weeds.

'North. Over the Bridge of Sorrows.'

The horn blew again, and a corpse pulled itself free of the broken ground. One skeletal frame at a time, the streets were filling with the silent dead, laughing daemons capering around their feet, mutated monstrosities pushing through their ranks in a mass of horns and teeth and rotting flesh.

The horn sounded for a third and final time, and the damned began their advance.

'He knows we're coming, doesn't he?' Laskari said softly.

'Put it this way,' Ursula said, 'if he doesn't know already, we'll make sure he bloody knows when we get there.'

# XLVII

## DAMNATION

The dead shambled from every city street, some little more than bones and sinew, others still fresh and rotting, serving the Huntsman in death as they had as cultists in life. Chaos spawn whooped and gibbered between them, darting forward to attack only to be driven back by volleys of las-fire or a power sword's sparking edge, while all the time the grinding advance of the infernal engines drew closer. The ground was trembling, spitting out scalding vapour from cracks still narrow enough to step over. They wouldn't stay that way for long.

Laskari took careful aim, and shot a cavorting cultist squarely between the eyes. She had thought dying would be easy, but as it turned out it was just as difficult as everything else. The pain was burning like unholy fire in her hand, sending tendrils of flame shooting up her arm with every movement. Meraq had found two injectors of morpholox in Ossian's discarded medkit, but Laskari had refused to take a dose before they left. She was saving them for later. Right now she needed to be sharp.

'You all right there?' Harapa asked.

'Right as rain, sarge.'

'Good kid.' He glanced over at Meraq, who was firing carefully controlled bursts as she retreated over the cracked earth. 'We're getting out of this place soon. All of us.'

'All of us,' Laskari echoed. It didn't matter that they were both lying. It felt good to be part of something worthwhile.

'There's the bridge!' Van Haast shouted. The huge edifice of the Bridge of Sorrows loomed out of the ruins a few blocks away. Steep banks plunged down a hundred feet to the river that bisected the city, its waters deep and blood-red where they reflected the fiery skies.

The lord castellan stepped forward and cut down a cluster of the dead with a flare of blue-white light. She was breathing hard, her face scarlet, her hair a wild corona about her face.

'Keep it up, trooper,' she said, offering Laskari a frag grenade. 'Let's clear ourselves some breathing room, shall we?'

The explosives were a precious and diminishing resource, but there was no doubt about their effectiveness. The grenade blew a path between the swarming cultists, clearing their way to the bridge. It was beautiful even now, its gothic arches a prayer of adamantine and astrogranite reaching up to the Golden Throne like beseeching hands.

'How many… poxwalkers… can there be left?' Argent gasped. He wiped the blood from his eyes, but the stream from his scalp refused to slow. Everyone was on their feet, but the stigmata of battle were starting to show on them all. Colonel Van Haast's left sleeve was soaked through with blood.

'Depends how many we had to start with,' Harapa said. His arms were covered in a latticework of shallow incisions, the grip of his combat knife stained red with blood, and when he smiled it didn't quite reach his eyes. 'I'm on forty-five kills. More if we're counting cultists.'

'Score them separately,' the lord castellan said.

'Chaos spawn?'

'Them too.'

'Respectfully, my lord,' Van Haast said, turning an outraged face towards her, 'is now really the time for this?'

'Worrying about your score, Hadrian?' Despite her dishevelled appearance, the lord castellan was the most relaxed Laskari had ever seen her, almost euphoric. That made a certain amount of sense. Now that the odds were so far stacked against them, there was nothing to lose, no wrong decision to make, just survival from moment to moment, each breath the God-Emperor's gift.

'I am worried about nothing of the sort,' the colonel said. 'Considering I have already killed more than both of the two of you put together.'

'And here I was thinking I was the one with the head injury.' The lord castellan paused to snap a quick shot from her one functioning pistol into a darkened alley. The shadows flared green, and something with too many teeth ruptured like a ripe ploin. A robed figure scrambled over the seeping carcass, and Laskari dispatched it with a single bolt through its misshapen skull.

'That's me up to forty-two, my lord,' she said, and Ursula Creed laughed.

'Good shooting. We'll make an officer of you yet.'

The lord castellan came to a sudden halt.

'Is there a reason why we're stopping?' Argent's voice was tight. He was the only one of the senior officers who didn't seem to be enjoying himself.

Creed held up her hand and bent down over the cultist's

corpse, peeling back the bony fingers to expose the small object clutched in its hand: a device like an oversized chrono. The control device for a penal legionnaire's collar.

'Frekk...' she said softly, and buckled the device around her wrist.

'What are you doing with that?' Argent asked.

'Keeping it.' She tucked the strap beneath the cuff of her fatigues. 'If Ossian's alive, we can use its proximity sensors to find him and take back that bloody crystal.'

'Isn't it more likely he's dead already?' Argent said. 'What are his chances of survival in a place like this?'

'Perhaps.' The smile was gone from her face, replaced with a cold-eyed determination. 'Better for him if he is.'

'Ursula, I need to know. What *is* your plan?'

Argent was at her shoulder as they headed onto the bridge, a jittering, distracting presence that she could have done without. The problem was that she *didn't* have a plan, only a series of disastrous ideas she'd already ruled out. With the assets at her disposal – a colonel of Hussars, a middle-aged staff officer, a suspiciously well-informed Catachan sergeant, a wounded trooper so green you could still see the white paint on her helmet and a traumatised teenage soldier raised by sappers in an underground bunker – a full assault was out of the question. The power swords were their only weapons capable of cutting through the Huntsman's armour, and she'd already failed in one-on-one combat against him. If she still had the bolt pistol they might have stood a chance, but she might as well wish for the *Wrath of Olympus* to come lumbering over the horizon. They were on their own. There were no miracles on their way, just an ever-encroaching tide of damnation.

'We get close. Scout the area. We have explosives. Perhaps we can find an unstable building and crush him beneath it.'

'We dropped a mountain on him before and that didn't take.' Argent shook his head. 'We need a better plan–'

Behind them, something huge gave a deafening roar, followed by a crash as a building crumpled into rubble.

'I'm open to alternatives!'

The bridge shook. A vast silhouette, larger than any tank she had ever seen, moved forward out of the maelstrom of smoke and dust. The three-headed flesh hound raised its frilled heads and roared. It was bigger than she had thought, bigger even than when she had seen it in the tunnels. It had been growing since the moment they had released it from the bunker in Kasr Gallan, feasting on their horror and fear, following their scent across the blasted remains of Cadia. A malign light shone from its hooded crimson eyes, glinting off the black iron collar on its neck.

It was on the bridge.

Four hundred yards stood between them and solid ground. Ursula risked a look across the parapet to the river far below. At that distance hitting the surface of the water would be like falling onto astrogranite.

'I can slow it down.' Harapa was already unslinging his backpack and pulling out a spool of detonation cord. 'Get moving. I'll set the charges to blow out the bridge.'

Ursula allowed herself a second to consider. 'Is this an attempt at heroic sacrifice?'

Harapa grinned around the piece of fuse wire in his teeth. 'I'm twice as fast as the rest of you. I'm just giving you a head start, that's all.'

Behind them, the monstrous beast slammed a forefoot down against the bridge with a resonant clang that shook the world and set the air vibrating in her chest. It threw back its head and roared. A bolt streaked from Laskari's long-las and bounced uselessly off its leathery hide.

'Save your charge,' Ursula said. Then, to Harapa: 'God-Emperor protect you, sergeant.'

Harapa nodded, slammed a melta charge down onto the vibrating surface of the bridge and spooled out his detonation cord.

'Go. Move. Now.' Ursula broke into a run, cursing every moment of her life spent seated in a command throne or behind a desk. Rho had been offering her augmetic limb improvements for years. For the first time she wished she'd taken them up on the offer.

Another shriek rose from the monster's throat. Ursula coaxed a burst of speed from her burning muscles, envying Van Haast his effortless stride. What if Harapa set off the charges too soon? Worse, what if the engine reached Harapa before he could set off the charges, or the charges failed to go off at all? Munitorum-issue explosives were delicate enough even when they hadn't been jostled through three days of snow and bloody rain.

Ursula risked a look over her shoulder. The daemonic hound filled her vision, a vast and malevolent shadow against the fiery skies. There was no sign of Harapa. She forced her attention back to the bridge, to the yards vanishing beneath her pounding feet, the far bank still tantalisingly out of reach. Laskari and Meraq were on solid ground already, their lasguns stuttering futile bolts of bright light. Van Haast was running a step ahead of her, Argent two steps behind.

A wave of heat and sound crashed over her, lifting her into the air. She hit the ground feet first, stumbled and kept running, the smell of singed hair filling her nostrils.

'Harapa! You still with us?'

The bridge had ruptured across the middle, leaving two ends of tattered metal. The daemon was dangling from the near side, then, as she watched, the metal beneath its claws shrieked and gave way, sending it plummeting to the water below.

'Harapa?'

Still nothing.

The waters below parted, and the daemon rose up from the river like a leviathan. The three great heads turned upwards, forepaws failing to find purchase as it scrabbled up the bank.

'Down here, chief.'

A hand reached up from lower down the bank. Harapa was clinging to the torn earth, his limbs spreadeagled.

'Well done, sergeant.' She reached down and offered him her hand, but with a single powerful movement he took hold of a jutting metal bridge-strut and swung himself up beside her. In the gorge below, the daemon shrieked and roared, its eyes blazing with hatred and warp-fire.

'It'll claw its way up eventually,' Harapa said. 'Still. That should slow it for now.'

Kasr Arroch was tearing itself apart. The ground had cracked open, rippling bands of heat and light rising from the magma-filled chasms below, the burning air full of scorching sulphur. It was almost beautiful, Ossian thought.

'Master,' Liga was saying. 'You promised you would make him one of us! You promised his freedom!'

'Freedom is a lie.' The Huntsman raised his scythe to channel the lightning down. The cloud was so low that the strikes had become a flickering net of light, connecting the heretic to the sky.

'What's he waiting for?' Ossian muttered.

She shook her head. 'Bend the knee, doc. Swear your fealty and you can have that collar off your neck. There's still time.'

'He's not listening.'

Ossian tried for the hundredth time to force himself to his feet. He had hoped the Huntsman might be distracted by the ritual, but the grip around Ossian's will stayed locked tight.

He had no weapons, no vox-bead, no way out but the collar around his neck, and no way of triggering that. Something huge that stank of death moved behind him, heavy lumbering steps shaking the ground.

'What did he mean, I'm the bait?'

'I don't know. He's been in all their heads. Reading their thoughts. Nudging them towards him. All of this...' She waved a hand around the dais. 'It's all part of the plan. Part of the *hunt*.'

'You shouldn't have brought me here.' Ossian was too tired to be angry, but the helplessness smarted.

'I did my best! I'm trying to give you a future.'

'I know. But it's not a future worth having.'

The Huntsman turned, lightning still coruscating over his armour. 'The time is now, Chirurgeon with the Bloody Hands. Surrender your will to me, and I will show you worlds beyond your imagining.'

The pressure holding him on his knees vanished, and Ossian rose, weightless with relief. For one last moment he entertained the thought of accepting the Huntsman's offer, of freedom from the collar, from the Astra Militarum, from a God-Emperor who only ever demanded and never gave.

But all that was on offer was slavery of another kind.

'No.'

Liga got to her feet, reaching out a hand in supplication. 'Wait. Lord, you promised–'

'I promised nothing. His life is mine, as is yours. The games are over. Do it, little daughter, or die with him.'

Liga stepped forward and drew her knife. 'I don't want to do this.'

'Then don't!' Ossian raised his hands. 'For the sake of your soul if nothing else!'

'He can be useful to us,' Liga began, but the Huntsman cut her off.

'I grow tired of waiting.'

Something punched Ossian in the back, just over his right kidney. He looked down and saw the blade of a bayonet protruding from just below his breastbone, the rusty surface gleaming with blood. With a sickening tugging sensation an unseen hand pulled the blade free. That was when the pain began. He stumbled, fell forward onto one knee and looked up at Liga. The look of horror on her face was directed neither at him nor at the Heretic Astartes beside her, but over his shoulder to the looming shadow behind him. It moaned.

Blood was pouring from the wound in his abdomen in a steady stream. He half turned, the world spinning around him, and looked up into a familiar face, marked with a neatly punched-out hole in the forehead between two glowing eyes. The skin had partially sloughed away from the facial bones, revealing the heavy brow ridge beneath. Thick horns the colour of necrotic bone sprouted from her shoulders and back, piercing through the remains of a rotting orange jumpsuit.

Her hand slick to the wrist with his blood, the thing that had once been Clavie raised the bayonet again.

The last of the Eighth Regiment fought their way through another knot of poxwalkers without breaking stride, through a narrow series of alleyways and staircases that wound up the mound towards the palace. Ursula could no longer distinguish one aching muscle from the rest, her legs on fire, her lungs burning, the heat stiflingly intense.

'I've got... a plan.' Ursula stopped, bent over, and tried to catch her breath.

'Delighted to hear it.' Van Haast was breathing hard too,

smoothing down the flyaway strands of his hair. Damn the man, he still looked appallingly fresh.

'Didn't say it was a good plan.' She stood upright and instantly regretted it. 'The Huntsman has to be outside. Those lightning strikes, they're part of what he's doing. Calling down the storm. You have been to the governor's palace here, haven't you, colonel?'

'Naturally.'

'There must be an outdoor space. A cloister? A churchyard?'

Van Haast shook his head. Ursula stood up and braced herself for yet more stairs.

'Come on. There's got to be something.'

'Nothing. Except… a landing pad, for the governor's personal gun-cutter.'

'Then that's where he'll be.'

They started up another flight of steps. She counted them down in her head, one step after another. Each one was a step she'd never have to take again. One step closer to leaving this damned planet, one way or the other.

'We have explosives,' she continued. 'Harapa, when we get close, find somewhere to set the mines. A spire, a tower – something you can set to blow. Crush as many of them as we can, disrupt the ritual. Then the moment the clouds part we trigger the beacon and hold our position until help comes.'

'And if it doesn't?' Laskari asked.

'It will come. We've fought through too much to die now.'

The baying of daemonic voices ripped through the air, followed by a heavy thud. The flesh hound was moving again. A bubble of laughter forced its way up through Ursula's chest. If everything on this thrice-damned planet wanted her dead, she'd make them fight for the honour of the kill.

She paused again for breath at the summit, and looked down.

The city stretched out before her, a final memorial to a dead planet. There would come a time when even the memory of Cadia was gone, lost to time and the warp. On the other side of the city, a sharp-edged cliff fell into nothingness, fog and bloody rain trailing away with the atmosphere into the void below. She had come to the edge of the world.

It was time to finish this.

# XLVIII

### THE CANONESS, REVERSED

Ursula propped herself up on her elbows and squinted across the landing pad from beneath her pile of rubble. Laskari and Meraq were out of sight in one of the ruined towers to her left, from which they should have a clear view of everything that was about to happen. Their job was simple: to take out anything that looked likely to stand between Ursula and the Huntsman once the explosion went off.

*'In position, lord castellan,'* Laskari whispered.

The Huntsman stood in the middle of the landing pad surrounded by a host of warp-born atrocities, ragged cultists gazing up in ecstasy around its feet.

'Any sign of Ossian?' Argent asked.

Ursula scanned the huddled masses, looking for the telltale blink of the diode on his collar. The module on her wrist was silent, its tiny machine-spirit satisfied that the collar was close by. Maybe he was dead already.

'I don't see him.'

'*Charges are set, lord,*' Harapa voxed, from somewhere to her right.

She looked at the soldiers beside her. Van Haast was checking his laspistol, his power sword resting dormant at his side. Argent's eyes were closed, his lips moving in silent prayer as his hands touched each of his weapons in silent benediction. Laspistol. Knife. Chainsword. He had used the blade more in the last day than in the preceding twenty years.

'Ready?' she whispered.

'Ready.'

'Emperor protect. And I'll see you on the other side.' She smiled. 'Whether that's the *Oriflamme*, or beside the Golden Throne.'

There was one final part of her plan, but she had kept that to herself. The timing was so far out of her control that she had barely allowed herself to take it into account at all, but if what Harapa had said about the daemon hound had been true – and if things came together the way she had dared to hope – then it might just give them the edge they needed.

Roll the dice. Deal the cards. Spin the wheel, and if she was lucky, maybe this time her luck would hold.

'Sergeant, now.'

'*On it, chief.*'

Ursula held her breath. One second. Another. And then the great towering skull-face atop the governor's palace erupted like a volcano, smoke billowing from the eye sockets and open jaw, the cultists scattering in alarm – but the stone didn't fall.

'What now?' Van Haast asked.

'It's supposed to blow the whole frekking thing–'

She broke off as a horizontal crack appeared in the stone facade between the orbits of the skull, spreading and branching to the sides until the whole cranium broke free and slid forwards. There was a howl from the cultists below, then the massive dome of rock smashed to the ground, obscuring the landing pad in a thick cloud of dust.

'Go!'

Ursula scrambled to her feet, activated her power sword and sprinted headlong through the smoke. Argent's chainsword roared into life behind her, and the sparking blue ghost of Hadrian's power sword shimmered out of the fog on her right like a will-o'-the-wisp of death. Something stinking lumbered out of the darkness towards her and she cut it down without a thought, shoved the rotting body to one side and kept running. A geyser erupted in front of her, and she ducked out of the scalding spray. These hot springs had powered the kasr for generations. Now that same buried energy was tearing it apart.

'Where are you?' she shouted into the smoke. 'Come out, you thrice-damned bastard! Aren't you supposed to be a Huntsman? Out you come and do some bloody hunting, then!'

The dust cleared. In the centre of the landing pad was a broad dais, the hulking figure of the Huntsman half-buried in rubble, the scythe protruding in one outstretched hand.

'We got the bastard!' she shouted. 'Throne damn it, we got–'

The Huntsman shrugged off a groundcar-sized rock as though it were made of foam, sending it thudding to the ground to crush a poxwalker's twitching remains. The heretic rose to his feet, lifted his scythe and snared another sheet of lightning.

'No, Daughter of Creed, you did not.'

She fired her single functioning laspistol, discharging bolt after bolt into the Huntsman's chest, throat and helmet, until smoke was rising from the muzzle and the charge-pack was empty. The Huntsman waited patiently until she had finished, then stepped forward and removed his helmet.

The Astartes' face was blanched and waterlogged like a long-drowned corpse. Sometime during the millennia of his existence, his lips had been gnawed away, exposing yellowed, broken teeth and bleeding gums. In place of a nose there was only a raw, suppurating cavity beneath the sunken, jaundiced orbs of his eyes. He wore the literal face of damnation, but worst of all was the ghost of what he once had been. The face had been exquisite, once: high cheekbones, a broad forehead and a well-formed jaw suffused it with the same terrible majesty she had seen in the lord regent, light years away and a lifetime ago. But the Huntsman's beauty was long gone, offered up with his soul on an altar of corruption and despair.

'All right, you heretic bastard.' Ursula raised her sword. 'Where is it?'

If she could keep his attention on her, maybe the others could get round behind him. If they flanked him they might – *might* – manage to take the heretic down, like a pack of canids at the heels of a Cthellean cudbear. If he charged her she was dead, but if she could just keep him talking a moment longer then a miracle of sorts might present itself.

'Where is *what*?'

'The data-crystal.' She glared at him. 'I want it back.'

The Huntsman laughed. 'You are mistaken, Daughter of Creed. I have no need for trinkets and baubles. You have brought me all that I need, by walking willingly into our midst. Now you surrender, and I ascend.'

The heretic was lying, but that didn't come as a surprise. She raised an eyebrow, risking a glance to either side. Argent and Van Haast had melted back into the fog.

'And what if I don't like the sound of that?'

'Your agreement,' the Huntsman said, his voice bubbling with satisfaction, 'is irrelevant.'

Dozens of cultists lay crushed beneath the rubble, but some were standing, clustered close behind their monstrous protector. The Huntsman raised a hand, and the rotting reanimated remains of an ogryn lumbered forward, a human figure in each hand dangling from the scruff of the neck, one in a blood-soaked legionnaire's uniform, the other in a robe the colour of rotting pondweed.

Ossian. Yager.

'A gift for you,' the Huntsman said. 'Your betrayers. You have been a worthy quarry, Daughter of Creed. In recognition of that, I offer you the deaths of the traitor and the chirurgeon in exchange for your oath of fealty.'

Ossian's lips moved, but whatever he was trying to say was too soft for her to hear. A protest of innocence or a confession of guilt? It didn't matter now. The Huntsman's voice was in her head, tangled so intricately in her own thoughts that she could no longer tell where his ended and hers began.

*Raise your sword. Kill them. Cut their throats and let the warm gush of blood wash away all the shame, all the regret.*

'Yes. Your soldiers betray you. They do not follow you. They do not love you. Cadia has fallen, to rise no more.' The heretic's voice was still thick with pus and grave-dirt, but it had taken on a new sweetness. It held the promise of new beginnings, fertile soil watered with blood in which to plant the seeds of the future. 'Cling no more to the past. Let us sanctify this covenant with blood.'

She looked down at the power sword, humming gently in her hand. It would feel so good to plunge it into Ossian's throat. He had lied to her, betrayed her, hidden his nature behind lying smiles. Now he would pay for his disloyalty with his life.

He raised his head, and his eyes met hers. His face was a ghastly shade of grey that suggested more of his blood was outside his body than in it. His lips moved again, and this time the words were audible.

'I'm ready.' He drew a ragged breath, his face twisting in pain. 'But do it in the Emperor's name, not his.'

She lunged forward with the power sword, but instead of plunging it into either of the legionnaires she stabbed it directly into the ogryn's pendulous gut. Ropes of grey-green intestines spilled out in a gush of purulent fluid, and the ogryn fell back, taking its prisoners with it to the ground.

The Huntsman's face contorted in anger. 'If you will not serve, your blood will suffice.'

The two vast gauntlets locked around the scythe, drew it back, and swung. Ursula darted back out of reach, bringing up her sword in a clumsy parry. Ossian and Liga were already lost in the press of bodies. There was no time to worry about them now. If she lost this battle, they were all dead anyway.

The scythe arced down again with impossible speed, the air tearing audibly around its leading edge. She didn't bother trying to deflect it this time, instead darting inside the reach of the weapon and lashing out with her sword in a blow to the knee that would have crippled a lesser opponent. Instead her blade gouged a bright score out of the ceramite leg plating, and she dashed back just in time to avoid the blunt end of the scythe's handle as it descended towards her unprotected skull.

'Any help coming?' Another green flare of las-fire painted the heretic's armour, but it was barely enough to scorch the surface.

*'Doing my best, my lord!'* Laskari voxed.

The distinctive rasp of a chainsword rang out from the ground to her left. Argent was toe-to-toe with a headless horror, a circular maw ringed with rows of needle teeth where the head should have been. Long ropes of muscle lashed from its back, each one ending in a hooked talon. Gouts of purple blood sprayed into the air as he hacked at its limbs and torso, the teeth of the chainsword frothing blood, meat and marrow into a fine red mist. Van Haast was fighting his way towards her, but the surviving cultists were swarming him, tearing at his clothes and armour with their bare hands, slowing his progress to a crawl.

The heretic ducked out of the way of a las-bolt from Laskari's sniper nest – how could it move faster than light? – and swung the scythe again. This time as she stepped back her foot caught on a jagged chunk of astrogranite. She stumbled, and the tip of the scythe cut through her pauldron to bite deep into the meat of her left shoulder. A scream tore its way from her throat, hot blood gushing across her chest and arm.

That wasn't right. The crackling energy from the scythe-blade should have cauterised the wound immediately, but there was no smell of roasting meat, only blood. The pain spread through her shoulder into her chest, driving the breath from her lungs, and she took a desperate step away, trying to buy time to gather her composure…

And the first scarlet droplet hit the ground.

'Yessss,' the Huntsman hissed, the word sinuous and elongated as it emerged from between the tattered lips. 'Creed's blood, spilled at last on unholy soil.'

The astrogranite smouldered as though her blood were acidic. Sheet lightning arced from the heretic's armour to the earth around it, and he screamed in victory.

'The rite is complete.'

The ground beneath his feet shook and split, rising like a plinth into the air. The Huntsman himself was growing too – swelling and distorting as he filled with sorcerous energy. The plates of his armour cracked and bulged, sloughing off in fragments with the last vestiges of humanity, until what was left could no longer be described as remotely human.

Ursula turned and ran. The ground was cracking beneath her feet, geysers erupting around her as the landing pad transformed into a fractured series of astrogranite islands in a boiling sea.

The thing that had been the Huntsman threw back its head, and screamed into the rising wind.

'Grandfather! Accept these gifts to you! With the Blood of Creed I seal my right as lord of this world!'

The storm fell silent, and the clouds parted.

**'CREED.'**

She looked up into clear skies. There were the familiar stars, there the Eye of Terror, blazing down brighter than she had ever seen it before. The massive scar of the Cicatrix Maledictum split the heavens from horizon to horizon, unholy light spilling from the wound that had torn the Imperium in two. And there between them was the vision from her warp-dream, only this time it was real. Tentacles roiled at the edges of the rip in reality, clutching at the sky as though they would pull it piece by piece into the void, while in its centre a thousand bulging eyes opened with vast and malign intent.

'Lord of Decay!' the Huntsman bellowed. 'Grant me your blessing, and Cadia shall be yours!'

A column of bilious light seared down from the sky, engulfing and filling the Huntsman's mortal form. The heretic was twenty feet tall, now, its rotting armour fracturing into a segmented bile-green carapace over the pulpy flesh beneath. Its eyes bulged outward into two huge, multifaceted globes, its mouth distorting into a pair of serrated mandibles and a long glistening proboscis, as pairs of segmented legs punched their way free of its abdomen.

'*Grandfather! I accept your blessing,*' it sang, in a voice like the buzzing of a gargantuan fly.

'*He's done it,*' Harapa voxed in awestruck tones. '*Bastard's actually done it.*'

*'Behold, my apotheosis! Behold, you who doubted, my ascension and my reward!'*

The column of light vanished, and the great eye closed, revealing a sky that was shockingly clear and filled with stars. The Huntsman let out a buzzing laugh, then stopped abruptly as a shriek of almost equal volume rang out from the far side of the crater. Ursula turned her head to see the three-headed daemon hound ripping its way through a heavy stone wall, its eyes blazing with hunger.

She tore her gaze from the sky and scrambled another few feet higher up the crumbling stone, pausing to rifle through the pouch on her belt, searching for the tiny metal sphere of the beacon. For one desperate moment she thought it was missing, then her fingers closed around the cool metal and pressed the stud at its base. The metal vibrated against her hand as the machine flared into life, cogs whirring deep inside like a pulse.

The skies were clear. If the *Oriflamme* was still in orbit, their message might reach them. There might be a way out after all.

A grating pain shot through her ribs as bone ground on bone. She risked a glance over her shoulder, and saw the daemon hound prowling on the far side of the crater, its haunches tensed, ready to spring. If it decided to move around the perimeter rather than spring across, she was done for. She had to hope it was going to take the direct route.

Or she could give it an incentive.

'Abomination!' She waved her arms, the powerblade crackling in the scalding air. 'Come and feel Cadia's wrath!'

The three great heads snapped around as one. Its speed was terrifying in so large a creature. It roared with all three of its throats at once. She answered its roar with one of her own.

'Cadia stands!'

The beast gathered its haunches and sprang.

# XLIX

### DEATH

The trouble with stab wounds, Ossian thought deliriously, as Liga dragged him around the crumbling astrogranite crater, was that you never knew how deep they went. Unless you could get your hands on the weapon responsible, the size of the cut in the skin was no indicator of the damage it had done. A meat-skewer could be more dangerous than a machete, its delicate puncture wound belying the tissue damage underneath. That wasn't the problem with this wound, though. This one went all the way through, and the real problem with it was that he was bleeding to death.

'I'm sorry,' Liga was muttering under her breath, the words repeated over and over with the air of a litany. 'I'm sorry. I tried.'

Behind them, the abomination wearing Clavie's skin struggled to rise, tripped on a loop of its own intestines and crashed to the ground again. Liga dragged them both another yard forward.

'Didn't expect you to hang around,' he managed. 'Thought you'd be out of here in a cloud of flies.'

'It's gone. All gone.' Liga was shaking. 'It was always the Huntsman's power, never mine. He promised me the world, that bastard...'

A jolt of agony caught him beneath the ribs, as though the knife had plunged in again. He drew a sharp, shuddering breath and tried to focus on anything except the pain.

Anatomy. That was as good a subject as any. Plenty of relevance to the task at hand. If his guess was right the knife had passed smoothly through skin, fascia and muscle, and missed liver, aorta and spleen, damage to any of which would have been fatal by now. That still left plenty of structures to hit, any one of which promised an unpleasant death. Cold sweat beaded on his skin, and his pulse was racing. Hypovolaemic shock. That meant he was four pints of blood down already, with more to come. Catecholamines flooded his system, his body's desperate attempt to maintain blood flow to his vital organs, turning the whole world bright and brittle.

'I'm sorry,' Liga said again. She stumbled, lost her grip around his waist and sent him sprawling painfully to the ground. 'All I wanted was for you to see sense.'

The ground was warm under his hands. They had made it as far as a narrow ledge on the side of the crater, while the shrieks and crashes of daemonic combat shattered the air behind them. He tried to push himself upright, but all the strength had gone out of him.

'There's no... helping some people,' he managed.

Liga was stepping back, her bloodstained hands held up in front of her. 'I can't carry you. The ground's breaking up. I–'

'It's all right. Go.'

'I'm sorry,' she said again, and then she was gone, climbing hand over hand up the crumbling rock. He didn't know where she was going, but he hoped she made it.

Ossian rolled onto his back and gazed up at a startlingly clear sky, the stars dancing in the superheated air. One of the stars was getting larger, shooting down towards the earth, as though the God-Emperor's holy angels were coming to bear him to the Golden Throne on their snow-white wings.

No. He might be dying, but he wasn't an idiot.

It wasn't an angel.

It was something far more welcome than that.

Teeth gritted against the pain, Ossian dragged himself up the slope, his eyes fixed on the falling star that held all the hope in the world.

The daemon hound's leap took it onto the Huntsman's rocky island, now jutting a full twenty feet above the scalding pool. Its clawed hindquarters scrabbled for purchase, then the claws locked into a fissure and it sprang upwards to claw at the Huntsman's pendulous underbelly.

'*Leave this place,*' the Huntsman said, its gleaming, multi-faceted eyes staring down on the three-headed hound. '*Creed's daughter is mine to devour.*'

The central head opened its mouth and vomited a gout of flame directly into the Huntsman's abdomen. The Huntsman shrieked, lifted a foreleg and brought it crashing down on the hound's neck, the force enough to drive it down into the rock. The daemon writhed away, the jaws of its two other heads gnashing as it tried to bite down on its tormentor's limbs, while the Huntsman stamped down again and again with its claw-tipped forelegs.

'Any sign of the damn Valkyrie?' Ursula shouted, hoping her vox-bead would be able to pick up her voice over the roar in the air.

'*Not yet, lord!*' Laskari voxed.

'Get yourselves onto solid ground. It's going to need a place to land. You need to be ready when it does. Got it?' Ursula's throat was raw. She spared a glance behind her, and saw the two daemons locked in a titanic battle of muscle and chitin. The Huntsman had the hound pinned through the shoulder, dribbling acid from its open mandibles down onto the leathery hide.

The hound gave a shriek of agony as the acid ate the flesh of its heaving flank down to the bone. The Huntsman bent down and punched its proboscis deep into the hound's belly, holding the twitching creature down as its convulsions weakened, drinking deeply of its vital essences. When the daemon was nothing more than a three-headed husk, the Huntsman flicked its head contemptuously to the side and sent the desiccated remains into the bubbling sea.

The huge insectoid head turned.

*'Now, Creed's daughter. Now you are mine.'* The power armour on the Huntsman's back ruptured in two vigorous gushes of pus, and a pair of glistening, membranous wings unfolded, their iridescent surface stretching and firming in the searing air.

*'Lord!'* Laskari shouted. *'There's a drop-ship coming! I see the lights!'*

A ragged cheer came through the vox. Ursula thought she could pick out the voices of each of her squad. She spared a thought of blessing for the *Oriflamme* and her crew, even for Mariet Thysia. They had kept their word.

The Huntsman's wings were almost dry now. In a moment it would be airborne, easily large enough to rip a Valkyrie out of the sky. A las-bolt shot through the air and burst against a translucent wing, punching a tiny hole that instantly sealed.

'Laskari! I told you, get yourself to solid ground!'

Harapa's voice cut over the vox, quick and urgent. *'There's a flat patch on the eastern slope. Colonel Van Haast and I are there already. The ship's coming in. Even if they can't set down they can drop ropes.'* A shudder passed through the earth. *'If we're quick.'*

*'My apologies, lord castellan,'* Laskari voxed. *'I needed to try something.'*

'You can't hurt it.' Ursula scrambled another few painful feet up the scalding rock. Her gloves were a smouldering ruin now, her palms already blackened and blistering.

*'You're right, lord. I can't hurt it.'*

'Then get moving while you–'

*'Not directly.'*

A tiny beam of blood-red light shot through the air and alighted on the Huntsman's monstrous face, no larger than a buzzing fly.

'What are you doing, trooper?'

Laskari's voice was triumphant. *'The laser targeter, lord. I still have it. I thought I might as well get some use out of it after carrying it all this way.'*

'Laskari, you bloody genius!'

Engines roared overhead, and a burst of heavy bolter fire ripped down through the sky. The Huntsman's wings exploded into tatters of membranous flesh. It threw back its bloated head and howled, reached up with one taloned foreleg and sent a beam of lightning scorching into the air to illuminate the undercarriage of a compact-looking gun-cutter. The gun-cutter returned fire, sending a missile into the stone plinth beneath the monstrous feet. A second missile followed, its impact within a yard of the first.

'It missed,' Ursula said softly. 'How the frekk did it miss twice?'

*'It didn't miss,'* Laskari voxed. *'Look.'*

A wide crack spread across the astrogranite beneath the Huntsman's legs, the rock crumbling piece by piece into the boiling lake below. The Huntsman beat its ruined wings furiously, but the tattered flesh was only half re-formed, their lift not enough to free its bulk from the tyranny of gravity. The gun-cutter blasted its multi-laser at the base of the rockcrete plinth, and it blew apart in an explosion of rock and fire.

'*No!*' the Huntsman howled. Superheated liquid bubbled up around its legs, the plates of its exoskeleton sloughing away, revealing pale, raw meat beneath. Its multiple eyes clouded over one after the other, hissing and boiling in its head. '*No! Creed's daughter is mine!*'

'Not "Creed's daughter,"' Ursula said, as the waters closed over its head. 'That's "Lord Castellan Creed" to you.'

The air burned in Ursula's lungs. Kasr Arroch was falling apart around her, the ground disintegrating into rockcrete islands as the hot springs beneath the city rose in jets of blistering steam. The Huntsman had vanished entirely, and what had once been the governor's citadel was collapsing in on itself, forming an ever-expanding crater around the roiling, sulphurous water. Muscles screaming, she dragged herself onto a narrow ledge, painfully aware of the bleeding scythe-wound in her shoulder and the rising tide of death in her wake.

'*You coming, chief?*' Harapa voxed.

She grunted. 'Coming. Hold the gun-cutter as long as you can.'

'*We'll get someone towards you, chief. Keep climbing, we'll send down a rope.*'

The ledge she was on was two feet wide, midway up a sheer, vertical cliff. Ten feet away from her was a pile of fallen rubble. It looked firm enough to climb, and if she was able to scramble up to the top then the edge of the crater would be within reach, assuming the ground didn't collapse entirely before she reached it.

Something was lying on the ledge in front of her. The unnatural shadows cast by the Eye of Terror made it difficult to see exactly, but when she looked closer it was unmistakably a human body. One of the Huntsman's cultists, most likely, used up and discarded on its path to infernal apotheosis.

It moaned. She ignored it and moved on past, but it reached up with a filthy hand and caught her ankle. She jerked her leg away in disgust, then stopped as she recognised the figure.

'Ossian?'

He looked like he should already be dead. 'Wanted you to know...' he said, from a mouth filled with blood, '...didn't betray you.'

In the moment, all she could do was stare. Then she bent down, grabbed him by the shredded remains of his tunic, hauled him upright and propped him against the wall of the crater.

'Never thought you did.' What was the harm in another lie? 'I told you I was getting you out of here. I keep my word.'

Ossian shook his head. 'Not even you can pull that off.' He drew a painful breath. 'I'm going nowhere. Do me a favour. Trigger the collar. Make it quick.'

The collar. Her eye fell on the little control module on her wrist, with its buttons and dials.

Its *two* buttons.

'You die when I say so, legionnaire, and not before.' Blood loss and exhaustion were making her giddy. How many more bad decisions did she have to make today? There had been so many that one more didn't seem to matter.

Ursula leaned in close and pressed her lips to his. Then she took a deep breath, offered up a prayer to the God-Emperor, and pressed the switch.

# L

## THE WARMASTER

Ursula's lips were rough and hot against Ossian's mouth, the smell of her skin – sweat, soot and a faint sweetness that was indefinably her own – filling his senses. He'd been a dead man walking for weeks now. As final moments went, it could have been considerably worse.

The collar's mechanism clicked. He flinched, waiting for death, but instead of the promised explosion he felt a bright stab of pain in the side of his throat. Icy liquid snaked down his neck into his chest, and then his heart was jackhammering against his ribs, every part of his body flooding with heat, his thoughts sharp and clear and…

…*angry.*

Ossian opened his eyes. A woman was looking back at him, a wary look of expectation in her blue-violet eyes.

'Still with me, Mac?'

He knew her face, but the name refused to come. His thoughts

471

were a swirling maelstrom, the drug flooding his system driving all rational thought away in a tide of righteous, cleansing rage.

Ursula, that was the woman's name. She was important, though he couldn't remember why. He managed a nod, the drug spreading through him like a cleansing flame, his muscles surging with a toxic strength that he knew in some dispassionate corner of his mind he would pay for later. If there was a later.

'There's more than one device in a legionnaire's collar,' the woman said. 'The frenzon's not going to last long given the state you're in. Get climbing.'

And then she was gone, scrambling – not gracefully, not exactly, but with a strange ungainly elegance – up the crumbling rock. His vision turned to red and amber as the drug took hold completely. It washed away months of fear and pain and guilt. He'd never felt like this before, never known this glorious abandon. He should have taken it days ago, before fatigue and injuries had taken their toll on him, when there was something there to fight. He wasn't armed, but that didn't matter. The next enemy he saw would die with bloody hands wrapped around their heretical throat.

A spray of boiling steam erupted behind him, spattering his exposed skin with tiny boiling droplets. The pain felt good.

'Hurry up!' the woman shouted over her shoulder, and he scrambled after her, the frenzon in his veins burning through his failing body one breath at a time.

The gunship was low in the air as it prepared to drop ropes. It wasn't a Valkyrie as Laskari had thought at first, but a compact black gun-cutter with elaborate golden trim along its bodywork.

The Huntsman was dead. The battle was over.

'It's dead,' Meraq said, in tones of utter disbelief. 'You killed it.'

'*We* killed it.'

'We need to go. Now.'

Laskari looked out at the remains of the kasr, the bubbling crater at its summit and the crumbling rock all around. A tremor shook the tower, and a wide crack appeared up the wall by the window. Her hand burned like it had been dipped in acid.

'Head for the gun-cutter. I'll be right behind you.'

'You won't be,' Meraq said. 'You're staying here to die.'

Laskari closed her eyes. Why did Meraq have to make this so hard? 'I can feel it,' she said. 'The contagion. It's in my blood. The medicae can't cut that away.'

'You don't know that.' Meraq's jaw was set hard.

'I do know.' Laskari was exhausted. 'I can feel it.'

Meraq folded her arms. 'All I'm hearing is that you're too scared to try.'

'I'm *not…*'

There was a flicker of movement in the corner of her eye. Anka's warp-ghost again, the skin sloughing away from the flesh of his face, his eyes locked on to hers. She turned to him, her frustration boiling over.

'What is it? What do you want?'

The milky eyes were full of sorrow. His rotting lips parted. The word bypassed her ears to arrive fully formed in her head.

'Go,' he said.

'What do you mean?'

Anka shook his head. *'There is no peace here. Not even in death.'*

'Who are you talking to?' Meraq demanded.

Laskari's stomach churned. Her hands were shaking. A moment ago she had been ready to lie down and die, to close her eyes and wait until the nightmare ended. But it wasn't going to end. There had been no escape for Anka. His remains were lying by the martyr's wall in Kasr Gallan, but his soul was trapped in Cadia's hellish ruins, perhaps forever.

'*Go*,' Anka said again, the single syllable laced with agony.

She had thought she was ready to die. But this wasn't death. This was far worse.

'I'm going,' she said, not sure if she was speaking to Meraq or to the dead trooper, but the decision was made. She grabbed her long-las, slung it on its strap over her shoulder, and ran.

Another choice made, another set of consequences to deal with. Ursula tried to put it all out of her mind and focus on climbing the scalding rocks, the animal sounds from behind her an additional incentive not to slow down. She had no idea what a combat dose of frenzon would do to a dying man's physiology – she would have needed the medicae in his right mind to tell her that – but she was pretty sure it couldn't be anything good. It had to be better than leaving him to fall into a pit of scalding water, she told herself, or trying to carry him to safety. One last-ditch gamble for survival. One last roll of the dice.

The edge of the crater was close, now. The ground shook again, sending a torrent of scree down the slope towards her. She braced herself and tried not to flinch as sharp edges gouged at her face and hands, then managed a burst of speed, shoving herself upwards with desperate determination. She was so close that she could see solid ground and the gun-cutter's lights.

'We're nearly there!'

Someone moved to the edge of the crater. She looked up and saw Gideon Argent leaning over, silhouetted against the descending craft's lumens. She reached up with one hand.

'Gideon! Pull me up!'

Argent crouched down, leaned over and flicked the vox-bead from her ear. Startled, she recoiled and almost lost her grip on the crater's edge. Her feet scrabbled impotently at the rock face,

but succeeded only in dislodging the rock that had been holding most of her weight.

'Gideon, what the frekk do you think you're doing?'

'Only what I should have done years ago.' He placed one
booted foot on her fingers, and crushed them hard against the
basalt.

'Throne's sake!' Pain seared up through her burned palm into
her wrist. She tugged at his ankle, but it didn't move. There was
still a pistol holstered on her belt, but trying to grab it would
mean trusting her weight to the hand pinned beneath Argent's
boot.

'Stepping out from your shadow,' he said.

'*Really?*' A clumsy blurt of laughter escaped her lips. 'That's
what you're doing?' The situation was too ludicrous for fear. She
was sore, exhausted, and above all astonished that this was how
it was going to end. 'The Huntsman's dead, Gideon, you don't
need to listen to it any more.'

Argent leaned down so that their faces were almost touching. 'It's not the daemon doing this, Ursula. It's me. It's time for
*me* to be the hero, to bring Lord Castellan Creed's last orders
home.' He tapped a finger to his abdomen. 'You didn't think to
search there, did you? Bit of a struggle swallowing it down after
I knocked you out and took it off your neck, but I managed.
Persistence. Patience. I've got good at those over the years.'

It didn't make sense. His kindness in her darkest moments,
when the mission had seemed over before it had begun. His
gentle persistence, encouraging her to continue the search when
her courage had faltered. He hadn't been looking out for her. His
eye had been fixed on the contents of Creed's bunker the whole
time, and she had been nothing more than a means to an end.

She searched his face for any sign of the old friend she had
once known, and found nothing at all.

'You've been planning this from the start.'

'There are people who want to see me succeed, Ursula. People who're ashamed of the mess you've made of your legacy. People who want the Astra Militarum to look forward, not back.'

'And who are they? Loyal servants of the Throne don't make deals like that behind everyone else's back.'

Argent laughed. 'When you're as powerful as they are, the ordinary rules don't apply.' He levelled his lasgun at her forehead. 'Such a tragedy the lord castellan never made it out of the crater. But I'm here to carry on your work. Who knows, maybe your death will inspire them more than your life ever did.'

A raw grunt of exertion came from the cliff face to her left. Gideon's attention flickered to the side, an expression of surprise crossing his face.

'I had no idea the convict would still be alive, though. You really don't give up, do you, Ursula?'

Argent pulled the lasgun's trigger. The bolt streaked past her ear and struck Ossian in the shoulder. He lost his grip and slipped backwards over the edge.

White-hot fury boiled through her. With strength born out of anger, Ursula grabbed Argent's ankle with her free hand and used the leverage to swing herself up onto the crater's edge. She got to her feet and her rising head smacked into the underside of Argent's jaw, sending them both reeling, but before she could swing a punch Argent brought his lasgun around. She knocked the muzzle aside as he pulled the trigger, and the hot barrel seared a fresh line of pain across her forearm as the las-bolt went wild.

Argent stepped back and brought the lasgun around like a club. It caught the side of her head, hard enough to rattle her teeth together. She stumbled, then the ground went out from under her and she fell.

'Look at yourself, Gideon!' Her head ached, her shoulder ached, her ribs ached, the palms of her hands burned like unholy fire, but the betrayal cut deeper than any of those. She had trusted him with her life. They had been closer than siblings. She would have died for him a thousand times over. But *this*? 'I thought we were *friends*.'

'No. Not friends. Not any more.' Argent touched his fingers to the cut on his jaw, then aimed the lasgun at her forehead. 'I'm tired of dancing to your tune, scrabbling for the scraps from your table. I'm *better* than that, and it's time the Imperium knows it.'

Emotions churned in her guts: astonishment, disgust, even pity. How had she failed to spot this? The Argent she had known – or thought she had known – had been her ally against a hostile world, someone she could stand with when the wolves came howling at the door. This man was ready to throw her to their waiting jaws.

Words failed her. She looked up. The barrel hung in front of her eyes, wide and dark as the void of space.

'Goodbye, Ursula.' Gideon touched the barrel to her forehead. 'I'll tell them you died with your eyes open.'

The tower was crumbling as Laskari and Meraq sprinted down the spiral stairs, chunks of masonry falling away to expose the nightmarish landscape beyond. The crater that had once been the summit of Kasr Arroch was expanding at terrifying speed, the roiling geyser stained blood-red in the light from the Eye of Terror. Laskari kept well away from the open edge of the staircase, her left hand rasping against the stonework in her need to keep away from the precipitous drop. A fall from this height would be fatal even if it wasn't into a boiling lake.

The gun-cutter was low in the air above the crater's edge. Ropes were spooling like spider-silk from its undercarriage, and two tiny figures – too small to make out their identity – were sprinting towards it. Her arm throbbed in time with her hammering footsteps, but she ignored it and ran. In a few seconds they'd reach the bottom of the tower. After that, one final sprint and they'd be off-world. Now that she had taken the decision to live, she found that she wanted nothing more than to breathe the *Oriflamme*'s tanked air again, to travel through the starry void, even to return to Shukret-Dhruv.

They were almost at the base of the tower. A green las-blast flashed two hundred yards away, and she paused, the defect in the tower's stone walls giving her a clear view of what lay below. Two figures were standing at the crater's edge. The rising heat haze made it difficult to tell who was standing there, but the longer she looked, the less it looked like a friendly reunion.

She raised her rifle and looked down the sights, just in time to see Major Argent swinging the butt of a lasgun directly into the lord castellan's face. She went down hard, rolled, and didn't rise.

'What are you *doing*?' Meraq asked urgently. 'We have to run!'

'My lord?' she voxed, but there was no reply. Argent was advancing, the lasgun aimed squarely at the lord castellan's forehead. Laskari had no orders to follow, no one to instruct her on the correct course of action, nothing but her own judgement.

'God-Emperor guide my hand,' she whispered, and took the shot.

The tiny green dot of a laser-sight appeared on Argent's face, then his head snapped to the side as a las-bolt vaporised his lower jaw. His arms spasmed upwards and his finger tightened convulsively on the trigger of his lasgun, sending a bolt of his own searing across the side of Ursula's neck. A raw, animal howl ripped its way from his throat, and he fell in a spasming heap, clawing at the open-mouthed ruin of his face. She got to her feet, leaned down to pull the vox-bead from his ear and shoved it into her own.

'Lord castellan?' Laskari's voice cut across the static. 'What happened?'

'Long story, trooper.' She lifted Argent's lasgun, her crushed fingers protesting as she wrapped them around the forestock. 'I owe you my thanks yet again. Sergeant Harapa, if you're on the gun-cutter tell them I'm at the crater's edge, and I would be obliged if they would come to me and not the other way around.'

Ursula stared down at her old friend, then to the ledge at the crater's edge where Ossian's battered body lay. She watched him carefully until she was sure that the movement of his chest was real, and not an artefact of the flickering light. He was breathing. The tension in her own chest eased.

'One additional casualty for retrieval.'

'Message received and understood, chief,' Harapa voxed. 'Hold your position. They're coming towards you now.'

'And one corpse.'

Argent turned his face towards her, his eyes open in mute appeal. Breath gurgled helplessly through his shattered mouth, blood welling from the base of his half-severed tongue.

'There's something in its stomach that we're going to need.'

The shot blew Gideon Argent's skull apart like a frag grenade. Under the circumstances, she felt she was being more than reasonable.

'Keep running,' Harapa voxed. Laskari didn't need telling twice. Meraq was already through the doorway at the base of the tower, so she clattered down the last of the steps, her lasgun swinging wildly over her shoulder, her hand throbbing in time with the hammering of her pulse. One more sprint and they would be there. Escape was so close she could feel it.

Laskari skidded through the doorway, and stopped. Someone was blocking her path. Someone wearing a filthy green robe, with a blood-slick knife in one hand and an Aeronautica-issue laspistol in the other. Meraq lay crumpled at her feet, blood welling around her head.

'This is all your fault,' Liga Yager said.

Laskari took a step back, horror and fear welling up in her. She reached for her lasgun, but Yager pointed the pistol between her eyes.

'Go for your gun and you die.'

Laskari raised her empty hands. She had to find a way to get to Meraq, find if she was still breathing. Yager had to want something, otherwise she would have shot the moment that Laskari came into view. That meant she had to keep the legionnaire talking.

'What are you doing?' Laskari asked.

'What does it look like?' Yager spat the words. 'Payback. You killed my friend. Now I've killed yours. You're next.'

'The ogryn?' Laskari blinked. *That* was what this was about?

'Her name was Clavie!' The legionnaire's voice was shaking, her eyes two pools of darkness. 'She was my friend! She mattered! And you killed her like she was nothing at all.'

'Killing Meraq, and me, won't put that right.'

'*Nothing* will put it right!'

A huge shape was moving through the shadows behind Liga. The legionnaire didn't notice, all of her hate concentrated on Laskari. The shadow moved without rhythm or grace, heavy footsteps scraping across the floor, dragging something in its wake that slopped wetly over the stone.

'If you're going to kill me, you'll have to be quick,' Laskari said. Whatever was coming, it might be a distraction she could use. Alternatively it might kill all three of them, but that was a step up on letting Liga shoot her down like a wounded dog.

An earthquake shook the ground. The crater was getting wider by the second, chunks of rock tumbling from its sides towards the spreading crater and its venting plumes of steam. A jet of lava rose up with it, painting the world a vivid orange. Soon they would all be swallowed by the hungry earth.

'Quick?' Liga bared her sharpened teeth. 'Quick is too good for you–'

Her voice cut off abruptly as a huge shadow lurched from the stairwell to wrap a hand around Liga's neck. The stench of decay from its flesh was so strong that even a full six feet away Laskari's eyes flooded with water. Liga let out a strangled scream. The massive poxwalker raised her into the air by the throat, holding her at arm's length with inhuman strength.

Laskari had seen the ogryn before. Before, she had looked at a living soldier and seen a monster. Now she was looking at the monster, all she could see was the woman it had once been. Sometime after her death, the ogryn's abdomen had ruptured to spill out great coils of viscera, now half-pulped where they had been caught beneath her dragging feet.

'Clavie…' Liga managed through her constricted throat. The ogryn's mouth stretched in an impossible daemonic grin, then it leaned its face in close and bit Liga's face off from the nose down. Liga's screams turned to a wet gurgle.

Laskari put a mercy-shot through her skull, and the screams fell silent.

The poxwalker threw the body to one side and turned its bloody face to Laskari. All trace of the dead ogryn was gone, the piggy eyes filled with daemonic hunger, devoid of intelligence or personality.

Laskari unshouldered her rifle, put the stock to her shoulder and pulled the trigger. The las-bolt tore off the flesh covering its forehead, but the bone beneath remained intact. It raised its bloody bayonet, opened its mouth in a bestial roar, and charged towards her. Her second shot blew off the bone-yellow horn protruding from the side of its skull, and the huge head jerked to one side, but it kept coming, so close now she could smell the stench of rotting meat on its breath. It drew back its huge bayonet, ready for the killing strike. She had time for a single shot, and perhaps not even that.

Mustering all her courage, Laskari stepped inside its reach and shoved her long-las directly towards the punched-out hole between the eyes. Her aching finger tightened on the trigger, the ogryn's skull exploded, and its massive corpse thudded to the ground.

Laskari didn't pause. She dropped to the earth and checked for a pulse at Meraq's throat. The bayonet had slit her from ear to ear, and the blood had already stopped flowing.

The world was shaking itself to pieces. She focused on the pain in her hand, glad at last of the burning agony spreading up her wrist. It made it easier to stay numb to everything else: Meraq's death, Liga's mutilation, the horror of the reanimated ogryn, Anka's tormented spirit, trapped forever on unholy ground.

She cast one look back to the tangled corpses at the tower's base, then broke into a painful run. There was no time left for self-deception. To stay on Cadia would be to die, but even making it to the gun-cutter would be no guarantee of survival. Even if the medicae flensed her wounded arm to the bone she could easily die during the attempt, or perish afterwards like Strahl. She might not even be given that slim chance at life. Her reward might be the Emperor's Mercy the moment she stepped onto the *Oriflamme*.

Nothing was certain.

Except that wasn't true. One thing remained: a tiny sliver of hope, the merest shard of it that refused to die in the face of insurmountable odds. Before Cadia she had thought that hope was a nebulous thing, but this was a tangible force, as real as the agony in her hand. Death had soaked into every part of Cadia's remains, but so too had the force of will that had kept their soldiers standing fast against an unstoppable tide of darkness, nothing more than the faith that that tide would one day turn, that the sun would rise again, that their final deeds still had meaning even when none but the God-Emperor would bear witness.

That there would be a future, even if she never saw it.

Laskari cradled her ruined hand against her chest, clinging to that last hope. She was close enough that she could hear the roar of the gun-cutter's engines over the roiling geyser, their tone rising in pitch as the craft took to the air, its lights flaring.

'Wait! I'm coming!'

Silence on the vox-link stretched out for an eternity. Then it crackled with static, and the lord castellan's voice came through, raw and hoarse, sounding almost as exhausted as Laskari herself.

*'Keep running, trooper. We're not leaving without you.'*

# ACT FIVE

*'Thence we came forth to rebehold the stars.'*

> – Fragment from an ancient text,
> kept in the Great Library of Terra

# LI

### DELIVERANCE

The *Oriflamme*'s briefing room was dark, lit only by the flickering light of the hololith. There were light years between them, but Ursula could feel the lord regent's presence, his calm air of unassailable authority, as though he were sitting in the room. The only other item there was a bundle of drab green cloth, sat on the table beside the holo-projector.

'*My congratulations on your success, lord castellan,*' Guilliman said.

She inclined her head, and bit down so hard on her lower lip that she tasted blood. She had been preparing for this conversation from the moment she had stepped back onto the *Oriflamme*, while the medicae had pieced together the tattered wound across her shoulder and chest, grafted the worst of her burns and covered the rest in unguents that stank as badly as they stung, and she still felt woefully underprepared.

'Thank you, lord regent. It is my honour to serve.'

What else was there to say? He had sent her into hell, and she had returned, scorched and bleeding, but still breathing. The information she had retrieved had been paid for in the lives of good soldiers, and at least one bad one.

*'Have you studied the contents of your father's data-crystal?'*

She shook her head. 'Not yet, my lord. My enginseer is extracting the data as we speak. I understand the process is a delicate one and cannot be rushed.'

*'If it contains what you have told me, lord castellan, then the information you have recovered is more valuable than any weapon.'*

'And will you let me put it to use?' She blurted the question out without thinking. Oh well. There was no unsaying the words now. 'Conquering a New Cadia will require more troops than I presently have at my disposal. Will you allow me to withdraw the Cadian regiments from their present deployments to this end?'

The great leonine head tilted to one side. *'I will give the matter due consideration. Once the full facts in question are known.'*

'Then I will await the results of your deliberation.' She tried to keep the impatience from her voice. If she was to make use of what her father had promised, the quicker they acted upon it, the better.

Guilliman leaned closer to his pict-caster. *'How do your companions fare?'*

'As well as can be expected, under the circumstances.' She thought of the frenzied activity in the *Oriflamme's* infirmarium as they had arrived, mechadendrites flailing through the air, Ossian's scorched and battered body vanishing beneath a sea of scarlet robes. He had suffered significant organ damage, both as a result of direct trauma and the toxic effects of the frenzon on an already overtaxed body, but the medicae still thought it was worth the effort to repair what they could and replace the rest. Whether he'd be fit mentally for anything other than servitorisation when they were done, no one was willing to say.

Laskari was alive, too, recently relieved of her right arm as far as the shoulder and under careful surveillance to assess for any evidence of corruption. The others had been patched and checked then consigned to careful isolation to await the arrival of the Ecclesiarchy for the rites of purification. They'd tried to do the same for her, but rank still had some privileges.

'Did you know about Argent? Who was he working for?'

Guilliman shook his head. *'There are always those who wish to place their own goals above those of the Imperium. Which one it was on this occasion I cannot say.'*

'Cannot say, my lord, or will not?'

Guilliman didn't reply.

'I gave his body to the magos biologis to dissect,' Ursula said. 'If there are any secrets there, we will have them before long.' Along with the data-crystal, she thought, already freshly scoured of gastric contents and handed to Rho on a gleaming silver specimen dish.

Another question shoved its way to the front of her mind.

'Sergeant Harapa turned out to be a useful man to have around, even if he knew far more than a Catachan sergeant is supposed to.'

The lord regent's mouth quirked, so briefly that she might have missed it. *'He is loyal to his masters, as they are to the Golden Throne. They are committed to the success of our mutual endeavour, but you must remember there are those amongst my father's servants who even I do not command.'*

'The Inquisition, then.' She rolled her eyes. 'Throne, that's not even his name, is it? They waited until I'd chosen from the list of transplants, and then sent whichever of their agents matched the correct description. Was there *anyone* in that squad telling the truth about who they really were?'

It seemed the primarch decided to treat that question as rhetorical, answering it only with another small, knowing smile.

'*The penal legionnaire. Have you decided his fate?*'

Ursula squared her shoulders. 'I request your pardon for him, lord regent.'

The heavy sculpted brow shot upwards in surprise. '*I have no objection in principle, but a formal pardon from the lord castellan of Cadia herself would be sufficient under almost any circumstance.*'

'They'll argue with me. They'll ask questions. No one will dare question a pardon issued by the lord regent himself. No one argues with you.'

Guilliman laughed. It was a surprisingly pleasant sound, rich and mellifluous, flowing around her like a tide of clear water. '*Very true, lord castellan, though I would count you amongst the few exceptions to that rule. I will grant him a pardon. May he make good use of the days you have returned to him.*'

'If he survives.' She looked down at her hands, and changed the subject. 'And my thanks for the coat, lord regent.'

A look of genuine surprise crossed his face. '*The coat?*'

'I found it in my quarters on my return. I assumed…'

She trailed off. The coat had been sitting on her bunk on the *Oriflamme*, neatly folded and still smelling faintly of cigar smoke. There had been a half-full bottle of amasec in the pocket, still good after all those years.

'I assumed you had arranged for my father's coat to be sent to me.'

'*An intriguing gift,*' Guilliman said. '*But I was not its source.*'

Something moved behind the lord regent. He looked over his shoulder, then returned his attention to the hololith with a sigh that was almost imperceptible. It was a comforting thought to know that even the Angels of the Emperor grew frustrated with the incessant demands made on their time.

'I've kept you too long, lord regent,' she said.

'*And I you, lord castellan.*' His smile returned. '*We will speak*

*further of your father's legacy and how best we honour it in the days
to come, but for now we both have duties that press upon our time.
I believe a ceremony is planned in the Oriflamme's cathedral, for
you to welcome the newly re-formed Eighth Regiment in its entirety.'*

And to hand out the medals, she thought. Let's not forget
about that. The Honour of Cadia for Hadrian Van Haast, the
Brazen Eagle for Vanatu Harapa – or whatever his name really
was – the Order of the Gate for the rest, the dead included.

*'We will speak again, Ursula Creed.'*

The hololith vanished. The silence lasted no more than a
moment, and then the door opened again and Hadrian Van Haast
entered, spurs jingling and Lieutenant Fletz trotting anxiously at
his heels.

'Are you ready?' Van Haast said.

'I'm coming.'

Lord Castellan Ursula Creed rose to her feet, and pulled on
her father's coat. The doorway stood open. Her people were
waiting on the other side.

Cadia had fallen, but it would rise again.

She would make sure of that.

# EPILOGUE

*Shards of crystal litter the floor of the chamber, spattered with the diviner's blood. He stays low to the ground, unresisting as his patron pours out wrath in a torrent of blows. He has suffered it all before. He has seen in the Tarot he will suffer it again.*

*'You told me–'*

*A boot strikes the diviner beneath the ribs, the force enough to roll him onto his side. He curls up by reflex, arms protecting his head and neck as another kick follows, and then another.*

*'You told me they would succeed! That I would have it!'*

*Memory is a fickle thing. His patron remembers only chosen details, discarding whatever parts of the prophecy do not suit. But there is no sense in arguing. The diviner's life hangs on a thread of his patron's goodwill. To correct his patron now would fray that thread to its breaking point.*

*'As I have said, the cards are not always clear.'*

*His patron turns away, shattered crystals crunching underfoot like freshly frozen snow, before aiming a final vicious kick at the diviner's skull.*

*'Attend to your prayers, witch,' his patron snarls. 'Pray that the God-Emperor grants you His mercy, for I find mine in short supply.'*

*The diviner's eyes are open as the slow darkness rises to claim him. His gaze rests on a broken piece of psychoreactive crystal, its surface rippling and moving under the stress of his regard. Images swim out of the haze, indistinct at first, then clearer, one giving way to another as though emerging in procession from thick grey mist.*

*The Bloody Queen. The Throne, reversed. The Catacombs. The Dead-That-Do-Not-Sleep. And then, unfamiliar images: a spinning blue world. A blood-soaked banner. A mortar shell exploding like a star.*

*Futures and pasts flicker before his eyes. He drinks them in like cool water as the tide of unconsciousness pulls him down.*

*The future is not yet written.*

*But when it comes, it will be written in blood.*

## ABOUT THE AUTHOR

**Jude Reid** lives in Glasgow with her husband and two daughters, and writes in the narrow gaps between full-time work as a surgeon, wrangling her kids and failing to tire out a border collie. In what little free time she has, she enjoys tabletop roleplaying, ITF Tae Kwon Do and inadvisably climbing big hills.

# YOUR NEXT READ

### MINKA LESK: THE LAST WHITESHIELD
#### by Justin D Hill

Cadia has stood in grim defiance against the enemies of the Imperium for ten thousand years, an indomitable bulwark against the forces of Chaos… but now, the 13th Black Crusade has come, and there will be no victory. Here, Minka Lesk will be tested in the very fires of a world's destruction.